THE
SCAM

A NOVEL BY BEST-SELLING AUTHOR

JAMES BYRON HUGGINS

STORY BY JAY B. MANN

THE
SCAM

WHITAKER
HOUSE

F
Hug.

This is a work of fiction. Names, characters, places, and incidents are either the product of the author's imagination or are used fictitiously, and any resemblance to actual persons, living or dead, events, or locales is entirely coincidental.

THE SCAM

ISBN-13: 978-0-88368-817-5
ISBN-10: 0-88368-817-4
Printed in the United States of America
© 2006 by Wild Horse Entertainment, Inc.

WHITAKER
HOUSE

1030 Hunt Valley Circle
New Kensington, PA 15068
www.whitakerhouse.com

Library of Congress Cataloging-in-Publication Data

Huggins, James Byron.
The scam / by James Byron Huggins.
p. cm.
ISBN-13: 978-0-88368-817-5 (alk. paper)
ISBN-10: 0-88368-817-4 (alk. paper)
1. Conspiracies—Fiction. 2. Government investigators—Fiction.
3. Americans—England—Fiction. 4. Washington (D.C.)—Fiction.
5. London (England)—Fiction. 6. New York (N.Y.)—Fiction. I. Title.
PS3558.U346S28 2005
813'.54—dc22
2005004845

1 2 3 4 5 6 7 8 9 10 11 12 **ᄖ** 15 14 13 12 11 10 09 08 07 06

Prologue

H e stood at the edge of darkness, but it meant nothing. He owned the darkness.

With a frown he moved forward, and the glistening sheen of grass made little sound as he crossed it toward the house.

The deep pockets of darkness surrounding the house were inviting to him, and in moments he reached the back door and used the security code that had been delivered to him.

Soon he was inside, and moving up the stairway. As he ascended the stairs, the dog rose, but it died silently. He withdrew the ice pick and turned to stare into the room that held the child.

No...not yet.

He moved down the corridor to the man and the woman.

Enough...Time to do what must be done.

He moved slowly to the bed, gazing down at the man. He raised his hand in the air, the ice pick frozen to his fist, and brought it down. A roar of pain shattered the dark and the man half-rose, struggling, and then the woman screamed. But at her move the Iceman struck, knocking her to the floor. Then he violently withdrew the ice pick from the man's chest though the man still struggled, and moved around the bed toward the screaming woman.

He did not need to watch the man die. He knew the man would die. The man's strength was only the strength of death—the strength of fear. As it was with all of them.

The woman's scream was hideous as the Iceman descended upon her and then he heard a sound in the doorway, as he anticipated. Grabbing the woman's throat, the Iceman turned. Waiting.

The child cried out in fear.

Not ten years old, he didn't even look at the room as he rushed to his father's side. Instantly the Iceman killed the woman, turning away before she even fell. He came around the end of the bed, moving to the boy. But then the boy saw him coming and screamed as he backed away, staring wildly.

Such easy prey...

Before the boy ran.

Moving swiftly, the child was out the door and flying, screaming down the hallway. He turned for the briefest moment as he reached the stairway to see the cloaked shape emerging from darkness, a grinning skull followed by its own night.

Then the boy screamed again as the darkness exploded and the grinning skull fell forward. Crying out in fear, the boy turned and ran with all that was within him, fleeing down the stairs.

Immediately understanding what had happened, the Iceman rose to see the dark profile of the father leaning in the doorway, smoke billowing from the handgun.

Another blinding flash exploded in the hall and the Iceman winced at the light. He drew his pistol and the silencer dulled the sound as the man fell into the shadows, crying for *his son...*

Enraged, feeling the warmth of his own blood beneath his cloak—no pain yet because he had prepared for that—the Iceman turned again to the stairway, descending.

But the child was gone, the stairway empty.

Quickly the Iceman moved down the steps, slightly deafened by the thunderous blast of the man's gun. His eyes were wide and white to see through darkness.

Scanning, searching more quickly now because he knew he was almost out of time, the Iceman moved through the house. But the house was large, so large, and there were so many places a child could hide...

Still, the Iceman knew, he would find him.

He would find this child.

Terrified child eyes stared at the chessboard, the figures glowing red in the dying embers of the hearth. He heard the dark man descending, coming for him, and he crept further beneath the table, hiding against the wall to become smaller and smaller. But he could never, never become small enough...

A tall shadow moved past him without sound and his trembling increased. Unable to breathe, he watched the dark man walk silently past the table, angrily turning his face away from the light, from the chessboard set before the flames, a game left unfinished—a game his father promised they could finish tomorrow. But now, the boy knew, tomorrow had been taken from them.

For a moment the black gleaming eyes of the dark man appeared to gaze down at the unfinished chess game. A long white hand hung in front of the boy's face—bone-thin and strong and the boy saw something else there, something *black*.

A black ring as black as the black king. Then the man's skull-face split in a grin, laughing silently at their game, before he moved away and there were only flames, the game.

The black king, the game, the game game *game*...

The game.

The child's gaze focused on the game. And, slowly, his eyes narrowed, desperate and concentrated. It was a moment that lasted, forever burning fear and flame into his mind beneath the game, remolding his heart and soul.

As silent as death, the dark man moved from the room.

And the boy entered the game.

Entering the darkness, he crept from beneath the table to step in perfect silence on the wooden floor that burned with cold, moving in the very steps of the dark man. With wide eyes the boy cast a cautious glance at the towering shape that walked only steps away, searching, searching, always searching.

Then the dark man seemed to sense something behind him and he whirled even as the boy eased through a doorway, disappearing past the corner with his face chilled in sweat, his nightshirt sticking to his back, thinking, thinking in the game, and the boy moved fast and silent down the corridor, searching for escape even as he felt dark wind rising in his steps.

Suppressing fearful tears, the boy saw the shadow darken the portal behind him and he reached a door that led to a stairway. He opened the door but did not enter before slamming it shut. Then he was across the hall and through another doorway, hiding behind the frame.

The dark man appeared at the stairway, opening the door and ascending the stairs in the shadows as easily as his father would have ascended in the light.

Blinking tears, the boy waited until the shadow was gone. Then he ran quickly down the corridor, his bare feet making little sound, searching for the back door, for he knew that if he stayed in the house he would die as his father and mother died...

The Scam

As he ran he heard the dark man descending the stairway in almost perfect silence. Then he reached the end of the corridor, his tiny hand settling on the latch. He didn't hesitate to look back.

The child fled into the night.

Arctic rage burned in white eyes.

The child had deceived him!

Had deceived *him!*

But not for long.

The man bowed his head, listening, slowing his heartbeat by sheer will. And in the night he recognized danger—a siren approaching. It was only one, he knew, but his prey had been an important man. Other sirens would follow, and soon.

He poised, debating, but he did not have time to search for the boy now. No, the child had escaped him to hide somewhere in the aged recesses of the cathedral manor.

Wrath rose within him and the Iceman knew, for the first time, that he had failed; he had never failed before. He had killed all of them—*all of them*! He had killed over and over again, so many of them. But tonight, he knew, tonight he had failed. Tonight the darkness had betrayed him.

As the siren reached the estate the Iceman made his way to the back of the house, moving down the short stairway to the door he had used for entry. He did not hesitate to decode the alarm and then he was in the night again, moving away from the manor to the trees. But as he came into the black night air the Iceman sensed him and turned.

The child stood in the grass.

Motionless. Terrified.

Staring.

A heartbeat passed between them, hot and hating. With a

grinning, hideous laugh, the Iceman raised the silenced pistol, focusing on the child.

And then the night violently vanished in a blinding, glaring white strobe of light—light somewhere close and piercing and then there were the distant sounds of men running and screaming, screaming, warning the child, warning him away.

With a roar the Iceman threw his arms over his eyes and whirled into the darkness of trees and the child was saved by shouts and light, light just—

So much light...

Chapter One

Judgment was delivered.

Logan stood to be sentenced.

Convened in the J. Edgar Hoover Headquarters in Washington D.C., the seven highest agents of the Federal Bureau of Investigation stared over Logan as if were a harbinger of plague. Logan returned the stares impassively. Unrevealing. Untouched.

"We are here to deliver a letter on the alleged theft of government property," intoned Richard Webster, gazing at Logan with a faint air of disbelief. "Over the past week I have investigated this matter and explored evidence and testimony. But before I deliver a decision based on the OPR report, I will like to ask the accused a question."

With dignity, Logan lifted his chin.

"Special Agent Logan," Webster began, "you do not have to answer. That is your right. But I will ask, nonetheless." He paused. "Can you offer any explanation, Agent Logan, why you have been accused, during your long and remarkably distinguished career, of violating so many rules and regulations?"

Standing straighter, Logan allowed the look of a man who had been egregiously offended beyond his station.

"I have no idea, sir," he answered. "I can only emphatically attest that I am innocent. I did not steal any shipments of Wild Turkey from the semitrailer confiscated in the Mancini raid. Nor did I use the aforementioned cases of whiskey to bribe New York City Police officers for the donation of stolen Jaguars subsequently used by agents of the New York field office.

"Further," Logan raised a hand, pointing, "I am amazed that I have been accused of such a malicious action. And I state that there is absolutely no evidence to back these charges." He dismissed them with a wave. "These accusations should never have seen review. They are without substance."

A ghost of a smile overlaid Webster's face, indicating satisfaction that his powers of anticipation had not disappointed. "And that is your answer?" he asked.

"Yes."

A pause.

"Very well." Webster lifted a sheet of paper. "Then this is the letter of finding. But, to preempt its delivery, I must say that I have confronted extreme collateral contingencies. The engineering of an undisputed decision was not possible."

Webster's frowning demeanor said it more forthrightly. "Your long personal history of revolving charges speaks for itself, Logan, as does your excellent record as a criminal investigator. So it was left for me, alone, to find you guilty or not guilty." His face tilted forward. "Nor was it an easy thing to do."

Dead calm, Logan waited.

"However, since all New York City police officers denied possession of said property, professing under oath they would *never* use their official positions for personal profit, and in light of the fact that all inventory sheets of the confiscated Wild Turkey have...*mysteriously* disappeared, I conclude there is insufficient evidence in the matters of theft and conduct unbecoming."

Logan nodded.

Webster rose. "Special Agent Logan, you are transferred to WMPD effective immediately. You are to report to Quantico forthwith to see the ASAC upon arrival."

"Transferred?" Logan asked. He searched Webster as if the statement were a vengeful joke. "To Quantico?"

"That's right." Webster folded the file, glanced up. "You're going back to work, Logan. Big time."

Logan leaned back into the plush leather chair and allowed his fingers to drum the mahogany table. Gazing across the chamber, he mused that Conference Room in the Administration Building at Quantico, Virginia, was the epitome of dignity. He didn't know why he was reporting here, but those were the orders. Logan glanced over at the only other agent in the room.

Gray-haired, stocky, and muscular, Blake Woodard was the image of a professional linebacker gone soft. His dark three-piece suit fit closely around his heavy torso to accent the obvious width and natural power of his massive shoulders and arms. His hands were large and his deeply tanned face was wide and craggy and creased by smile-lines that deepened beneath bright, friendly eyes.

Overall, Woodard was thoroughly disarming, warm, and likeable, with an aspect that compelled people to confide secrets in him. He was widely regarded inside the agency as not only a consummate investigator but also a highly skilled diplomat—a man who could resolve tariff disputes at a duck hunt.

Woodard had thirty-three years in the job and held the post of Legat in the Bureau's London office. He was responsible for coordinating all of America's investigations with Scotland Yard, Interpol, or any other European intelligence service. His squad of twelve FBI Special Agents—the largest FBI squad located in any foreign nation—occupied the entire fourth floor of the American Embassy at Kensington Square. He smiled, "So tell me, Logan, how are things in New York?"

"Just great, Woodard. Fine and dandy."

Woodard's eyes gleamed. "So how did the Wild Turkey fiasco wind up?" He laughed. "Come on, Logan, you know that you can trust me."

Logan sighed. "Woodard, Wild Turkey ended like everyone expected it to end. They accused me of conduct unbecoming and theft of government property."

"What'd you get?"

"Unsubstantiated."

"I heard OPR even got involved."

Logan drummed fingers on the table. "Yep."

"I heard *Webster* even got involved."

"They drafted him to make the finding."

Woodard's face was alight with admiration. "I tell you, Logan, that stunt was *creative*. But how well did it work? I mean, how many Jags did you guys get for the Bureau?"

"Eleven."

"*Ha!*" Woodard slapped his massive hand on the desk. "Worked pretty darn good then, didn't it?" He waited, frowned. "Until you got caught."

Logan looked for a moment at a portrait of former FBI director J. Edgar Hoover, who probably broke more national and international laws than anyone in the history of America. "Well, you know what they say, Woodard. You lose some and then you lose some."

Woodard nodded, "And some get rained out."

Strangely, Logan felt slightly swayed by Woodard's apparent admiration. But he wasn't about to be affected by it any more than he would have been affected by criticism. He was inherently skeptical of both, always doubting the source and motivation. And to add to his suspicion he still didn't know why he was here, so he was in a high self-defense mode. They rose to their feet as the wide wooden door opened and Webster entered. Logan wasn't surprised.

Webster waved them back to their seats and took his place at the head of the table. Then he abruptly slid a stack of manila envelopes to Logan and leaned back. "Congratulations on escaping Wild Turkey," he said casually, "but I don't think you're going to escape this."

Logan watched the files skid across the table. Woodard chuckled.

Webster was a formidable figure. His short, black hair was close cut and he wore an immaculate but humbly tailored dark suit and tie. His eyes, black as coal, focused on Logan. Logan knew that gaze could switch from friendly persuasion to utterly cold command in an instant.

Long ago, mainly because Webster had always been reluctant to take part in the witch hunts leveled against him, Logan had decided that he could be half-trusted. Further, he knew that Webster had risen to his exalted position of Assistant Director by the power of his formidable intellect, his professional skill, and his exemplary field record as a Los Angeles Special Agent in Charge, and not by playing politics.

Further, Webster's reputation for honesty and integrity were legendary. It was rumored that he once issued a Letter of Censure to *himself* because he lost a cell phone. So Webster was one of the few FBI directors in Washington who had actually earned his rank. And Webster's presence in the room was the only thing that made Logan feel comfortable. Still, he found himself gazing cautiously at the files: "I'm supposed to look at these?"

Webster smiled. "Get yourself in gear, Logan. You're about to take the wildest ride you've ever had. Maybe the wildest ride any of us have ever had."

Logan nodded, thoughtful. "And do I have the option of refusing this assignment?"

"No." Webster's tone became more intense. "And neither do I. Which I would, if I could. So open up the files before you find yourself transferred to Butte, Montana."

"I like Montana."

"Open the files, Logan."

Logan cast a glance at a file and read "Top Secret." He nervously recalled the State Department's criteria for the classification: *Information that could cause serious damage to the security of the United States...*

Cautiously, he reached out and opened the flap, quickly reading the first page of the Teletype: "By the authority of the Director of the Federal Bureau of Investigation, an undercover investigation is authorized into the threat of a worldwide banking takeover by..."

Logan closed his eyes.

Something told him that this had always been coming, that this was God's vengeance for all the sins he had ever committed or *would* ever commit. Just as he knew that it was long, long overdue and that he utterly, utterly deserved it.

"You know, boss," he said quietly, "this seems to me like a job for our Special Action Crime Unit. Yes, sir, I'll bet those guys could figure this out in no—"

"They've tried, Logan," Webster stated morosely. "They've tried and they've failed. Interpol has tried and failed. The CIA. MI6. MI5. The Israelis, the Russians." He paused. "Everybody has tried and everybody has failed. And that's the end of it. This thing is too big."

Logan didn't move. "How big?"

"Big."

Logan still didn't move. "How big?"

Webster's face transformed from persuasive to wrathful. "Logan, do you think I'm here with you because I want to be? This thing was handed to me by the *director.*" He leaned forward. "And let me tell you, I didn't *want it.*"

"So who put him in charge?"

"The president."

"Never heard of him."

"Well, you're about to, Logan." Webster reclined again. "In more ways than one."

A long moment passed but Logan knew the look that hardened Webster's face. Knew it was set in stone. Finally he glanced at the two other manila envelopes that appeared to be...*personnel* files? He raised his eyes without touching either of them.

"I've got two men for this? With all due respect, sir, that's ridiculous. We used over a hundred agents in the Rabini Banking operation alone. And that wasn't half as—"

"You've got *two men,*" Webster replied. "And I don't like it, either. But I'm not calling the shots. This was passed down to the Bureau after a meeting with...another agency."

"What other agency?"

"You don't want to know."

"Sure I do."

"Logan, you do *not* want to know. Is that clear?"

"Sure," said Logan, after a moment. "I don't know why I asked about it. Twice."

Webster obviously didn't want to hear about it, either. "Believe me, Logan, it'd just make you more nervous than you already are. But to continue, this is going to cross investigatory lines paralleling both banking and counterintelligence like international tic tac toe."

"Did the Bureau select me for the job or did you?"

"You were selected," Webster said, leaving it at that. "But there weren't that many agents qualified to do the job. We needed someone who can work around...restrictive situations. And since most of those agents are in prison or dead, there weren't many to pick from." Webster was dismal. "It was a cellar battle: You won."

"Or lost."

"Whatever."

Logan realized that it was moments like this that defined a man. How he found the faintest reason for celebration at a funeral. How he found self-respect when he lost home and hearth. He held his ground. "Yeah, well, just how complicated is this thing liable to get?"

Webster rested his hands on the chair. "Apparently, from what I understand, this is going to cause an international scandal the likes of which have never been seen, nor ever shall be seen forever and ever again, amen. And you were supposedly selected because, among other things, you know better than anyone how to do this job and still cover your butt." Webster's glare was threatening. "Which is *our* butt, Logan. And even more important, is *my* butt."

Woodard cleared his throat and Logan suddenly understood why the Bureau's legal attaché to London was here.

"This is going over the water, son," he said gravely. "Going over big time before it comes back to crap all over us. We've got connections in Luxembourg, the Grand Caymans, Paris, Rome and every other city on the Continent. And we're going to be mixing it up with Interpol, Scotland Yard, the Saudis and some of the biggest old-money moguls in America." He nodded hard. "It's gonna be a big mess, Logan, once this gets up to speed."

Staring at the files, Logan said nothing for a moment. Then he shook his head with, "I want a promotion for this. I mean it. A promotion. I want a transfer to Quantico where I don't have to do anything but collect a paycheck the size of good ol' J. Edgar's, God rest his miserable, crooked, black soul."

Webster leaned back and laughed. "Well, I'm glad to see your priorities haven't changed, Logan. And I'm sure you'll be adequately compensated." He chuckled. "If you live."

Logan glanced at the mission file. He didn't want to read anything else about the scope of the operation. He'd seen enough to keep him from sleeping. He opened a personnel file. "Jonathan Malone?" he asked. "Who's Jonathan Malone?"

"He's graduating from the Academy today," Webster replied.

Logan's eyes flared. "Today? *Today*? That's against regulations, boss. I can't use a newbie for an investigation like this. I have to get people who have field experience. This kid's still on probation. He's doesn't have field time. Geez, I need somebody with time in—"

"You've got Malone." Webster pursed his lips, as if he didn't understand it, himself. "You've got Malone and you've got that guy out of Phoenix. The Indian. Cherokee or Navajo or whatever he is. The hacker we hired because he was too dangerous *not* to hire."

Logan stared evenly. "I don't like this."

"Look," Woodard growled, "this ain't gonna work with regular investigation methods. Between Interpol and Task Force and the British, there have been over five thousand men on this case and we *still* can't break it. So the time has come to get...*creative*." He paused, cocking his head. "This is a last-chance, make-it-or-break-it power drive, Logan. Just like the good-old, bad-old days. You know what I'm talking? Keep the thing in a glass case and only break it for war?"

Logan didn't smile. "Sounds like a suicide run."

Woodard continued, "Listen, partner, and listen good because what's on the line here isn't some Mafioso or some drug cartel or even some scumbag gold-smuggling operation. This is the big one, Logan. The real one. The *last* one."

Sighing, Logan took a second to reply. "If we're going to do it, let's do it right. Let's put a task force together and go after these people with a coordinated effort. But this is too wild. It's...too narrow."

"No," Webster said flatly. "This is the way it has to work if it's going to work at all. All our coordinated efforts have been crippled by leaks, so we need a team that can go undercover with minimum supervision. A team that won't be telegraphing their next move because nobody's going to know, exactly, what their next move is. You've got six sets of identification for you and each of your men and a half-million dollar operating budget. You can use the resources and whatever methods you deem necessary to run these people to ground."

"Listen, Logan," Woodard interjected, "everything seen before this has just been smoke and mirrors. But this, forgive me, is the godfather of the mother of all conspiracies. It comes down to a whole lot of money and who's controlling it. And, I'm telling you the truth, where there's this much money, there's blood in the hand holding it."

Logan grimaced. "What does *that* mean, Woodard?"

"That means," he answered, "that these people are covered far and deep and wide, son."

"How do you know that?"

With a slight hesitation, Woodard leaned forward. "All

right, listen to me on this. Cause this is one of the things that prompted this little war council. Six days ago a conglomerate of Middle Eastern banks took a whole ton of uncut diamonds off the market, shooting the cost of diamonds sky high all over the world. That's illegal, if you don't know, since banks can't work in unison to corner a market. But nothing could be proven, there's no joint ownership, whatever. But what it did was cripple six big-time American industries that use these diamonds for the production of some of that black op military machinery, lasers and stuff. So half our not-so-secret weapons are crippled."

"So what?"

Woodward gaped. "Dangit, Logan, that's not the point. The point is that someone was sending a message."

"What kind of message?"

"I'm trying to tell you!"

"Get to the point already."

"I'm trying to!" Woodard paused to gather his thoughts, "Now, I've got a man inside one of these banks in Jordan. He's trying to find out what little company started this little flea-market shutdown, and then he finds something. He signals for a drop." He paused. "You know what a drop is?"

Logan rolled his eyes. "Yes, Woodard, I've seen one on TV."

"Sorry. I forgot—you been around."

"A while."

"Okay, so my man—a good man—he schedules a drop and our team waits up for him. It's supposed to be inside a hotel in Cairo. He shows up, takes a stairway, then he don't come out like he's supposed to."

Looking aside, Logan saw Webster listening patiently, though he seemed to know everything.

"After an hour we go in," Woodard continued, distinctly morose. "We find him inside a storage closet on the sixth floor. A single stab wound through the heart. He had his gun, everything. But he didn't get a chance to pull it. No witnesses, no clues. Except his eyeballs had been cut out and stuffed with uncut diamonds."

He waited as Logan processed that information.

"About a million bucks worth," Woodard added.

Webster's expression was still unrevealing. After a moment Logan looked back at Woodard. "So...leave me alone, huh?"

"A million dollar warning," Woodard nodded. "He shuts down the diamond market to threaten us. He kills an agent because we want to know how he shut down the diamond market."

A tense silence filled the room.

It didn't need to be said that whoever did this was, indeed, covered far and deep and wide. To shut down the diamond market required unimaginable power. To uncover a FBI agent required the brutal manipulation of that power. To kill an agent required a fearless execution of that power. In all, it meant that this man, or men, could cripple nations, had access to classified secrets, and did not want anyone challenging his actions. And to leave a million dollars in diamonds as a warning meant a fearless contempt for enemies.

Slowly, Woodard continued, "Right now we've got leaks we can't *begin* to trace—from the Hill to the IRS. These people know what we're going to do before *we* do!" He shook his head again. "I don't know who this guy is, son, but I know that he's got access to all our secrets and that he controls a big chunk of the world banking system. And I know that no man could get that any way legal."

For no truly logical reason, Woodard lowered his voice. "These people can get to any of us, Logan. Individually or together—it doesn't make any difference. They can take our jobs or send us into bankruptcy with a phone call. So I'm telling you, buddy, we are in danger. And we have been, for a while. And that's just on a personal level. I'm not even talking about the international dangers. These guys can break countries as easily as they break people. And they enjoy doing it."

"Why hasn't anybody shut these people down before this?" Logan ventured.

"Logan," Woodard's was angry, "MI5 has lost three agents in the past four months, all of them good men. Experienced. Hard to kill. The French, running their own investigation, lost eight. A couple of other countries have lost more. It's not like nobody's tried."

Webster's reply was equally discomforting. "And we think we've lost more agents than the one in Cairo," he said. "Two months ago our legal attaché in Rome was killed in an automobile accident. The brakes of his car failed but the subsequent investigation revealed nothing empirical. It could possibly have been an accident. Or it could have been murder.

"Then, last month, one of Woodard's agents went sailing in the English Channel. His body was washed up on shore, no marks of foul play." He paused. "That seems to be the way it goes. Whenever someone is getting close to this thing, they die. But no one had actually been murdered outright until Cairo."

"Which means this guy is getting angry," Logan muttered.

"Which *means*," said Webster, "that he has already shut down the diamond market. Which means he's beginning to shut down the gold and silver markets. Which means that, before long, we might be paying a hundred bucks a barrel for oil. Which *means*," Webster stressed, "that we can't let this one slide, Logan."

The three men fell silent. The heavy, stressed atmosphere inspired a feeling like nothing Logan had ever known. He felt more alarm than he had known in a long time, but also faint pride that he didn't reveal the cold that gripped his bones. Then a latent detective-reflex caused him to ask: "What about the CIA?"

"We don't know about the CIA," Webster said. "They've said they don't want to participate and they've refused a liaison on the grounds it would compromise covert enterprises currently underway."

Logan expected it. "But if these crooks are involved in an international conspiracy to control the world banking system, then it's basically a counterintelligence investigation."

"No," Webster answered. "Counterintelligence is a finely controlled process to protect information. But to discover the name and location of a man when there are no leads whatsoever is pure detective work. So this is a job for the real thing, Logan. It's a job for a detective who can walk in where there's nothing, find the clues, and then the truth. As someone recently explained to me."

Logan didn't argue; Webster was right.

The faintest anger was visible in Webster's tone. "I don't like this plan, Logan. You're going to be pushed into traffic, and I'm not sure about your backup. But this has been assigned and passed down." He hesitated. "And you're the point man."

Logan lightly tapped the top file folder. He considered what he was up against and knew that, win or lose, this would be his last move. After this he would be finished forever or the rest of his career would be gravy.

A long silence passed.

"We'll start with the kid," he said, frowning. "Tell me about Malone."

"You're up, Jonathan!"

Rising, Jonathan lifted the shotgun, chambering a 12-guage round. Then he casually ensured the SIG Sauer P-226 semiautomatic—standard issue for candidates in the Federal Bureau of Investigation Academy—was secure in its holster.

He walked to the line.

"The line is *ready!*" shouted the instructor, putting on his earmuffs. He turned to wave at a bulletproof booth located atop a tower and Jonathan knew that the Range Controller was programming a new series of pop-up and moving targets.

"This is your first attempt at qualifying, Jonathan!" the instructor shouted—a burly, muscular man in his mid-forties who would forever resemble the marine drill sergeant he had once been. He was stern and impatient, but in spite of his gruff exterior, the students loved him, and he was affectionately known as "Paps" at the Academy.

"You've got five rounds from the Remington and three fifteen-round magazines for the SIG!" Paps shouted. "You'll have two minutes to finish the course!"

Jonathan nodded.

"*The line is hot!*" Paps shouted to Jonathan's classmates. All of them shifted nervously, donning ear protection. Then the big firearm instructor turned back. "You ready, Jonathan?"

Jonathan scanned the hundred-yard range located at the end of Hogan's alley. He would have to hit targets as they emerged from the ground or sped past him on the belts, discriminating in a split second between friendly and unfriendly paper silhouettes. And he would have to claim at least fourteen clean kills without a single wrongful shooting or he would be disqualified from the Academy.

Jonathan hefted the Remington and stepped past the line of the alley and onto the range. "Let's get on with it."

Paps raised a stopwatch. "GO!"

Instantly a woman with a child popped up to the left and Jonathan identified it before it was even vertical, knowing the real threat would come from the other side as he saw the silhouette with a gun rise from the ground and he fired from the hip, the massive .00 buck round shredding the target center-mass.

Into it with the first blast, Jonathan racked the round hard. He glimpsed the red shotgun shell sailing over his shoulder and he instinctively chambered another, walking forward.

Four more rounds.

A hostile target rose close and Jonathan swung right to left, hitting dead-center and he racked again, slamming in his third shell and counting, always counting.

"*Look quick, Jonathan!*" Paps shouted but there was nothing there and Jonathan continued steadily forward, the Remington set hard against his shoulder. He wouldn't allow himself to be disoriented.

A hostile target moved fast forty feet out and Jonathan calculated the time it would take to reach safety as he fast-drew the SIG, aiming high and to the left because the bullet would fall and then the semi-automatic erupted, recoiling hard, again and again.

Two rounds hit dead-center before the target reached safety and he de-cocked the SIG to slam the pistol into his holster, lifting the Remington to the ready position.

THE SCAM

"Sixty seconds!" Paps shouted. "Hurry it up, Jonathan! Find a target! Find a target or *you won't qualify!"*

Eyes on fire with something inside him rising and heating as it *always* heated to combat, Jonathan moved steadily and unhurried down the range, sixty seconds and counting. He stepped lightly and sensed a host of moving targets emerging left and right.

The next thirty seconds were a cacophony of thunderous blasts from the Remington and then Jonathan hurled the smoking shotgun hard to the side and contemptuously dropped the SIG's empty magazine to slam in another, moving forward and counting.

Six dead. No wrongful kills.

Paps' voice was at his back. "Look out, Jonathan!"

A silhouette spun close.

"Hit quick!"

Jonathan scowled as he sighted the unarmed woman. He moved another two steps before a target came up and he took his finger off the tightened trigger at the last second: A plainclothes cop excitedly extending a badge.

Grimacing in heat and overheated control, Jonathan turned to face the other side of the range as—

A silhouette rose *behind* the police officer: *Hostile!*

Jonathan fired from the hip, knowing that he didn't need sight-eye alignment and the round went past the officer at an angle, hitting the silhouette's 10-ring—the heart.

He turned to confront three targets speeding across his path, all armed. Raising the SIG and leading each, Jonathan emptied the last magazine for three 10-ring shots to claim three more kills for a total of fourteen.

Now, he could finish the course early or he could stay and claim more kills. But if he stayed and accidentally hit a friendly silhouette, he'd still be disqualified.

"What are you going to do, Jonathan?" Paps shouted, dark eyes flashing. "You've got your kills! What are you gonna do! You gonna crap out on me and run across the line or are you gonna kill some more?"

Finding his place in the conflict, here and now and somewhere in the past, Jonathan didn't reply as he dropped the empty magazine to the dirt, slamming in his last fifteen-round clip.

He moved up the range.

"*Ha!*" Paps laughed. "I knew you'd want to finish it! But you're out of *time!* You've only got twenty seconds! Go across the line! Go on! Hurry it up!"

Jonathan waited.

Paps shifted in panic. "Don't be screwin' around on me! I mean it! Get across the line!"

Jonathan waited. It would come for him; it would always come for him. Then a target emerged far left and Jonathan fired cross-body to hit it solidly as he glimpsed another threat and dropped, no longer on a range but somewhere else—the place where he always returned, again and again—to where his rage was born and still lived and he fired to hit the heart, the heart, head, head, head...

Dead, dead, dead.

Paps ran forward. "Jonathan! How many rounds you got left? How many rounds?"

Jonathan waited on his knees. "Three."

"*NO!*" Paps shouted. "That's the kind of thing that gets you killed, son! You've got five rounds *and ten seconds!* So finish it! Go across the line! You're done!"

Jonathan knew he wasn't done. Then he saw the target: the one he'd been waiting for. It was the killer, the cold-blooded *skull-faced* killer holding the gun barrel to the head of a help-less, unarmed woman. Jonathan had waited for him and he had come as he always came, coming to him *for him* and Jonathan never missed.

It was an optional shot because of the technical difficulty and this time it was longer than ever before.

Jonathan raised the SIG to aim high. He centered on the left of the gunman's head because he knew the .9 mm. slug would fall low and right at the distance but he was at home, here, had *always* been at home here and his finger tightened. Hit through the forehead.

Cold kill.

Ten feet remaining. Two more shots.

"Five seconds, kid!" Paps was shouting now with genuine alarm. "Get across the line and *stop screwing around!*"

Two hostile targets, each optional and moving toward the other and Jonathan fell to a knee. He raised the SIG, waiting calmly until the targets crossed each other and he fired his last two rounds.

Center-mass.

The slide of the SIG locked and Jonathan walked forward, crossing the line of the range to turn stoically as Paps raised a burly arm into the air, staring at the stopwatch.

"TIME!" he bellowed.

Shaking his head, the firearm instructor glowered with unconcealed anger. With the slightest smile Jonathan dropped the last magazine, letting it hit the dirt. He laughed, "I thought you said I had five shots, Paps. Looks like I only had three."

"Yeah, yeah, I lied to you, boy. I wanted you to *know* how many shots you had left," he lectured. "And screwing around like that was stupid, Jonathan. They've spent a lot of money putting you through this Academy, and it's my job to make sure you get through the course."

Scowling as he walked forward, Paps added, "But you shot good, I'll admit that. We don't see too many hundred percents on this range." He turned to the bleachers. "And I can tell you the *rest* of that crew ain't gonna pull it off. I'll be lucky if they don't shoot me!" He was pleased. "Yeah, boy, you did all right. You kept your cool. And that's what counts in a gunfight. Keeping your cool."

Jonathan's eyes were focused on a spot downrange. He was the first of his classmates to qualify, and the rest were shifting nervously on the bleachers. "How many options do I get to qualify, Paps?"

"You've qualified, Jonathan." Paps motioned, as if he sensing the doomed direction of this conversation. "Go to the house."

"How many options, Paps?"

Paps eyes narrowed like gun sights.

"You *know* you've got three options, Jonathan. But you just ran it and you shot a hundred percent, and that's as good as it gets." He paused. "If you try and run it again and you shoot less than a hundred then...Well, I'll have to put that score, or the *last* score, in your file. Or you might even fail the darn thing, boy. Which means you'll be out of the Academy. I don't like it, but those are the rules."

Jonathan glanced at the bleachers. Most of his classmates were staring at him...waiting to see what he would do. He knew they would talk about this later, but he didn't care. He had never fit in with them, anyway.

Most of them were accountants or lawyers or computer specialists who, for whatever bizarre reason, wanted to be special agents. They came from good families and solid backgrounds, were college educated, and had enjoyed the best the world could give.

He barely had enough college education to qualify for the Bureau, and to make his relationship with them even worse, he'd earned their contempt by conquering academy exams that could drive a lawyer insane.

Jonathan had found new respect for his own intellect by rising to the number one academic position of his class, winning valedictorian without effort—a coveted position that he cared absolutely nothing about. So he knew that he was as smart as any of them. He just didn't have the benefit of a good family, or any family at all, for that matter. But he was comfortable with it. He didn't need a family. Hadn't, for a long time.

Jonathan dropped the slide on the SIG, a steel crack that communicated his intent. "I tell you what, Paps: What do you wanna bet I'll shoot another hundred on the next run?"

The muscular firearm instructor chuckled. "No, sir, Jonathan. I wouldn't bet anything at all against you on this range." The ghost of a smile appeared on his face. "No, sir. I wouldn't bet anything at all."

With a laugh Jonathan walked toward the line.

"Then let's shoot it again."

Chapter Two

Logan tossed the file onto the table.

"We've all seen scams like this before. It's good, but it's not that good. What makes these people so special?"

Webster's voice was low. "Just tell me what you think is going on, Logan."

Adjusting his coat, Logan settled back. "All right, this is a coalition of seemingly legitimate companies running a bogus loan-making operation. The coalition takes large cash payments from targeted companies as collateral against big-time loans that never materialize, and which were never supposed to materialize."

"That's where it starts." Webster rested his chin on a cupped hand. "Save me the trouble with the rest."

Logan continued, "This coalition recruits loan requests from companies by advertising in publications like *The Wall Street Journal* or the *New York Times*. The say they have an absolute truckload of cash available for commercial loans. And after reading these advertisements, companies contact..." He looked at the file.

"World Finance," Webster offered.

"World Finance, thank you, and World Finance says, 'Do we have *money*? Do *we* have money? Are you kidding? We've got money out the wazoo! You want some? No problem! Just give us a loan package so we can see how much you're worth,'" Logan grimaced, "'and we'll work out a loan that will make you a financial Tyrannosaurus!'"

"Exactly."

Logan laughed. "So, after this poor fool CEO gives his company's financial statement, World Finance knows *exactly* how much they can dupe him in flat loan fees, qualifying fees, fees for letters of guarantees, whatever. Basically they know how much they can scam out of the sheep.

"Except World Finance is just a point man. And within days World Finance puts this fool CEO of...uh...say, International Widgets, or whatever, in contact with an overseas company that will do the *actual lending*. And this overseas company sends the CEO of International Widgets a tentative letter of credit."

Webster appeared sick. "You're on the ball, Logan."

"Yeah, J. Edgar taught me, himself. Best scam artist to ever darken the doorway of any whorehouse in—"

"Just get on with it, Logan."

Enjoying himself, Logan continued, "So, Mr. Widget pays his half-million dollars and gets this Letter of Credit from an overseas lending company for a five million dollar loan. *But...* the Letter of Credit is only good for thirty days. Then Mr. Widget is informed by World Finance that the lending company wants him to get something called a 'Prime Bank Guarantee' so they can approve his five million-dollar loan. But Mr. Widget has to do it *quick* before the thirty days expire.

"Now *this* is a problem because Mr. Widget doesn't know what a Prime Bank Guarantee *is*." Logan laughed out loud. "Anyway, in the end Mr. Widget is stalled and stonewalled until he loses his down payment, his company, his house, and everything else he owns in a maze of letters and guarantee fees with ten different companies. It could work a hundred ways, but it's always the same."

"You're on track," Webster muttered. "On reflection, I think they may have been right to give you the job."

"How's that?"

"Because, Logan, you could have been a brilliant success on the wrong side of the law. It's a good thing for all of us, if you ask me, that you're on the right side."

"Well," Logan stared, "I'm not really sure this is the right side."

"Maybe not. But one thing's for sure."

"What?"

"It takes a crook to catch a crook."

Logan nodded. "Exactly."

Jonathan walked into the gym. He glanced out the window—six hours to sunset. Six hours to finish the match.

Mayamoto Matsumo, concentrated on his conditioning, did not look up. Holding a small sledgehammer, he rhythmically pounded one hand laid flat against a slanted piece of steel. Again and again, again and again, the big Japanese pounded his right hand, pounded slowly up his forearm, pounding, pounding, steel against steel.

Someone had told Jonathan that, as a young man, Matsumo had worked in a Tokyo slaughterhouse and had used the sledgehammer to kill cattle. But when he quit, the powerful Japanese took the sledgehammer with him to harden his hands, forearms, feet, and shins.

For thirty years he had beaten his body until his arms and legs were as hard as flesh and bone could become. His fervent devotion and fantastic skill in the martial arts were legendary—as indestructible as the steel held within his hands.

When he still lived in Japan, Matsumo was recruited by Japanese police to search the riverfront bars and apprehend the most violent Yakuza. And Matsumo had done his job well, beating the meanest, toughest thugs into submission. Then he would simply handcuff them to a rail or doorway until uniformed officers came along to transport them.

Long, smooth knife scars crisscrossed his forearms and face like a roadmap, traces of war. Nor did Matsumo try to hide them. He was what he was; the strongest of his kind. He metered out Old Testament justice, like Samson. And his body was witness to the fact.

"It is all I know," the big Japanese had muttered one day as Jonathan sat beside him. "If someone tries to break my arm with a club, what will I do?" He hammered slowly, frowning. "I will block the club with my arm, and the club will break."

Jonathan said nothing.

"The hammer and anvil are not for everyone," the Japanese growled. "It is the old way; a way that is lost."

Jonathan had sat attentively beside the massive martial arts master for half of his nights in the Academy and long past the hours when his classmates retired to study for exams. And he had learned a lot more, sitting and listening to Matsumo, than he would have ever learned from books.

Over fifty years old, Matsumo lived by his own highly developed code of honor, based on the code of Bushido from his youth and, surprisingly, the Bible. Knowing he had escaped death many times, he considered his life forfeit, and lived to help others.

"A death must be right," he said one night. "Even if a man lives a life of wrong, his death must be right. There is always one last chance for redemption."

Although Matsumo had never served in the FBI, the FBI had been quick to apprehend his awesome skills for Defensive Training—skills in karate, judo, boxing, escrima, knife fighting, even guns. It didn't matter; Matsumo was master of them all.

Initially, Jonathan had trouble reconciling Matsumo's fierce warrior persona with his discussions of faith. But finally Jonathan understood the apparent contradiction. The fearsome Matsumo was also a gentle man—a man who tended his garden with almost paternal affection. Matsumo was both a warrior and a gentleman. His body was virtually invulnerable, but his heart could be wounded.

Their initial friendship had been forged on the combat mat, where Jonathan earned his respect. For Matsumo had mercilessly beaten him to the ground, and yet Jonathan had always risen to his feet, fighting, fighting, fighting, never surrendering.

It was the place where Matsumo measured a man, the first level Jonathan had passed. Then on a slow day of training, when the class was resting from a six-mile run, the implacable Matsumo had invited Jonathan to dinner at his own home.

Stunned, Jonathan accepted.

As generous and concerned with courtesy as a fourteenth century samurai, Matsumo had prepared boiled octopus "beaten one hundred times against wood, to tenderize the flesh."

Jonathan shared the dinner gladly, sensing the beginning of the first genuine, close friendship of his life. It was odd, he noticed, for he had always been alone, had always found comfort in being alone. Yet despite his preference for solitude, he knew a friendship with the big Japanese that could not be denied.

That first dinner, Matsumo had bowed to say a silent prayer. Jonathan remembered something of his childhood— bedtime prayers with his father and mother. The room half-lit by his nightlight, his parents sitting on his bed. He had rarely felt safe in his life, but with Matsumo, he could revert to that simple, childlike faith. It was enough knowing there was someone looking out for him. Matsumo understood—he and Jonathan were the same. Alone in a hostile world. A friendship that had begun in martial respect had moved far beyond.

Defensive tactics was a unique unification of aikido, judo, wrestling, boxing, knife fighting, and handgun fighting that were the ultimate cutting edge of self-defense. It was a complex science of throws, blows, knife tactics, handgun tactics, ground fighting, and killing blows that had become, in the realm of those who *knew*, the ultimate fighting art. It was both tactical and physical, and only a few became truly proficient.

"You fight with fire," Matsumo said one day, standing over him. "But fire will destroy you if it's not controlled."

Jonathan said nothing.

"When you graduate from this school, come to me," Matsumo continued. "I will teach you how to control this fire."

Holding bruised ribs from where Matsumo's brutal fist had connected, Jonathan promised but then added, "When I finish my sixteen weeks, Matsumo, they'll be transferring me. I'm not going to have any more time to fight."

Matsumo laughed, turned away.

"It will not take much time," he said.

And now, one day before graduation, Jonathan had come for their last match. He walked forward, stepping silently upon the blue foam pad.

Matsumo looked up from his pounding. Then he smiled slightly, gently laying down the sledgehammer. With a quick jerk to straighten his gi, he laughed.

Immensely strong, as thickly muscled as an ox, the gigantic Japanese walked onto the mat. His face was dark and forbidding with eyes that unconsciously revealed a supreme physical confidence. He smiled slightly, a sliver of delight beaming in his slitted eyes. His bull-like chest was as wide and deep as a barrel, heavy arms descending to his sides. His hands were dark, callused, intimating the strength of stone. He stopped six feet away.

Jonathan tossed his gun belt to the side. He wore only his khaki BDU pants, blue FBI Academy T-shirt, and boots. He circled to the side, holding Matsumo's black eyes.

"So," he muttered, "you have come."

"Surprised?"

"No," the Japanese smiled.

Jonathan began circling slowly. "But you're wrong, Matsumo. This won't teach me anything."

"We will see."

Frowning, Matsumo unfurled a yellow sash from his hand. Then with ominous meaning he wrapped the sash around his massive waist, over his black belt. When he was finished he closed his huge hands, the first two knuckles of each fist making a wide wedge that Jonathan knew could shatter stone laid flat against stone.

"When I was a young man," he rumbled, "I survived the *One Hundred Man Kumite*." His face became severe. "One hundred rounds of full-contact fighting against seven black belts, each of them resting for six rounds while I fought without rest. Full contact, round after round. Bones and cartilage were broken, but there was no mercy. And I won, in the end. Defeating them all. Then I fought the Shaolin in the hills of Geigan. He was over sixty years old, but still as strong as he had ever been. He wrapped this sash around his waist and challenged me to take it from him before sunset." Matsumo's dark eyes glinted. "I did."

Jonathan was watching carefully.

A broad hand as hard as a brick caressed the yellow sash around Matsumo's waist. "Remove this sash from my waist, boy. Attack me. Use your fire. Your rage."

Jonathan knew that was all but impossible. "What is that supposed to teach me?"

"When you take the sash, you will know."

Jonathan said nothing. But he realized that Matsumo was one of the few people he had ever respected. And then he realized that he had wanted this moment for a long, long time.

"*KAAII!*"

Matsumo's punch would have shattered his ribs but Jonathan slipped right to return a straight blow that he effortlessly blocked with a granite forearm and they both retreated.

Slow. Unhurried.

Jonathan knew that it would be all but impossible to take the sash from Matsumo's waist. But he bent his head, he awoke his rage, and then he let the rage loose. He shouted as he leaped to kick Matsumo's thigh, the room echoing with the thunderous impact.

Matsumo didn't even sway and Jonathan felt as if he'd kicked a slab of granite. He came out of the blow and leaped away, trying to gain distance on the Japanese.

"*Now the game begins!*" Matsumo laughed, even larger in his wrath, surging forward.

Jonathan leaped back to evade a punch and instantly returned his own, solidly striking Matsumo's chest with a fist and then he retreated as he *had* to retreat before the incommensurate strength as he saw a place of fire and rage more rage to see himself...

At home.

Logan sat back.

"Not a bad scam, Commander. Taking hundreds of millions, even billions, from these companies and doing it legal. Except that I've heard of this for years and I know we've got some kind of task force on it." Logan stared Webster hard in the eyes. "So what's the real reason I'm here?"

"You catch on fast, Logan."

"I've been around the horn."

Webster raised his brow slightly. "Good enough, then. Let me tell you why we're—"

"No," Logan said, unfriendly. "Let *me* tell you why we're really here." Webster shrugged and gestured that he should continue. "We've got just about a hundred special agents on this, right?"

Webster nodded.

"And we, the most prestigious law enforcement agency in the entire world, have this grand international task force with mail opening and phone taps and surveillance, the whole nine yards. We're using Intelligence and Technical Services and Inspection and International Affairs Divisions and Justice and, despite the sieve of leaks, we've pretty much figured these goons out.

"*Except*...while we were figuring them out, we stumbled over something else. Something that scared everybody. Something that's as ugly as ugly gets. And the director shut the lid hard to keep it secret. Because it's scary. It's scary and mean, and the only thing anybody knows *for sure* is that *somebody's* got to do something quick or we are truly screwed."

Webster had the look of a wild animal backed into a corner.

"So what's got everybody so scared?" Logan asked. "Including you."

Woodard interjected, "We think there might be a new player."

"A new player?"

Woodard nodded. "And we got suspicions he's running something else. Something bigger than the money. Meaner than the money. And let me make myself clear, it's what's beneath the money that's costing our boys their lives. That's why the MI5 guys were killed. They were onto something bigger than the money."

"Bigger than the...?" Logan scowled. "Like *what*?"

"We don't know. But it's there."

"How do you know it's there if you don't know what it is?" Logan asked.

"A trail of dead bodies stretching halfway round the world lets us know its there." Woodard replied. "One of my best ASACs washing up dead on the shores of England lets me know."

No one seemed eager to break the silence. Finally Logan focused on Webster. "Something isn't adding up. If this new player is so new, how did he get control over this thing?"

"Well, he's not actually *new*," Webster replied. "That's a misstatement on Woodard's part. Actually, we have suspicions that this mystery man is the one who started all of this. But we don't know what he's doing behind the money. Or why." Webster sighed. "Or if he even exists. We only know that any time an agent—anybody's agent—gets close to discovering who this guy is, they get themselves dead."

"A suspicion," Logan stared. "That's it?"

"Yep."

Logan paused a long time. "And you want me to find him?"

Webster sighed, "That's about the size of it."

"I see," Logan said, clipped. "Would I be coordinating my efforts with any other team?"

"No. You'll be on your own. But Strike Six is spearheading the overall investigation." Webster was referring to a specialized federal task force comprised of agents from Treasury, Internal Revenue, and the FBI, all joined to make a unique team operating under the singular jurisdiction of the Justice Department.

"Who's heading up Strike Six?" Logan asked.

"Mark Hooper. You know him?"

"Yeah," Logan replied. "I know Mark pretty well. We've worked a lot of cases together. In the old days, that is. But I haven't seen Mark in four or five years."

"What do you think of him?"

"What do I think of Mark?" Logan opened his eyes, as revealing as a glass window. "I'm thinking Mark's about to retire and that he's earned it. I'm thinking he's one of the best agents that ever carried credentials but he's KMA. If you're not familiar with the term, boss, that means 'kiss my—'"

"I *know* what it means, Logan."

"Yeah," Logan continued, "anyway, Mark's a good man but he's KMA. And, more seriously, he tough and smart, but his health isn't what it used to be."

"Hooper was selected because we've got security problems. And Hooper, at least, can be trusted."

"*Executive* security problems?" It was one thing to have lower-level leaks. It was another thing to have heavyweights sold out. "Where?"

"We don't know, Logan. That's why your team is set up the way it is. We're hoping that a small, covert team will dig up what's being protected. Which is why you're totally covert with only distant supervision. I'll be your only contact."

Stunned, Logan took his time to reply. "And just how am I supposed to find this mystery man?"

"You're supposed to find him," Webster answered, a vague gesture. "But for my sake, please try to stay within the law."

"How high is security compromised?"

"We don't know. But we know there are numerous and sundry forces within this government that may well try and impede if they discover what you're doing." Webster seemed to consider his next words carefully. "This guy has got to go down, Logan. Even if we have to do something extreme."

"Uh huh," Logan mumbled. "Let me capsulize this: You want me to work with or around Mark and everyone else to find this mystery man who's killed every other agent sent after him. And to make it even prettier you don't have the foggiest who this guy is or what he's really up to. But you want me to deal with everything, stay within the law, and find this maniac, regardless." He waited. "That about it?"

"No." Webster responded. "That's not about it. Cause we want you to do more than just find him."

Logan nodded, "I figured."

Webster turned slowly toward the window. "We want you to discover why nobody can put him down, Logan. Find what's broken." He waited. "Understand?"

"Yeah. I understand. And I don't like it. Cause I think you want me to tug on Superman's cape." Logan stared hard. "You want me to stay alive long enough to find out what Superman is doing and how heavy he's covered. And I'm not the first choice for the job; they rest just got themselves killed."

No answer.

"Well, I can probably tell you right now why this mystery man has never been taken down by any intelligence agency, Commander. Might save you some time."

Webster made a faint gesture. "No, Logan. Let me tell you what you're thinking and save us both some time. Our mystery man has never been taken down by any of *us*, and I use that term loosely, because he *is* one of us. He's a senior man in FBI or CIA or Scotland Yard or MI6 or KGB or something else. But he's got equal numbers in competing agencies, and they're cleared above classified. It doesn't matter; he's one of us, somehow."

"Or," Logan added, "*all* of us."

A long time, no one moved.

Delicately, Webster rested his hand on the file. He stared at the pages in silence as if he were taken by dark thoughts. He didn't look up when he spoke again.

"You've got to find him, Logan. Any way you can. You'll have international jurisdiction, diplomatic immunity, the works. But remember; you can trust no one. Not our people. Not their people. Not CIA or Scotland Yard or whoever comes into the picture." He paused, a deadly gaze in his eyes. "And for your own safety, Logan, find him as fast as you can."

A silence passed and Logan wearily leaned his head back against the chair, slowly releasing a breath. He placed a hand against his forehead, rubbing. Suddenly he had a headache. For a brief moment he closed his eyes, didn't even look again at Webster as he spoke.

"If this guy is covered like I think he is, he'll have the local police in his pocket. Probably the nationals, too. He'll have a dozen escape routes and some high-class hitters that are gonna be coming after me as soon as he sees me coming after him." He paused. "I think it's an understatement to say I'm gonna need some backup."

Webster sighed, looked gloomily out the window.

"Well...I hope we've taken care of that."

The Scam

Sweating and beaten, Jonathan glanced at the window. Exhaustion gripped his bones, hot and close.

Again and again he had attacked the massive Japanese, roaring as he hurled blow after blow, throwing the endless anger of his soul to burn Matsumo to the ground. But even after six hours, Jonathan was as far from victory as he had ever been. And night was falling.

Jonathan lowered his head, teeth clenched, thinking furiously of a tactic, knowing he remained in the fight for only one reason.

Despite Matsumo's promise to fight full contact, the Japanese had never struck him with anything close to it. For if he had even once struck with that mountainous power, Jonathan would be dead, his skull crushed like a grapefruit or his back broken by a sledgehammer fist driven through his chest.

"A last exchange," the Japanese growled, gazing down. "A last chance." He nodded. "You fight with great anger. But you're not fighting me. You're fighting someone else that is always before you. When the time comes, do you plan to kill him with your great anger? Is that how you plan to defeat him? With your great rage?"

Jonathan grimaced.

"Well?" Matsumo laughed, crouching. "Use your great anger! Anger can defeat anything! Can it not?" His dropped into a crouch, a fist raised. *"Can it not!"*

Jonathan gasped, blinded by sweat and knowing that nothing, nothing on the face of this Earth could defeat Matsumo. Here was the place where strength ended, where flesh failed.

Matsumo took a slight step. Approaching.

A last encounter.

Matsumo's leaped forward, his hand lashing outward in *shuto* that would have shattered Jonathan's skull if he didn't retreat as he had retreated hundreds of times only to angrily attack again, trying to beat the massive Japanese to the ground and Jonathan suddenly understood...

He threw himself into the blow.

Matsumo's eyes widened in shock as his hand grazed the skin of Jonathan's skull. The Japanese shouted in alarm to wildly turn his blow away. Then Jonathan's hands lashed out to frantically rip the sash from Matsumo's waist and they collided chest to chest and spilled backward together, wild and off balance.

Nothing skilled, ugly and unexpected, they tumbled across the mat and Jonathan rolled far and away, glaring wildly at the sash, unbelieving of his victory even as he held it in his hands. He was too exhausted to feel anything at all and then Matsumo gained his feet, mountainous and poised.

The Japanese gazed down with impenetrable black eyes. His face was ultimately menacing.

Breathless, Jonathan brought a foot beneath him, not daring to stand. The sash was in his hands, but not because of skill. It was because Matsumo, at the last frantic, flashing moment had possessed the supreme skill to turn a blow that would have taken his life.

A victory won by mercy.

Silence enveloped them in the heavy, humid air.

Jonathan saw thin tendrils of mist rising from Matsumo's oxlike neck and wide brutal hands, smoldering in the cold. And Jonathan felt a quickening fear, knowing Matsumo could kill him without effort...before the Japanese smiled.

"So," he rumbled, "now you know."

Jonathan was breathless.

"Now...I know...*what*?"

"Now you know...that fire must be controlled." With a nod the Japanese turned and walked away. "Remember that when you find this man you seek."

Jonathan blinked and suddenly the room faded around him. Now he saw a house, darkness, a skeletal face and a game unfinished.

"I'll remember," he said.

For a man so big, he attracted an amazing lack of attention as he approached the mailbox, one among thousands in central London. He flowed unhurried through the crowd, his huge shoulders ox-like and brutish against the slim silhouettes of others.

It was difficult to explain how such nothingness was accomplished until one stood next to him and even looked upon him. But there was something Zen-like about him, as if he were not there. He did not look at anyone, nor did he look away from them. It was as if he simply did not exist in any real way. What was *him* was not here; it was somewhere else. He was not worthy of notice.

Cold blue eyes like arctic ice were half-closed, masking their piercing intensity. His beard, streaking with gray like his hair, was mildly unkempt, neither handsome nor offensive. His clothes were common and vague—clothes found everywhere, nowhere.

He stood before the box, opened it.

Not a flicker of emotion or thought crossed his face as he gazed upon the envelope. It had been almost twenty years since he had opened it to see a letter. He did not hesitate, though, as he removed his mail as if he removed it every day.

The only mistake he made, as he walked slowly toward the doors, was not looking to identify the sender.

Because he already knew.

Chapter Three

Immensely opulent, lined in glossy mahogany and glistening ivory, the office glowed with a pearly light, the very image of power and superiority and achievement, and the few who inhabited its subdued space were preternaturally focused, silently studying the glowing green computer screens.

Clad in a black three-piece Armani suit, the visitor entered without announcement and approached the rear of the floor, located on the thirty-second level of the National Commerce Building in New York City. He was not confronted as he neared a large, red-bearded man seated within a walnut office.

Beside the man were two doublewide walnut doors that obviously led into the last, and most important, domain.

The bearded man was powerfully built, like a weightlifter. His face, deeply tanned and weathered like some ancient mariner, was impassive, brutal, and dangerous. Halting before him, the gentleman gazed down and nodded curtly.

"Frazier," he said.

The man named Frazier reached over to touch a small button and spoke in a low tone. There was no reply but the wide double doors opened soundlessly.

With a dismissive nod, the man entered.

Logan set his empty beer on the table and motioned to the bartender for another. His movement was patient, but patience was the last thing he felt.

Nervous, now, Woodard sat across from him, bent morosely over his fifth whiskey. And although Logan thought his behavior was attracting attention in The Boardroom Bar, the favorite hangout of federal and military agents stationed in Quantico, he'd decided not to say anything. Better, he thought, to study it.

"Whoever this guy is," Woodard mumbled, "he's covered his tracks far and deep and wide. We've got people all over the country trying to find an *initial* and we got nothing." He belched. "Just rumors of a dark-haired guy who owns everything. A guy who gets things *done*. Some kind of Superman." He looked away, seeming to search. "A guy nobody can touch."

Logan glanced to the side, saw a couple of NAs, maybe foreign police officers training at the academy. There were also two marine drill instructors intently trying to follow the conversation and Logan decided he couldn't wait any longer. "Come on, partner. Your people just missed something."

"No!" Woodard shouted. Logan looked up sharply, realizing the whiskey had hit something else. Hard.

"I'm telling you," Woodard continued. "This guy owns half of England and half of America and we've checked everything but he ain't there! He ain't anywhere! You think fifty agents studying the same page are gonna make a mistake?"

Logan knew he had to defuse Woodard carefully because a drunk doesn't respond well to those who are not. "Only two eyes can study the same page at a time, Woodard. You know that. And anybody can make a mistake. Even if they do it one after the other."

"So what do you see?"

"All I see is a lot of talk about how this Superman can't be touched. So I'm going to take my time, go over the evidence myself. And the rest of it is flack. This guy hasn't perfectly covered his tracks. Nobody can perfectly cover their tracks." Logan took a slow sip. "He's made a mistake. I promise you that much."

"What kind of mistake?"

Logan laughed, looked away. "It's always the same, Woodard. There'll be a place where he reached too far. Where he got greedy. But it's going to be a few years back, I think. And that's probably the mistake your boys are making. They're looking at recent documents. But whatever mistake this guy made, he made it when he was young. Before he learned to play the game."

Sweat was visible on Woodard's forehead, and Logan studied it. It reminded him of the way rookie agents looked before they went into a gunfight. But Woodard had been involved in six shootouts since he joined the Bureau, so it wasn't a look he would easily wear. He asked, "You really think so?"

"Yeah, Woodard. I think so."

"That's where you'll start? In the past?"

Logan laughed, "Yeah."

"But how are you going to know where to look? Where are you gonna start? I mean, that's a gazillion documents to search for something like that!"

"We'll just start looking and keep looking until we find it." Logan grimaced. "You act like you're terrified of this guy."

Woodard leaned close. "You don't *get it*, Logan! This guy is *power*. He's *never* been caught! And he's been running a financial scam for forty years that's made him billions of dollars and we've got *nothin'* on him." He licked his lips. "This is out of my league, son. I'm telling you. It's out of my league..."

Quiet followed the outburst like a funeral dirge. It was as

if Woodard had been given a death sentence beyond appeal. Logan's voice was subdued. "Has this guy threatened you?"

"This guy doesn't threaten." Woodard clutched his whiskey for comfort. "He don't have to." He glanced around. "But you're right; this isn't the place."

Logan was still, watchful. "Has somebody tried something, Woodard?"

"Not yet. But it's coming. I can feel it. I know too much. I'm getting too close."

Logan tried to get him to relax. "We've got years in this business, partner. Our lives have been threatened a thousand times. But nobody ever tried to do anything. Most of the time it's just talk. And even if they do, we can give as good as we get."

"This guy is different, Logan. Nobody's safe. I've got thirty-three years in the field, son. Everyone knows I can't be scared anymore. Shoot, I can't even get drunk anymore, no matter how much I drink. But I've got a real bad feeling about this one. I...I think this is the real thing, buddy. This mystery man won't hesitate to kill all of us. And believe me, he can do it." He paused. "I'm too old for this."

Disturbed, Logan took a long swallow of beer. Then he gently set the glass dead center on the napkin before raising his eyes evenly. "Woodard, it doesn't matter if this guy stole a million bucks or a twenty off some wino on the street, he's still a crook. He is *not* Superman. He's a punk, and he'll always be a punk. He's just smarter than the rest." He paused. "Or luckier."

Woodard didn't move.

"Tell me about Malone," Logan said, leaving it. "I read the files at the administrative building, but not everything can be put in a file. What do you know about him?"

Woodard was grateful to talk about something that he actually knew something about. "No parents. Relatives in Charlottesville raised him. Got a degree at the university in political science. File says he's smart. Maybe too smart. He spent four years in the Army. He's real good at hand to hand. And real, *real* good with a handgun. I looked over his scores from the Army to police and through the Academy. He never shot less than a hundred percent on any course he ever ran."

He belched again. "He's, uh, real good with bombs, too. Explosive Ordinance qualified. Good in the forest and all that fancy fast-entry stuff. But I hear he's a stone-cold loner. Doesn't work well with teams cause he tends to improvise, thinking of things like a game. He was even recommended for Delta, but he didn't make it because they considered him too creative. After he got out of the service, he spent two years in regular law enforcement before applying for the Bureau. And..." he paused, "...when Malone was just a kid, I think he was considered some kind of chess prodigy."

"A chess prodigy?" Logan asked, genuinely interested. "Malone was a chess prodigy?"

"Yeah, he was considered some kind of genius." Woodard cradled a new glass. "A bona fide *genius,* son. He won the British Chess Championship when he was only nine years old. Beat some old geezer named Stanlov Sarkosky, a Russian Grandmaster, in the best of five games. A real mean match, I heard."

"Who'd you hear that from?"

"Webster."

"Well," Logan decided he could trust the source, "what'd Webster say about it?"

Woodard rubbed his chest with an acidic belch. "He said... uh, that Malone and Starkosky were two games for two and the whole thing came down to the tiebreaker. A real war."

"And Malone beat a Grandmaster? At nine years old?"

"Well, Malone and the Russian killed every player on the board but two pawns and two kings. That's all they had left—two pawns and two kings. In the end—I don't know how Webster learns all this stuff—Malone made some kind of brilliant sacrifice move and traded his pawn for a queen and put the guy in checkmate."

Woodard opened his eyes wider. "Webster told me that it's recorded as one of the best ten games ever played in the history of chess, or something like that. And we're talking about several *centuries* of games here, buddy. So Malone has the touch. He was nine years old and he played one of the greatest games in history."

Logan's eyes narrowed. "Well, why didn't Malone become another Bobby Fischer or something? What's he doing in the FBI?"

Woodard was silent.

"C'mon, Woodard. What's wrong with this kid? Cause I'll tell you this: If I had the ability to make millions with that kind of talent, I sure as hell wouldn't be in the FBI."

"Look, Logan, this kid got messed up. His parents were killed in front of him right after this game." He waved with irritation. "Some guy broke into their house, a big old place in England. Stabbed his parents to death. Malone saw it. Like I said, he was only nine years old and his father was the one who taught him to play chess. Played a game with him every night, so they were close." He paused, cleared his throat. "After his old man died, Malone couldn't play any more. I don't know why. They say he just couldn't play the game again."

Logan stared. "Why not?"

"I don't know. Some kind of traumatic shock association

thing triggered by symbolism. The psychiatrists got a fancy word for it; I don't remember. But it basically means he can't play chess anymore because it reminds him of the night his father was murdered. Or...or something about that night."

Logan nursed his beer.

"Hard thing for a kid," he whispered.

"Yeah," Woodard replied, "anyway, his father was MI6, so the State Department relocated him to America, where he was born. It's in the file." He added, as if in afterthought, "Webster said some old admiral out of MI6 supported Malone financially while he grew up in the States."

"An admiral out of MI6," Logan repeated, searching Woodard's drunken gaze.

"Yeah. The admiral was a close friend of his father. And, by the way, this is secure. Malone's name was changed when he was a kid. I think the admiral was worried that the kid was also targeted, but he managed to escape. They also thought he was a potential witness, so he was protected in England for a while and after things quieted down he was moved to America and given a new name. He was raised by some distant relatives of his mother."

Logan was silent. For the first time, a suspicious pause stretched between them. "All right," Logan said finally, "Malone understands games, but doesn't play 'em. Is that what I need?"

"Well, it *might* be what you need, Logan. And that's not a joke. You might just need somebody who's got the touch. Someone who can play the game and win. No matter what."

Logan shook his head. "This isn't a game, Woodard."

Woodard was somber.

"Or it's the most dangerous one."

Without sound, the wide double doors opened.

In a moment the tall gentleman in the Armani suit appeared in the exit. Then he reached into his coat and withdrew a handkerchief, wiping it hastily over his sweating face. With a hesitant step, he cautiously left the entry.

Silently, the doors closed.

Implacable and unemotional, the red-bearded man seated at the desk watched the visitor walk slowly toward the dark-tinted windows and expensive cherry-wood door. A cold voice came over the speaker at the desk.

With a wide hand the man touched the intercom, listening without a blink of emotion as the calm, infinitely controlled words came through the small speaker: "We have a grave problem."

The man's blue eyes glinted, but his face was utterly implacable as he pressed the button to reply. Upon his hand was a black ring—a black ring with a single eye like the all-seeing eye imprinted on a dollar bill.

"I will summon Charon," he rumbled.

Logan stared moodily at his empty beer.

"I'm tired of waiting for this kid," Woodard mumbled. "How long before Malone shows up?"

Logan glanced at the door to see a shadowed figure standing beneath the dark entrance. The shadow turned its head until it centered on Logan and Woodard.

Logan held the gaze; the shadow didn't move.

"Well, Woodard," he said, "I think the boy has arrived."

Stygian blackness cloaked the Queensboro Bridge, suspended high over silent Roosevelt Island, located a scant two miles from New York's Central Park. It was strangely empty of traffic, and white light from the overhead beams illuminated the bridge like pale frost in the palest summer night. Dark air rising from the East River smelled of dead things, of things ancient and dark and decayed.

Cloaked in black, the white-haired man stood unmoving at the corner of the bridge as the smaller, dark-haired man approached him. And as the man made his way down from the street, the white-haired man continued to gaze over the river, as if he found strength in the dancing, flashing light that cut across the East River like a frozen scythe.

A long silence passed.

"We have a grave problem, Charon," the dark-haired man said. Behind him, a long black limousine idled at the curb, and two bodyguards stood beside the fence that separated the walkway from the bridge itself, but for this single place where the earth verged with the sea, deep and dark and cold.

With a frozen laugh, the white-haired man turned.

His face was pale, his hair short and white as snow. Although he was at least sixty, his face was the sternest image of winter and cold and death. And his poise was mysteriously, almost mystically, strong. In the darkness he held himself as calmly and placidly as the deepest and coldest of the ocean's unexplored depths.

"I am here," he said tonelessly.

No expression crossed the face of the dark-haired man, and his voice was also controlled and subdued—a tryst of kings. The figure that stood before him was intimidating, yes, but the dark-haired man revealed no fear as he spoke.

"Woodard has come to America, Charon. He is meeting with another FBI agent. I don't know what he has told him, but we know Woodard has suspicions. I believe it would be in our interest if he were eliminated."

Freezing rain crowned Charon's head.

"Where is Woodard tonight?"

"He is in Quantico. He is flying to London tomorrow."

"No," Charon said. "He is not."

"This situation may already be out of control. Woodard met with an Assistant Director in the FBI. A man named Webster. He is leading the team sent to investigate us."

"Webster." White eyes narrowed. "We know of Webster. He cannot be controlled."

"No, he cannot. But there is another man, an agent named Logan. He has been assigned to lead the field team." He paused. "Logan is different from the rest, old friend. Different, even, from Webster. Webster is dangerous because he pursues the truth. Logan is dangerous because he is a detective of the highest caliber—a man who may very well discover what has not yet been discovered. I am convinced that he, too, must be eliminated."

Charon laughed. "Then he shall be eliminated."

"Be warned, Charon. These men are FBI."

"It is no matter," Charon frowned. "Have I ever failed you?"

There was a cautious pause before the dark-haired man spoke without a hint of fear, though any man would have felt fear. "Yes. You *have* failed me. A mistake you could not correct because the prey could not be found."

The Iceman's face seemed to freeze more solidly, hardening to reveal a true essence, haunting and surreal and infinitely, infinitely frightening. He clenched a fist, his hand bearing a ring that matched the ring worn by the dark-haired man—black rings with small diamond eyes slashed in the crests.

"A single mistake," he intoned. "It is nothing."

"This man, Logan, has an ally, Charon. An ally you might remember from your past."

A moment like a passing season blew across the bridge, and the white-haired man's face held no expression. But his eyes burned brighter with a light that melted winter within.

"The child," he said without surprise.

"Yes."

The Iceman turned to stare over the water, which no longer seemed to freeze at his gaze. He held the position a long time, his back to the dark-haired man.

"Logan and Woodard, and even Webster if necessary, will be done according to your rules," he said finally. "The child is mine."

"I don't know why you failed to kill him, Charon. In all the years you have served me, it has been your only mistake. And now he has come back to haunt us, as I knew he would. And this time he *must* be eliminated. But remember: He is no longer a child. He is a man. A man driven by rage because he remembers what you did to him."

Arctic rage blazed from the Iceman's gaze, and the dark-haired man involuntarily stepped back. And slowly, frighteningly, the skull-face solidified into immeasurable, forceful will.

The Iceman walked away.

"He will always be a child to me," he said.

Chapter Four

Logan knew the kid probably had a hard day with final qualifications, but he was a little shocked.

Malone's face was pale and he seemed perilously drained of energy, as if he'd run a marathon that he should have quit a long way before the finish. And when he turned to look at the crowd, Logan saw bruised ridges on his cheek and jaw.

"Who beat you up, kid?"

Jonathan took a swig of his beer, grimaced, and cupped his jaw—his fist also bore contusions, like he'd worked over a heavy bag without gloves. "I went a few rounds with Matsumo after qualifications," he said, leaving it at that.

"Why'd you do something stupid as that?" Logan followed. "You've already qualified on Defensive Tactics. The file says it's your strongest asset."

Wrapping both of swollen hands around the ice-cold bottle, Jonathan shrugged, "I just wanted a real match, one on one without all the rules and non-contact."

Logan considered. "Well, *that* was stupid."

"Yep."

"How bad did he beat you up?"

"Only as bad as he wanted."

Logan looked away, sighed. "Matsumo can *look* at you and put you in the hospital. Came out of Japan, beat everybody in every branch of the military and the Bureau hired him on the spot." He gazed back. "You didn't know all that?"

"He didn't bust me up too bad. I guess he was feeling soft-hearted."

A gut-laugh erupted from Logan. "Yeah, well, I wish ol' softhearted Matsumo had felt that way toward *me* when I went through in-service." He shook his head. "He was evil."

Jonathan nodded. "He's tough."

"Tough?" Logan guffawed. "No, kid, *I'm* tough. Matsumo's one of those guys you just shoot on sight and figure it self-defense. We do the paperwork after we've got our lies straight." Logan paused. "You know what I mean?"

Jonathan couldn't help smiling. He'd known a lot of street cops like Logan and, yeah, he understood.

Logan was ultimately practical. If his life was in danger, he was going to drop somebody and drop them fast, plain and simple. And he wasn't intimidated by the paperwork, either. He probably thrived on it, and was more than willing to make up whatever lies were necessary to protect his guys.

Yeah, Jonathan thought, Logan was more like a real cop, not an antiseptic Bureau agent. And he'd probably been burned by the system so many times that he didn't care about it anymore. He was loyal to people, not the administration. With him the final rule was that you always, always, *always* went home alive. The rest was sauce.

"I know what you mean," Jonathan nodded, agreeable. "We'll do the paperwork later."

Logan studied Jonathan with unreadable blue eyes, and nothing was said for a moment. "Anyway," he continued finally, "I've been looking at your 202. It says you make good decisions under stress."

"Good enough, I guess," Jonathan muttered. "Only, I can't decide why I'm here. I should have been transferred to San Francisco, then I got orders to report here." Jonathan didn't blink at Logan's appraising stare. "So what's the deal?"

"Beats me, kid. All I can say is you're here because somebody wants you here." He shot an irritable scowl at the man beside him. "When is Blackfoot supposed to arrive, Woodard? Didn't he get his orders?"

Woodard's massive shoulders and wrinkled jacket moved in an uncaring shrug. "He's teaching some kind of security class on how to access, uh, encrypted computer systems, or something. I didn't really get it. He's late. He'll be here."

"Encryptions?" Logan appeared impressed. "Blackfoot can beat an encryption system? How?"

"Logan, how should I know? Ask him when he gets here. I mean if you really...want to."

Logan froze. "What does that mean?"

"Uh..." Woodard's voice became more slurred, "well, I mean, Blackfoot ain't your typical support service guy. Blackfoot ain't typical, period. He's like, uh...like some kind of real brain with electronics and stuff. But I understand from some of the guys that he's a little...a little strange, I guess."

Logan's tone was serious. "Don't do this to me, Woodard. I'm already under stress. I don't need you joking about how Blackfoot is some kind of ape-crazy Indian."

"No, no," Woodard gestured, "I'm not messing with you, son. I heard Blackfoot's a real solid guy—a really good guy. I just heard that he can...uh..."

"Heard *what*, Woodard?"

"Good grief, Logan, I just heard that he's a little on the eccentric side." Woodard lifted a hand as Logan began to speak. "But everybody says he's a great guy! For real! Even the instructors in the Computer Response Team say he just likes to kid around. But he's smart. And even though he's not a special agent and can't carry a gun, he's going be an asset. Trust me."

Logan wouldn't let it go: "What kind of strange are we talking?"

Woodard, clearly, wanted to dismiss his offhand comment. "It ain't nothin' important, Logan. You're overreacting."

Logan looked at Jonathan. "Do you know Blackfoot?"

"Never met him."

"I can tell ya what Webster said," Woodard offered.

"What'd Webster say?"

"He said Blackfoot proved the old adage was true."

"What adage?"

"If you can't beat 'em, hire 'em." Woodard seemed happy that he'd survived the wrath of Logan. He smiled, "C'mon, Logan, Blackfoot passed the psych test, didn't he?"

There was no reply as Logan scanned the overcrowded bar, studying the room a moment before reaching for a pack of Marlboros. He lit one without taking his eyes off the room. Agitated, he looked back at Jonathan. "You carrying?"

"Yeah. Paps issued me my duty weapon."

"The SIG?"

"P-226."

The SIG-Sauer P-226, a double-action 9 millimeter blue steel semiautomatic, was the weapon of choice for federal agencies from the FBI to the Texas Rangers. It had a four-inch barrel, a fifteen-round clip, and only a three-inch drop at one hundred meters.

"You carry a backup?" Logan demanded.

"No."

"Own one?"

"Nope."

"Get one."

The way Logan surrounded the subject, Jonathan figured the senior agent had a preference. "Like?"

"Like a Smith .38 with a two and a half-inch barrel." Logan knew it by heart. "And don't carry it on your ankle. Put it in the small of your back, inside a snapped holster. And don't carry the SIG in a shoulder holster. There's never been a shoulder holster made that could stand up to professional use, no matter what anyone says."

"Kidney carry?" Jonathan muttered with a sip.

"No. Carry it on your hip. It's more secure, especially in a scrap." Logan seemed to find comfort in talking about anything but Blackfoot's imminent arrival. "Go by the Armory in the morning and pick up twenty extra clips and a thousand nine-millimeter rounds—Federal supersonic 138-grain hydroshock. Hollow-points."

Jonathan paused. "A lot of ammo..."

Logan's stare was hostile, then, "Son, believe me; if you think there's the slightest chance you might be in a gunfight, carry as much ammo as you can. As long as you've still got ammo, you've still got options. When you don't have any ammo, it's time to make peace with God."

"I understand."

"Plus that, pick us up ten 3,000-megahertz radio steel-clip holders with voice-activated microwave pick-ups so that we can hear each other without keying the mike."

"Yes, sir."

"We'll meet at eight o-clock in the Behavioral Science Unit subbasement, level three. Wear jeans and a T-shirt. Bring an old jacket to cover your hardware."

Undercover.

"Got it."

"And remember," Logan added, even more intense, "I know that you can handle yourself, Jonathan. But this investigation ain't worth dying for. You know why?"

Curious, Jonathan shook his head.

"Because there's a hundred more that look just like it," Logan said flatly. "And each of them are important. So don't take any stupid chances. Keep yourself alive. That's the golden rule."

"I won't forget," Jonathan replied. "I keep myself alive, keep you alive. Do what I'm told when I'm told, and don't ask a lot of stupid question. I can handle it."

"Good man. Just do what you're told, and we'll get along great. There will be no car chases or improvising or superhero stuff or hair-raising shoot-outs." Logan seemed to think twice about that one. "Don't get me wrong," he raised a hand. "If somebody takes a shot at us, we *instantly* kill them graveyard dead and ask questions later."

He watched carefully, and Jonathan tried not to reveal anything but competence and agreement. And, the truth was, he liked Logan's attitude and style.

"But we're not going to look for any of it," Logan added. "Understand? Our job is to investigate, not get into a street war. HR—Hostage Rescue—can do the killing after we point them in the right direction and leave town."

"Yes, sir."

"Any objections?"

"Nope."

"Okay," Logan said, and waited. "You've got good sense, Jonathan. Not an easy thing to find in the Bureau. If you use it, you'll go a long way." He glanced around the room again. "This is ridiculous, Woodard. That Indian was supposed to be here a half-hour ago; late for his first assignment. Where is he?"

"Logan, your guess is as good as—"

A shadow fell across the booth.

Gazing up, Jonathan saw an immensely tall, thin figure dressed casually in a cheap blue-plaid shirt and sadly faded blue jeans with the knees clean gone. Half-hidden by shadow, the face was smooth and hairless and aesthetically thin with soft edges like an adolescent's.

Jonathan knew this was the guy they'd been waiting for.

Blackfoot's eyes were almost totally black—not even the pupils could be seen. His long hair was intricately braided, falling in a maze of brightly-colored beads to the middle of his back. Then Jonathan noticed his hands. They were uncommonly long and thin with the slender fingers of a virtuoso violinist.

Although the voice that came from the shadowed face was not old, it was frighteningly intelligent, solemnly serious. "Logan?"

Staring up, Logan nodded once.

"I am here."

Logan responded with sarcastic politeness: "Well, Blackfoot, we're glad you could join us for this little—"

A voice invaded, "*Ooooooooiiiieeeee!*"

The crowd parted like wheat before a scythe as the invader staggered forward. His eyes were vacuous, gleaming as he focused on Blackfoot's wild attire like it was a present. He wore utility BDUs as if he'd just gotten off work and Jonathan recognized that he was a marine drill instructor—a big one.

Blackfoot turned fully into it, frowning.

"What do we have *here!*" the sergeant laughed.

Logan shook his head as he slowly rose. Crossing his arms, he gazed with a mixture of boredom and contempt at the drill instructor, completely blocking the path to Blackfoot. The Marine blinked at the defiance.

Low and distinct, Logan challenged, "Why don't you drag

your sorry drunk self back to your side of the room?"

Swaying, the man questioned, "Do *what?*"

"Why don't you go sit down." It was not a question this time and Logan said it directly enough to be threatening. "You don't have any problems with this man."

Impressed, Jonathan glanced at Blackfoot and saw that the Sioux was watching Logan intently. The marine blinked, shocked: "Boy, you are lookin' for a—"

"I'm *lookin'* to put you in the hospital if you don't go sit down," Logan said, his voice barely above a whisper. "If I want you to mess with this man, I'll tell you."

"Oooooo," the marine hooted. "Scary! Why don't we just *see* if you can do that! I've got some friends behind me who'll say you hit me first!"

Logan glanced at the sergeant's sewn-on nametag. "Okay, Sergeant Brainwaith, I usually charge for lessons like this, but in your case I'm going to make an exception."

The sergeant smiled. "Well, ain't you—"

Gaining Brainwaith's immediate attention, Jonathan rose to invade the DI's personal space, eye to eye. "Why don't you and me step outside?" he threatened quietly. "I don't want to bust you up in front of your friends."

And then Blackfoot was there, standing close behind Logan as the marine blinked dumbly, hesitating. Logan was merciless, quiet, and implacable: "Go sit down before you get hurt."

The Marine took a step back, glaring at all of them, angry but confused. "Pansies," he mumbled and turned away, weaving a wavy line through the cockeyed tables.

Logan placed a hand on Blackfoot's shoulder: "Have a seat, son. He ain't gonna be back."

Blackfoot slid into the booth, almost expressionless. But

Jonathan caught the narrow glance that he cast toward Logan and then Jonathan saw something that surprised him.

The Sioux smiled.

(O)(O)(O)

It was raining in heavy, waving sheets as Logan drove into the parking lot of the Alexandria Hilton in downtown Quantico. Drowsy and drunk, Woodard slouched in the passenger seat, mumbling about how dangerous this case was and how they were going to die.

For the most part, Logan ignored it, figuring it to be the booze and frayed nerves. He reached the front doors, put the car in park, and said loudly, "We're here, Woodard! Time for bed!"

Woodard shook his head, "There's stuff you don't know, yet, Logan. Stuff I ain't told you. But you need to know. You need to know...what I know."

Studying the man closely, Logan said, "I don't want to talk about killing and dying right now, Woodard. You've been talking about killing and dying all night. We'll go over it in the morning. When you're sober."

"Uh huh." A volcanic belch. "But it's stuff you need to know, son." He gazed out the window at the hotel, as if surprised. "We're at the hotel. Listen, too many people have been hit by this guy. You need to know what I know."

"All right," Logan said, a little heavy. "Tell me what's got you so upset."

"If we get close to this guy, we're gonna die," Woodard said with remarkable smoothness, his eyes saddened by the inevitable. "That's what I know, buddy. I know it in my soul. And it's eating me up. Cause I'm too old and too tired to end up another notch on this guy's gun."

"Woodard, you're too mean to die."

"Ain't nobody that mean, Logan." He bent his head as he spoke. "Ain't none of us as mean as...as..."

"As our mystery man?" Logan finished, wondering, somewhat unexpectedly, whether Woodard's paranoia might be justified. Then he shut it down because he knew drunks tended to exaggerate, and he didn't want to sort out the real from the imagined this time of night. They could do it in the morning.

"No." Woodard's answer was emphatic. "Not him. There's somebody else that we've got to...look out for."

Logan's eyes narrowed. "Who are you talking about Woodard? You talking about the guy who killed your man in Cairo?"

Woodard gazed out the car window. "I think so, Logan. But all I got are rumors. I don't know what he looks like. I only know what he's done." He seemed monumentally tired. "But you're right; I'm drunk. Now ain't the time. And I...I don't want to talk about it right now, anyway. It might make me sick." He sighed. "Anyway, how did you think the meeting went?"

"Good enough," Logan shrugged.

"What do you think of Blackfoot?"

"He's still a question mark," Logan answered flatly. "So is Jonathan, for that matter. But I'll find out soon enough if they can do the job."

"Good kids," Woodard repeated. "That's why you need to know what I know. I've got to tell you some things." Suddenly he looked cold sober, repeating. "I think we're gonna die, Logan."

Shaking his head, Logan leaned over the steering wheel. He knew that mindless repetition was the common faculty of a drunk. And for a moment he considered truly exploring what it was before deciding once again that he couldn't trust anything Woodard said right now.

"Look, Woodard, it's too late to discuss this. Let's get some sleep and tomorrow morning we'll talk about this guy that's got you so spooked. I'll pick you up for breakfast."

Woodard didn't like the sound of it. "Breakfast?"

"Yeah. An early one."

Silence fell in the car. Woodard stared morosely at the dash, and Logan felt a wave of strange anxiety. He'd known Woodard a long time, and he knew that he was a hard and experienced field agent. But Logan had never seen him like this. It was disturbing, and Logan considered for a moment that it might be the genuine see-your-doctor kind of paranoia. But, again, Woodard had been in the field a long time. Sometimes agents got to where they could pick up on a threat that they couldn't actually describe; it didn't make the threat any less real. And sometimes that little tiny voice in the back of your mind was the voice that saved your life—instinct, reflex, whatever. Did it matter?

Logan was not, by nature, a compassionate person. He gave little, and asked for none at all. But seeing Woodard like this saddened him. "What room are you in?"

"814."

He shut off the engine. "I'll walk you up."

"Ha!" Woodard boomed suddenly, laughing to break the mood. He reached for the door handle. "I ain't gonna let no...no two-bit *whiskey* thief put *me* to bed! You get me up there, ain't no telling *what* you'll do. You can't trust no moonshiner!"

Logan didn't quite smile. "All right, Woodard. We'll talk tomorrow about the rest of this stuff. "

Woodard stood in the door, stared a final time. "Be careful," he added quietly.

"Don't worry about me, Woodard. Self-defense is close to

my heart. And you need to go pass out. I would say *sleep,* but you passed sleep about a hundred miles back."

With a laugh Woodard closed the door, walking with a re-markable semblance of soberness across the long empty lobby. Then he entered the elevator, leaning tiredly against the wall.

Logan continued to watch, wondering.

Immediately entering the elevator behind Woodard, an elderly man with short-cut white hair moved hesitantly to the back wall, turning as the elevator doors began to close. Logan saw that the man's face was thin and extremely pale. Extreme-ly dark glasses hid his eyes, lenses deep black against bone white skin.

He held a long white and red cane by a white ivory pom-mel—the kind of cane a blind person carried. But he held it strangely, somehow, even though Logan couldn't understand why. And maybe it was Woodard's paranoia or maybe it was instinct or just too many years in the field, but Logan's eyes narrowed.

The doors closed and the elevator rose.

Logan cursed savagely. Knew what it was.

The man had held the cane too high—near the pommel—not in the middle like a blind person would hold it to save the strength in their arm. Not even hesitating to make a decision that might create a fiasco if he were wrong, Logan leaped out of the car and charged through the lobby, raising his creden-tials to the desk clerk.

"FBI!" he shouted, drawing his SIG. "Call police and tell them an FBI agent needs assistance!"

The shocked clerk fumbled with the phone.

Breathless and frantic, Logan pounded on the elevator button. He looked around wildly, whirled back. "Where's the staircase!" he shouted at the terrified clerk. "Where is it!"

The clerk threw up an arm.

Logan exploded in a run.

Inside the elevator, Woodard leaned against the wall.

Out of a keen survival habit honed from thirty years in the field, he studied the old guy dressed in black who was standing against the back wall. The old man's eyes were completely hidden behind black glasses. He held a cane by the head, his fist wrapped tightly around a white ivory pommel—*blind*.

Tough break...

Woodard relaxed the slightest degree as he leaned back against the wall, arms folded. He wondered if the old man could sense him staring. But he seemed oblivious to it—so old, so fragile.

Never underestimate anyone, Woodard thought, *but he sure is old. Maybe sixty-five—maybe older than that.*

As Woodard looked over the gaunt form he knew that, no matter what happened, he could take this old guy out. The old man seemed to have trouble standing, and there was a point where you just couldn't suspect every old lady and every old blind guy of being a hitter. He had to be selective or he'd be jumping at shadows and then they'd make him see a psych guy and he'd never pass the test with his nerves and that would be that—a diminished pension with diminished benefits.

No way, man. He wasn't gonna start clearing out elevators just because he was jumpy. No way.

"Excuse me," the man said politely. "Could you hit the button for the seventh floor, please?"

"Sure." Woodard glanced down as he hit the button. When he looked up the old man seemed to be even more unstable, balancing himself unsteadily as the elevator rose. "Thank you," he replied. "That was very kind."

"No problem."

The man was silent a moment, then, "Is it raining outside?"

Third floor.

"Yeah," Woodard looked down. "A real frog-strangler."

The man smiled. "I thought so. Forgive me, but could you tell me what time it is? I left my watch in my room." He did not need to say that he was blind and Woodard looked down, raising his hands to lift the sleeve of his jacket, trying to focus bleary eyes.

"Sure, old guy. It's—"

The old man exploded as if he were a gigantic black vulture with wings spread and Woodard was smashed against the doors but he came off them hard, enraged and shouting.

Instantly fighting, bellowing in rage, Woodard threw out a powerful hand to sweep the old man back even as his other hand folded around his gun, no fear there because it was all happening too fast and then something hit him high, pain streaking through Woodard's neck and spine and Woodard heard screaming, screaming as he fell against the wall to see a haggard face twisted in rage *blood everywhere* and he felt another impact inside his chest.

With a moan, Woodard's breath left him aching, and the old man savagely tore his hand away, skeletal face snarling in rage. Shocked, Woodard's head dropped down, and his bleary eyes focused on the man's hand: *ice pick.*

Ice pick in his hand...

That was all he knew.

Logan slammed the door open with a *boom* when he reached the eighth floor, his lungs burning.

Lightheaded and enraged he charged down the hall,

lifting the SIG in a two-handed grip as he saw the elevator doors open. They began to close and Logan leaped into them, shooting to kill at point blank range and saw...

Woodard sprawled in a blood-drenched corner.

Blood...

With a snarl Logan spun, leveling the SIG, searching. But the converging hallways were empty, silent. He cursed, slamming his hand against the doors as they tried to close again. Then he reached inside and pulled the stop button, freezing it. Emotions on fire, he ran back down the hall and charged back into the staircase, knowing the hit man would be escaping.

Legs numb from the exhausting climb, Logan was operating on pure adrenaline. There was a fleeting black shadow on the landing below him, something he didn't understand but sensed as a threat, and Logan twisted against the wall. Concrete exploded at the edge of the stairway as Logan rebounded off the wall and he threw his hand over the edge, cursing in rage to fire the SIG blindly as fast as he could pull the trigger.

Thunderous blasts from the SIG filled the concrete and metal silo and Logan could hear nothing as he rolled back away again, cursing, ripping out another clip from his waist to slam it in. Drenched in sweat, breathing too fast, he leaned sharply over the edge, more than willing to fire face to face.

Nothing.

The stairwell was empty.

Logan couldn't hear any Quantico police sirens but he knew that units had to be approaching. Then he heard a frantic scream from the hall above him and he ran back to the door, ripping it open to leap out. He saw a woman standing in front of the elevator, hands over her face, still screaming.

Logan cursed—*no time for this!*

Back into the stairway, he went down the steps fast, knowing he wasn't going to dive away from a second attack. He'd take it and he'd give it back and almost instantly saw shattered concrete on the seventh floor where his rounds had struck—*no blood.*

Taking a single second to orient himself, he ripped the door open on the seventh-level hall and entered, spinning, searching, SIG leveled. But there was nothing and he knew in his heart that he had lost the man in the chaos of combat.

Whoever had killed Woodard was gone.

It was chaos.

The first two Quantico cops to arrive on the scene were rookies and they tried to put Logan on the ground, not believing he was a federal agent.

Glaring and enraged, Logan entered the lobby and stared into two semiautomatics and faintly heard the screams that repeatedly ordered him to get down on the floor but he wasn't in the mood to get down on the floor.

Reaching for his credentials almost got him killed, but Logan couldn't have cared less. He drew them out and from then on it was a major crime scene with city and federal technicians and investigators turning the building upside down.

Webster arrived thirty minutes later to find Logan sitting on the back of a patrol car, morosely smoking a cigarette, surrounded by droves of sleep-eyed guests who'd been rousted from their beds. Locked in a hard, always-deadly calm, Webster walked up as if he couldn't believe Logan was still alive.

With red eyes Logan returned the gaze, released a cloud of smoke. "Woodard's dead?" Webster asked quietly.

Logan nodded.

Webster stared at the building, his face set in a dark mask. He didn't seem to know what to do, seemed amazed that the situation was already this bad. It was as if he hadn't expected it—not like this. He looked back. "Are you hurt?"

Logan's voice was lifeless. "I'm all right."

"Did you see the hitter?"

"I gave 'em a description."

"Did you get off a shot?"

"Yeah."

Webster paused. "You *missed*?"

Silent, Logan nodded.

"Why?"

"He killed Woodard on the elevator," Logan responded dully. "He must have seen me watching and figured I'd be coming. He exited the elevator on the seventh floor, waited for me to go up to the eighth. When I went after him he was waiting for me on the seventh floor landing. He took a few shots. I returned; I think I missed. He got away, somehow. I don't know. Probably went down the stairway. Nobody saw him leaving, but I'm pretty sure he's gone."

"Are they searching the building?"

"Yeah." Logan was grim. "Our HRT and Quantico HRT. But they aren't gonna find him. This guy's a pro." He stared at Webster. "Is this gonna put off the investigation?"

"No," Webster responded instantly. "Nothing is going to put off this investigation."

"There'll have to be a shooting review board."

"We'll see about that," Webster said, coming back to the patrol car. "Get back to the office, leave your statement on my desk and get out of town." He stared hard. "Do you still have it in you to find this guy?"

Logan nodded once.

"Then find him."

"And then?"

Webster was grim.

"Dead or alive is fine with me."

At three in the morning Logan was not the first one into Woodard's room, but taking advantage of his full authority and command over this investigation, he put the freeze on the Hostage Rescue Team and Crime Scene guys.

Ordering them outside, Logan took a long time memorizing the room, noting the location of every item, trying to find anything unusual. Woodard was not a particularly neat guest. He obviously depended heavily on the maid service, and it looked like he had been planning to stay a few more days.

Why would Woodard be in a holding pattern?

Logan walked forward, touching nothing, seeing everything—*half-eaten pizza on a paper plate, paper cups, half-bottle of Jack Daniels.* He lifted the Jack—mixed with Coke. He searched the mattresses, the pillowcases, drawers; he lifted the ceiling tiles, shone his penlight down the crawl space—*nothing.*

He stood at the door again, and saw something that had escaped his first search; a few drops of...Coca Cola?

Spilled on a distant coffee table—the one beside the balcony—were a few small drops of...yeah, Coca Cola. Logan bent, staring at them. He looked beneath, saw a tiny sliver of glass, crystalline and transparent—part of a broken bottle.

A quick search of the trashcans didn't reveal any bottle. But it was obvious that a bottle had been knocked over and broken, leaving the sliver on the floor. Certainly, Woodard wouldn't have gone to the trouble of discarding the glass downstairs or something. He would have trashed it in his room. But it wasn't here.

Whoever had broken the glass had wanted to get rid of it for a reason.

Logan opened the door and instructed the Crime Scene guys to search every waste receptacle between Woodard's room and the front door. Thirty minutes later the bottle was found in the third floor alcove and they dusted if for prints—none.

But Logan knew three things; someone had searched this room, had broken the bottle and had tried to hide any trace of their presence. But they'd left no prints so why had they hidden the glass? Unless they weren't certain that they were going to kill Woodard. Unless...they didn't want Woodard to know that he was being set up. Unless...they were waiting to see if this investigation was going to be launched, or not. Then Woodard was to be killed while he was still off-guard.

Simple enough; if the FBI launched this very secret investigation—obviously not so secret—Woodard was to be killed. If this very secret team of investigators—obviously not so secret—entered the field, they were next. And since this team was obviously so very secret, only the high holies in the FBI and the White House were need-to-knows.

Well, well...do tell.

As Logan left the hotel, it was almost dawn. He walked to his car in a bitter haze and knew one thing already: This chase might lead them around the world, but in the end it was going to come full circle with a vengeance. Cause someone inside was gonna pay—either someone in the FBI or in the CIA or the White House or hell.

Logan didn't care which.

To him, they were all the same.

After Jonathan picked up extra magazines from the vault,

he went by Medical to pick up some painkillers. It was there that he first heard about Woodard's death.

Stunned, he tried not to reveal anything as the resident physician, on training from the Marine Medical Hospital on the northside of Quantico, took one look at Jonathan's badly beaten body and strongly suggested that he take three weeks light duty.

Pondering Woodard, Jonathan refused. Then the doctor prescribed something Jonathan had never taken that he said would the edge off the pain. He also gave him some high-level ibuprofen to ease his torn muscles. He tossed in a bottle of Tylenol.

"A bottle of Tylenol-codeine No. 4 is routinely issued to Marine Recon units," the Doctor said. "It's probably the best thing there is for taking the edge off physical pain. Helps you keeping running and moving. But don't exceed the recom-mended dosage."

Jonathan was looking for something to say, just to keep the conversation off Woodard. "What happens if I exceed the dosage?"

"If you do, you'll accumulate so much aceptominaphin in your system that it'll destroy your liver in three or four days. Pretty gruesome. I've seen a few." He shook his head. "Faking a suicide with Tylenol is stupid. It turns into the real thing. And people have a lot of time to think about it before they die."

Jonathan looked away. "I don't need much. I have a feeling all this is going to be over pretty soon, anyway."

The doctor shrugged.

"It's your life," he said.

Jonathan saw Logan and Blackfoot standing together in the shade near the north side of the building. They were glum, but Logan was obviously trying to establish clear lines of operation. He looked impatient and Jonathan knew he was probably still on a rush from the shootout.

"Blackfoot, just tell me what you can do," Logan said as Jonathan walked forward. "From here on I'm dead serious. I'm going to take this guy down and I want to know how you can help."

With clear respect for Woodard, Blackfoot spoke, "I surf."

Logan stared. "Surf?"

"Yes, Logan. I surf. I can find gophers, and secret elements. I tame what cannot be tamed. I uncover what has been lost."

"What are you talking about?" Logan seemed frustrated. "What can you find?"

"Whatever can be found," the Indian replied. "I search Hytelnet and find what Hytelnet hides. I find the address and names of those who began what has begun. I know the Mother-of-all BBS by heart. I can sleuth beyond the web to find the subtle, the insubstantial, and the invisible. And where the enemy believes he cannot be heard, I can hear him. And I can defeat any firewall known."

"A firewall?" Logan asked.

"A firewall is a guru-thick, cyber-intensive line of software to prevent unauthorized interfacing with the target, Logan. It is the last and strongest line of defense." Blackfoot frowned. "I have never been defeated."

Logan concentrated. "So how would you break through the encryption system designed to protect something like, say, the National Security Agency?"

"I would not."

"So you can't break into the NSA?"

"Yes," said Blackfoot. "All that the NSA possesses is mine, should I desire it."

"Well, Blackfoot, if you can't break the encryption guarding the computer, how were you going to get inside the NSA files? That doesn't make sense."

"TEMPEST," said Blackfoot.

"What?"

"TEMPEST."

"TEMPEST?"

"Yes."

"And what is TEMPEST?"

"It is commonly known as a transient electromagnetic pulse emanation standard-frequency." Blackfoot's voice had assumed a darkly inhuman drone. "TEMPEST is a secret method for picking up the current display of any computer screen, regardless of the mainline defenses involving encryption and coding. It can be done through thin air from as far away as a mile."

"Are you kidding me?"

"No."

Logan was actually impressed. "That's incredible."

"Yes."

"How does it work?"

"It is simple," Blackfoot continued. "A computer screen operates along the same principle as a radio station, only on lower frequencies. Each computer sends the data to be displayed on the screen to the monitor over seventy times per second, over and over again, while you are staring at it. And these low-level RF frequencies are detectable with low-frequency collectors. Then, once the data is picked up, in much the same way a regular radio station is picked up, it can be read on another computer, and then translation begins."

"Can you get into a computer's memory with this?" Logan asked intently, sensing something there. "Could you, like, raid the hard drive and access the files?"

"In order to raid the hard drive files when the files are not on the screen, I would need to be closer to the source," Blackfoot answered with a faintly alarming air of experience. "Perhaps even a few feet, because the internal transmission frequencies are so weak. But they are there. Yes, it can be done."

"And would you have to have some kind of federally-licensed equipment for this? Something we'd have to requisition?"

"No," Blackfoot shook his head. "TEMPEST equipment is not classified under any FCC regulation because the equipment operates on such a low radio frequency. There are no federal controls that limit its possession." He smiled. "Or use."

"But," Logan pressed, "wouldn't you need a whole vanload of expensive equipment? I mean, this sounds like it's some kind of big deal. Finding the right frequency and all that."

"For any other man, that would be true. But I am beyond that. I can build what we need. And the expense would be small."

"Where would we get the materials?"

Blackfoot was obviously brilliant and knew it. And, finally, Jonathan understood. Knew why the government had hired the Sioux. Just as he knew that Webster was ultimately right. If you can't beat them, hire them.

"With five minutes inside a first-rate computer store, I can buy whatever we need," he continued. "I need only ten thousand dollars in my hand. Then I can build a microwave relay the size of a lunchbox that will read any computer screen the government possesses and also monitor what is displayed."

"So," Logan figured, "how will we get into a computer's memory or hard drive if we can't beat the encryption or coding?

The encryption will still be locking down the hard drive, won't it? I mean, I know that you can read the screen. But the information we need might not be on the screen." He waited. "Isn't that right?"

"We will watch their screens and copy the log-in codes and password formulas as each user logs them, Logan. Then we can use their own password codes and log-in identities to penetrate the system. And once we have taken what we want, they can blame each other. Because there will be no breaking and entering. No crude or amateuristic theft—only a legitimate entry under a legitimate code. Nor will it have come from a definite source. We will do it from a car. A van. Whatever. Driving while we work. The source will have come from the Interstate, if they manage to get a trace."

"God Almighty," Logan whispered. "Whose log-ins can we get?"

"We can get anyone's. A bank's. An electrical company's. Any corporation. The Federal Reserve. The FBI. The NSA. The military or the National Power Grid Control Board in New York. We will access satellite codes to penetrate NORAD or the CIA. Even the president, if he is not inside a sufficiently shielded room."

"Yeah," Logan said. "Lead walls would block transmission from the computer."

"Not always, Logan. There are ways to defeat even leaded rooms. I can devise an inexpensive means of lasering a pickup wave that can be directed through—"

"All right, Blackfoot," Logan raised his hand. "I got it already. That's real good. We can use you. But for now, I think, we need to get on with the agenda. Later on tonight, you can give me a real lecture." He turned to Jonathan. "You got what you need? You wearing what I told you to wear?"

Jonathan was suddenly nervous. "Yeah," he nodded, glancing respectfully at Blackfoot. "I got everything."

"Did you inventory the car?"

"Yeah."

"Good. You got crime scene gear? Report sheets? Two shotguns with extra rounds, a laptop, cell phones and transmitters?"

Jonathan nodded tight. He had checked it all with meticulous concentration before he took the car from the lot, anticipating that Logan would be methodical.

"Good job," Logan nodded, removing a small two-shot derringer from the front of the Chevrolet. "Take this derringer and put it in your jockstrap, right up front. It's a .44 and it'll give you two shots. Don't be caught without it."

Jonathan took it.

"Okay. Let's hit the road. We'll switch up drivers or change rides, but we'll always take two cars for backup." Logan was silent a moment, thoughtful. "Jonathan, on this trip I want you to take the LTD. Stay behind us and stay in code. Give me a radio check before we clear the city so we can still get back to the lot and change cars if there's any problems. Blackfoot and I are going to take the Chevy and talk about this some more."

"Where are we going, Logan?"

"Across the river to Justice."

"For what?"

"To talk with Strike Six," Logan replied. "I want a bigger picture on this mystery man. I want to know how he's stopped everyone else."

Jonathan and Blackfoot stared together. "What are we going to do then?" Blackfoot asked.

Logan hesitated at the car door, nodded.

"Then we're gonna rattle Superman's cage, boys."

Chapter Five

S trike Six was a complex of twenty offices that occupied a subbasement of the United States Justice Department's headquarters in downtown Washington.

Logan flashed his credentials and worked his way toward the back of the office, noticing an amazing array of computers and large capacity data servers. Clearly, no expense had been spared in setting up the team with a formidable array of tools and resources.

Having obviously received the bad news about Woodard, Hooper came out of his office and met Logan with an air of commiseration. Then introductions were made to "Special Agent" Malone and "Specialist" Blackfoot.

"All right, Mark," Logan continued without formalities. "I need to know what you've got on this guy."

Hooper took out a cigarette. He was not overly concerned about anti-smoking regulations in federal buildings. "There's already some problems, Logan."

"Like what?"

After reaching behind his desk, Hooper tossed a copy of the *Washington Post* on the desk. The front page had a picture of Woodard's body, the sheet widely stained in red, being carried from the Hilton. "Must have been a slow news day," Logan muttered.

"They're not the only ones, buddy."

"I'll bet."

"*New York Times, The Post,* FOX, CNN." Hooper leaned back, his gut expanding against his shirt. "It's one thing for some Jap to samurai one of us in Timbuktu. It's another for one of us to get cut down in an elevator by a 'professional assassin.'"

He lowered his chin. "That kind of stuff causes people—people like senators and congressmen—to get in on the act. Any time you put 'professional' and 'assassin' in the same sentence with the FBI, people think you are one step away from the White House. Which means they think we're one step away from another president. Which means a stock market collapse, canceled defense contracts, economic mayhem. *Locusts.*"

"So?" Logan stared. "This is an ongoing investigation. Congress doesn't have any need-to-know."

"They may not *have* a need-to-know, but they darn sure *want* to know. And if enough of them get together, they *will* know." Hooper threw his hands up in irritation. "Woodard's death changed everything. It's gonna be almost impossible for us to keep a lid on this now. And the more people know about what you're *supposed* to do, the less you can *really* do."

Hooper put out the cigarette, reached for another. As he waved out the match he erupted in a coughing spasm, nicotine-heavy mucus cracking inside his chest. Finally he gained control and finished: "Somebody with power is trying to shut you down, son."

Already at his mandatory 57-year-old retirement, Hooper looked as if he'd once been a truly formidable field agent. He was built like a retired heavyweight boxer. But he was unhealthy now, and old beyond his years from the life he'd led.

Jonathan remembered what Logan had told them: Hooper only had six more months before he went out, but he looked like he might not make it. Then Jonathan tried not to think about anything at all as Hooper suddenly looked them over, eyes narrowing with a level of scrutiny that matched Logan's. Despite his calm, Jonathan felt as if he were being submitted to a visual polygraph.

"So these are your boys?" Hooper rumbled in a voice weathered by far too much smoke and whiskey and late, late nights. "They look kinda green for backup."

"Yeah," Logan responded, taking out his own cigarette—so much for regulations. "They're young, but they're with me."

A smile twisted Hooper's face. "That's what ol' J. Edgar used to say, God rest his crooked, black soul." He attempted a broad imitation. "'Any attack against an FBI agent is considered a personal attack against me!'"

Logan rolled his eyes at the alarming parallel. "It was the only decent thing the maniac ever said. I already see what direction the wind's blowing, Mark, so I'm keeping my moves to myself. Not anyone—not you, CIA, State, or Justice is gonna know."

"So," Hooper nodded, "paranoid at last."

Logan didn't care to confide about the Coke bottle or anything else. "We'll see."

Falling somber, Hooper shook his head. "Poor old Woodard. He was a good man. Great field agent, once. But he was worn out." A pause. "I guess we all are."

"I need to know what you've found, Mark. I don't have a lot of time."

"Are you gonna be the ones to take him down?"

"I don't know." Logan exhaled a long stream of smoke. "First we gotta find him. And we need to find him as fast as we can. I know that much."

"Not like I know it."

"What can you tell me?"

Hooper propped his feet on the desk. "If we're getting down to it, I can tell you some good, and I can tell you some bad. What do you want first?"

"The bad."

"All right. The bad is that I've gotten three transmissions from State. And as of this morning I'm officially under orders not to give you any hard copy or computer files on this case. They said that I can talk to you, but I can't unlock the computer."

"Wait a second." Logan turned his watch, as if he'd remembered an anticipated date. "Before we get started, I need to send a Teletype to Webster."

Hooper's eyes widened. "In DC?"

"Yeah."

"He's running this?"

"Yeah."

"Really?"

"Yeah."

"Good Lord."

Logan sighed. "I need to get that message to him, Mark. We're running late as it is."

"Yeah, sure." Hooper snapped his fingers to an agent outside the window and Logan turned to Blackfoot: "E-mail Webster. Make it short and encrypt it."

"Yes, sir."

Not wanting to expose them, Jonathan lowered his head and stared at the carpet. He didn't trust himself not to express shock because he knew Blackfoot was about to raid the FBI's own files and nothing on the face of the Earth could stop him if he had two minutes on a terminal.

The agent that Hooper had summoned came through the

door. "Take this man and help him sign on so he can communicate with Washington." Hooper reached for another cigarette. "Then leave him alone so he can send his message."

"Yes, sir," the agent said and Blackfoot followed him from the room. Jonathan heard Logan say, "All right. Give me a rundown on what you've got."

Hooper released another deep draw. "I'll tell you, Logan, but you'd better have a seat."

Logan sat on an opposite desk and placed his hands flat on the metal top. He looked utterly at ease with the posture, as if he could sit there and talk for hours.

"Some of this is classified," Hooper said. "You might want to hear it for yourself before you decide what to tell your crew."

Without expression, Logan turned to Jonathan. "Go help Blackfoot with the message."

"Yes, sir." Jonathan stood, meeting the challenge quickly and moving out the door. "I'll take care of it."

"I want to know what kind of investigation is underway."

Richard Webster stared stoically at the man who had summoned him, not because he did not comprehend the gravity of the situation—he knew exactly where he stood. He also knew this man did not needlessly summon other men for council. The man turned.

Barely over forty years old, his face was aristocratic, tanned, and intelligent. His Seville Row suit was immaculate and appropriately dark, and his cold, clear gray eyes focused on Webster with an icy chill. His silver hair was close-cut and carefully groomed.

Webster didn't blink as he returned the stare. He knew

his station would never be equal, but he was a heavyweight, too. And the life he had behind him was testimony to that. Further, he reminded himself that the man standing before him had never earned a promotion in his life. He had been elected.

"I asked a question," said Harold Stanton, president of the United States. "I expect an answer."

Webster glanced around the chamber of the subterranean War Room located seventeen hundred feet beneath the White House—built to withstand the detonation of a ground-zero nuclear weapon.

Surrounding him were some officials he knew vaguely and some he didn't know at all. Of course, the president wouldn't summon him to a private briefing. But FBI Assistant directors, and even technical experts, were sometimes ordered for reports that might involve more in-depth analysis than a director could provide.

And, although this summons was unexpected, it wasn't Webster's first. He was only surprised that there were so many witnesses. It was disturbing to know that secrets from the highest tiers of this nation passed through these men without any restraint or apparent need to know.

And again, as he did every time he was in the room, Webster noticed that the dark paneling along the walls of the War Room were apparently comprised of some kind of ceramic-steel mix that seemed to absorb whatever light emanated from the overhead circular ceiling fixtures. He thought that they could never throw enough light into this room to make it appear anything but dark. It seemed appropriate.

"Webster?" Stanton asked.

Webster chose his response carefully. "This team is an addition to Strike Six, which you've authorized to investigate an international banking takeover."

"Yes, yes," the president replied, "I understand that, Webster. I want to know what, specifically, this team is designed to accomplish. A federal agent is dead. I take that personally. I want to ensure that the investigation is worth the risk."

"Mr. President, the information on this investigation team should come from the director. I have neither the authority nor the legal release of my supervisor to speak of it. I'm sure you appreciate my respect for the chain of command."

"Yes, I'm quite aware of your devotion to the Bureau and your respect for the chain of command, Webster. Your reputation precedes you. But when a federal agent is killed, it causes dangerous domestic focus. I must know specifically what type of dangers might arise from this team's efforts."

Webster sighed. "There are, as of this time, no developments. And, though Woodard's death is a great tragedy, we're not certain it has anything to do with Strike Six, or Logan's team. It's premature, and just plain wrong, to make that determination."

Gray eyes returned Webster's gaze, searching and unrevealing. "Yes..." Stanton replied finally. "I understand...with utter clarity...what you are telling me, Webster."

Webster remembered the Bureau's interdepartmental meeting two days earlier with General Ariel Ben Canaan of the Israeli Army.

In his mind, he could still see the desert warrior...

Holding the table with the authority of the veteran soldier he was—a soldier who earned his stripes on the Egyptian frontier commanding a tank battalion—Canaan gravely stressed the need for absolute secrecy.

"That's the end of it, gentlemen," Canaan had said at last.

"And make no mistake; this man has profoundly compromised the security of my nation, not to mention what he has done to your banking system. He must be found or Israel will soon find herself at war. And America's singular control of its banking system will be lost forever."

"This sounds like a counterintelligence situation, general," Webster had frankly remarked, chin on hand. "I'm not sure the FBI can be of any service to you."

"No," Canaan had replied instantly, explaining to Webster something he had never quite understood before and which he later shared with Logan. "To discover what this man is ultimately planning may be counterintelligence, yes. But to discover the name of the man himself is a matter of pure detective work." He paused. "My people have tried, and they have failed because they are spies, not detectives. That is why we need your absolute, finest detective. Your best! A man who can go where there is nothing and yet find something. A man who can see what others cannot see. A man of superior intelligence and ability."

Canaan had suggested using Logan, and Webster didn't like the idea but was overruled. So Logan was chosen to head up the team and then Canaan had suggested Malone and Blackfoot for the reason that "only those no one had yet trusted could *be* trusted."

That, too, was accepted, and the team was formed. Then Canaan presented evidence to document an allegation that upper levels of the American intelligence community had been penetrated by this man, so security was a particular concern. He suggested, even, that knowledge of the team should be kept from the White House.

Already familiar with security problems in State, FBI officials agreed, and "Endgame" was the suggested cryptonym for the team, given by Canaan himself, which everyone accepted. But in the last half of the meeting Webster suggested that an unsupervised team could be very risky and possibly even irresponsible.

Under Canaan's stone-cold gaze, Webster said that he didn't like any of his men, even veterans, operating without on-site supervision and sufficient backup. The threat of over-exposure was too great and placed agents in unjustified peril. But, again, Webster's objections were overruled, and now he had to live with it.

Webster felt himself growing angrier and angrier at the situation because he had been the only one at the meeting to express reservations. And now, for some inconceivable reason, he had been selected as the very one to oversee and organize the thing.

◉ ◉ ◉

The president was speaking...

"Understand me, Webster, I want this mission to succeed. And I am prepared to provide whatever resources are necessary. I can even set up a secure relay here, which will be totally impenetrable."

"Thank you," Webster answered, returning to the present. "But Endgame's operating costs are coming out of the Bureau's reserve budget. We don't need financial assistance. And we've already worked out secure communications."

"Just tell me what I can do." Stanton crossed his arms and stepped forward. "I want to know about this team."

Webster sighed, "The team is simply an interdepartmental assignation of agents, Mr. President, and I'm not prepared to speak about specifics. If you want more information on it, I'm sure the director will talk with you."

A tense moment passed as the president crossed his arms.

Although no definite expression crossed the man's face, Webster saw the image of anger before he turned away.

"I wonder," President Stanton said, "if this situation is not developing into something beyond your agency's capabilities." He paused. "We've lost one agent. I'm not sure that I can tolerate the loss of another."

"I'm sure the Bureau will manage the situation professionally and responsibly, Mr. President."

"Yes, I'm sure. But...what would you say, Webster, if I told you I had a premonition that this situation was about to become too complicated?" His words were weighty, drawn out, giving plenty of time for his implication to set in. "What if I warned you that this investigatory team is in a position to make serious mistakes in judgment and cause security dangers that might rock the highest tiers of this nation?"

Webster's gaze was unblinking. "I'll tell the American people they did right to trust me, Mr. President."

With a contemptuous laugh, the president ruffled papers on the long table. None of the men around him revealed anything at all. Even though they were watching Webster's most minute gesture, probably recording his every syllable, Webster saw not even the faintest tic of emotion or thought in their eyes.

Anger leveled the president's tone.

"You're dismissed, Webster."

Jonathan walked up as casually and calmly as he could to where Blackfoot worked on the "Teletype" to Washington. But when Jonathan looked down, his heart almost leaped out of his throat because the screen contained a bright red list of classified files.

Hands stuck deep in his pockets, Jonathan gazed around

the room. "How much longer you gonna be?" he asked non-chalantly.

"A second," Blackfoot replied softly, dark eyes flaming with the reflected displays. "A minute, and I'll be finished here."

Jonathan didn't look down but suddenly wished to God that he wasn't standing beside Blackfoot as he performed a felonious raid on FBI computer banks. Then he noticed the small external attached to the computer, copying files.

Suddenly he realized that this was the reason Logan wanted to drive up from Virginia with Blackfoot. From the very beginning, when they were standing in the parking lot, Logan had planned this. And Jonathan abruptly felt a new level of respect for the man, understanding that Logan was a natural-born crook who simply landed on the right side of the law. He could have been another Al Capone, if he had chosen. Yet there was also something about Logan that was inescapably honest—some inherent, iron cell of character.

Also, there was something about the way Logan defended them that compelled Jonathan's trust. And what Logan had done in the bar had obviously won Blackfoot's dangerous allegiance.

"Jonathan?"

"Yeah?"

"Can you hear me?"

Jonathan gritted his teeth. "Of course I can hear you, Blackfoot. Tell me what you want, already."

"I can't copy the rest of these files without setting off an alarm." Blackfoot's words were as soft as his fingers flying over the keyboard. "So very...*very* inconspicuously...walk over to the printer in that corner. See if you can read a number on the top, so I can select it. It'll probably be somewhere near the print button."

Jonathan glanced down to see "Classified Code Index: Encryption and Code Selection for Strike Six" on the screen and then he began walking, utterly gray and boring and uninteresting, toward the printer. He watched with peripheral vision to see if he had attracted attention but no one cast him a look. When he reached the printer he glanced down to get the number and strolled, again very gray and boring and uninteresting, back to Blackfoot. He didn't risk looking down.

"P-6 3738."

Instantly Blackfoot typed and hit "Enter" and the screen went black before it flashed a plaid screen saver message about maintaining honor and public trust.

Blackfoot leaned back, glancing to the side as the first pages began printing. He laughing shortly, his long arms hanging limp along his faded and tattered jeans.

"I have no equal," he smiled.

Lighting a second cigarette to Hooper's eighth, Logan tried to get a feel for this scam. But he had the distinctive impression it was about to get complicated.

"All right," Logan said, "I know how they take honest people for everything they've got. I want to know what else is involved in this network."

"Money laundering," Hooper replied.

"For who?"

"Drug cartels. Arms smugglers. And our mystery man only works with heavyweights."

Logan considered it. "So this guy is running an international loan scam *and* a money laundering operation? He's taking honest folks for their life savings at the same time he's laundering money for drug runners and arms smugglers?"

"Yeah," Hooper said. "And that's just the tip of the iceberg,

Logan. This guy's got more dirt under his fingernails than a gravedigger. To him, honest folks—folks who make less than a million a year—ain't nothin' but meat. He is, by far, the most powerful crook in the world."

"Maybe, maybe not." Logan tried to focus. "First, tell me how he's laundering the drug money. How does he make the money disappear?"

Hooper gestured. "It's simple, because the money laundering scheme, drugs or arms—it doesn't make any difference—works basically the same way as the loan scam. What happens is this: These dopers set up little mortgage companies, or gas and oil companies—all high-risk ventures. Then the dopers go to World Finance for a loan. The only difference is that these dopers know that the loan companies are bogus enterprises. And, of course, the dopers want big loans. So they're putting down *big* down payments on the package."

"How much?"

Hooper shook his head, as if the sum were nothing against the true scope of the operation. "Three hundred million bucks down payment for a billion dollar loan. The important element is that all payments are submitted to...what have you been calling this guy?"

"Superman."

Hooper laughed. "His official DS is 'Phantom.'" He moved a hand rapidly across the desk. "You know, he makes you look in one direction while he's doing something in the other. Magic."

"Whatever," Logan grunted. "Go on with the loan part of the laundering."

"OK," Hooper continued. "This is how it works; the cartels fill out a loan package for a billion dollars so that they can drill oil wells on the moon or wherever. But the dopers have to lay down five hundred million on a billion-dollar loan. Then the loan package goes overseas where it's stalled, and so forth. It goes to Luxembourg, England, Switzerland, the Caymans, all of 'em. There are delays, more down payments. And when it's finally over the loan is turned down because the dopers didn't meet the deadline. And they've *legitimately* lost five hundred million on a bad investment."

"Just like they wanted to," Logan remarked.

"Yeah," nodded Hooper. "Just like they wanted to. And after Phantom stashes away something like ten or fifteen percent for his services and pays the bills at World Finance, the five hundred million that was allegedly lost overseas is wired and rewired to twenty or thirty banks over a period of days and finally dropped in the Caymans or somewhere else that won't cooperate with us.

"Then, when the IRS comes to the doper's front companies to study his books, the doper says, 'I've had a real bad year, boys. That's a fact. I've lost all my money to this scam!' And the doper says, 'Why don't you IRS people do something about this? This is a crime!' Except the doper knows there's nothing the IRS can do because *he's* the one who failed to meet the deadline."

"So," Logan commented, "not only does the doper look honest, he looks like a victim."

Woodard leaned back. "He just laundered a half billion dollars in drug money and the doper can legally claim it as a tax deduction." He lifted his hands. "It's a good system."

"As good as money can buy." Logan imagined a web of fake loan companies and underwriters and banks controlled by an unknown criminal genius to clean money, hide money, make money. It reminded him of an old hit by Pink Floyd—*money, money, money, money...*

And Logan sensed something else: "You said this was just the tip of the iceberg. If that's true, this guy's got to have a major-league bank at his disposal—a mothership."

"He does."

"What is it?"

"BCCI. The Bank of Credit and Commerce International, New York City. Or the Bank of Crooks and Criminals International, take your pick."

Logan wasn't surprised; rumors had plagued BCCI since its inception. He walked across the office. "Have your people checked the CEO, the VPs, the board, trustees, all of BCCI? Did you find a trace of anybody who might be Phantom?"

"We checked everything. He ain't there."

"How do you know he ain't there, Mark? You don't even know who this guy is."

"He ain't there, Logan."

"I want a copy of Phantom's file."

"I can't give it to you."

Logan's gaze was distinctly unfriendly. Hooper raised both hands. "Come on, Logan. Give me a break. You've covered me and I've covered you. But I can't do it. Not this time."

"Why not?"

"Cause this place has no security, man. It ain't like the old days. Seriously; you don't know who to trust anymore." He suddenly rasped, coughing. Then, "Do you think 'specialist' Blackfoot is done with his 'Teletype'?"

"Yeah," Logan smiled faintly. "Probably."

"Good. Cause you're gonna need it."

Logan turned away. "Take care of your health."

"Logan? You want some advice?"

"Sure." Logan paused. "You were always full of it."

Hooper leaned forward. "Leave it alone, son. Cause it's like you always said: None of this is worth getting killed for. There's always another case, and then another. Just do the job, make the moves, close it up, and say you couldn't find this guy. Like I'm gonna do."

"Only one thing wrong with that," Logan said. "Woodard is dead. You gonna let that go?"

Hooper ignored his cigarette. "Woodard ain't the only one who might get himself dead."

There was a moment that seemed like silence, but everything was communicated. Logan spoke flatly: "This guy has got you scared, Mark."

Hooper had obviously reached a place where he no longer had an ego. "You're dealing with somebody bigger than all of us, Logan. This guy can crush you in a heartbeat. He can take your job and ruin your credit rating and make it so you can't even get food stamps. He can make it so you can't even buy a loaf of bread, just so you'll have to watch your kids starve to death. And then, six months after you bury your kids, you'll find yourself in prison for tax evasion. He won't lay a finger on you, Logan, and he'll kill you dead as dead gets." Hooper stared with a dead edge. "Do you know what happened to Woodard the last few months? There's not a lot of people who do."

Logan shook his head.

"In the last three months Woodard was interviewed five times by the IRS for suspicion of tax evasion." He searched for the right expletive, couldn't find one. "Woodard! They hauled him into their office and presented him with so much evidence that even ol' Woodard started to think he was guilty!" He paused, angrier. "I swear, when it comes to malicious prosecution, those guys in the IRS are lower than the

FBI. I couldn't believe it.

"Woodard had a ten-year-old kid and a wife that he knew couldn't make it without him and the stress was killing him. That is, until *Webster* heard what was going on and got involved." Hooper nodded with astonishment. "*Personally.*"

Logan didn't move. "What'd Webster do?"

"He went ape."

Logan still didn't move. "What'd he *do*?"

"Webster got Mr. IRS Director on the horn forthwith and told Mr. IRS Director could he kiss his big, white, FBI butt." Sweat glistened on Hooper's forehead. "He told Mr. IRS Director that if he even gave Woodard a phone call again without legal justification that would stand up in the United States Supreme Court he would be hauling him in front of a Senate Intelligence Subcommittee Hearing inside twenty-four hours to charge him with Obstruction of Justice. Then he told Mr. IRS Director that he was in a hot mood to put *somebody* in jail, so it might just as well be him."

Logan laughed. "What happened then?"

"Well, Mr. IRS Director suddenly discovered evidence, as if by miracle, that proved the charges against Woodard were unsubstantiated." Hooper paused. "Just like a miracle."

Shaking his head slowly, Logan grew more somber, then, "If Phantom was really smart he would have killed Woodard a long time ago and avoided the confrontation with Webster."

"The only reason Phantom didn't kill Woodard before last night is because he was still trying to defuse the situation without the danger of a conspiracy-to-commit-murder charge. Lower-end agents are expendable, but Phantom doesn't use violence against honchos. It causes too much heat. But that doesn't mean Phantom doesn't understand the danger of killing a low-end agent, either. He does. It's just that Woodard was senior Legat with the London Bureau. He was the kind of name that can cause problems."

"They still killed him."

Hooper stared. "Yeah. Because he was talking to *you*, Logan. Because they're afraid of you." A pause. "Listen to me; if this guy can hurt Woodard, he can hurt anybody. Just remember: Webster can't be everywhere at once and Phantom can kill you anywhere he chooses. You're chasing a ghost in a fog, Logan. He ain't out there."

"He's out there," Logan muttered. "And I'm gonna find him."

"And then?"

"Then I'll notify HRT and step aside."

"You don't know what you're messing with."

Logan froze; his eyes narrowed. "What are you afraid to tell me, Mark?"

Hooper glanced down, away.

"Watch your back, Logan."

Walking down the outside hallway, Logan glanced casually and openly at Blackfoot who stared back, unexpressive.

"Did you do it?" Logan asked quietly.

"It is done."

Logan smiled slightly. He had been uncertain about them until now, not knowing whether they would truly go to the wall for him. But they'd proven themselves with this—a felonious raid on the FBI's computer system. They had done exactly what he had asked without complaint or hesitation, standing on their loyalty like the rock of Gibraltar, proving themselves as *everyone* in police work had to prove themselves before they could be trusted.

THE SCAM

Logan was more relaxed as they left the building.

There was just nothing like a good, well-coordinated lie to bring people together.

CHAPTER SIX

L ogan rented two adjacent suites at the Washington Hilton, rationalizing luxury as compensation for this miserable assignment. The mood he was in, there wasn't going to be a penny left in the half-million operational fund.

He trusted Jonathan to go through the rooms and balconies, checking everything from roof access to wall access. Logan himself walked the entire hotel to familiarize himself with the layout. Then he found a pay phone three blocks away and attached a magnetic microwave transmitter that Blackfoot would use to raid more of the FBI's protected files on Phantom.

According to Blackfoot, whom Logan had come to admire as a thief almost equal to himself, these were classified files that the Sioux couldn't raid when he was at Justice because there was no way to do it without tripping an automated alarm. And when that happened, the Systems Administrator would telephone to make sure the correctly cleared person was actually doing the entrance, and in this case there would be a negative search. At that moment, Blackfoot explained, a satellite and phone line search would be launched.

Logan was impressed by the absolute concentration Blackfoot possessed as he worked the laptop computer the Sioux had bought earlier in the day after Logan had the unfortunate impulse to mutter, "Don't worry about it, son. We got all the money we need."

THE SCAM

With a broad smile Blackfoot emerged from the computer store with a $15,000 laptop, TEMPEST laser-antenna and portable Pentium antenna receivers, an assortment of encrypted high frequency and laser satellite communicators, a dozen phone modems that could be electronically linked to another FM-connected phone modem that could be attached via magnet to a pay phone for long range transmission, a laser printer, and a case of Hammermill paper.

Logan had gone ballistic swearing to take something *like that* out of Blackfoot's salary. Still smiling, Blackfoot loaded the equipment into the LTD and they found the hotel.

Only minutes after arriving, the Sioux had the computer linked up, programmed, checked for bugs and running. And now his hands flew across the keyboard like a machinegun, pausing only as he read before hacking, hacking...

Logan crossed his arms and watched. The Sioux was poetry in motion with a keyboard, reading faster than Logan could even scan before he hit another command to find his way to the next level. He used the "unbreakable" codes and encryptions as easily as most people used a phone book. But sweat was visible on the Sioux's face, and Logan sensed something.

"What is it, Blackfoot?"

"They're on me, Logan."

Logan stood. "What!"

"They're—" He hit a command and the screen went temporarily blank before it switched back to more data; not a file, a list. "They're trying to find the source of the intrusion."

Alarm flooded through Logan. He didn't mind violating the law—he'd done it plenty of times—but he didn't want to get caught. "Well, shut the thing off, Blackfoot! And get Jonathan back in here with that receiver!"

Blackfoot hit a command and a light on the laptop's B-drive began blinking. "A second," he whispered, "I keep putting them off. They think I've reached their files through MajorDomo list on the Teletype UNIX system. Which I have. But I've rerouted the system through a couple dozen Washington log-ons."

Logan's alarm became an anxiety attack. "Whose log-ons did you *use*, Blackfoot?" He raised his fist. "By God, Blackfoot, you'd better not tell me you used—"

"The White House."

Logan bowed his head. With a tired moan he began massaging his temple.

"A lot of people are going to be questioned!" Blackfoot laughed. "But it won't be *us!* Ha! Those fools are trying to find me on the Internet! We've probably fifteen minutes before... Oh, no."

Logan spun. "What?"

"Wow. They're good."

"*What!*"

"They've locked down the transmission."

Logan stepped forward. "How much longer do you need before you can break the transmission?" He raised a fist again, shouting, "Blackfoot, I'm going to pull the plug on this machine right now if you don't—"

Blackfoot snatched up the radio. "Jonathan!"

"Yeah?" came the reply.

"Get out there fast! They're closing on you."

"How far?"

"Can't tell. Just move."

"I'm going for the receiver."

"Make it fast, man. You're out of time!"

No reply.

Logan stepped forward, electrified. But he shut it down because he couldn't allow himself to lose it in front of these rookies. He tried to be calm as he turned away.

With a lightning quick movement Blackfoot snatched the phone off the modem, staring at the computer. Then he hit a command and the printer began to discharge pages.

Logan didn't congratulate him on the good work. He tried to turn his mind from what was going on outside and felt an impulse to make sure Jonathan got back. But he knew that two of them caught outside were worse than one.

Trying to stay calm, and even more importantly, to *look* calm, Logan walked over and picked up the first page that came out of the printer. He scanned with what concentration remained, but it was a lost cause. He turned to Blackfoot. "Raise Malone and see if he's clear. Make sure you're in code."

Blackfoot was on the radio and Malone came back across, clear and startlingly precise. "Yeah, I'm two blocks away, but I can see six cars of agents. They found where I attached the transmitter to the phone, and they're scraping for saliva. They think I used a suction cup instead of the magnet."

Logan snatched up the radio. "Do you copy me, Jonathan?"

"I copy."

"Move slow and make your way in another direction." Logan tried to make his voice calm but stern. "*Do not* move back toward the hotel. Move toward a restaurant. When you're sure you're clear, get back in here. We're locking up for the night."

"Understood."

Logan picked up his jacket and went toward the door. He tried not to think logically about what he was going to do—he might talk himself out of it.

"What are you doing?" Blackfoot asked.

"I'm gonna make sure Malone gets back here alive." When Logan reached the door he turned to Blackfoot, who was wearing a quizzical look. Quickly, Logan walked to the table and took out his SIG Sauer, laying it down beside the computer.

Blackfoot looked shocked. "You're giving me a *gun*? Don't regulations say that I can't carry a..."

"Forget regulations," Logan said, amazed that he was already bathed in sweat. "Just remember this: *Do not* shoot any of our people! But we don't know who else might be coming. Do you understand me? *Do not* shoot any special agents!"

Blackfoot nodded.

"You remember the description of the guy that killed Woodard? Tall, white hair, about sixty?"

"Yeah."

Logan pointed at the door. "If he comes through that door, don't even bother with a warning. Just start shooting and keep shooting until he drops and then get me on the radio. I'll be back here in a few seconds. I'll handle the paperwork myself and cover you. You got it?"

The Sioux's dark eyes blazed, cold and controlled. And he seemed to meet Logan's concern with new loyalty. "You can count on me, Logan."

Logan nodded and laid down two clips. "Turn off that computer and put your back against the wall and keep your eyes centered on that door and your ears open to what might come through the balcony." He placed a hand on the SIG. "Do you know how to use this?"

"Yeah, I've used one."

"You sure?"

"Yes, sir."

Logan nodded as he turned.

"School's out, kid."

Jonathan was moving toward a restaurant and suddenly realized that he hadn't turned off the frequency finder in the magnetic modem. Without expression, sweating and trembling, he tried to remain calm. He reached into his pocket and searched the fist-sized device, hoping that he could shut it down by feel. Then, a brown Chevy roared past and slid to a halt forty feet in front of him. Four men in dark suits leaped out, armed with shotguns and MP-5 fully automatic weapons. They erupted instantly in a run, dead toward him.

Waving weapons, they bellowed at Jonathan to lay down on the sidewalk. Whirling with a curse, Jonathan saw a dozen more men charging up the street from the pay phone, an army with an arsenal.

Frantic, he spun, but there was nowhere to run.

Logan heard the sounds of gathering sirens as he exited the lobby of the hotel. Moving with stunning slowness because he didn't want to attract attention to himself, he turned toward the commotion like a curious tourist.

Feeling faint pride in his creativity, since he was far beyond jaded and curiosity was orphaned in his life, Logan even had the presence of mind to freeze in the revolving doors, staring with everyone else as if he were suddenly concerned for his own safety. Then he began walking down the street, hands in his pockets.

Yes, among the curious...

He had no idea what he was about to do. But he knew he'd blow the roof off this entire mission and drag the scandal into the daylight before he let either of his boys get hurt. *Forget that,* he thought, *if it goes that far, I'll give interviews to CNN.*

Nobody was going to kill his people.

Nobody.

Logan had made his way a full block when he saw a nest of blue suited special agents running up the block. And then in the distance he heard an entire army of police sirens approaching. They were coming from all over, mobilized to help the federal agents. In seconds this place would be swarming with uniforms.

He walked quickly into a parking garage.

Jonathan whirled and searched but there was no place to go—no alleys, fire escapes, nothing. Then he noticed the huge plate glass window behind him—a restaurant.

"FBI!" screamed a cacophony of voices. *"Get down on the ground! Get down NOW!"*

Jonathan took five hard strides and launched himself into the air, powering through the plate glass window like a locomotive. Then he came down on the other side in a sparkling rain of slicing white light and he was running, overturning tables and slamming a waiter backward to sustain his momentum. He was in the middle of the room when he heard others scrambling through the smashed opening.

Screams of panic and chaotic orders were all he knew and Jonathan saw blood on his hands but he was too frantic for emotion. He vaulted a counter and slammed the kitchen door open to see the back door.

"Stop or we'll shoot!" screamed an agent. *"STOP!"*

Jonathan ignored the threats and slammed the door outward to find an alley parallel to the street. He hurled himself north, away from the hotel and heard them following through the kitchen door.

Jonathan increased his speed, running to burn out because he knew that he couldn't win any long distance race with these people. There were too many of them; he had to lose them with pure speed and a single, cunning move. There wouldn't be time for anything else.

He cleared the exit of the alley, coming out on a street he didn't recognize. More shouts echoed behind him, perhaps a hundred yards away now but he knew they wouldn't fire—not yet. They were bluffing, part of the street psychology of bringing a man to the ground and FBI regulations didn't *allow* deadly force against a fleeing felon simply because he was attempting to evade arrest.

Jonathan turned east, weaving through the crowds and tiring quickly because he had used so much speed in the alley and lactic acid was building up. His vision was bright but fading, sweat burned his eyes, and his chest felt raw. In every direction he heard sirens; the FBI had called in support from the DC police.

No good—in seconds an army would have him surrounded.

He could outrun some of them, but the ones who fell back would radio ahead so others could pick him up—others cops who would be fresh and eager to snatch the suspect who had evaded everyone else, a golden arrest.

Reaching a large intersection, nothing he recognized, Jonathan saw a subway and without hesitation leaped down the stairs, descending into the florescent haze. He vaulted drunks to cover the last few steps in a rush, smoothing hair from his sweat-plastered face.

Trying to appear normal, he walked quickly forward and saw two uniformed guards in the train's entranceway. They didn't seem to be paying attention to their radios, which echoed with the chaotic pursuit. Obviously, they didn't think they would be getting involved.

Grimacing, Jonathan didn't hesitate.

With a fast clip, timing it so that he would reach the cops at the same time the FBI agents reached the station itself, he moved forward. His teeth came together as he heard the shouts and sudden rushing down the steps, so close.

No more time.

The transit cops looked at the chaos on the stairway.

Jonathan clenched his right hand in a fist.

Preparing.

Logan nervously rubbed sweat from his eyes, waiting for the moment he needed. Listening to his own radio, he sensed what Jonathan was going to attempt.

Shadowed and silent, Logan stood in the stairway on the second level of the parking garage, waiting for the move. But they *had* to lose a visual on Jonathan, even for a moment, before he could make his play. He looked across the garage, sighting what he needed in the far corner—a four-door brown late-model Buick that looked like it'd been there a long time. Isolated. Ready for sacrifice.

Inside his coat, Logan folded his hand around his knife and lighter. "Come on, kid," he whispered. "Lose 'em for just a second...Just a second..."

Jonathan reached the turnstile as Special Agents flooded down the stairway and the DC Transit police turned, walking toward the commotion.

With a lunge Jonathan hit the first one—a big guy who could have been a linebacker at any college in the country—in the chest to knock him flat. Then the second cop shouted in alarm and reached for his Mace but Jonathan closed instantly.

A frantic intertwining of arms and Jonathan turned, pivoting and lifting the cop from his feet. Then he twisted down hard and the smaller man came over his shoulder. Jonathan slammed him hard and then leaped the turnstile.

A train was on the platform but Jonathan didn't have time for it, knew they could corner him. So he ran through the terrified crowd and *felt* the big cop so close. Then the narrow darkness between the train and the platform was in front of him and Jonathan hurled himself into the tight opening.

Ignoring the slashing storm of bruises and cuts that came from the jagged fit, Jonathan scrambled forward, his mind not even working anymore, too tired and shocked from the ordeal to have any coherent thought. He pushed himself away from shouts and curses and then he saw the rear of the train and he leaped, trying to land in the middle of the tracks and clear the electrified third rail.

Exhausted now, he knew that he didn't have but a moment to find his way out because the others would follow fast when the train departed. Stumbling and falling, he ran violently for two hundred yards. He knew one knee was hurt and bleeding, his pants torn, but he was too adrenalized to feel it.

Rage rising, he ran, searching, searching for anything that would give him a chance.

Logan heard the call and knew Jonathan was clear. He moved from the stairway but didn't remove anything from his pocket until he reached the Buick. He glanced around, searching the empty garage, and dropped to the pavement.

He thumped the gas tank: half-empty. Good. The more

fumes, the better. He took out his folding knife and stabbed upward, making a ragged hole, wrenched sideways, enlarging it. Quickly gasoline began to run out of the fissure and over his hand, flooding onto the concrete.

Smelling of gas, Logan stood and wiped his hand on his coat. Then he walked back, and when the stream was twenty feet from the Buick he took out his lighter and bent. With his clean hand, he lit it.

Burning toward the Buick in an amazing blaze of light that illuminated the entire rear section of the garage, the fire reached the vehicle as Logan reached the stairway. Bending reflexively, Logan felt the stunning force of the explosion, a massive *boom* amplified by the close ceiling of the garage.

Trying to catch his breath, he crouched on the stairway. Amazed despite his superior ability to remain calm, he saw the Buick was now an inferno, superheating the air. Breathing cautiously, he leaned against the wall of the stairway, waiting a moment for the blaze to ignite the sprinkler system, as it did.

Logan knew the fire department, police department, and probably even the FBI would know instantly of the commotion. It would give him the edge. He raised his radio, switching off the coded frequency to talk to the Bureau agents who had lost Jonathan in the subway.

"2101!" he shouted, using the roar of the blaze for cover. He intentionally made his voice garbled, so they couldn't follow the exact code. There was a pause and then the supervisor commanding the pursuit responded: "All units hold transmission until pursuit is terminated."

Logan stepped closer to the Buick, his voice all but lost in the roar of the flames. "2101! I've got him in the parking garage at Howard and 23rd! He came up a manhole! Request assistance! He's got a...!" Logan snapped off the transmission.

"What!" shouted the supervisor. "What unit is calling for assistance? Repeat your transmission! Repeat!"

Logan stepped perilously close to the flames, hearing the distant sirens of fire engines approaching. "This is 21—" he garbled. "He's at Howard and 23rd! Howard and 23rd! He's in the parking garage! Second floor!"

"All units respond to Howard and 23rd!" commanded the supervisor. "I repeat! All units respond to Howard and 23rd! Subject has been cornered."

Logan estimated: *five seconds to get clear.*

He was instantly on the street, moving like a man who, quite rationally, wanted to get out of a burning building. He ran lightly across Howard and into the rolling crowd, doing his best to look shocked. He didn't answer questions as squad cars slid to a halt beside the stairway and FBI agents raced up the steps.

Clearly, all agents not inside the subway itself were responding here. And even though he didn't turn his radio back to the utilized frequency, Logan knew the FBI supervisor was screaming right now for 2101 to give his exact position.

"That's the best I can do, kid," Logan muttered as he threaded through the rushing crowd. "I've cleared the streets, so get back on 'em and keep moving."

His next words surprised even him.

"Come on, Jonathan, play the game again..."

◉ ◉ ◉

Jonathan knew that they were at least a half-mile behind him, somewhere near the platform. They were moving cautiously through the darkness, prepared for an ambush.

Light was scarce, coming from a distant subway station where a train rested. Jonathan moved quickly forward, but he didn't want to emerge on the platform because he feared that any Transit cops would be looking for him. Recovering his breath, he crouched on the railing, trying to think clearly, to think of, think of...

...The *game*...

Bowing his head, Jonathan concentrated; *in chess, position is everything*...

He couldn't go back, couldn't go forward. So he had to... *open* something. He had to force them to make the move that could give him the path that he needed to win.

Make them break their position!

Grimacing, Jonathan knew that retreat was no option. Better to take his chance by advancing, by threatening. He had to push them into a time problem, had to make them think they were going to lose him if they didn't move fast enough, and moving fast would force a mistake, opening a line..

Force them to react to attack, and they'll sacrifice defense...

Jonathan scanned the darkness surrounding him with almost surreal concentration, something emerging and everything else fading as he studied what he had to work with.

It wasn't much. But he had been here before, and he studied with the attitude to win. He had...darkness, a tunnel, rails, timber, electricity, a train and a platform...

A train?

Yes! The train!

Use it!

Whirling, Jonathan saw a dozen flashlights moving up behind him, knew that he had maybe two minutes. *Use the train!*

How?

He turned back to the train, studying the crowd as they finished loading. Not knowing what else to do, he ran forward, trying to stay low and in the dark, waiting for the exact idea to come to him. He reached the train as the doors were seconds from closing.

Don't jump on it! That's what they'll expect! They'll have people waiting at the other station! Attack, attack, attack, and they'll break defense!

He laid low and to the side, raising his radio as the engineer began switching on power. Jonathan raised the radio, switching off the coded scrambler. Then he shouted frantically into the microphone just as he knew the other agents *had* to be shouting in the chaos.

"He's on the train!" Jonathan screamed above the engine and heard an entire symphony of roars and shouted instructions come back across, trying to get an exact location. "I've got an eye! He's on the train!"

Then he cast a quick, furtive glance to see the two Transit police lifting their radios and drawing guns as they ran forward with shouts and almost lost his breath as they came *too* close to missing and then the doors closed. The train left the station.

Broken defense!

A line! Attack!

The train was hurtling down the tracks toward the pursuing agents, but Jonathan knew that they would just step to the side. And when the last car cleared the trestle he ran quickly forward, rolling over the edge of the platform to his feet.

He walked to the exit, trying not to attract attention, and then he reached the turnstile and was past it, noticing peripherally that the ticket taker was talking frantically on the phone. But she hadn't seen him and he knew for certain that no one from the tunnel could have already reached the trestle.

On the stairway he harshly traded his sweat-soaked

leather coat with a wino for a cheap, urine-stained United States Army fatigue jacket and a blue New York Yankees hat. Then he threw a twenty-dollar bill to another wino and roughly snatched a pair of cheap sunglasses from his hand, wasting no emotion or time to discuss the fairness of the trade before he hit the street, moving away.

Logan got back to the hotel at ten p.m. He half-expected to find Blackfoot dead, and decided that his own paranoia had risen to the level to poor ol' Woodard's. Suddenly Logan regretted not listening to him on that gloomy night.

Holding his knife low and concealed, Logan went quietly through the door to come into the suite.

All the lights and lamps were burning. Obviously, Blackfoot was taking no chances. Then Logan saw the Sioux sitting in the chair, his back against the wall—asleep.

Logan shook his head, walking forward. He stood over the Sioux, knife in his hand, staring down, wondering how to teach him a lesson. Carefully, he reached out and lifted the SIG from the desk. Then he leaned forward, staring into Blackfoot's snoring face.

"BANG!"

Blackfoot shot from the chair with a shout, scrambling for the SIG to send papers over the desk. He leaped back before he identified Logan's scowling aspect. The Sioux's hand was on his heart, chest heaving: "What was that for?"

"I though you might live longer if you were awake." Logan slammed the SIG back into his holster. "What are you doing, Blackfoot? I told you keep a lookout."

"Well...Uh..."

"Yeah, I've used that one myself." Logan walked to the bar and poured himself a stiff whiskey.

"Where's Jonathan?" Blackfoot asked.

"I can't tell you, son."

"Well...is he alive? Did he get away?"

"I can't tell you, Blackfoot." Logan took a swallow and grimaced. Then he sighed and leaned on the bar. His voice sounded tired, then he recognized it was concern. He gazed into the bottom of the empty glass.

"We'll know soon enough," he said.

It was midnight and Logan, chain-smoking at the table, was still awake. He had done severe damage to the refrigerator's stock of Old Forester, trying to defuse the overload of adrenaline from today's activities. But despite the fact that he had worked hard with booze and cigarettes and tiresome pacing, he had never felt more sober or distracted. He focused on Blackfoot, still on the computer. A seven-inch thick stack of reports on Phantom, BCCI, the rest, lay beside him.

The Sioux was preternaturally focused, but Logan sensed that Blackfoot was as worried as he was. He was just channeling his energy into work.

Glancing down, Logan looked at the hundred or so documents—documents that created more questions than answers.

He had already gained a general understanding of World Finance's financial infrastructure. But he needed hard proof that the company was working with BCCI with the intent to defraud, something that had escaped Strike Six and which had not been revealed in any 302s—work interview reports filed by special agents. Oh, sure, there was tons of allegations, accusations, and suspicions, but nothing he could use in court.

Taking another sip, Logan concentrated on the facts. Fact: World Finance issued Letters of Credit to back phony loans.

Fact: the Letters of Credit were legal because they were backed by a three-billion-dollar World Finance account at BCCI.

Clearly, it was this huge stockpile of available funds that enabled World Finance to launder the vast amounts of drug money.

With a three-billion-dollar surplus of liquid cash, World Finance could easily accept loan requests for hundreds of millions and no one would raise an eyebrow. But something about it bothered Logan, and he kept returning to it. There was simply something *there* that didn't make sense, and he was finally getting tired.

He took another sip and gazed at Blackfoot, amazed that he'd kept at it for this long. "Why don't you give it a break, Blackfoot?" he asked. "You've been hacking on that thing all night."

The Sioux sighed and blinked tiredly. Logan could see small dark rings under his eyes. His face was slightly pale beneath the dark brown skin. "C'mon, kid, give it a break."

Blackfoot was solemn. "Do you think he made it?"

Logan sighed. "Jonathan's smart, but I don't know. I've tried to raise him on the radio—he's not answering. So if he's clear, he's being real cautious."

Blackfoot closed his eyes.

"Let it go, kid," Logan's tone was fearless. "You did what you could, and I did what I could. If Jonathan's half as smart as I think he is, he got clear."

"How long do you think he'll stay out there?"

"Not much longer. He's going to have to get back here to get some rest."

Blackfoot walked to the window. He edged back a curtain to stare over city lights that lit the space below them in a continuous florescent haze. Headlights filled every street as far as they could see. "There's a lot going on down there," he muttered.

"The Bureau's still got agents out," Logan answered. "I'd say there's probably forty or fifty of them along the streets, waiting for Jonathan to surface."

"What about police?"

"They have to work for a living. But if Jonathan is spotted, they'll respond."

Logan looked back to the documents. He was still bothered by something about World Finance's account with BCCI. Something that wasn't *logical* for a crook to do, and yet Phantom had done it. He leaned his head back against the chair and closed his eyes, allowing the whiskey and the idea to settle inside him.

It was—he became certain—something that had been done with the money that shouldn't have been done. Logan tried to go with the flow of it, sinking into the finer intricacies of the scam.

He tried to put himself in Phantom's place, to imagine the financial depth of the operation. But after a moment he knew he wasn't going to succeed. He was having too much trouble concentrating, and there was simply too much money, too much...

Logan opened his eyes. *Too much money?*

Slowly, stunned, he leaned forward.

Too much money?

That's it...There was too much money. From beginning to end. There was too much money connecting World Finance and BCCI.

Logan stared at nothing, letting the idea work itself. It didn't sound right, but he knew it was. There was simply too much money connecting the two organizations. Somehow, he knew, no scam artist like Phantom would ever stash three billion in a BCCI account to *legitimately* back up illegitimate loans. If Phantom were intent to promise bogus loans, then the guarantee behind the loans would be bogus as well. It's the only thing that made sense.

"Blackfoot..."

The Sioux turned.

"Run a global reference of all the 302 reports to see if Strike Six ever investigated whether BCCI actually contains the three billion it used to guarantee those loans."

Walking across the room Blackfoot bent over the computer. Obviously, such a mean task didn't deserve his full attention. In a few seconds he stood, shaking his head. "According to a 302 report filed on 13 September, 1999, Strike Six investigated the financial holdings of the World Finance account at BCCI and BCCI confirmed in an interview that there was 3.4 billion available to back World Finance's loans."

"Who confirmed it at BCCI?"

"Frank Fincher. The president. He told agents that..." Blackfoot read for a moment. "...that World Finance has more than enough real money and bonds in the bank to cover all the loans."

"Huh," Logan grunted, "World Finance never *made* any loans." He paused. "Did the Bureau obtain a subpoena for the account? Did they actually *look* at the cash and the bonds themselves?"

Blackfoot hit another key. "On 15 September, 1999, a request for a subpoena was submitted to United States district attorney, Southern District of New York, to visually confirm the assets. It was refused on grounds of insufficient cause."

"Did the Justice Department resubmit the request to another court and file a reconsideration?"

"No," Blackfoot answered. "A supplemental memo filed

the day after the request by your buddy, Hooper, says that Justice didn't think the financial search merited a reconsideration. Hooper says that...that Justice refused to back his suspicions."

Logan stared away, blinked slowly. "Good ol' Mark. No wonder he's scared. He knows." A long pause. "Who received Mark's memo?"

"It went straight to the director."

Logan nodded, then, "Tell me something, kid, and all this is classified, have you ever heard of FIN-CEN?"

"Sure—Financial Crimes Enforcement Network. It's a top secret complex located in Vienna, Virginia, run by a contingent of federal employees who monitor the international banking system. FIN-CEN tries to keep track of where all the money transferred in the world goes, who it comes from, whatever. And they report directly to the Treasury, although in reality the National Security Council and the CIA run them. FIN-CEN can't follow all of the money, but they do their best and they follow a lot of it. SMART is the software program they use to monitor the system. It's a pretty complex program. Not easy to access."

"I'll bet," Logan appreciated a plan as it came to him. "Have you ever broken into it?"

"Never had a reason."

"Can you?"

"Sure," the Sioux replied, an amazing lack of hesitation. "What for?"

"Because I want to know if there's actually any money in World Finance's account with BCCI. I want to know if World Finance's account actually holds three billion dollars."

"What makes you think World Finance's account at BCCI is empty?" Blackfoot questioned.

"Because none of this makes sense. No bottom-feedin' scum like Phantom is going to tie up three billion dollars in an account designated to guarantee loans that never need to be guaranteed. It's a waste of money, and Phantom's too greedy to waste money. He wants it to be working for him, not lying around in an account to confirm loans that are never going to be confirmed."

Blackfoot looked confused. "But don't lawyers and banks call BCCI to confirm that World Finance's account is big enough to guarantee their loans before they let their companies make down payments?"

"The honest folk would call, Blackfoot, but if BCCI is crooked to the bone, like I know it is, then whoever takes those calls would lie to lawyers as quickly as they'd lie to anyone else. So if a lawyer called and asked if World Finance had three billion in an account to guarantee a loan, the crooks at BCCI would just say that it did. They wouldn't tell other bankers the truth. They wouldn't tell *anyone* the truth."

"And if the money's not in the account?"

"Then it will prove that both World Finance and BCCI have conspired to defraud investors of hundreds of millions for fake loans that were never legally guaranteed."

A moment of silence, then Blackfoot walked to the desk, removing the phonebook. He thumbed through it quickly, running his finger down the page until he froze, dark eyes narrowing.

"What are you looking for?" Logan asked.

"The phone number of First National Bank of Washington. I can access FIN-CIN through their direct phonelink once I bypass their fire wall."

"Can you do it from the hotel without a trace?"

"No. In the end, it'll be traced. It might take them some

time, but they'll figure it out. Even if I network a dozen lines and go through a couple of satellites, there's always the last link in the chain. They know it and I know it."

"How long would it take them to find us?"

The lean shoulders shrugged: "An hour."

"Then we'll wait until morning and we'll drive to the outskirts of town to use a payphone. I don't want anyone tracking us here. We've got six sets of fake ID, but we can't risk compromising any of them."

Blackfoot set the book on the desk. He looked at Logan a moment. "I heard what you said, but how can you be certain Phantom is using an empty account?"

Logan turned his glass, and it threw out a brilliant spectrum of color far too complex to be called light or dark.

"That's what I'd do," he said.

⊙ ⊙ ⊙

It was late in the morning and Logan, still awake, reached instantly for his SIG as the door opened and a shadowed form shambled into the suite.

And Jonathan emerged into the light Logan saw that he was covered with cuts and bruises and dirt. He was dressed like one of the ubiquitous homeless that covered Washington streets. He was wearing a green Army Jacket that smelled strongly of urine, blood, and garbage.

Without words Jonathan bent over the sink, and Logan watched as he drank a glass of water. Then Jonathan wheeled tiredly and sat down, gasping. With an effort he slowly shed the jacket, dropping it to the floor. He bent slowly forward until he was resting his elbows on his knees, breathing hard.

"You okay, kid?"

"I lost them...in the subway. I went east...ducked into a theater, lost myself in the crowd." He released a tired breath.

"When it got dark, I made my way back. But the streets are crawling. It took a while."

Logan nodded steadily. "You did good, Jonathan. I don't know too many agents who could have pulled that off, and that's the truth."

With a faint nod, Jonathan rose and walked to the couch. He roughly drew the SIG, holding it reflexively in his right hand. "Thanks, Logan," he mumbled, "but I gotta get some sleep, man. I'm wasted.... *Wasted.*"

Logan nodded, and then watched until Jonathan's chest rose heavily. The kid was almost instantly asleep, still covered with unwashed cuts and gutter smell.

Still holding the SIG, Logan checked to make sure the door was locked and chained and walked to the back of the hotel room. Fully dressed, he lay down on the bed and stared at the ceiling, estimating their chances.

Their enemy was a megalomaniac with untold billions of dollars and an army of professional assassins—a Superman who had control over everything from the Justice Department to the White House.

Logan had only his instincts and skills, an utterly unstoppable Sioux and a true genius that was beginning to play the game again.

Logan closed his eyes, knew only one thing.

It was going to be one heck of a fight.

Chapter Seven

Logan awoke before dawn and took a cab from the hotel, exiting at a closed entrance of Pennsylvania Avenue. Then he caught another cab and doubled the city to sanitize his trail.

He exited at the Washington City Zoo and walked to a payphone at the corner of Randolph and McMillian. As he was dialing Webster's number he saw a copy of the morning edition of the *Post*. Beside a follow-up story on Woodard, there was a story about the SEC launching an investigation into the gold market.

Logan dropped some change, lifted a copy: The NYSE's computer monitoring equipment had picked up an incredible flood of gold ore into the market. It looked like the price of gold was now slightly more than dirt. He was still reading when Webster answered.

"This is Webster."

"Logan."

There was a pause. "Well, are your people still alive?"

Logan felt slight anger emanating through the line. "Yeah, they're alive."

"That's good. Because we had a *major* scene yesterday in downtown D.C. Somebody broke into Strike Six files and the NSA documents involving your investigation. Then, apparently, they blew up a car in a parking garage to create a diversion so that one of them could escape a pursuit. And I was really, *really* concerned for a moment that you might have been involved." A hard silence followed. "I'm glad you *weren't*."

"Yeah." Logan said quickly. "Me too. Did you see this morning's article in the *Post* about this gold?"

"It's our man. He's trying to counter you, Logan, like in a chess match."

"What'd he do?"

"He flooded the market with high-grade gold ore, which sent the price of gold through the basement. Consequently, as everyone discovered with not a little alarm, five hundred billion bucks in Fannie Mae bonds crashed and a dozen American towns are facing bankruptcy."

Logan grunted, "Smart..."

"Yep."

"So he's destroying entire towns to warn us off."

"Almost. At the eleventh hour the Federal Reserve announced that we had enough reserve gold on deposit to cover the loans even with the deflated price." Webster released a tired sigh. "Needless to say, though, this is a knife fight. Do you know yet who killed Woodard?"

"Not yet."

"What do you have?"

"We don't have anything on the hitter, but we've got a good lead on this mystery man. And I've learned that Justice is compromised all the way to the top. This guy is evil, boss. He's got control over just about everything. And Justice is doing everything they can to protect him." He thought of something. "Do you know this guy by his official code name? Phantom?"

"Yeah. I know it. I just don't like to use it. It gives a cheap crook too much credit."

"Yeah, well, that's what they're using." Logan gathered his thoughts. "Next, I'm going to try and confirm that—"

"Wait, Logan; I'm not sure this line is secure, so keep your moves to yourself. Just tell me this: How close are you to pinpointing this mystery man?"

"A couple of days, maybe. I think I know how to rattle his cage. Get him to stick his head out."

"All right," Webster said, "then listen to me very carefully. The director has placed CI-3 on standby. He's got a helicopter at Quantico that'll get them to Dulles where a Lear jet is prepped to take them anywhere in the world within a half-hour's notice." A subdued warning was evident. "Do you understand what I'm saying?"

CI-3 was officially known as Division Five, Squad Nine, Counterintelligence Team Three. It was the FBI's official team for international body snatching or counterinsurgency. Its authority was far, far more comprehensive than Hostage and Rescue and it was supposedly comprised of the best killers in the world. Logan had also heard that, for whatever dubious reasons, CI-3 had never brought anyone in alive.

The activation of CI-3 made Logan nervous, but there was something else in Webster's tone that disturbed him even more. "What else is happening?"

"Nothing for you to be concerned about," Webster answered without patience. "I'm dealing with it. But you need to get on with this, Logan. I'm not sure what certain people are going to do in the very near future to terminate your team. And without your team we don't stand a chance of finding this man."

"I need three days."

"I can buy you three days," Webster responded. "But heat is coming from everywhere, so time is a priority. Right now they don't have the foggiest what you're really doing. But if they realize you're close to nailing this guy, they're going to do everything that they can to terminate your team. Officially or otherwise."

Logan took a second. "Tell them I only get in touch every seventy-two hours. But don't let them shut us down, sir. The only thing we've got going for us is that we still have a chance of finishing this guy. If we walk away from this without nailing him, I think he's going to take vengeance and then some. I've played this game before."

"I'll cover you as long as I can, Logan. But things are burning down fast and I've already been pushed to the wall." Webster intensified his tone. "So *find* him."

"What if CI-3 can't get to him before he goes under?"

Logan heard Dead stand up. "Don't let him go under, Logan! No matter what! Don't let this man go under! This is our last chance!"

"So...what are you telling me to do?"

"I'm telling you to do your job!" Webster responded. "That's what I'm telling you. Find this man and put him under arrest. Arrest him dead if you have to but arrest him!"

Logan wanted to be utterly clear. "Are you telling me that... that this guy would be better off dead?"

"Logan," Webster said very, very distinctly, "we are the FBI. We do not assassinate people. That's the CIA. What I'm telling you is this: Find this man and put him *down*. And if he places you or your men in danger, throw everything you've got. Don't worry about the complications. Don't worry about anything. And if you need more backup, get on the horn to me. Am I making myself clear?"

"Yeah," Logan almost smiled, truly beginning to appreciate the full scope of Webster's integrity. "I understand."

"Good," Webster said. "Now get to work. You're on the clock."

With a faint smile, Logan walked away. But something told him where this train was headed, told him that he was on a dead-ahead collision course with the most powerful player in the world who was even now patiently waiting for Logan to come into the crosshairs. And he knew that only one of them would survive.

As he remembered something else.

"It all came down to two kings, and two pawns..."

Jonathan finished breakfast in the hotel room and went down the hallway for some ice, but the ice machine was broken, so he took the elevator to the lobby, noticing with faint nervousness that no one cast him the faintest glance as he went into the kitchen.

He filled the ice bucket, and didn't bother to lodge any kind of complaint because he didn't want anyone to remember him, and entered the elevator again. He punched the button for the thirtieth floor as a tall, somberly dressed gentleman wearing a dark coat stepped onto the elevator behind him. The man held a long cane in his hand and wore extremely dark glasses, utterly black against skeletal skin.

Jonathan knew.

Knew!

With a control that surprised him, Jonathan placed his back to the wall. He almost reached for his SIG but realized instantly that any overt action would explode in close combat and he wanted more room to maneuver. He knew he could get at least one shot off quick, but also knew he would probably take the same.

The old man stood close beside him, solidly commanding the center of the elevator, the long wooden cane with an ivory pommel in his hand.

The elevator rose.

Breath under tight control, Jonathan attempted to look oblivious. But as he took in everything about the man there was another image he had in his mind, an image he saw when he was a child, hiding from his father's murderer.

Shadows...

Shadows, darkness and...something *more...*

Skeletal face coming from darkness.

Frowning, Jonathan glanced up to see a small black ring on the man's left hand. It was ebony, polished like bone and strikingly powerful. It had a small eye, an all-seeing eye that reminded Jonathan of the eye on a one-dollar bill. Black ring, black *king...*

Father...

Jonathan raised his face to stare fully at the man.

Smiling, the old man turned to nod politely, thick black glasses shielding his eyes that still seemed to somehow burn coldly through the darkness.

Cold as ice.

Logan entered the hotel fast but casual, eager to check on the status of his men. He hit the button and the second of the hotel's parallel elevator doors opened. Without hesitation he hit the button for the thirtieth floor. He knew something was amiss, something that even Webster was too rattled to mention. And it bothered him, because Webster wasn't shaken easily. He had a lot to tell his boys.

It was going to be a long three days.

Only one of them was getting out of this elevator alive. Or neither of them. It didn't matter anymore.

Jonathan stared at the elevator doors. He knew that as

soon as the doors opened he would move. Then he would turn and fire a full clip and keep firing until there was nothing left. It took all his control, standing so close *so close.*

Then he felt something else—something he hadn't known since he was a child. He tried to control his breathing, his face a frozen mask, fear itself the only control he had. *Come on, make a move, and I'll blow your brains all over that wall.*

But the old man didn't move, and for a moment Jonathan wondered if he weren't somehow mistaken. Then he remembered the ring *black king* that he had never forgotten and he was certain.

He prepared, quick and alert, as the elevator rose.

Then the man turned. "By the way," he said with a heavy German accent, "do you have the time?" He laughed. "*Dolt* that I am, I left my watch in my room."

Jonathan had a watch on his left wrist, hidden from view. "No," he said. "I don't have the time."

"Ah," the man laughed. "It is my fault." He was utterly disarming. "I should be more careful, no?"

The old man turned back to the doors as the lights passed the twentieth floor. Then he dropped an envelope from his jacket as the thirtieth floor approached, and bent. An almost albino white hand, long fingers stretched like bones, gripped the fallen object and then the doors opened and Jonathan moved fast.

"I wonder—" the man said, stepping forward.

Jonathan drew the SIG as *it* came over him. He shouted as the man struck with a knife and fired a close shot as something tore savagely through his shoulder *white pain...*

Jonathan spun away from the blow and the SIG left his hand and there was skull-white rage before him, a skeletal force beyond anything human and Jonathan struck the man's right forearm—his weapon hand—aside. He read the wide angle of the neck-blow and slid inside it, lashing out with a punch that connected hard in the man's chest. The blow was perfect; the whole weight of his body in his arm and the man's feet fully left the floor as he sailed back.

Rebounding from a wall, the man stabbed and Jonathan kicked, taking out his knee. The man cursed loudly in German and connected with a hard backhand. Turning away from the blow, Jonathan crashed against the wall, stunned and off balance. He grimaced as he focused through the blood cascading from his cut forehead.

Just from this encounter, fierce as it was, Jonathan knew he could take this guy one on one. But the old man had used some kind of hidden backup weapon to cut his forehead and now he was half-blind. Then he glimpsed blackness closing. He turned into it, but the man was already inside his elbow and his chest lifted with his arm. Jonathan felt breath leave his chest.

The Iceman smiled; his skull split. "Do you remember me, child?" he whispered. "Do you remember?"

Jonathan frowned as he sensed deeper pain and glanced down to see an *ice pick* wedged through his ribs. It was driven tightly into the skin, locked hard, and numbing pain was everywhere—pain that came from deep within and had no origin yet took his breath. He looked dead into the glacial eyes.

"Yes!" Jonathan said. "I *remember!*"

"We started a game but we did not finish!" the man smiled savagely. "But now I will—"

Twisting in a bolt of pain that separated his mind from his body, Jonathan tore his skin from the ice pick and spun with another blow that slammed into the old man's chest, hurling him back.

The Iceman shouted in pain and fell into the elevator with the bloody ice pick raised high as the doors closed, slamming on him to separate them again.

The parallel elevator opened and Logan stepped off, eyes instantly opening in shock.

"Logan!" Jonathan screamed.

Logan's SIG magically leaped into his hand as he sprang forward with an agility that belied his fifty-something years to come down solid as stone between Jonathan and the elevator as the doors began to open.

The Iceman drew a pistol.

Logan fired first—a full magazine as the doors closed and Jonathan saw the Iceman fall backward, roaring in pain. He collapsed against the wall as the doors shut and Logan kept firing, rending the door with rounds, blasting holes in the steel and the elevator itself until the slide on the SIG locked and the elevator descended. The corridor was heated with gunfire, smoke clouded the air.

The Iceman was gone.

Logan whirled. "You okay, boy?"

Jonathan gasped, gripping his ribs as Blackfoot charged out the door of their room. Naked and soaking wet, the Sioux was holding a shotgun.

Logan glared. "Load everything *fast* and get Jonathan downstairs! Go north on Rhode Island Avenue but don't go past Riverdale. Stay on Channel Three and I'll catch up to you in the Chevy. You got it?" He stood. *"You got it!"*

Blackfoot nodded.

"Move it!"

In a flat run Logan went for the stairway.

"Logan!" Jonathan gasped. "You're gonna have to kill him!"

For a split-second Logan paused in the stairway, dropping the empty magazine from the SIG to slam in another with vengeance and his face blazed with the purity of murder.

"Good."

Blackfoot grabbed Jonathan's SIG from the floor and jammed it in the doors of the second elevator. Then he slung the shotgun over his back and ran into the room, quickly pulling on his pants and shoes and not pausing for a shirt as they heard sirens.

In a whirlwind Blackfoot hurled documents and weapons and ammo and computer gear onto the trolley and in thirty seconds he was back in the hall, shoving the trolley before him.

Still electrified, Jonathan leaned against a wall as Blackfoot exited the room and then he reached down and pulled the SIG from the door, holding it open with his shoulder. In another split-second Blackfoot was inside it and Jonathan hit "basement." It descended quickly as both of them fell against the wall.

Still soaked from his shower, Blackfoot snatched shotgun shells from his coat, quickly loading the magazine of the 12-gauge. "How many of 'em were there?" he shouted.

"One."

Blackfoot whipped his hair back. "What? Just *one*?"

"Yeah."

"Did Logan get him?"

Jonathan blew sweat from his lips. "I don't think so. I know he was hit but he was wearing a vest. He's a pro. He's not going to..." He grimaced in pain. "...make a mistake."

They reached the parking garage and Blackfoot pumped a round hard into the chamber and instantly swung the

Remington 870, centering on the doors as they opened wide.

A startled bellhop stared down the barrel of the shotgun.

"Back up!" Blackfoot shouted as the bellhop took three quick steps away, hands raised.

Jonathan knew that he wasn't a hitter—his fear was too real. But then again, as Jonathan watched Blackfoot commanding the situation, he realized there weren't many people, hitters or not, who wouldn't be afraid of a half-naked Sioux emerging from an elevator with a shotgun.

Sirens were closing.

"We've got to move!" Jonathan said, finding more strength as he recovered from the initial shock. Blackfoot swung the barrel of the shotgun to the bellhop. "Get lost! *Now!*"

With a wild cry of relief the bellhop turned and ran. "I'll get the car," the Sioux said instantly. "We've got to clear this garage inside two minutes or we're history."

"Go!"

Seconds later the LTD slid to a halt beside Jonathan and together they threw everything into the back seat, keeping their weapons up front. Shotgun close at his side, Blackfoot hung a hard turn to follow the down-ramp but the ticket booth was—

Blocked by cars!

With a Sioux-accented curse Blackfoot spun the steering wheel to the right and they roared airborne over a concrete barrier, propelled by the LTD's momentum to clear a two-foot drop and land in the first floor of the garage. They recovered and surged forward in the wrong lane, shredding a path through oncoming traffic. Shouting, Jonathan slammed a hand hard against the dash.

"Hang on!" Blackfoot screamed.

They skidded wildly through a turn and Blackfoot took the bumper off a parked car. Then they hooked another right to head down into the lower level of the building as an angry maze of sirens converged on the entrance of the parking garage. Jonathan glared wildly as the Sioux threw the LTD into a screaming left turn in the basement and they flowed under a haze of artificial light.

"Blackfoot!" Jonathan shouted. "We're underground!"

"*Nothing's* underground in this city!" he yelled, skidding hard right to avoid another vehicle.

Jonathan saw it: *Up ramp!*

Up ramp to the street!

"*There!*" he yelled.

Blackfoot was howling as they hit the up ramp at sixty miles an hour and Jonathan knew they would be *absolutely* dead if there were any oncoming traffic. Then they were airborne with a red and white beam flying over their heads, big air, howls, bodies diving, screams, white day and night.

Miraculously *truly miraculously* they came down on an open street. In a thunderous collision of wheels rebounding against the frame they slammed forward, sliding to a full stop. Shocked, they tried to reorient themselves and stared at each other as if they couldn't believe they'd survived. Then, together, they saw the tunnel.

One block away.

"*Go!*" yelled Jonathan.

With the virtuosity of a violinist Blackfoot cut the steering wheel hard, hands flying and slapping and then they were spinning again, evading sirens.

The LTD hit the tunnel at seventy and Blackfoot cut left to pass a semitrailer, barely evading another oncoming semitrailer that took off the LTD's sideview mirror and then they were in the daylight again, angling right to gain another interstate—it didn't matter which.

Jonathan grimaced in pain, heard Blackfoot: "What about Logan?"

"Logan's as smart as it gets," Jonathan answered, teeth clenched. "He can take care of himself."

"Do you think he can get out?"

"If *anybody* can get out, it's Logan."

"I hope so," said Blackfoot, becoming more subdued as the moments passed. "He's the only one we can trust."

"Yeah."

Making a smooth lane change, the Sioux slid the LTD between two semitrailers, using them for cover. Now it would be hard for anyone at all to observe them. "Who was the guy that tried to take you out?" he asked. "I didn't see him."

Jonathan leaned his head back, closing his eyes.

"Somebody from my past."

"From your *past?*"

"Yeah."

"But why was he trying to take you out? Was if for something in your past or was it for what we're doing now? I thought that he was the same guy who killed Woodard."

Jonathan concentrated.

"Jonathan? Did you hear me?"

"I heard you."

"Why did that guy hit us?"

Jonathan gazed down as his hand tightened on the SIG.

"To finish a game," he said.

Logan holstered the SIG as he hit the lobby, trying to be inconspicuous.

He noticed a large crowd staring at the shot-to-pieces

elevator. Trying to catch his breath, profoundly feeling the damage done by cigarettes, he moved forward. The elevator doors had already opened; it was empty. Bloodless.

Concealing his rage, Logan searched the lobby, knowing he'd finish it here and now if he saw the white-haired attacker. He turned as hotel security rushed to the front entrance to meet a cadre of Washington police. A sergeant shouted instructions, pointing upward.

Logan knew it would be easy to find the room with all the blood in the hallway and fifteen 9-mm shell casings littering the floor. Plus, he was certain that Jonathan and Blackfoot probably made a wide trail as they departed, leaving the door open with clothes scattered all over the room.

A crime scene analysis would quickly reveal that the 9-mm casings on the floor were special FBI issue. And a print of the room would reveal that they had been involved. Then accusations of misconduct would fly, heaping even more tension on Woodard's death at the Alexandria Hilton in Quantico.

Logan thought of calling it in to take steam out of their enemies' stride. But if he did he'd be placed on leave pending a Shooting Review Board, and he couldn't lose three days on a shooting investigation. He couldn't even lose an afternoon.

He was violating so many rules and regulations that he'd never beat them all, even with Webster's help. Yet another thought dominated: He had to find his boys quick or they might get hit again and the odds were decidedly against them.

Logan moved for a side door that had not yet been secured and, knowing he couldn't go into the garage now that the exits were sealed, searched for whatever officer was watching the east side. He saw a scared-looking uniform, no more than twenty-two.

A rookie, for sure.

Logan went fast down a hallway, coming out the glass door to directly approach the rookie. Immediately the boy raised a hand, his other hand settling on his gun.

With an air of authority Logan theatrically displayed his FBI credentials. "Is Captain Briggs on the scene!"

He knew Captain Stephen Briggs was Commander over the entire uniform division of the DC police.

There was a pause; the rookie's mouth hung open. His confusion was evident.

"*Son!*" Logan said sternly, "I'm Special Agent Roberts with the Bureau. I've got a situation inside. I need to know if that paper-pushing Briggs is on the scene yet."

"I don't know." the rookie responded. "I just got here. He might be around front."

"Good enough." Logan took a step and spun back as the rookie raised a hand.

"Secure that door!" Logan commanded. "Nobody gets in! Nobody gets out! Not until I talk to Briggs! You got it?"

"Yes, sir!"

"Good man!" Logan paced onward, job to do. "I'm going around front to see if I can find your captain."

"Yes, sir!"

When Logan was near the front of the building he angled right until he was in the flowing row of cars and then he was lost from view. In a moment he was on Howard Avenue, then he was clear and moving away and no longer concerned about the evidence left behind in the hallway or in the room. He'd face the music later.

He didn't worry about the Chevy, either. He'd find other means of transportation. He just had to find it quick and get clear of this town because there would be no turning back now, not for any of them.

An incident like this raised everyone's level of commitment, permanently changed the game. It was something he had seen before, even in professionals.

Once blood is drawn, it's personal.

Chapter Eight

Black rain cast a somber tone that disturbed Webster even more than this abrupt meeting. And as he made his way down the honeycomb streets northeast of the capital, he searched carefully to discern surveillance, but saw nothing.

It'd been a while, but Webster found himself sliding back into a combat mode with surprising ease. He even enjoyed it in a youthful sense, feeling like a real law enforcement officer again instead of an academic or, worse, a bureaucrat. He was in the action again, watching his back—alert, afraid...alive.

For the first time in a long time he was solidly aware of the Smith and Wesson .45 he carried on his hip. For years it had been mostly adornment, far more cosmetic than practical—it wasn't likely anyone was going to attack him on the third floor of the J. Edgar Hoover Building—but now he was comforted by the weight. Then he saw the saloon, the half-functional neon lights burning even in the day, and the door was open for drinks to those who couldn't wait.

Webster went slowly through the door, letting his eyes adjust to the gray, smoke-filled interior. The room already bustled with people trying to get a jump on the night, and that's what this place was, Webster thought, as he stood without moving. It was where night never died, where those who needed the night to feel comfortable with their sins could find it. A place where they could wait patiently for the sun to set so they could move back to their world.

Seated in the rear of the building, Webster recognized the man he'd come to see—the man who had left a terse message on his pager only an hour earlier.

General Ariel Ben Canaan did not move. His hair, shaggily cut and the color of pale oak, was uncombed.

His face was darker than Webster remembered it, and he judged that the room gave it a more of its true desert hue. Otherwise, Canaan was obscurely dressed in a plain white shirt and gray dress pants, not recently ironed. His shoes were black and worn; a man who moved quickly. Beside him, a gray dress coat was heaped over something solid that he obviously did not want Webster to see. Yet.

The general nodded charmingly as Webster came through the smoke to reach the table. He sat as Canaan motioned to the bartender. "It's a little early for me," Webster said.

"The FBI is notorious for its high moral standards."

Webster wasn't sure if it was respect.

"It is not so in my country," Canaan said more quietly. "Soldiers drink because they are soldiers. It helps a man forget, sometimes." His eyes narrowed as he lit a Marlboro.

Webster's laughed. "I'll take a beer."

"Now I can trust you."

"You don't ask for much."

"It is early."

After the waitress left, Webster lifted the beer glass, saw gruel flaking along the edge. "Nice place you picked here."

"I prefer real places and real people." Canaan released a perfectly timed cloud of smoke as he took another sip of whiskey. "War has made me what I am. Some things a man cannot change, though they may change him. You agree?"

"Yes."

"Even you are a man who changes, I think."

"You think so?" Webster replied mildly.

"Yes," Canaan rumbled, eyes focusing with a gaze that Webster knew could reach across long miles of sand, to mountains. "I think you are a man who is changing. Even now."

That was inspiration for a sip. With a slight frown Webster set the glass down. "How's that, general?"

"You are a man who is loyal to his country, Mr. Webster. A man of honor. You have regarded the FBI and your country as the same—until now, I think. But now I think you are realizing that, perhaps, they are not the same. You are thinking that you cannot be loyal to both."

"An intriguing thought," Webster replied.

"Still, only a thought." Canaan gestured. "There is more to patriotism than loyalty, and there is no honor in loyalty when a man is loyal to a lie. I think you, too, are realizing things have changed, and it is changing you. Because you have realized that what you have always served can be served no more. You are a son who must choose between two parents."

Webster pursed his lips. Without doubt Canaan got to the point quickly, even if he spoke around it, instead of to it.

"The old ones in Israel have a saying," the general said, with a strangely becoming smile. Webster realized it was the smile of a man who rarely smiled, making it all the more impressive. "Would you like to hear it?"

"Sure."

"It is said that the future of the world, at any time, hinges on the lives of six men. It is said that these six men control the destiny of us all. They say it has always been like this."

"Another intriguing idea."

"Knowledge and secrets make a man intriguing." The Israeli tank commander laughed, gesturing to indicate his fatigue. "I know too many secrets."

Webster said nothing.

"I will tell you a secret, Mr. Webster. Perhaps you will also find it intriguing."

Glancing down, Webster traced a drop of moisture on his glass. He knew that Canaan was Mossad, so he would be suspicious of everything that he might hear—especially if it sounded like the truth.

"I'm listening."

"Then I will tell you a story," Canaan began, like a man confiding Aesop's Fables. "It begins in a small village in town in American, just after World War II. It is the story of a boy who wanted to be a king. But by unfortunate birth, he was born a slave. So he chooses to become a thief, to steal from others what he did not inherent by right. But he does not come from a family of thieves. He comes from a good family—a family with a loving mother, a strong father. And yet the boy is neither strong nor loving. He is a monster in his heart, if he has any heart at all. He is a curse to those he should honor, and idealizes the Nietzschean code of the Uberman—a man who by sheer force of will, and the lack of any conscience, can and does do whatever needs to be done to make his dream a dark and terrible reality."

Webster hoped the voice-activated tape recorder strapped to the small of his back was working.

"In time," Canaan continued, "the boy becomes a man. A man who learns that only by taking what does not belong to him will he ever become the king he dreams himself to be. But he does not know how. He is unskilled. So he joins the United States Army, hoping the United States Army can teach him. But they do not teach him to steal. They teach him to shoot, to obey orders, to fight for his country. But the boy-king does not want to obey orders. He wants to give orders. He does not want to fight for his country. He wants to be a king without a country. So what does he do?"

Webster shrugged and waited.

"He becomes the mythical alchemist, Webster. He takes a gun and tries to make gold out of lead. He becomes an ordinary and stupid thief who is quickly caught and sentenced to a short term in an American military prison in Germany. This was in January 1945."

"Near the end of World War II," Webster interjected.

"Yes," answered Canaan. "The war that killed more than six million Israeli men, women, and children."

Taking a sip, Webster nodded.

"In 1945," the General continued, "this man left the American military prison. But he is not the same man who entered that prison. Yes, now he is experienced in devilment and has a dark wisdom. Now, he knows how to take what does not belong to him. He knows how to build his kingdom." He lit another cigarette.

"Two months later he marries a woman, a British citizen whom he has never seen and obtains a British citizenship. He divorces her six months later. But now, as I have said, he has learned to play the role he coveted for so long. He has been trained. And three years later he is the proud owner of a large British bank off Dublar Street, five insurance companies, and two Rolls Royce. He possesses an American passport, a Canadian passport, and a British passport. He had strong connections to the American Mafia and the English Mafia."

"English Mafia?"

"Yes. Not so smart as their American cousins, but smart enough to do the kinds of things that must be done."

Webster didn't blink. "Like what kinds of things?"

Canaan squinted through another cloud of smoke. "This man that we speak of—"

"What is this man's name, general?" Webster presented the clear impression he didn't care to continue unless he'd be given something more substantial.

"Silman," the general answered plainly, almost as an afterthought. "At the time of his incarceration in an American prison, his name was Simon Silman. But he changed his name years later, after disappearing."

"When did he disappear?"

"About twenty years after he was released from your American Army prison."

Despite himself, Webster was hooked. "Why did Silman begin working with the English Mafia?"

"Several persons needed him to market seventy thousand dollars in stolen Canadian bonds," the general responded. "Silman, at that time, was a proficient smuggler of gold throughout the Middle East and Europe. He was put in contact with them through another British banker who lacked connections for the task."

"So Silman smuggled gold?"

Canaan squinted through a cloud of smoke, nodded. "A great deal of it, apparently. He was said to have operated a gold smuggling ring of disturbing volume after his release in prison in 1945 until 1967. He is also known to have smuggled art and precious stones. He laundered the profits so well that they were virtually untraceable and deposited the profits in Geneva or Brussels."

"How about Russia?"

"No," Canaan shook his head. "Silman is not a politician. He simply owns them."

Webster pondered what was laid before him.

"Even as early as January of 1950, only five years after his release from prison, Silman was a mystery," Canaan continued. "He was rich beyond reason. He was, without any hint of how he obtained such skill, extremely skilled at laundering and hiding vast sums of money. He had Middle East connections with arms smugglers and gold smugglers, in addition to a seemingly unlimited amount of gold." The general paused. "Many said he was a spy."

"For whom?"

"Spies do not discuss whom they serve," Canaan laughed. "But the best spies have more than one master."

Webster heard the bar bustling with subdued, angry energy. He recognized an impulse to look over his shoulder. He didn't. Outwardly stoic, he searched the Israeli's obscure aspect, but he was dealing with an equal. Neither would unintentionally reveal anything.

It had been a long time since Webster earned his stripes, but he remembered dogging it, interview after interview, deposition after deposition, to make a case. And he knew from experience that it was exhausting work. Just as he knew that there was only one way to do the job—stone on stone until you built the wall.

There were no shortcuts. There never had been. And whenever investigators tried to move ahead without doing the homework, they lost the case. Then it occurred to him that the Israelis were not fools in this type of thing and that Canaan wouldn't be here if they hadn't already tried the same thing and failed.

No, Webster realized with simple clarity, he wasn't going to find what he needed in the facts. If it were that simple, the Israelis would have done it without the Bureau's assistance. What they both needed was *hidden* by the facts.

Holding silence, Canaan drew steadily on his cigarette, sipping his drink at frequent intervals. *Whiskey,* Webster thought...*a hard-drinking man, this early in the morning. It's amazing what characteristics can be noticed in casual—*

Webster blinked: *Characteristics?* His face hardened slightly, dark eyes focusing on nothing. Canaan noticed the air of concentration, leaned back. "Yes?"

"Tell me," Webster began, "what do you know about Silman's characteristics? His habits?"

Canaan scowled. "Why do you ask?"

"Just curious."

"He..." Canaan looked away, brow furrowed, "...he is an uncommonly placid man. He is brilliant at what he does. He is utterly calm, even in disaster. He has no fear. He is neither liked nor disliked. And yet he has forged unalterable alliances."

"Alliances with whom?"

"We don't know for certain."

Webster took a moment. "All right, what else?"

"He...I suppose...he enjoys his money a great deal. He lives in high custom. He is addicted to wealth and power. He is, to use a common word, an aristocrat."

That's what Webster suspected. "So why did Silman work with the English Mafia?" he asked. "Someone as proud as Silman is careful whom he associates with. He wants to rub shoulders with equals. If he's a spy, then he would deal with spies."

Canaan considered this. "Silman apparently used them for protection from other criminals who threatened his life. Something the English Mafia was glad to provide in exchange for his assistance in forging certificates for the stolen bonds."

Webster laughed without humor. "So Silman needed untrained lowlifes out of the English Mafia to protect him from some lightweight hitter? I don't buy it."

"How do you know the man who threatened Silman was a lightweight?"

"Because heavyweights don't threaten."

"Yes," the Israeli nodded, thoughtful. "That is correct. You certainly have more experience than I in this."

"Silman never enlisted the support of the English Mafia for protection," Webster continued. "A man like Silman doesn't hire two-bit thugs for protection. If he feels he's in danger he hires the best hitter in the world and puts him on standby. He gets somebody with class. Somebody who doesn't miss."

"There is that, too. There is a man who works for Silman. A man who is said to be responsible for the extermination of entire cultures—a monster in its truest sense."

Webster sensed this was important. "What's this man's name?"

"I don't know."

"What's his nationality?"

"He is German."

"How old is he?"

"He was apparently born in the early years of World War II. He may even have been one of the Ubermen bred by Hitler's 'superior mating.' I would guess that he's at least sixty. "

"What does he look like?"

"No one knows."

Webster stared. "What *do* you know?"

"I know without question that he is the best assassin in the world," Canaan said simply.

"How can you say that?"

"Because no one I have ever sent after Silman has ever returned." Canaan paused solemnly. "And I have sent many."

Webster paused in respect for Canaan's men, then, "What's this hitter's cryptonym?"

"He is known as 'Iceman.'"

"Iceman? Why Iceman?"

"Apparently because he has no fear, even no emotion. There are also rumors that he is somehow...inhuman."

"Inhuman?" Webster asked, a touch incredulous.

"Not 'inhuman,' actually," the general said. His eyes hardened in anger or hate. "He has some kind of ability—I do not know what it is—that makes him far more difficult to kill than a normal man. I have only heard rumors. Nothing substantial."

"That's the guy who killed Woodard," Webster said.

"Yes," Canaan replied. "I suspected as much. I also fear that he will kill even more of your men before this is over," he added gravely. "In fact, I can assure you that he will."

Logan caught up with Jonathan and Blackfoot at the intersection of 495, just south of Riverdale on Baltimore Avenue. They had made it past three city police departments and the highway patrol without any incident. Jonathan was sweating with pain but alert as Logan walked up to the car. He leaned down to the window: "How you doing, kid?"

"Fine," Jonathan grimaced. "How about you?"

"Not good at all. He got away from me."

"He's good."

"It doesn't matter; his day's coming." Logan opened the door, kneeling. "Show me where you're hurt."

Jonathan lifted his shirt, revealing a six-inch gash. No ribs were visible and the bleeding had mostly stopped. But Logan knew he was in a lot of pain and needed stitches. That's why he hadn't simply *asked* Jonathan about it.

If he had just asked, Logan knew, the kid would have said something like "fine" even if he'd been bleeding out. Rookies tended to do that idiot-hero stuff, whereas a senior field agent, like Logan himself, would tell you that he's *dying* (what are you, blind?) *and why aren't we at the hospital yet?*

Okay...a hospital.

Logan knew these people couldn't have *everything* wired. He could probably get Jonathan into a hospital and out again before anyone got wise. Nor was he, personally, such an international fugitive yet that he would attract undue attention.

The only hurdle would be the doctor himself who, according to law, was required to notify local police on all knife wounds so they could investigate the incident. But the doctors probably wouldn't do that if Logan told them it was government business and that the Bureau had already notified the proper authorities.

On balance, he thought he could pull it off.

It might be closer than he preferred, but he did have his own not completely useless charm. For good measure, though, he'd get on the phone, dial the weather number and fake a show of calling headquarters with a full report, all within easy listening distance of doctors and nurses.

Yeah, it could work: Get Jonathan in for some stitches, charge it to the Bureau, grab some painkillers at the pharmacy, and hit the door. By the time a bill was filed in Washington, this case would be in the grave. Or *they* would be.

"C'mon, Jonathan," he said. "I'm taking you to the hospital."

"Logan, I don't—"

"Don't argue with me, boy. How are you gonna cover me when you're bleeding out?" Logan smiled, and Jonathan nodded. "Good, now, let's get you sewed up and ready to run." He turned. "Blackfoot!"

"Here, Logan."

"Take that Lincoln that I rented in Washington and steal a license plate from a used car lot—something near the back that won't be reported missing for a few days. Then put that shotgun in the trunk and meet us at Riverdale Medical Center in one hour. And don't get caught! Don't break any traffic laws either!"

Blackfoot smiled. "Yes, sir."

Logan walked around the car, pointed sternly. "Remember what I said, Blackfoot! Don't get caught! If you do, I'll deny everything! I'll say I've never *seen* you!"

Still smiling, Blackfoot nodded, "I got it."

"Let's roll."

It still didn't come together.

Webster asked, "How come Silman didn't do time when this gold smuggling operation was uncovered by Justice?"

"Silman's story was that his international gold smuggling operation had already been discovered by agents of the United States Treasury. He said the Treasury recruited him to work undercover to obtain evidence to convict the English Mafia. He also said that American Treasury agents threatened him with incarceration if he didn't work undercover for them as an, uh...an *agent provocateur*."

"What year was this?"

"1967."

"You're saying that Treasury wanted Silman to work undercover in 1967 in exchange for a lesser charge? That they'd cut him a break if he did what they wanted him to do?"

"Yes."

"That doesn't make sense," Webster said. "Why would the United States Treasury Department care about some crime in London? That's Scotland Yard's turf."

"According to our reports, your Treasury Department was concerned about the inflow of narcotics into America, which was their responsibility before Nixon created the DEA. The English banks involved in the gold smuggling were also laundering drug profits for American organizations through the late sixties."

There was silence as Webster ran it through his mind. "So why was Silman so close to American law enforcement agencies?" he finally asked. "What'd they gain from it?"

"My people do not know."

"Then tell me this," Webster concentrated, "who actually placed Silman in custody for smuggling the gold?"

"Scotland Yard."

"Scotland Yard? You're sure about that?"

"Yes," Canaan frowned. "Why?"

"How did Silman escape prosecution?"

"He told Scotland Yard that he had been working undercover for Scotland Yard itself for over two years." The Israeli regarded Webster closely. "What are you thinking, commander?"

Webster shook his head. "Not yet. Tell me this; do you know if Silman really working undercover for Scotland Yard?"

"I doubt it."

Silence.

"Go on," Webster said, tight.

Canaan crossed his arms over his chest. "The enigma becomes even more convoluted. As I said, Silman alleged that he had been an informant for Scotland Yard for two years, and consequently produced documents to prove it. Also, he produced documents to prove that he was an agent for the United States Treasury Department?" He shrugged. "Who knows?

He was never prosecuted for either gold smuggling or money laundering, so perhaps it was true."

"But you said he probably wasn't working for Scotland Yard," Webster countered.

"Probably not for Scotland Yard, itself. But he was, in fact, working for someone inside Scotland Yard—that much is certain. Silman's power and influence betrayed him."

"Did Silman disappear after his arrest?"

"No."

"Where did he go?"

Canaan smiled. "He went into your federal witness protection program, Mr. Webster."

Webster slammed his hand on the table, leaning forward. "Are you telling me that we've got this man who's killing us under *witness protection?* Are you telling me that we've been spending millions of dollars to find a man that I'm protecting?"

Canaan laughed. "No, not any longer. As of 1978, he was terminated from your program. But he was, indeed, there for some time before he was eliminated as a reliable informant."

"Who placed Silman in witness protection?"

"The Department of Justice."

"Who requested it?" Webster pressed.

"The Secret Service."

"*Who* in the Secret Service?"

"No one knows. Everyone denies."

"What year was Silman placed in witness protection?"

"1977."

Webster leaned back, teeth clenched. He cursed, trying to remain calm. Amused, Canaan laughed. "You see, Silman has used your government the same way he used the English. Or Scotland Yard. Or even the Secret Service, or Treasury, whom he also served at the same time to allegedly combat narcotics trading. He has constantly and skillfully played one organization against the other, always for his own interests. Though he did indeed, on occasion, deliver sufficient evidence to send powerful underworld figures to prison. For in truth Silman is quite skilled at setting up deals. I understand that there is even a documented incident where, for sheer enjoyment, he set up a deal where your CIA bought drugs from your FBI. A deal where, at the culmination, everyone present pulled their guns to arrest the other only to discover that they all worked for the same government. I heard from reliable sources that Silman walked out of the rendezvous laughing. He found it quite amusing that he could manipulate you so easily."

Webster didn't say anything.

"That, in essence, is who you are dealing with," the Israeli continued. "You are dealing with a man who has cunningly used virtually every intelligence agency in the world. He professes to have, and does in fact possess, significant alliances with the Federal Bureau of Investigation, the Secret Service, the Treasury Department, the Internal Revenue Service and, most of all, the State Department. In addition, he has worked extensively for Scotland Yard and both the American and European Mafia. Also, he has international ties to arms dealers and the largest drug cartels in the world. He has worked for them all and against them all, all at the same time. He is a master manipulator and that is why I say...he must be killed. He is too dangerous to live."

Releasing a deep breath, Webster leaned back. He stared into his beer a long time. "What was Silman's name in the witness protection program?"

"He never changed his name for the program."

"Fine." Webster didn't question it. Had almost expected it because he knew Silman never entered the program for protection. There had been a deeper reason. "Where did the government place him?"

"Nowhere at all. Silman simple became part of witness protection—something he could use for his own purposes. For a while, that is. He lived by his own significant means and according to his own skills. Nor did he change his name at all until late in 1978, just before he was thrown out of the program."

"Yeah, you said that. Why was he thrown out?"

"Because the Attorney General of Arizona indicted him for bank fraud in the Phoenix area. An operation of bank fraud very similar to what you are investigation now."

"How could the Attorney General of Arizona indict him when we can't even find him?"

"He was not hiding at the time. Also, he had not chosen, for whatever reason, to use the Iceman. From what I understand of that charge of bank laundering, the Attorney General already had too many witnesses for even the infamous Iceman to kill. The situation was out of control. And after that Silman disappeared for good. Then, later, he began his worldwide banking takeover with BCCI."

Webster sighed. "What connection does Silman have with World Finance?"

"We do not know. But reliable sources tell us that he is, indeed, deeply involved."

The *we*, combined with the highly secretive nature of the information, only confirmed it for Webster: Ariel Ben Canaan was Mossad and he was operating on American soil without State Department sanction. Also, Webster knew there was a good reason for it, just as he knew the war-tempered General did not allow the *we* by mistake. It was done to communicate the seriousness of the situation in a manner only a serious man would understand.

"I understand," Webster nodded, calming with an effort of will. "Please continue."

Canaan dropped ashes in the tray. "You have my respect." He hesitated. "After Silman was abruptly terminated from the witness protection program, he apparently decided that the enormous wealth he had accumulated, and which never left his hands throughout his long dealings with your intelligence community—"

"Wasn't enough," Webster interjected.

"Of course not; it never is. And so Silman's ambitions enlarged, propelling him to play some part in this global banking takeover that you are currently investigating. We do not yet know what role, exactly, was his. Or how much control he retains any more than we know how Silman went into an Army prison in 1945 a heartless fool and came out a heartless wiseman with an international gold smuggling network at his command."

Webster took a moment. "How do we find Silman now?"

"If I knew the answer to that question, we would have found him ourselves. And, as of this moment, Silman would have been relieved of the burden of his life. Unlike your people, we have no compulsion against taking the lives of our enemies."

There was something else there. "Why does Israel want this man so badly?"

"That is not a question I can answer." Canaan released smoke. "At least, not now. But for the record I can say that he threatens Israel's God-ordained sovereignty, and the land God has given us." He paused a long time. "Make no mistake, Mr.

Webster. I am a patriot. I fight for love of my country. But I will destroy this devil because God has returned us to our land, and I consider it my duty to God to defend the children of Israel upon the land he promised them. I may be a spy today, but I will be a soldier forever. A soldier who does his duty as God gives him understanding of his duty, however hard that duty becomes."

Out of courtesy, Webster took another sip and waited for the Israeli to continue.

"To end this conversation, let me say that your government has been bought and sold." Canaan was utterly convincing. "Even your president is a vassal. And be warned; Silman will take every precaution to protect his empire. But, if that fails, he will resort to using his friends, and your Justice Department will not prosecute.

"This man has strong influence in the highest tiers of your nation, and he knows secrets that cannot be compromised. So, if his frontline defenses fail, he will simply allow himself to be arrested, just as he has done in the past. And, like before, his cohorts will be a sacrifice. Flesh for freedom." A pause. "Do you know what happened to Silman's cohorts when he was charged with bank fraud in Arizona?"

"They went to jail."

"Yes, but do you know what happened to Silman himself?" Canaan smiled as he took a sip.

"No," Webster responded, flat. "Tell me."

"Silman was placed under house arrest until trial," the Israeli replied, setting down his glass. "And the judge granted him the rather amazing right to travel to three places in the United States. He could travel to Phoenix, Arizona, New York City, and..."

"Washington," Webster said.

Canaan laughed. "I see how you earned your rank."

"What happened to Silman at the trial?"

"Well," the Israeli continued, "at the moment of trial, as if by miracle, Silman's case was transferred to another venue, where he received a judge of your government's careful choosing. And the judge did indeed find him guilty, but was careful to protect him. He delivered to him a very lenient fine and set him free."

Webster searched the desert eyes.

"Yes, Mr. Webster. Your government is ultimately compromised, and I do not know whom you can trust. Or if you can trust anyone at all."

It was time to meet the issue head-on.

"I understand you, General. But let me make myself succinct. We are the FBI, not the CIA. I will not order Logan to kill this man. We do not purposely set out to kill people."

Canaan almost said something. Webster could see the thought begin even as it was subdued. The general leaned forward, arms on the table as he spoke closely.

"There are far more questions than answers, Webster. For instance, how did Silman make intelligence connections when he was interned in an American army prison? How did he enter prison destitute and emerge with a gold smuggling ring at his disposal? How did he gain such contacts inside the global intelligence community? How deeply do his tentacles reach into your government? What is protecting him? And why? And what secret does he know, Webster? What terrible secret does Silman know that makes your nation tremble? What terrible reason does he have that compels him to destroy Israel?"

Webster released a deep breath. "I don't know, General."

"Neither do we."

Silence, and Canaan rose, dropping a fifty-dollar bill on the table as he lifted his coat. Beneath it Webster saw a thick mound of papers, documents, depositions. Canaan lifted them all and set them down on the desk. "The answer to Silman's whereabouts may lie within these papers," he said. "I confess that I myself cannot find it."

And as Canaan came around the table, he stared down. "My people have a saying, Webster."

Inexpressive, Webster gazed up.

The hate of a nation was in the Israeli soldier's gaze.

"Never again."

Blackfoot was waiting outside Riverdale Medical Center, north of the hospital itself when Logan walked out of the Emergency Room with Jonathan.

Logan glanced quickly at the tag on the Lincoln; Blackfoot had changed it. The date still legal. He looked piercingly at the Sioux: "Anybody see you?"

"Nope."

"Good, let's go. I'll drive Jonathan. You stay close because all we've got now are the handhelds and the range is only a few miles."

Blackfoot walked to the LTD. "Where are we going?"

"North, to Laurel. We'll find a place there for the night and head into New York City tomorrow."

"Then we're gonna hit BCCI?"

Logan's face turned mean.

"Like the wrath of God, boy."

Chapter Nine

Exhausted, Jonathan slept in the back room, resting on a doubled dose of painkillers as Logan walked to the front of the Hyatt suite he rented in Laurel. Blackfoot had unloaded the cars and was at the computer again, hacking away. The only difference tonight was that he was working with a shotgun at his side.

"What else are you trying to get?" Logan asked the Sioux.

"Something keeps bothering me."

"Like what?"

"Like why wasn't BCCI seriously investigated by Treasury? It seems like an easy thing to do. I want to find out what Hooper was told to do by the State Department."

Logan noted Blackfoot's dedication to the cause. He gazed down. "Blackfoot, you almost make me want to stand up and salute the flag."

"Yeah, right."

Logan dropped his coat over a chair. "But don't worry about it too much, kid. Hooper didn't look closely enough because Treasury ordered him not to. Simple as that. There won't be any incriminating documents. And even if Treasury *had* decided to look hard into BCCI, they wouldn't have found anything."

"Why not?"

"Because the investigators in Treasury would have a hard

time understanding how a bank can be *designed* to expressly serve the entire criminal element of the world. Treasury agents only understand the regulation of banking procedures and violations of those procedures." Logan grunted. "More than anything, Treasury is just a watchdog over banking regulations. They're basically just bankers who watch bankers. They wouldn't know a crook if he kissed them."

"But aren't these guys at BCCI breaking banking regulations?"

"Yeah, yeah, they are. But not like you think," Logan picked up a document. He was still wearing the SIG on his side; he'd decided to sleep with it. "And not in a way that Treasury would think. You see, these guys at BCCI are using the banking regulations *themselves* to launder billions of dollars. Or they're using existing loan laws to make the money disappear. But it's the *misuse* of regulations, not the actual violation of regulations, that's the criminal part of this. The illegal part comes after you tear the label off the product."

Blackfoot nodded but the word *criminal* struck something in Logan, and he froze. He still held the document in his hand. He was staring at it but he wasn't reading. He stood a long time before he faintly heard Blackfoot speaking to him.

"Logan?"

Logan looked down. "Yeah, kid?"

"What is it? Looks like you were in a trance."

"No, I'm fine." He paused. "Tell me something, Blackfoot. Can you tap into the local police department's NCIC line? Can you obtain user log-ins and get me a list of all of the high dollar, white collar criminals in New York and Europe, South America and the Middle East and run them against a list of BCCI clients?"

Blackfoot shrugged. "Yeah, no big deal. You want their

criminal records or just a list of suspects?"

"Just a list."

He began hacking. "No problem."

"How much time will it take?"

"All night, probably. I'll have to access the telephone company central office to get into the National Crime Information Computer, the Bureau files and a couple of terrorist think tanks in New York. Academic stuff, really. But I'll have to access the lines."

"Good." Logan placed a hand on his shoulder. "You're a good man, Blackfoot. If I had ten more guys like you and Jonathan, we might have made the FBI worth something."

Blackfoot smiled.

"And run the list of criminals against the list of BCCI clients. Work as long as you want and then grab some sleep. And do whatever you have to do to keep them off our backs until we check out in the morning."

"What do you think we'll find?"

"I think we're going to find the Almanac of the world's greatest criminals." Logan walked to the kitchen table. "Something to make old dead-and-gone Benjamin Franklin roll over. I think we're going to find that BCCI is expressly designed to serve the biggest criminals in the world from the Saudi arms smugglers to the Mafia to Colombian cartels to Hitler if the murderer was still alive. A bank of international crooks and criminals." He laughed bitterly. "Plus that, I think we're going to find a whole truckload of congressman, senators, and State Department workers on the payroll as lobbyists and influence-peddlers. It'll probably read like a who's who of professional criminals and professional politicians, all of them in league with the devil." He grunted, staring at his whiskey. "Suddenly I could use a drink."

"Will that be proof of a conspiracy?"

"It'll be a start, kid. Have you broken into BCCI's account on World Finance to see if there's actually any money in it?"

"I'm working on it."

"Work harder. I want to know by morning if World Finance actually has any money in that account with BCCI or if they're granting these billion dollar loans from an empty account."

Nodding, Blackfoot bent over the screen.

"It's coming," he said. "Believe me, it coming..."

In the morning, Logan traveled over five miles from the hotel before calling Webster. Answering on the first ring, Webster sounded as if he had little hope of ever sleeping again.

"Logan? We've got seventy seconds. Talk fast and make good sense."

"What is it?" Logan asked, half expecting to see a 1972 Dodge Charger 440 gunning across the median to run him down with a spectacular disintegration of glass and steel and blood.

"We have to meet," Webster stated. "And we have to meet *now*. Who hit you in Washington yesterday?"

"Same guy that killed Woodard. He looked older in Quantico but I'd say now that he's not more than sixty. But he's strong. Fast. Moves like a pro. He almost took Jonathan out before I threw a clip at him."

"Did he have a German accent?"

"Yeah." Logan paused. "Jonathan said that he spoke with a German accent."

"Watch out for that guy, Logan. That guy's taken out a lot more people than Woodard. He the real thing and he works for Phantom."

"I figured." Logan glanced around but saw nothing but gray fumes of traffic, cars rolling past, an early morning orange-tinted sun. He was utterly deserted at the isolated phone booth but somehow it didn't make him feel more comfortable. "How bad are we compromised?"

"We need to talk," Webster repeated.

He can't say it on the line...

Logan tried to think of a way to set up a rendezvous without alerting anyone who might be listening. It would be all too easy for a sniper to wait and pick them off when they arrived. Yet he couldn't think of anything before Webster interjected.

"Logan," he said distinctly, "we've got thirty seconds. Are you listening closely?"

"Yeah."

"You know," Webster continued, "I didn't just fall off the turnip truck. I've been in the Bureau a long time. And I know a lot more than I let on. I know what really goes on in the field, and I know agents sometimes take shortcuts. Did I ever tell you that?"

"No," Logan replied impatiently, not knowing where this was going. He hoped desperately that Webster wouldn't say something so obscure that he'd never figure it out.

"Yeah. I know a lot, even if I decide to let it go. And sometimes I really need a *drink*." Webster paused for a split-second. "So tell me, you got anything to *drink*?"

Logan froze. Then, "Yeah. I think I know where I can find something."

"Good. Meet me there tonight."

Logan hung up, making sure he had stayed under seventy seconds. Then he smiled slightly, touching the phone a moment before he turned to the LTD: Wild Turkey.

An entire *truckload* of Wild Turkey housed at the New York

City Police Department's Impound Lot. The same truckload he'd used to bribe the NYPD guys for donations of seized Jaguars. The same truckload Webster always knew that he had used. Logan laughed out loud as he walked toward the car.

Sometimes trust was a beautiful thing.

Chapter Ten

With a slight whisper, the doublewide doors at the opulent office opened and a man walked through the portal.

Of medium height, in his early sixties, he was unimpressively slight. His hair was thinning, though still dark. A sad, thin-looking mustache and goatee were carefully groomed, and he wore an immaculately tailored three-piece English suit with a gold watch-chain suspended across the vest. His cuffs glinted, and he held a long, slender black cigar in his hand. Standing with utter calm in the door, he stared at the red-bearded man, who looked up without expression, always without expression. His eyes focused on the small man, implacable and observant.

"Frazier," the man said calmly. "I wonder if I might have a word with you."

Without hesitation the man called Frazier rose, following the other into the inner sanctum of the office as the doors slowly closed. The office was immensely rich and immensely dark throughout with cherry and mahogany and a huge, extravagantly carved black desk that commanded the exterior wall before solid rows of books, books, and more books, all first editions, all hardcover, all polished. And he knew when these were out of date they would be replaced, unopened, with more first editions, all hardcover, all polished.

Behind the desk, gleaming white elephant tusks were poised on both sides of a huge leather chair unique in design.

The tusks rose into the air and curled majestically—the kind of tusks seen on Mastodons, giants of another age.

With a casual air the man walked to a bar, dropping ice cubes in two glasses. He poured a drink and walked to Frazier, who respectfully took it into his thick hand. As the man turned back to the bar he spoke with perfect pronunciation, tossing the words over his shoulder: "How long have we known each other, Frazier?"

No hesitation. "Almost twenty years."

"Do you remember how we met?

"I remember."

Frazier recalled that dark night. He was young, barely out of his teens. Part of a gang of street thugs who terrorized the neighborhood. Then came a chance meeting with a wealthy man, looking for a bodyguard. Frazier always felt that the man had saved him from a hard life on the streets, and since that time, he defended the man with his life.

"Yes, Frazier, of course you remember. How could you forget? Me delivering instructions and your consummate hand dropping heads like the wrath of a slaver's barracoon?" He laughed. "Those were the days, weren't they? The Wild West, so to speak."

Expressionless, Frazier held his glass.

"You were the ultimate killer, Frazier. The perfect soldier. Eliminating our enemies in the Middle East. Eliminating our enemies in America. Teaching those pompous cretins of terror, the KGB, what terror truly was—a one-man slaughterhouse, I used to say." He turned, sitting casually on the arm of a sofa. "Behind your back, of course. Did you know that?"

"I knew," Frazier said. He took a slow sip from the glass and stood without moving in the middle of the room, waiting until the shorter man spoke once more: "Tell me, Frazier, do you know who the best scam artist in the world is?"

"No."

The man laughed. "It's not anyone you suspect, I assure you. He is a man who will live and die in obscurity of his greatest talent. He will be known as a great philosopher, a philanthropist. He will enjoy his wealth and the luxurious leisure of his labors. He will be seen as a kind, benevolent, loving soul. Wear the finest suits; inhabit the finest surroundings—a devil with the face of an angel. But do you wish to know a secret?" He smiled. "It is this: No matter how high this man rises, no matter how finely he dresses or how expensively he lives or how much he wishes to remove himself from what he is, he will always be a con artist." Smiling, he took a sip. "As all of us, I presume."

Stoic as granite, Frazier focused uneasily on the goateed man before he said, "Mr. Dumont, why don't you just tell me what you want me to do."

"I need your protection again, old friend. As you protected me in the old days."

"I understood that Charon was handling the situation."

"Oh, make no mistake, Charon is determined to handle the situation. But I wonder if the old man might be slightly past his prime. He attempted something yesterday and failed. He did not tell me that he was, in fact, injured, but I believe it is so. Remarkable, don't you think?" He shrugged. "I suppose we all get old."

"Charon is patient, Mr. Dumont. I'm sure I couldn't accomplish any more." He paused. "He's always been better than me."

Dumont waved a hand. "You're too humble, my friend. Unreasonably humble. But in any case, that's not what I had in mind. I do not want you to replace Charon. At least, not yet."

He paced slowly across the room. "No, I simply believe this situation is escalating rather alarmingly and that we must... retreat somewhat."

"What do you have in mind?"

"I wish for you to accompany me to England, as you used to do before you rose to your present position. I want you to insure my safety and make certain that our enemies cannot reach me. I doubt that you have lost your edge in these matters."

Frazier's blue eyes froze. "I will do what must be done."

"Good," Dumont smiled. "Please, be aware, Frazier; I understand that you no longer possess any desire to fight in your old arena—'si riposi vecchio gladiatore.' And I remember my promise, made after you and Charon battled over Justinian's assassination, that I would never again ask you to use your strongest skills. I understood your position at the time; I understand it now."

Frazier's face was stone. He would never reveal his thoughts to his employer or the fact that he was still torn between two loyalties. Justinian had been a true friend, saving him from prison and showing him there was another way. But, though he could fight and kill with brute strength, he wasn't as brave as Justinian. He couldn't turn his back on Dumont, the only father figure he had ever known. Since that day, he had never used his skills as an assassin. He vowed that he would not kill the innocent.

"You and Charon were at each other's throats because you, Frazier, felt something for Justinian. And you lamented his death because it was Justinian who insured the release from your life sentence in Stalwart. In exchange, of course, for your brief service to MI6." He sighed. "So you were understandably upset at his death, necessary as it was. But, then, that is behind us now and you have proven your loyalty to me time and time again. I only ask this final favor because this situation truly disturbs me, and I believe we must return to England for a while to wait out the storm."

"I'll make the necessary arrangements, Mr. Dumont."

"Good," said the man known as Lazarus Dumont. "Contact the staff in Waltham and tell them we shall be arriving tonight. Then contact the airport and make arrangements for the jet. I'll leave the rest of the security details to your extraordinary competence."

Frazier set the glass on a marble table and stood back. Built like an ox, his chest and shoulders and arms were thick, heavy, hard, and scarred. His neck was almost lost in the heavy mound of muscle that surrounded it. He walked toward the door.

"At your service, Mr. Dumont."

"Oh, and Frazier?"

Frazier hesitated.

"Do bring your weapon."

Logan drove a lot faster to the hotel than prudence would have allowed. He unsnapped his holster as he went into the room, his hand settling casually on the SIG.

Blackfoot was leaning back in a chair, precariously tilted against a wall. He lifted sheets of paper as Logan came forward. Another stack was on the desk. Logan glanced toward the back of the suite: "Is Jonathan up yet?"

"He got up after you left."

"How's he doing?"

"He's—"

Jonathan came out of the bedroom. He was freshly showered, dressed in faded blue jeans and a dark T-shirt and ankle-high hiking boots. His belt was heavily laden with the SIG and four extra clips. His stance was poised and rested, ready for a fight.

Logan focused. "How ya feelin,' kid?"

"Pretty good," He rubbed the back of his head with the towel.

Logan grunted, "You sleep okay?"

"Good enough. I've still got a little adrenaline going."

"You ready for the field?"

"*Been* ready."

"Good."

Logan told them about the conversation with Webster. He told them what he'd learned about the German assassin and how slim their chances had become, holding back nothing. Stoic, both of them failed to move until he was finished and then Logan waited in silence, giving them plenty of time to decide.

"So that's the deal, boys," he continued, tiredly sitting down in a chair, lighting another cigarette. His smoking had escalated from three cigarettes a day to three packs a day since he'd seen Hooper. Logan didn't worry about it. Somehow he felt that cancer wasn't going to have a chance to kill him.

"We've been targeted and things have changed. *Massively*. So I'm giving you this chance to get out while the gettin's good. And I'll tell you this; if I were in your position, just rookies with a future, I'd hit the door. But I've already used all my career moves. I'm used up and this is going to be my last case, one way or another. That's why I'm staying. But if you want to leave, that's fine. I'll figure you're a lot smarter than I am." He paused, stared a moment at nothing. "Poor old Woodard was right as rain."

Jonathan leaned against the doorjamb. It was clear that he wasn't going anywhere. Blackfoot laid papers down and placed his hand flat over them, long slender fingers almost covering the page.

"I've got a present for you," the Sioux smiled.

Logan glanced at each of them. They'd made their decision just like that—if it was any decision at all.

Rubbing his eyes, Logan felt tired and exhilarated because he knew, for certain, that they'd stand beside him to the end. "All right, Blackfoot." He tried to switch to a commander's mode. "Tell me what you've got."

"I've got a list of internationally known criminals who all have accounts with BCCI. All of them are heavy hitters—the heaviest. And all of them are using BCCI for complex loans, or loan losses. The same scam, over and over—big down payments and then the loan falls through, the big down payment is lost, yadda yadda. A lot of money goes through that place that never comes back."

"How many crooks are involved?"

"About two thousand heavyweights. We've got Saudis and Colombians and a whole bunch of Americans. We've got the Mafia, South American drug runners, South African diamond smugglers, a lot of scumbags that like to break the law. And BCCI takes care of all of them. Makes their profits disappear." The Sioux gazed at the papers. "Logan, if these people pulled all their money out of the bank, Wall Street would fall through the floor."

Logan wasn't stunned.

Still, though, two thousand criminals were outrageous. And it was even more outrageous because BCCI must have known that such a coalition of underworld figures would eventually attract attention. Yet the bank didn't seem to care. Which meant they had government sanction. Which meant, *ergo*, they had government *protection*.

He read the names with gathering amazement, thinking of the facts: BCCI was a bank of criminals with probably more than twenty billion in annual revenue, and it wasn't even worried about investigations. Of course, there was a reason—the worst.

Logan recognized some of the names, but knew Phantom wasn't there. No, Phantom would be as hidden as hidden could be, buried beneath them all, using them for cover. "What did you get on World Finance's account with BCCI?" he asked, expelling a heavy stream of smoke. "Any money in it?"

Blackfoot picked up a sheet of paper, laughing as he floated it across the desk.

"World Finance's account at BCCI is flat empty," Blackfoot smiled largely. "I had to go though hell to get it, and probably broke every banking law there is. But I'm sure of it. World Finance doesn't have a dime in BCCI."

Logan stared. "You're *sure*?"

"Yep," Blackfoot affirmed, and proud of it. "World Finance's account at BCCI is as empty as empty gets. There isn't a dollar to back up those billion dollar loans."

"Smart guy," Logan muttered. "He doesn't tie any of his money in the account because he knows he doesn't need to. He just gets BCCI to tell lawyers and investigators that the account has a few hundred million to guarantee World Finance."

Blackfoot looked at Jonathan. "A ghost account to back up ghost loans. And nobody knows it."

"Nobody but us," Logan added. "All right; this is what I want you to do. Put all this, the list and the information about World Finance's account at BCCI, on three CDs. Mail one to a relative's address and keep the other one in your pocket."

"You want to mail one to Webster?"

"No. They'll be watching for that. Mail one to a friend's address that nobody knows about. But make it someone obscure. Don't make it someone on any list of friends and relatives that you gave to the Bureau during your security check."

"I'm on it," Blackfoot said, quickly getting back into the swing, "would you like to know what else I found?"

"You've got *more?*"

"Yeah. I've accessed a record of all fax transactions from World Finance to BCCI."

"What'd you find?"

Blackfoot was into the game. "I found out that, unlike the other organizations involved in this, over eighty percent of all fax transactions from World Finance were sent by a code or encryption to Fincher, the president of BCCI."

"What does that mean?"

"That means that World Finance has a relationship with Fincher that none of the other children share," Blackfoot smiled. "And that's not just conjecture, Logan. It means that somebody with power at World Finance has a direct line to the president of BCCI. World Finance has sent over three dozen faxes in the last three months. On an increasing crescendo. Which means..."

"They're scared," Logan muttered. Then, "Who did you say was the president of BCCI?"

"Fincher."

"Can you monitor Fincher's screen?"

"Sure."

"Without tripping an alarm?"

"Sure. I can use TEMPEST."

Logan knew the general method. "How close would you have to be to make TEMPEST work? You said that you could do it within a half-mile."

"Not in New York because there's going to be a lot of different machines to laser in on. We can't be so far away that we might get electromagnetic interference."

"How close, then?"

"Three hundred feet. And it would help a lot if this guy has an office window."

"I'm sure he does. All these guys have offices with windows. They think it's a mark of success." Logan was thoughtful. "Now, this is the crux. Can you monitor an *outgoing* Telex from BCCI at the same time you're sending a panic-fax from World Finance?"

"Why?"

"To see who BCCI contacts after we send the message."

Blackfoot appeared dazed. "Logan, that's going to take some coordination. I'd have to get BCCI's and World Finance's phone lines and monitor the fax lines without alerting the systems."

Logan paced the room.

Jonathan asked, "What are you planning on doing?"

"I'm planning on scaring them," Logan answered. "You ready for a rematch with the German?"

Jonathan stood away from the wall.

"Good," Logan nodded.

"What are we going to do?" Jonathan asked.

"We're going to scare them and then we're going to tell them where we are. We're going to let them know that we're on dead on top of them and dare 'em to come after us."

"Why?"

"Because," Logan said, sullen, "I want to stare that Nazi assassin in the eye when I kill him. He killed poor ol' Woodard, tried to kill you, and that means he *must pay*."

Jonathan was still. "He's mine, Logan." He waited; Logan held the gaze. "I owe him, Logan. More than you know."

There was silence as Logan searched Jonathan's determined face. It was clear—he wasn't backing down. "All right, kid," he replied. "But when you put him down, I'm gonna be there to make sure you drive a stake through his heart."

Jonathan's gazed down as he slowly clenched his hand into a fist. He held it tight a moment, held something else inside it.

"There won't be anything left to drive a stake through."

Paps, the firearms instructor at the FBI Academy in Quantico, looked up as Matsumo approached, moving across the concrete floor of the armory with surpisingly graceful strides for such an obvious warrior.

A curt nod was all Paps gave as Matsumo came to the counter, lifting a black bag and removing two semiautomatics. Wordless, Matsumo ejected the clips and locked the slides on both pistols before placing them on the counter. Laying down a clipboard, Paps said, "Well, what do you think?"

Matsumo nodded, "A good weapon. Para-Ordinance made the frame well. And the slide and barrel are Colt, so it functions easily. There were five feed jams until it was broken in. But it functioned smoothly with Federal hydro-shock."

Paps picked up one of the .45s and began breaking it down for cleaning. "How was accuracy?"

"Similar to the SIG .357 and the P-229. Aim to point of impact dropped one inch at twenty-five yards. Velocity was slightly less than one thousand feet per second at twenty. Energy impact in pounds per foot measured five hundred pounds at ten yards, dropping to four hundred at twenty-five. Beyond that, we did not test."

"That's one heck of a weapon," Paps commented, holding it admiringly. "Jonathan should have taken one of these babies on his undercover assignment, instead of that Sig. Those things throw a lot of rounds but you have to shoot somebody fifteen times to put 'em down."

No expression crossed Matsumo's face as he reached into the bag and removed unused ammo. "Jonathan went on an undercover assignment?" he asked.

"Yeah." Paps dropped the slide on the second .45. "Some sort of grand-secret assignment he caught last Friday. I had to open up the armory to issue him a SIG. Then he came back the next day for six extra clips. He must be going for bear."

Matsumo acted uninterested, merely making conversation. "Jonathan was supposed to leave for San Francisco for field training. He is not ready for a high-risk assignment."

"Yeah, I know. The kid is good, probably the best I've ever seen, but he's not ready for the field. Makes me wonder, you know—Jonathan coming in here and loading up like he did." He shook his head. "And he seemed nervous, too. Sometimes I think the Bureau doesn't have the foggiest idea what they're doing."

Matsumo poised. "Did Jonathan say where he was going?"

"No. He just said he would be working undercover. He didn't know anything else."

With a frown Matsumo turned away.

"Oh," Paps added, laying down the .45, continuing to inventory the equipment. "He said he had a meeting at The Boardroom last Friday night to discuss the situation with the AD. Said it was his first night in the field and that he almost had to bust up some Marines." He lifted empty hands. "That's it."

Matsumo nodded. "I want you to find a firearms instructor to finish testing the .45s." Without another word the gigantic

The Scam

Japanese walked across the armory, the muscles in his tree-trunk arms rippling as he clenched his fists.

"Where are you going?"

Matsumo's voice rumbled across the concrete.

"Vacation."

Chapter Eleven

F razier scanned the field at Dulles International Airport and noticed nothing out of the ordinary. He had already searched the area for high-megahertz transmissions and found no unauthorized traffic. He looked up as German Shepherds and handlers exited the twin-engine, white Lear LC-88 jet, fueled for takeoff. A uniformed guard approached, keeping his hands in plain view. "It's clear."

Frazier nodded and quickly entered the private lounge of the airport, instantly sighting the man known as Lazarus Dumont. He was dressed in a black cashmere overcoat and an Armani suit with black lace-up Oxfords. "Everything is ready," Frazier rumbled.

"Thank you, Frazier." Dumont stood smoothly, always moving with dignity and poise. Two plainly dressed bodyguards picked up his luggage, walking before him.

Frazier, far beyond them in station, strolled beside his employer, his hands empty. His eyes questioned everything as they exited the building and crossed the tarmac. Suddenly Dumont looked across, his face curious but hard. "Tell me, Frazier," he asked, "why do you never look at me when you protect me?"

Frazier studied men loading a distant trolley with luggage. His voice came back faint and subdued. "I know what you are doing, Mr. Dumont, so I don't need to look at you. I need only to know what others are doing."

182

A laugh. "You are the consummate professional, Frazier. And I have seen many. But tell me, old friend, don't you miss the bloodshed and the action somewhat?"

"My job is to protect you, Mr. Dumont. That is all that concerns me." He hesitated. "I miss nothing."

"But if I may ask, Frazier, tell me something else. I know that you and Charon have never enjoyed each other's company. He dislikes you. He distrusts you. I would go so far as to say he even hates you. And he worked for me many years before you came into my employ, so you knew you would have to deal with him in order to deal with me. So why, if I may ask, did you decide to work with him?"

Frazier did not hesitate. "My feelings about Charon are nothing. I can work with him." A pause. "I can work with anyone."

"But you do not like Charon."

"It is not my job to like or dislike Charon. I will work with Charon or anyone else, and do what you tell me to do."

"So nothing matters to you, Frazier? Nothing at all?" Dumont slowly shook his head. "You simply do your job and do not complain. Nor are you sentimental or emotional. If I ask you to do something, you do it. Without emotion. Without anything at all. You will simply do it." He paused as they continued forward. "But tell me, Frazier, what do you truly think of Charon?"

"Charon is the best at what—"

"Yes, yes, I know, Frazier. Charon is the best in the world at what he does." Dumont's smile continued. "I am not a fool— that is why I hired him. But does he not also amaze or frighten you? Are you not sometimes simply stunned by Charon's utterly pure commitment to his murderous profession?"

Frazier scanned another distant party of loaders. "I give

credit where credit is due, Mr. Dumont. Charon is the best of his kind. He does not make a mistake. He waits. He is patient." Another pause. "He is better than me."

"But could you could kill him?" Dumont's asked casually, a question thrown with the utmost relaxation, as if it meant nothing at all though Dumont steadily searched Frazier's bearded face.

Frazier did not look. "I am a professional, Mr. Dumont. I do not kill without a reason."

"And, yet, what if I ordered you to kill Charon after this latest assignment is finished? What if I told you that Charon had outlived his usefulness and knew too much about our operations? Do you think, then, that you could kill him?"

Frazier did not have to think about the question. He was a bodyguard, and would do what he had to to protect his employer. Charon would kill regardless. He served only because it ultimately served his own purposes. Charon needed to answer for his actions, and Frazier would be more than happy to bring justice to him. His tone was certain.

"If you told me to kill Charon, Mr. Dumont, then I would kill him."

Webster settled his Colt .45 in his holster, making sure it was firmly snapped to his belt. Then he reflexively reached to his left to insure the twin magazine holder was closed and filled with two extra clips for the semiauto. As he reached for his keys, the phone on his desk beeped. Webster reached over. "Yes?"

"Director Fletcher is on the line, sir."

Webster answered. "Yes, sir."

"I've got some bad news, Richard." The director's smooth, diplomatic voice was unmistakable, but there was, for the first time, a hint of anxiety. Webster had never recognized fear in that voice, but wasn't surprised.

The director continued, "I anticipate that, within the next 48 hours, there is going to be an edict passed from the State Department that is going to, in effect, terminate the authority of the team."

Webster swore beneath his breath.

"Further," Fletcher continued, "I believe that we are in a precarious position with the shootout in Washington. I trust your word that it was within regulations. But we don't have Logan or the others to confirm it. We don't even have a *statement!*" Papers were shuffled. "This is ridiculous!"

Webster waited.

"Have you seen today's papers?" Fletcher finally asked, not quite a panic attack. "Those goons are all over this thing. And you know there's only so much heat those guys on the Hill can take. First, we have an FBI agent killed on American soil by a professional assassin. God Almighty! Then the gold thing! Then, this morning, oil prices went through the ceiling and the stock market went through the floor! What's next? Is this madman going to rob the Federal Reserve?"

No response.

Fletcher continued, "Richard, listen to me. I am absolutely serious: The networks are beginning to tie all this stock market descent, the banks pleading for federal assistance, the sudden oil scare, even the gold thing into some kind of big picture." He sighed. "Not that it takes a genius, but we do not need that kind of exposure—not now. If the American people find out that this headline investigation of Logan's is somehow, God help us, tied to the crash of Wall Street and a threatened oil embargo we...are...*dead.* And I do not mean figuratively."

"I understand, sir."

"Let me be succinct," Fletcher pronounced. "Unless we can prove that we do not have some kind of out of control operation that is making the American dollar worth used toilet paper, we are placing ourselves in a position that is not only civilly dangerous, but which could also permanently cripple the FBI! Am I making myself clear?"

"Crystal clear, sir."

"So what's your plan?"

"To finish this assignment within seventy-two hours."

Fletcher paused. "Can you do that?"

"Yes, sir."

"Good," Fletcher added. "I can assure you that I do not want to go head to head with the United States Congress. Having the president on my back is bad enough."

"I understand."

"See to it, Richard. You know what's at stake."

Webster gazed without seeing the papers on his desk. "I know all too well."

"Good. Now tell me this: Do you know how to find Logan?" Fletcher's tone was faintly alarmed. "I mean; can you warn Logan that he's almost out of time?"

"I'm...not sure, sir," Webster lied. "Logan and his team are undercover and I don't know if I'll be able to meet with him or not. It's complicated."

A fatigued curse. "Richard, be aware that there are...*monumental* forces on a collision course. We do not know who they are but we do know they are *not us*. Logan and his team are outgunned and out-manned. CI-3, God forbid, has been placed on standby. But CI-3 is absolutely our last resort. I do not want to put that team in the field unless it is necessary to avoid a world war or something equally catastrophic. Am I making myself clear?"

"Perfectly, sir." Webster looked down at the phone, knowing already what he was going to do. "I'm going to see this through as quickly as possible."

"Good. See to it."

"Yes, sir."

Webster's finger instantly touched a button on the phone as he hung up. The secretary's voice came on the line. "Yes, sir?"

"Get me a scrambled line to the security office of the Israeli Embassy in Washington." Webster was impressed by his own calm. And one moment later a bland Embassy official answered, speaking perfect English.

"This is Richard Webster, Assistant Director of the United States Federal Bureau of Investigation. I want to leave a message for General Ariel Ben Canaan."

"I'm sorry, sir, but General Ben Canaan is not in the Embassy," responded the officer too mechanically. "We can call Jerusalem through the YAMAM office if you care to—"

"Tell him to meet me tonight at six at the Metro Art Museum in Central Park," Webster interrupted.

"I'm sorry, sir. But General Ben Canaan isn't—"

Webster hung up, walked to the door.

Knew he'd be there.

Logan stood outside the towering BCCI building at New York's 5th Avenue and 86th Street. Jonathan stood beside him, studying the street.

Walking quickly, Blackfoot came up the crowded sidewalk, his long black hair lifted by the wind. He was wearing ankle-length boots, blue jeans, and a quilted plaid shirt. He could have faded into any poverty-stricken area of the city without a hitch.

"I've found it," he said tersely.

No words were spoken as Jonathan and Logan followed him down the street. But Jonathan scanned to detect any overly familiar faces, trying to catch the images of people in windows as they passed. He looked behind them and across, trying to find someone following them on the sidewalk bordering Central Park. But there was nothing. They were alone, it seemed. And they blended perfectly into the crowd as they walked up 5th Avenue to 87th. Then Blackfoot nodded to a corner building, his face unrevealing. "That's it."

Logan studied the building. *Manhattan Inc.* was printed in large blue letters over the entrance and the revolving door bustled with activity. *"That's it?"*

"Yeah." Blackfoot was nervously watching the crowd. "Fincher's office, is on the southwest corner of the BCCI building, on the high side of 86th. I've checked the angles. It's narrow, but we can use a laser to pick up the electromagnetic field from Fincher's computer and Teletype from here. All we have to do is get an office high on this side."

Logan sighed. "All right. I'll rent us an office and—"

"The higher, the better," Blackfoot interrupted nervously. "There's a lot less interference as you climb." He searched the streets. "Do you think the German is here, Logan?"

Logan stared indulgently at the Sioux. "Don't worry about it, kid, I'm gonna shoot him on sight and claim it self-defense." He waited until that seemed to calm Blackfoot down. "I want the two of you to scope out the streets. This is my city and I know it like the back of my hand, but you don't. So get to know it. I want you to be able to move without me if you have to. Understand?"

They nodded.

"Good," Logan nodded. "Be alert, boys, because that German is out there. And I assure you he's trying to reacquire us right now. He's probably even figured we'll be scoping BCCI, so he's scoping BCCI to scope us." He looked at Blackfoot. "You don't have a weapon, so stay close to Jonathan. Hear me?"

"I hear you."

"Good man." Logan turned away. "I'll catch up to you in an hour right here. Stay alive."

"Got it."

"Let's do it."

Darkness was falling as Jonathan and Blackfoot finished reconnaissance. They still hadn't heard from Logan and figured he was shelling out a bundle, especially on such short notice. Around them, the streets were crowded. Droves of people moved quickly in the early shadows of night.

The sky was alight with a spectral, shadowy haze, distinctly different from the blue that overlaid the city during the day. Jonathan lifted his head to wind, caught the scent of pollution and distant rain. "A storm's coming in," he said.

"Yeah," said Blackfoot. "I know."

Jonathan looked over. "Really?"

"Yeah, man. Knew that a few hours ago."

"Can all Indians do that?"

"Sioux."

"Sorry." Jonathan waited. "Well? Can all Sioux do that?"

"Do what?"

"Smell rain coming like that?"

"What do you mean?" Blackfoot gestured at the window. "I saw the weather report while you were—"

"Good grief," Jonathan said. "Come on. We've got to—"

Jonathan saw the Iceman standing motionless on the far side of the street. Cloaked in a long dark coat, his glasses again concealed his eyes, black against a skeletal face.

Black king...

Jonathan reached for his SIG to pull down and then he remembered; the people, the people, so many of them. If a shootout began here, there would be no way to avoid killing an innocent bystander, not in the heat of combat.

The Iceman smiled.

He had probably always been close, had anticipated from the first they would be scoping out BCCI, just like Logan warned. But he had waited until dark to emerge. Now they were separated by four lanes of traffic, measuring one another—the battle had already begun.

Jonathan heard Blackfoot complaining about how long it was taking Logan and then the Sioux turned and saw the tall, white-haired figure. Blackfoot looked at Jonathan, back across the street. His chest deflated. *"Oh, man..."*

"Come on," Jonathan said, walking backward. "Blackfoot! Come on!"

Quickly the Sioux came up beside him, keeping an eye on the Iceman and then the old man was walking slowly across the street, hands shoved deeply into the pockets of his black coat. Jonathan knew if the hit man got close enough for a clear shot he'd just take it and vanish into the crowd. Jonathan walked faster.

"We've got to get distance on him."

"Do you have another gun?" Blackfoot asked.

Quickly Jonathan handed the Sioux his backup weapon, the .38, and then grabbed Blackfoot's shoulder to suddenly push him into the doorway of a Chinese restaurant. He snarled, "Go out the backdoor and *run* back to where Logan is cutting the deal on the office! Stick close to him and tell him I'm going to take this guy out!"

"What are you gonna do?"

THE SCAM

"Kill him!" Jonathan shoved Blackfoot violently through the door. Then he turned to see the old man less than a block away, coming steadily, and knew he could outrun him but he had to make sure the old man came after him instead of Blackfoot. He slowed even more, luring the Iceman forward, walking backward.

Jonathan noticed something at his side and glanced down to see a cardboard shelter of the homeless. One of the weathered homeless was warming a plate of beans over a can of sterno. Without a word Jonathan threw the man a twenty-dollar bill and snatched up a coffeecup-sized container, keeping one eye on the killer.

Fearless, the Iceman advanced.

Within twenty steps Jonathan suddenly noticed a grocery store and he was in and out in less than a minute, leaving an astonished clerk with a hundred-dollar bill. But now he had everything he needed: an 18-ounce bottle of Coke, a fist-sized bag of potassium nitrate, instant coffee, a tiny box of Tide detergent and a quart of kerosene.

He went out the door to see the tall black figure of the old man almost on top on him, eighty yards away. But there were still too many people for him to take a clear shot. Turning cautiously away, Jonathan was walking again, knowing the predator was much, much too close to let his prey escape.

Jonathan felt death on his spine as he moved, quickly pouring out the Coke and mixing in the potassium nitrate. Then he placed the kerosene under his arm and poured in the Tide before reaching into his pocket to remove a careful measure of coffee.

People passed him on the street but no one seemed to notice and then Jonathan poured in a careful volume of kerosene into the glass. Finishing in forty seconds, he tossed the remainder far into an alley and turned back as he neared a tunnel, the crowd thinning dramatically. By the time he reached the darkened entrance, he was alone. Turning back to the implacable figure, he lifted his chin in a challenge.

The Black King smiled, and came forward.

Like before.

As soon as Jonathan hit the darkness he was running to find a good place for an ambush and he reached an indentation in the wall.

Sweat freezing in the cool of the tunnel, he leaped into the crevice and drew the SIG. He whirled back to see the tall, terrifying image pausing at the entrance. Reaching up slowly, the old man removed the thick black glasses that hid his eyes, and came into darkness.

Vanishing.

Webster leaned against the entrance of the Metro Art Museum in Central Park and noticed General Ariel Ben Canaan immediately as he came down the curving, shadowed walkway.

The big Israeli had his hands shoved deeply into the pockets of a long dark overcoat. His face was pale, his wild hair swept back by a gathering cold wind. He came up to Webster without expression. "Sooner than I expected," he rumbled.

Webster's eyes were obsidian. "Are you armed?"

Canaan fell in beside him, hand still shoved in the pockets of his coat. "Of course."

"You should be."

"Of course."

Webster's next words took a little steam out of the Israeli's stride. "I know why Logan was selected for the team, general.

I know why Blackfoot was selected. What I don't know is why you selected Malone. I want an answer."

"Malone is a ferocious fighter," the general said with admiration. "He reminds me of—"

"There's a time to speak the truth, general," Webster said, low and without emotion. "Tell me the truth or you and your men will be on the next flight out of this country."

Silence.

"Malone is of interest to us, Webster. He has an element that gives him extraordinary power. Moreover, he has a unique motivation that no nation can instill by military training. We need him, Mr. Webster. And *you* need him."

It was only by a phenomenal level of control that Webster didn't turn and slam the Israeli against the wall. "I'll give you one more chance," he said. "Why Malone?"

Canaan understood. He responded with a faint frown. "You know, of course, that Jonathan's parents were Amelia and Justinian Falken, and that they were murdered in their manor in England. What you did not know is that the man who is hunting Logan and your team is the same man who murdered them."

"Charon," Webster said to sweep back his disbelief.

He had suspected it, somehow. But it had been only the wildest intuitive guess that something in Jonathan's past linked him to this. He had just never been confident that such an instinctive premonition could be correct.

"Yes," the general answered. "This man, this Iceman, killed Jonathan's parents as they slept. But Jonathan himself evaded the assault to play a very deadly game of cat and mouse with Charon inside the house—a chess game they did not finish."

A revolving collision of connections swept like whirlwind

inside Webster. The same instinct that told him there had been a special reason for Jonathan's inclusion also told him that he would not leave this meeting with the full truth. Nor did he reveal that his anger was slackened by Canaan's mostly forthright admission.

"Keep talking," he said.

The Israeli shrugged. "What do you want to know?"

"Why didn't you tell me earlier that this man killed Jonathan's parents?"

Canaan sighed. "A cult of secrecy breeds men who consider everything to be a secret. It is the easiest road, when fatigue and despair make a man question what he can and cannot confide. It is the answer for everything: tell nothing. Israel uses such a devotion to secrecy in much the same manner the FBI uses rules and regulations. To maintain standards. 'Never get personally involved. Always go by policies and you shall never make a mistake.' With us, we reveal nothing. Our first rule. My conscience is relaxed to it. I harbor no compulsions against lying to those who trust me."

"I've seen that."

Canaan shrugged. "Jonathan's father was a skilled agent for MI6, but he was also a devoted agent of the Mossad, and a Jewish patriot." Canaan spoke like a man sharing a dark family secret. "A day before his death on November 1, 1984, he covertly contacted the Israeli Embassy in London and spoke with a senior Mossad operative."

"Why?"

"Falken intimated that he had uncovered something concerning Silman. It was Falken himself who provided the history of Silman, which I gave to you yesterday. He had compiled another file."

"Did Falken deliver this file to Mossad under orders from

MI6? Or did he do it without their approval?"

"He did it because he knew that Silman and his compatriots were planning the destruction of Israel through financing a joint Syrian-Egyptian invasion. And I suspect his actions were unsanctioned M16."

Webster pondered it; the implications were far-reaching. "What did Falken do after he delivered the file?"

Canaan was taking a long time with each reply.

"Falken set up a clandestine meeting for the next day to tell us tank divisions, troop numbers, details that would have insured Israel's survival. But he was assassinated that night. And we have never been able to hypothesize what else he might have known. Nor have discreet diplomatic inquiries yielding anything of substance."

"You don't have any intelligent assessment about what else Falken knew?" Webster asked, glancing casually at a man and a young woman, raven-haired and stunningly beautiful.

She was sitting and talking with a man on a park bench. They looked as if they were from the Middle Eastern and they were trim, athletic, and a bit too stylish to be so lovingly involved in a public place—Mossad guards.

"This, I remind you, is only my theory," Canaan said. "I have no proof that Charon murdered Jonathan's parents. But I believe it is the truth." He paused. "Only Jonathan knows."

Webster had no argument. "Did the Mossad believe at the time of Falken's death that Silman was responsible for the murder?"

"Yes."

"Why didn't your people retaliate?"

Canaan shook his head. "For diplomatic reasons, we were forced to leave retaliation to MI6 and, for whatever reason, they never choose to punish him."

Each revelation only revealed another question. Webster said, "Why didn't Falken turn a copy of the file over to his people in M16 as a backup?"

"Falken was British. He did not want his people to know he was so fiercely protective of Jewish freedom. He wanted to maintain relations. To betray his own by delivering such a file when he had been expressly ordered not to would have been a mortal sin."

Mortal sin—an unforgivable betrayal in the counterintelligence community that was punished by death without trial.

"Treason?" Webster couldn't keep the intrigue out of his voice. It seemed inconceivable. There was no profit, no obvious purpose except exposure of a supposed threat to an allied nation.

"Not treason to his country," Canaan replied. "But Falken did betray someone, I believe. It is only safe to conclude that he did not trust his people enough to turn over the file to them. Perhaps he believed that it would have assured his death."

Webster didn't like any of it. "None of this makes sense," he said. "Why would England want Israel to fall?"

"Not all of England," Canaan seemed to have thought about it to some length, "but it was someone among the holies of MI6."

"I can accept that. But if MI6 was working with Silman to kill Falken, why would MI6 then relocate Jonathan in America to protect him from Silman? That doesn't follow."

"It makes masterful good sense if you look at if from the standpoint of a man who cannot trust anyone at all. Whoever rescued Jonathan and relocated him in America worked for MI6, yes. But that does not mean he also worked for Silman. *Someone* in MI6 was Silman's man, but not *everyone*. Clearly, Falken knew that he was not the only one on Silman's list. But he did not know the second name. Whoever rescued Jonathan also knew this. So, when he hid Jonathan, he concealed the location from his colleagues in MI6 and from compromised intelligence agencies in America. It is the only explanation."

Webster followed, and agreed. "All right, but tell me; why was Falken's entire family targeted instead of just Falken? Family is sacred with professionals. Why would Silman suffer the complications of violating that by killing a woman and a child?"

"That answer is obvious," Canaan replied, as one who is experienced in such a question. "First, it is because Silman is not a professional intelligence agent. He is a thief and a murderer—a man who bought and sold the services of intelligence agencies. He does not honor the sacred code of leaving family out of a war. Amelia Falken was killed because Silman feared Falken had possibly confided to her. Unlikely, since Falken was a professional. But Silman knew that it was Amelia Falken's homeland that was threatened by Silman's arms shipments. So he took no chances."

Webster stopped. Stared. "Her homeland?"

Canaan also stopped. "I thought you knew."

"No. I didn't."

Now it made sense. Webster knew that according to Jewish law a child was only Jewish if the mother was Jewish. The ethnicity of the matter was of no consequence.

A laugh. "I am not easily surprised, Webster. It is something I long ago abandoned as a luxury I could not afford. But, yes, this is a surprise. A cunning omission. What did Jonathan's file include?"

"It said his father was killed in a botched burglary and that Jonathan was a possible informant for the British government. It said MI6 requested the State Department's assistance and the State Department provided it. Who, exactly, is unknown. It's still a classified agreement between opposite numbers."

"Anything else?"

"Just psychological tests on Jonathan when he was a child. Stuff on his problem with nightmares, problems in school. A lot about how he was some kind of chess prodigy but can't play the game anymore because of what happened. Had stuff about some severe child-psych treatments that didn't work on him." Webster frowned. "It had more about how big a loss it was to the world that he couldn't play chess anymore about than the kid, himself."

The Israeli general nodded.

"So," Webster muttered as they began walking again, "Jonathan is Jewish." He shook his head with a mute curse. "I should have *known*."

Canaan chuckled. "Yes."

Silence descended for a dozen steps.

"Still, General, why did Silman consider it necessary to kill Jonathan? He was just a child. His father wouldn't have told him anything."

"Perhaps," Canaan hesitated, "that is something more akin to the nature of my people. It is only a guess, but I believe it the correct conclusion. Silman feared that Jonathan would one day investigate the murder of his father and discover the truth. An eye for an eye." He paused. "Israel is not a nation disposed to demonstrate mercy, Webster. We cannot afford it. Silman knew that there was a possibility Jonathan would one day seek vengeance for his father's murder. So Silman chose to avoid the possibility of future complications."

Utterly practical thoughts like that, Webster realized, gave a man a black advantage.

"Nevertheless," Canaan continued, "we are not thwarted

in our designs. Whether we discover the truth or not, we will ultimately succeed in sanctioning Silman. He cannot escape."

Which brought Webster back to where they started. "So why has Israel decided at this time, without proof of Silman's guilt, that it's time to kill him?"

"We have currently not killed Silman because assassinations never remain secret in the intelligence community, and always exhort a high measure of diplomatic influence. But we tire of the game. It is time for Silman to die. And he will, when we find him." Canaan frowned bitterly. "Webster, you said there is a time to talk. I say there is a time to do what must be done. Silman has murdered my people. He remains a threat to all of Israel. And now, we must kill him. I am prepared to answer to the God of Israel for my actions."

A descending rhythm in the words informed Webster that there was nothing more to say. "All right, general. I won't get in your way. Just tell me this; how many people do you have in this country? Do you have a fully operational unit?"

The general hesitated, then: "Yes."

"Can you use your unit to protect Logan and my team until they run Silman to ground?"

"If we knew where Logan was, we could do that, yes. But you also have the availability of your revered CI-3 unit. Our people are not superior."

"I don't trust my lines of communication anymore," Webster answered. "And I can't activate CI-3 without word getting back to the president inside forty-eight hours. At which time, unless we're in a life-threatening situation, he will execute some kind of jurisdictional override. I need an independent source to protect my men in the field."

Canaan was sympathetic. "First we must know where Logan and his men are located. It is impossible to protect them if we cannot find them."

"I'm meeting Logan tonight in the New York City Police Impound Lot. There's an eighteen-wheeler there that contains a load of Wild Turkey. I want your men in the area early. As far as I'm concerned, you've got a standing green light to kill anybody who's a threat."

Canaan nodded his understanding. "There is no one you can trust, is there, Mr. Webster? No one but an Israeli spy who, as far as you know, might be working for the other side."

Webster was unshakable. "I know you're not working for the other side, General. As you said, Israel won't let the Holocaust happen again. It's as simple as that." He paused. "And they shouldn't."

Canaan's face reflected the suffering and the deaths of six million Jews. And a royal oath to God—*never again.*

"I'll be there at 10 o'clock," Webster looked at his watch. "Use infrared scopes because—"

"We shall deal with the details," Canaan interuppted, then smiled without warmth. "My people are skilled."

"Fine." Webster leaned forward. "No mistakes, general. My people are valuable to me. And I don't want to see any of them wasted by this German. So use whatever force is necessary."

"There is only one level of force." Canaan's words held a fatal aspect. "Let that be understood. Israel does not indulge her enemies."

Webster knew he was crossing a line he vowed never to cross but he didn't hesitate. He was into it, now. Into it so deep that he'd never be free again no matter what happened. He walked back up the path.

"You're right," he said.

Canaan walked to the raven-haired woman that had been poised with such delicacy on the park bench. But now, in stark contrast to her earlier demeanor, her expression was no longer gentle. It was cold and merciless—utterly devoid of human feeling. She said nothing as Canaan walked up; her eyes waited.

"Yes, Daniela," he said. "You will soon have your revenge."

Daniela stared after Webster's departing form. "He will let Malone remain in the mission?"

"Yes," Canaan nodded.

Her face reflected the purity of pain.

"Good," she said, and her hand tightening on the Uzi hidden beneath her coat.

She turned away.

⊙ ⊙ ⊙

Matsumo cradled a beer that he had not yet tasted at The Boardroom Bar. Watching. Waiting.

His sleepy, lionlike gaze roamed over the rows of military, FBI and Secret Service agents, and trainees occupying the establishment. He had talked to no one, observed everyone. He was waiting for a chance to approach whoever appeared to be a regular, who might have been in the bar Friday night.

Finally, near a back booth, he recognized the face of a man, a gunnery sergeant from Quantico that he had instructed in close-fighting skills. A man who might talk easily, if prompted in accordance with his weakness.

Gripping his beer, Matsumo stood away from the bar and walked across the red brick floor, finally smiling as he drew near the table.

"Matsumo!" the sergeant boomed as the mountainous Japanese parted the crowd like a ship slicing water. He gestured emphatically, honored that the legendary Matsumo would approach him in a social setting. "How ya doin'!"

Gunnery Sergeant Brainwaith, remembered Matsumo as he smiled easily and sat, relaxing. Then, using the full measure of his considerable charm, he approvingly commended Brainwaith for how well he had mastered defensive training. Matsumo offered to buy him another beer. And another.

Time passed, nothing important discussed.

More beers, and more.

Matsumo learned that Brainwaith and his Marine Corps friends had, indeed, overheard a heated discussion at The Boardroom on Friday night, a discussion between two "lowlife" Bureau agents. Then the two veterans were joined by two rookies: a young guy, about twenty-five. Tough. Mean. And an Indian.

Matsumo laughed, shaking his head as Brainwaith guffawed and slammed his hand on the table.

Ordering more beer.

As sober as he was when he entered, Matsumo exited The Boardroom, moving toward his car. He knew more than when he arrived, but also knew there was more to discover.

In the end, Brainwaith had described how the two veteran FBI agents had argued over some "Superman" and how dangerous it would be to take him down. Finally the "kid" arrived and they had talked more, but Brainwaith had heard nothing of that.

Matsumo was discouraged until Brainwaith recalled, in a drunken stupor, that the original two agents had mentioned something about "Superman" being in *England.*

England.

Matsumo only vaguely understand why he was doing this. He was not a sentimental man, but he knew that he felt something in his heart, something paternal and reckless and protective for Jonathan.

Brow furrowed, he headed for his car, reaching for his keys and reflexively checking reflections in the glass for anyone following. And although he saw no one, he felt a thrilling winter-cold that chilled fear into his bones.

Disregarding all he knew, Matsumo spun around, already searching, his fists tightened into stone as an instinctive growl rumbled from his chest. But he saw nothing.

Nothing but shadows.

Jonathan searched the shadows.

The Iceman had vanished as purely as darkness itself.

Holding his breath, Jonathan listened, trying to find the slightest whisper of an approach in the encompassing darkness. But there were only surrounding sounds of the city echoing through the tunnel, the tunnel itself framed by night-light at the far ends. There was no movement, no shadow breaking shadow.

He squinted, turning his head to listen more closely. But there was so much sound from the city that he could hear nothing soft. He feared that, with echo to cover his approach, the hit man could virtually walk up beside him without any warning.

He had planned to keep a visual on the German as he came down the tunnel. But that had gone the way of all good combat plans—in the trash. Now, he couldn't wait for the German to come to him. He had to force the old man to move. He had to create a situation that would put the hitter in such alarm that he would have to move quickly.

Then Jonathan would have him. He'd hurl the bottle and upon impact it would explode in mushrooming napalm, the Tide adhering the ignited kerosene to everything it touched, the oxygen-rich potassium heated by the coffee grains and sterno to violently detonate upon compression. Then he would start firing, carefully placing every shot dead in the Iceman's head.

He slid as silently as possible to the ground and moved from the wall, coming quickly behind a cement column. Overhead, freeway traffic made the roof tremble; rumbling thunder, heavy air. Cautious, Jonathan leaned around the corner of the pillar to see if—

A cold gun barrel pressed against the back of his neck.

The old man's voice was calm. "That was an excellent game, Jonathan," he whispered. "You are very good. But then you always were—even as a child."

Closing his eyes against the adrenaline surge, Jonathan thought wildly about trying for a shot. But he knew he'd never make it. He turned his head to stare into the old man's eyes.

Opaque even in the gloom of the tunnel, his eyes were pale and milky. And despite his spiraling fear, Jonathan understood—*understood* the reason for the thick black glasses, why the Iceman always protected his eyes from the sun. Why he was at home in darkness.

He couldn't see in the light.

Charon laughed, dry and rasping. "Please drop the hammer on your weapon," he whispered. "Yes, thank you. And now, please, toss it to the side. I do not think it will discharge."

Jonathan heedlessly tossed the SIG aside, holding the bottle of napalm in his left hand. The Iceman glanced down, the pressure of the barrel increasing slightly on Jonathan's neck.

"Desperate, Jonathan? Were you planning to assault me with a broken bottle?"

"Something like that," Jonathan whispered.

"Grandmasters do not make desperate moves."

"I'm not a Grandmaster."

"No," the old man smiled, "but you would have been. Yes, most assuredly, you would have been." He laughed. "I lost you for many years, child. They hid you from me. But now I know who you have become. I have even studied your file." The skull-like face became curious. "Tell me, Jonathan, why did you never play the game again after that night?"

Jonathan frowned. "All I could see was you."

A laugh.

"Perhaps," the old man continued softly, "it was because we began a game that we never finished."

Jonathan's fear was quickly fading. He gazed into the death-white eyes—eyes that seemed more than shark-like than human. There was power there, unrestrained and unmerciful.

"I'm going to kill you," Jonathan said.

A slow shake of his head and the Iceman began to squeeze the trigger—

"I want to know your name!" Jonathan shouted. "You owe me that much! I want to know the name of the man who killed my parents."

"Of course you would." The old man paused. "Since you have known me, my name has been Charon. And I say this with genuine respect, Jonathan. You have been, by far, my most difficult prey. But now, at last, you are in checkmate."

"The game's not over." Jonathan shifted the bottle.

"Oh, yes," Charon smiled, "yes, it is. It is time to finish the game we began so long ago. It is time to—"

Jonathan tossed the bottle to the side, throwing it so the napalm would scatter across the breadth of the tunnel and Charon turned away from the explosion with a shout, lifting a forearm over his eyes. Then Jonathan twisted desperately down as the gun discharged, the explosion behind him splintering his back with slivers of concrete. He kicked but the old man expected it and blocking with his shin, reorienting instantly.

Diving fast to the side, Jonathan couldn't even understand how the second bullet missed as he hit to roll away, coming up on his feet, assessing the situation.

The old man was between him and the SIG, and he'd given his backup to Blackfoot. All he had was the two-shot derringer and in a few seconds the napalm would die down. Then Charon would have the advantage because he was master of the dark.

Jonathan knew he didn't have a choice; it was suicide to fight him on those terms. So he angled behind a column and squinted back to see Charon placing the black glasses on his face.

Jonathan removed the derringer, holding it close. As a last resort, he knew, he could fire the weapon pointblank into Charon's chest. But the weapon had no accuracy beyond ten feet, so he'd hold it back for a desperate moment. Moving away, relying on speed, Jonathan ran down the tunnel angling back and forth between columns to make a hard target and he felt two impacts near his back.

In twenty seconds Jonathan made it to end of the tunnel, angling instantly around a wall to see the crowd close and he hesitated, holding his place and knowing the old man was getting closer each second.

Go!

You can't win this!

The Scam

With a snarl Jonathan moved, knowing the old man was following but also knowing that he could lose him fast in a flat run and in seconds Jonathan was surrounded.

Lost in the crowd.

Chapter Twelve

After leaving Canaan in the park, Webster worked four hours to sanitize his trail. He used every trick he knew and even created a few new ones. He descended into six subways stations, moved through hotels and restaurants to take different exits only to grab another cab as soon as he hit the street again

Too many times he thought he saw the same beige and blue cars, and maybe a white van. There was no way to be certain, but he didn't question it. He had to lose them.

Moving fast, he used the entire city to his advantage; traffic jams, crowds, multi-exit buildings, fire escapes and carefully timed subway pickups and drops, moving quick and constant so they would tie up radios with updates. It was a long time before he felt comfortably that he was clear. He looked at his watch—he was late for his meeting with Logan.

○ ○ ○

After Jonathan returned, Logan's wrath was biblical. He stalked back and forth across the office, smoldering, holding the SIG in his hand like he couldn't let it go.

Finally Logan kneeled beside Jonathan and Blackfoot, both of them holding shotguns, shoulder to shoulder. They were sitting beneath a window where the TEMPEST equipment was aimed at the window of Fincher's BCCI office.

Clearly, Logan was reluctant to leave. "I can't stay any longer," he said. "I've got to meet Webster."

"I'll go with you," Jonathan said. He had used up a lot adrenaline in the tunnel, but the crash had come.

"With what?" asked Logan. "You don't have a gun anymore, son. You gonna carry that shotgun all over Manhattan?" He waited; Jonathan shrugged. "Just stay here with Blackfoot and get some rest. I'll take care of this."

"What if Charon is there?"

"That's his problem."

"C'mon, Logan," Jonathan's voice approached insubordination. "You need to take me with you. That guy's better than all of us put together."

Logan wasn't hearing it. "You're staying. Blackfoot's going to be on that computer and he can't be watching the door at the same time. As good as that Nazi is, he could come up right behind both of you if you're not careful. That is..." He glanced behind his back, "...if he knows where we're at, yet."

Blackfoot started. "You think he knows where we are?"

"There are ways," Logan muttered, distant. "But we're in a good position. Locked door, one entrance. He'll have to fight for it and that's not his style. He likes to ambush, hit from the dark."

Remembering Charon's white eyes staring with surreal force through the darkness, Jonathan murmured, "Darkness... Yeah, I guarantee it."

"You did a good job on him in the tunnel," Logan nodded. "You went head to head and you're still alive. I just wish you'd blown his brains out but..."

"It wasn't from lack of trying."

"I'll bet," Logan laughed. "All right. Lock this place up. I'm going to meet Webster. I'll pick up some food and drinks on the way back." Abruptly, he was contemplative. "Listen to me," he added cautiously, "if I'm not back by morning, take everything you've got and deliver it to every newspaper and TV station that has an address. Then book yourselves on every talkshow you can find."

"What about security contracts?" asked Jonathan. "They'll put us in prison."

"Just tell everybody, including the government, that you're talking about a fictional novel. And then tell the television people off the record that it's a true story," Logan smiled. "The government can't shut you down if you call it fiction. But everybody will know you're talking about something that really happened, and that's how they'll use it."

They nodded.

"There's only one really good defense against these people," Logan continued. "If you're a nobody and you cause problems, they will kill you and nobody cares. They do it all the time. But if you're a celebrity, if you've gone so far across the line that you're actually a *liability* to kill, then they'll hold back until they absolutely have to do something. They don't want it to look like they're trying to cover something up. It's a game."

Blackfoot sighed. "The only game in town."

Webster flashed his credentials at the New York City Police Impound Lot and moved cautiously inside the gate. A haze of streetlight illuminated the compound and, in the distance, beside the tractor trailer, stood the silhouette of a man.

Webster cast a glance at surrounding rooftops but saw nothing—not Israeli snipers or shadows moving or reflections from a scope, no roofline silhouettes rising or falling, stark against night.

These guys are good...

He reached Logan, who stood relaxed, leaning against the truck. Webster laughed as he saw a bottle of Wild Turkey and two glasses set delicately on the bumper. Logan smiled and reached down to pour a shot for each of them.

"Sorry I'm late." Webster took the glass.

They clicked a toast.

"Just got here myself." Logan took a sip. "Jonathan went up against the Nazi again."

Webster stared. "Is he hurt?"

"He's all right. But the old guy almost took him out. You said his crytonym was Iceman. But his real name, or as real as it gets, anyway, is Charon."

"Yeah, I picked that up, myself." Webster sat on a hood. "In Greek mythology, Charon was Lord of the Dead. He ferried souls of dead guys across the River Styx, into Hell."

"Are you serious?"

"Yeah. Charon demanded a bronze coin, or *obolus,* in payment for the trip." Webster glanced again into the dark. "That's why the Greeks put a bronze coin under the tongue of their dead guys. According to superstition, if the dead guy didn't have a bronze coin with him, Charon wouldn't take him across the river. Then he'd have to wander around until he could convince Charon to take him to Hades."

Logan enjoyed the slight reprieve from talking about the case. "So Charon carried the souls of all those dead guys to Hell, huh? Sounds appropriate."

"Well, *mostly* dead guys," said Webster, abruptly so grim that he seemed to surprise even himself.

There is a time when something is said with such a sense of impending tragedy that it obliterates everything that would otherwise be deemed important. Logan realized he'd just reached it.

"Mostly dead?"

"There was a guy," Webster continued. "His name was

Aeneas. He was a Greek soldier. The story goes that he was the only living man to ever force Charon to take him across the river into Hell."

"Why did he do that?"

Swirling the whiskey, Webster suddenly studied the glass as if he wasn't sure what was in it. His words were somber.

"He wanted to see his father again."

○ ○ ○

Jonathan closed his eyes and saw his father, the only person he had ever loved, dying in darkness, slain again and again by Charon, so many times. Saw it as clearly as if it had happened tonight.

Dark blood...

"Jonathan?" It was Blackfoot. "You alright?"

"Yeah." Jonathan opened his eyes. "Yeah, I'm fine. Why do you ask?"

"You said something."

"No." Jonathan didn't want to hear it, no matter what it had been. "I was just thinking."

Blackfoot gave him a concerned look, then muttered, "Whatever you say."

He concentrated on the computer screen again, reading blips and flashes like an air traffic controller. Occasionally he would reach out and make a minor adjustment on a lunchbox-sized device that was supposed to pick up and translate the electromagnetic field emanating from Fincher's office, making sure that they could read everything he was doing on his computer screen.

Jonathan spoke, "What have you got?"

"His log-in. He's not really doing much. Just working on some financial stuff. But he sent out a few fairly important Teletypes."

"How do you know they're important?"

"He coded them."

"Can you read them?"

"Sure. They're not coded until they leave the screen and go into the net. The code is to protect the messages from theft or deciphering while they're being downloaded."

"How is he coding them?" Almost instantly, Jonathan regretted it. "Don't get technical on me, Blackfoot. Just give me the *Reader's Digest* version."

"It's simple. Fincher is using a 3.5 floppy that codes his Teletype transmissions with a specific cryptology. Sort of like the Enigma coding system that the Germans used during World War II. More complicated, but similar."

"Huh," Jonathan grunted. "Have you ever seen the code before?"

"Yep."

"Where?"

"It's one of the disks used by the CIA."

Jonathan sighed. "So much for democracy."

"*Democracy*," Blackfoot spat. "What's democracy?"

Jonathan knew the Sioux was about to start talking and he didn't try to stop him. And he sensed, somehow, that he was about to hear what he had wanted to hear for a while.

"Do you know where I come from, Jonathan?"

"A reservation?"

"Yeah. A reservation. I was raised near Four Points, the place where Arizona, Colorado, Utah, and New Mexico meet. There's not anything there. Just desert. Hills. Heat. Sun. A bunch of poor, dumb Indians living on the Res. The place is so dry a broken bottle laying the middle of a field can cause a forest fire. The suns hits it just right and the glass focuses the sun and then you've got another fire that burns up another ten thousand acres of land. Nothing but bones and rocks and fire. That's why they gave it to us."

Blackfoot revealed an essence, angry and focused. "But I was educated on a Sioux reservation, near Apache land." He laughed softly. "You can always identify the Apaches. They're pretty short but they're strong, and they have these long, hooked noses. And the Navajo are tall, big people. They make this jewelry—necklaces and earrings that they sell out of the market at Four Points. They make a lot of money there, too. And some of them travel all over the nation, doing shows with real silver and turquoise. Not the fake stuff you find in white people stores.

"Anyway, when I was a child, I sat a horse at Four Points, day after day in that mean sun, posing with the white children who wanted to be photographed beside an Indian. And let me tell you something, it was a hard dollar."

Jonathan found himself intrigued, but wanted to know where it was going and why Blackfoot worked now for the FBI.

"All day long I sat on my pony, posing with the white people while my father worked in the reservation casino outside Cortez," the Sioux continued. "Then, when I was thirteen, my father tried to have federal law changed so people could gamble at the casino with more than *two dollars* at a time. He said the federal government shouldn't have the right to set gambling limits at an Indian casino if they didn't set gambling limits at a white man's casino. But the government wouldn't do it. They said they'd *study* it. Then they harassed and persecuted my father until he died of a heart attack at forty-two."

Blackfoot became still. "Afterward, my mother moved us to Cortez, just to get us off the Res. She was a fighter, man. Proud. She tried to clean up a toxic chemical dump outside the Res that was draining into Navajo land. Children were dying.

Everybody was sick from the water, the food. Even the animals were sick. It was a killing field. But the EPA wouldn't close the dump. They didn't care. So my mother got some lawyers and tried to use the American Superfund Policy for cleaning up chemical waste."

Jonathan blinked. "Superfund Policy?"

Blackfoot laughed, but it was black. "Superfund was a piece of legislation passed in the late 1970s that was supposed to pool money from chemical industries to clean up waste sites. It looked good on paper, made good press, fooled most Americans. But the chemical industries didn't actually put any money in the fund. The Environmental Protection Agency would ask them for a few thousand dollars here and there, whatever they were willing to dish out, but the EPA didn't push it. And as far as Cortez went, the EPA said the site wasn't toxic. They said there wasn't anything in the dump that could threaten the environment."

"How could they say that?" Jonathan asked.

"Industries *control* the EPA, Jonathan." Blackfoot stared, and Jonathan must have looked surprised because he added, "You don't believe me? Think about this: in twenty years the EPA has only regulated seven of two hundred and seventy-five toxic chemicals. And almost all of 'em are stored beside Indian land. That's a fact. And twelve years after its passage, only seventy-three of the twelve hundred toxic chemical sites listed in the Superfund Policy have been cleaned up. The rest contaminate the children, the animals. The federal government doesn't care." The darkness that descended upon Blackfoot was frightening. "Until I *made* them care."

Jonathan didn't move. "What'd you do?"

"I took their heart," Blackfoot whispered. "I took what they loved."

Jonathan waited, then broke the tense silence.

"What'd you take?"

Blackfoot looked to the computer screen. "My ancestors fought with the bow and arrow." His smile was cruel. "I fought with this. Because I knew that *this* could break them."

"How?"

"When my mother died, I used the money from her insurance to buy my first computer. Then I taught myself to use it. I bought books. I read. I studied. Then I made contact with others that knew more than me and met with them, and learned from them until there was nothing left to learn. Until I mastered what they knew. And then I learned more. I lived and worked on the computer until my fingers bled. Until my eyes couldn't focus. I experimented and pushed and learned more and more. More than anyone before me. I dreamed about the Internet. And then, seven years later...I claimed my revenge."

Despite his friendship with Blackfoot, Jonathan had a new, somewhat alarming appreciation. He repeated, "But what'd you do?"

"I began with simple theft," Blackfoot answered. "Then I realized the secret to stealing millions instead of thousands was just adding more zeros. So I stole millions from the chemical companies. I changed their inventory reports, crippled their supply lines. I blew substations with direct feeds from nuclear plants. I knocked out the power for entire cities over four states, over and over again, until I grew tired of it." He shook his head, wild and unconquered. "I made them pay over six hundred million dollars in repairs and maintenance until...until I thought of things far, far more diabolical."

Jonathan's mouth hung open. "Like *what*?"

"Like *relationships*," Blackfoot smiled. "*Sacred* relationships. I attacked what was holy. I attacked what protected them."

Jonathan's question hovered unasked.

"The United States Government," Blackfoot said.

Jonathan was mesmerized. "How'd you attack the relationships between the chemical companies and the government?"

Blackfoot laughed his scary laugh. "They didn't think anyone would challenge them. They are fools. So I stole the government's internal reports on the toxic effects of chemicals, reports the government refused to release. Then I gave them to newspapers that would print them. I put light where this... this *democratic* government wanted darkness. I let the people know what the government was hiding. And that's when the hunt truly began...for me."

Jonathan leaned back, listening.

"They used the FBI. The NSA. The CIA. They recruited the Japanese." He laughed. "They used low-intensity microwave satellites to find the source of my transmission. But I defeated them all. Again and again. And then I remembered my father and I decided...I decided that if my father could not make money with an Indian casino, then *no one* would make money with a casino. I targeted Las Vegas."

"Oh, man," Jonathan whispered.

"Yes," Blackfoot nodded. "They were not happy with me."

"I'll bet."

"I took back what they had taken. Each day I took money from every account of every casino. I caused the IRS to owe billions in tax refunds to the poor. Entire bank accounts were wiped out in the countless tapeworms I turned loose." Blackfoot's face was grim. "The rich do not care for the poor. They do not care for the Navajo children who have nothing and never will. But they care about their money. So I took their money. I made it disappear and reappear in the American Indian Defense Fund. Over seven hundred million dollars in six months. I gave it to the United Negro College Fund, the Society for Thailand Refugees. Anyplace I wanted to send it."

"And they never found you?"

"They tried," Blackfoot laughed. "They used helicopters. They used the Marshall Service and, in the end, the Tribal Police." He shrugged. "By then, they knew where I was, but they could not find me. I had worked out a system with friends where I could access any line in Colorado with microwave hookups and cellular modems. By the time the trace was completed, my communication was broken, and everyone would vanish into the crowd. We moved through the countryside, often on horseback, to avoid checkpoints." He bowed his head. "I did not do it alone. There were many who worked with me."

Jonathan grunted: "And one of them was caught."

"Yes." Blackfoot's eyes glinting like volcanic glass. "My younger brother—he waited too long to break away, and I underestimated their distance. The Marshall Service caught him as he was walking down the street."

"Did he turn you in?"

"No. My brother would never betray me. He is my brother. He loves me." Blackfoot paused. "As I love him."

"What happened?"

"Within hours," the Sioux continued, "I contacted the FBI Command Center in Colorado. I gave them an ultimatum. I told them to immediately release my brother without charges or I would take my vengeance. I told them that, until now, I had been merciful. But the time for mercy had passed. I told them that, unless they let my brother go, I would reduce this nation to ashes. I gave them one hour to make a decision. Then I gave them the emergency self-detonation codes for the nuclear missiles housed in silos on the Jornada Military Reserve in New Mexico. My last failsafe."

Jonathan realized he wasn't breathing.

"Within thirty minutes," the Sioux continued, "my brother was released without charges. But they never came for me, though by then they knew who I was."

"Why not?"

"They feared what I would do."

There was a long interval of quiet. "What happened then?"

"I contacted the FBI and made a deal," Blackfoot answered with a sigh. "To defuse the situation, I told them that, if they would clean up the chemical site and provide compensation for the children who had been injured, I would stop. In their fear, they did more. They restored what had been lost, as best they could. They cleaned the site and relocated the chemicals and provided medical service for the reservation. Then, to make peace, they said it would be better if I worked *for* them instead of *against* them. They only made me vow that I would never again wreak havoc on the American financial system."

"And you agreed?"

"Yes," Blackfoot said quietly. "I agreed. I had accomplished what I intended; there was nothing left to do." He frowned. "I am not a monster."

Jonathan gazed quietly at the Sioux. "No, buddy," he said tiredly. "You're not."

"And, yet, this man," Blackfoot whispered, "he *is* a monster. A monster that takes from the poor and gives to the rich. Even worse, he's protected by those elected by the *people*." His voice was filled with contempt. *"That's* democracy."

Suddenly Blackfoot's hand lashed out to strike a command as the screen instantly vanished in a message; a message coded and sent to the source. His smile was exultant.

"Hello, Phantom," he whispered.

◉ ◉ ◉

"What do you know about Jonathan's father?" Logan asked to break the haunting mood of the moment. But he realized, if anything, his question only made it worse.

Webster muttered, "You're not going to like it."

"I believe you."

"It was a contract killing."

Logan hesitated. "What makes you say that?" But he knew where this was going, and now, finally, suspected why Jonathan wouldn't back down from this fight.

"Charon killed Jonathan's parents," Webster said bluntly. "And I think Jonathan knows it."

Logan looked away. "Yeah," he whispered, "I figured it would be something like that."

Webster's expression reflected his dark thoughts. "Jonathan's father was an agent for MI6. But he was also loyal to Mossad. He was loyal to Israel. He was also after Superman."

Logan closed his eyes, shook his head. "How long have you known this?"

"Since today."

"How'd you get it?"

"The Mossad."

"Uh-huh." There was no surprise. "And Mossad is the agency that picked Jonathan for the job, right? That's the agency you referred to at the meeting in Quantico." It wasn't a question. "The agency you couldn't talk about."

"Uh huh."

"So how come you can talk about them now?"

"Because this is the place where the map ends, Logan. Things have gone beyond the place where promises are binding."

Logan followed the facts and didn't like where they led. "The Mossad picked Jonathan because they think blood is stronger than duty. I'll bet they've watched Jonathan since he moved to America, just so they'd know what he was capable of, always planning for this contingency. Might have even helped train him. They were hoping that Jonathan, once he recognized Charon, would give the Nazi the last fight of his life. They were hoping that Jonathan would take Charon out, leaving the door wide open so that they could take down Phantom."

"Yeah, but Charon's not Phantom's last defense," Webster countered. "Phantom's got more than the Nazi in front of him. He's got our judicial system. He's bought off the White House and a big piece of Congress and probably a host of federal judges. He doesn't want to use them unless he has to, but he can cut a deal. He can do anything he wants to anybody at all. Believe me."

"I've already figured that out," Logan muttered. "BCCI has got over three hundred federal judges on the payroll. Consultants, investors, whatever. You wouldn't believe the people working for this guy. Ex-secretaries of state. Defense secretaries. Ambassadors. Ex-*presidents*. A whole lot of very powerful people are more than happy to take what he's got to give. I never thought it was possible for so many people to be owned by one man. But if you've got the money, I guess..."

Mutual contempt for the legal system was wordlessly communicated.

"But something doesn't make sense," Logan continued. "Even if Jonathan was relocated here by MI6 without the knowledge of most of our people, it couldn't have been done without *somebody* knowing. How come Phantom didn't track Jonathan down and finish the job? If Phantom has the power to get the files on this investigation, then he's got the power to have gotten something on Jonathan."

Webster didn't say anything.

"So why didn't he?"

Webster toyed with his whiskey glass, then gave his best shot. "I guess because Jonathan's file was classified."

"*So?*"

Webster blinked. "*So,* Logan, I don't just mean his file was 'classified.' I mean Jonathan's file was so classified it wasn't even *listed* as classified. I'll bet there wasn't even a *file!* This was a deal between opposite numbers, man. This stuff *never* gets written down or put into a computer."

Logan didn't seem convinced. "There's got to be some kind of procedure for this. Everything has a file, some way to track it."

"No," Webster answered. "Whoever moved Jonathan to America knew who could be trusted in our government and who couldn't, so he didn't alert any of Phantom's people. He probably told one person—the one man he trusted." The senior FBI agent shook his head in disbelief. "Logan, Jonathan's relocation is probably the only thing that *has* remained secret in this."

"Meaning," Logan proceeded, "that whoever hid Jonathan from Phantom...works for Phantom."

From his face, it was clear that that hadn't occurred to Webster, though it surely would have, in the end.

"Yeah," he said with reflexive calm, "whoever hid Jonathan works for Phantom, and knew how to hide Jonathan from Phantom." Webster slammed his hand against their makeshift table; he'd had just about enough calm. "I can't believe this!" He turned and walked away, back again. "Only someone who *worked* for Phantom would know who could be trusted in the

American Intelligence! I can't believe it! One of Phantom's *own people* hid Jonathan from Phantom!" He closed his eyes. "Man oh man, I never saw that one coming."

Logan leaned his head back, sighed heavily. "Well, I don't think we're gonna be finding any of these people in church." He laughed. "There's just no end to this. Each time we think we know something, it turns into something else. But Jonathan is the key, somehow. Israel picked him because they thought the blood of his parents would cause him to take out Charon, no matter the odds. But there's more to this, Webster. I can feel it in my—"

Gunfire blazed in the night and Logan ducked, trying to understand whether he was hit.

Instantly Webster was beside him, both of them pressed against a car. They glared as more gunfire erupted from a nearby roof, flame spiraling in a staccato burst before the night air echoed with sonic booms, the shouts of a man screaming, and...silence.

Sweating and breathless, Logan looked across the huge bumper of the semitrailer at an adjacent roof. At the guard shack, the civilian gatekeeper could be heard shouting into the phone.

Logan turned to Webster, saw the Washington AD holding a Smith .45 and scanning the darkness, vivid and angry. Webster appeared far more enraged than frightened. His teeth were clenched. His hand was tight on the semiauto as he looked at Logan. "It's the Mossad," he grimaced. "They've been hit."

"The *Mossad?*" Logan hissed.

"They're supposed to be covering your team!"

"Now you tell me?" Logan tossed a CD-ROM to Webster who caught it and shoved it in his pocket. "It's got information you're gonna need if I don't make it out of here!"

Sounds could be heard, the pounding of men racing across roofs, screaming in Hebrew, moving to the location of the conflict that now contained a terrible emptiness.

Webster crouched, squinting into the darkness. "We've got to move for that roof. Charon is up there."

Trying to catch his breath, Logan wiped sweat from his eyes. "Well," he said, "nobody lives forever."

They ran toward the gate.

◉ ◉ ◉

Logan went through the door of the roof, aiming at dark silhouettes, moving shadows, moving weapons. Webster raised his gun simultaneously.

"FBI!" he shouted as stress electrified the air and then another voice came from the far side of the roof—an angry voice that bellowed a single brutal command: "*Saleba!*"

The Israelies lowered their weapons.

Shaking with fear, holding an aim that shifted from one shadow to the next, Logan saw Webster suddenly lower his .45, gazing at a big man who strode forward with an air of command. Logan also lowered his gun and rose from his crouch.

"What happened?" Webster said and Logan saw the face of the man—old, maybe sixty, but big like a heavyweight. His hair was gray, wild, windswept.

Two bodies, dead, lay on the roof.

"Now you see why none of my men have returned," the old man said in a thick Hebrew accent. "Now you see why I want to see this Nazi assassin as they are, now."

"How did he know about the meeting?" Webster asked.

"He followed one of us," General Ariel Ben Canaan answered. "It is the only explanation."

Logan walked forward to gaze at the dead men and rain

began to fall. Quickly the entire roof was wet and Logan's brain fired the thought that he had never been able to tell the difference between blood and rainwater in the dark.

One of the Mossad had been shot from behind, the bullet exiting his forehead in a mushrooming blast. The other had fought for a moment before he was cut down. A sniper-version of the Galil semi-automatic assault rifle lay beside them—it had done him no good. Charon had come upon them unseen and without sound.

Logan shoved the SIG in his holster.

"Let's get out of here."

Chapter Thirteen

Blackfoot hit a command and Jonathan saw the screen flashing continuously, almost unreadable. Finally it lit with a lockout code and Blackfoot leaned back, biting his lip.

Jonathan was afraid of breaking the Sioux's surreal concentration, but couldn't stop himself from whispering, "What is it?"

Blackfoot said nothing, but his lips moving silently as he seemed to memorize a thin line of data at the top of the screen. Jonathan didn't repeat the question but he knew whatever was at the top of the screen was important.

Hands flying over the keyboard again, Blackfoot continued, face hard in concentration. His mouth was a tight line, his eyes like coals lit from within with ghostly thin tendrils of electronic flame. After thirty seconds the screen opened again and Blackfoot typed a solid message. He instantly hit Enter.

"I'm in," he whispered.

Jonathan couldn't keep from asking: "Where are you *in*?"

"London," the Sioux said as if he were physically there. "Looks like I'm in a bank."

Jonathan was confused. "I thought the message was sent from Fincher's office in BCCI to World Finance and back for instructions."

"It was, at first. But I anticipated World Finance's Teletype would relay the message as soon as it was received. This guy hides deep."

Jonathan had never felt so far out of his league and realized Blackfoot's skills had to require some kind of mystical gift.

Suddenly the Sioux froze.

"What is it?"

"I've accessed Bell South's mainframe. I'm trying to nail the destination through the Teletype line but there's another firewall and I don't have time for it." Sweat appeared on the Sioux's brow. "All right. I'm gonna retreat and use the SMART code authorized for FIN-CEN."

"What's FIN-CEN?"

"Don't worry about it. It's just a system that has access to all the banks in the world. It monitors stuff like financial transactions."

"But this wasn't a financial transaction."

"No. But the SMART code got me into the bank. Got me past the firewall. Now I'm scanning to see if I can access the phone modem to see if they're sending the message out again."

They waited two, three, five minutes. Blackfoot's concentration never wavered. He didn't even seem to blink; his hands were poised like withheld lighting over the keyboard. Finally, he shook his head in frustration.

"This isn't right," he said. "It should have gone out by now to another destination. Should have been forwarded to where Phantom is hiding."

Jonathan was catching on. "He's not there, Blackfoot. This guy's not going to take a message from the bank. It's another attempt at misdirection. That's why they call him Phantom."

"But why would Fincher send the message to London if he's not there?"

"Oh, he's in London," Jonathan replied and leaned back,

resting now. "He's just not at the *bank*. The bank is cover for something else, like always. They probably had a courier waiting to carry the physical message to where Phantom has gone to earth." He rubbed the back of his neck. "We're still a long way from catching this guy."

There was a disappointed air.

"Why do you think he's in England?"

"He's there." Jonathan paused grimly before he added in a faint voice. "Somewhere..."

Blackfoot must have noticed something in the tone. He was watching Jonathan carefully. "What is it?"

"Nothing," Jonathan shrugged, a bit too obviously. "I was born in London. I never wanted to go back."

"Why?"

"It's not important."

"You got family there?"

"No."

Silence.

"I'm sorry, man. I didn't know."

"It's in the past," Jonathan said softly.

Blackfoot tried to change the subject from family. "Okay, got any friends over there?"

"Yeah," Jonathan said quietly. "An old admiral out of MI6, a guy who worked with my father. He's probably eighty, by now. I haven't talked to him in a long time."

"What's his name?"

"Haitfield."

Jonathan had no compulsions talking about the admiral's background. "When I visited him in London in the late seventies he told me that he'd worked real close with my father until he was killed by..."

"By Charon," Blackfoot said, simply.

No surprise—it had already been said in a dozen ways. There was a silence that lengthened until Blackfoot looked back at the screen: "What was it you said?...An unfinished game?"

Jonathan stared at nothing in the room.

Charon's skull-face emerging from darkness.

"...feels unfinished."

Three hours later, clear of the impound lot, the Israelis and General Ariel Ben Canaan settled into a low-budget hotel room on Broad Avenue, near Palisades Park.

Entering the room last, with Webster slightly in front of him, Logan looked around carefully to inventory their arsenal of weapons and surveillance equipment. There was almost no contingency that this team had not anticipated.

First, their selection of accommodations was superior in its inferiority. Instead of the Hilton, they'd rented two adjoining corner rooms at a seedy hotel. They was no security and its mere location guaranteed a slow police response. They also enjoyed the luxury of knowing that they could pay a little extra not to be remembered. And, tactically, the location was perfect.

It was centered beside a two-hundred-acre park within easy access of Highways 93 and 46 and Interstate 95, all offering a rich choice of retreats. Also, should the need arise, they could be inside the gates of Teterboro Airport within fifteen minutes. And Logan didn't doubt they had a boat waiting on the Hudson, less than a mile to the east—probably a three-minute run for this crew. Comprehensive and efficient—they'd covered every contingency.

Logan stared at Canaan as the general gave terse instructions to his men, apparently telling them where to take the bodies of the fallen Mossad agents. Then he barked orders to another agent, a young woman of astonishing beauty who immediately began typing messages into a laptop computer hooked into a modem.

Seconds later, two of the Mossad left the room and Logan knew they were going downstairs to the van that had rushed them from the impound lot—an utterly forgettable, beige van that contained the bodies of their two comrades.

Webster loosened his tie and poured himself a drink as Logan took it all in. Then, finishing with his instructions to the girl, Canaan smiled: "Are you surprised by any of this, Special Agent Logan?"

"Just call me Logan."

"Yes," Canaan said, the smile continuing. "A man without pretense, even when forced to play games."

"I've eaten enough lies for fifty lifetimes, general. And I've played plenty of games, just not when my life was on the line. When my life is on the line, I treat people a little different. And right now I want to know what's going on," Logan replied matter-of-factly.

Webster dropped two cubes of ice into his drink. "I've told Logan what you told me, general. But he's got his own questions."

"Questions?" Canaan looked back, smiling. "Yes; I expect that he would. You are an exceptional detective, Logan. We are fortunate they gave you this—"

"*Investigation?*" Logan stepped forward, daring the Israeli to tell the truth. "This isn't an *investigation*. It's a shooting gallery!" He walked around the unmoving old man as if he were circling a rattlesnake. "What are you people doing here?" Logan added. "Why do you want Silman so badly?"

"We have studied him for years."

"That's not what I asked."

Canaan stared a moment, then, "You are quite capable, detective."

Logan pressed, "I want an explanation, general. Why does Israel want Silman so much?"

"I have told you all that we know."

"No, you haven't."

"Why do you say this?" Canaan frowned, almost angry. "We have already told you about Silman. His arms shipments represent a threat to Israel. I have told you about—"

"Charon?" said Webster.

"Yes, Charon." Canaan pronounced the name with venom. "Yes, that is his name. But, to proceed, we have told you all that we know of Silman."

"Israel wouldn't go to all this trouble to find Silman if you didn't know more than you've told us." Logan raised his hands in supplication to either the tile ceiling or God. "Good Lord, *everybody* represents a threat to Israel! You'd have to kill two-thirds of the Middle East if that was your reason!"

"There is war and then there is *war!*" The Israeli general scowled. "We are always in conflict, yes. But the weapons Silman has provided our enemies are capable of destoying our Air Force! Entire tank batallions could be lost in minutes! That is *war*, Agent Logan! Not random shots fired into a government building!"

Logan was unaffected by the passion. "You're not selling it, general. Everything about you says you're lying. Why don't you try the truth?"

Webster was smiling.

There was a discomforting pause. "Perhaps I have not shared more," Canaan began, "because I am a professional. I do not offer conjecture. And I try to stay within the parameters of what is a hallowed secret for my agency. We do not offer surreptitious intelligence as fact or even hypotheses. It would be irresponsible for me to vaunt unverifiable speculation."

"Suspicions lead to clues, general." Logan was suddenly still. "And clues are how we're going to find Silman."

Abruptly, the woman leaned back. She seemed to possess an intensity of focus that caused her dark eyes to glaze. Logan couldn't imagine her smiling.

"Silman will die for what he has done," she said.

"Daniela!" Canaan shouted. He added something harsh and stern in Hebrew, but the woman named Daniela didn't blink. Her gaze at Logan was solid black light.

Staring into those coal eyes, Logan knew this woman was dedicated to killing Silman, and he wondered what horrendous price she would pay to see it done. But her voice said it for her; it was hoarse and ravaged, as if she had pushed herself again and again to limits that no one should endure.

Breathing heavily, Canaan was gravely disapproving when he turned back to Logan. "What you ask is difficult," he said. "You are disinterring the bones of my people. I am not certain that I shall tell you, no matter what you threaten."

Logan glanced at Webster and they made a silent agreement without words. Neither of them would back down. Logan gazed at Canaan without any compassion.

"I see," the general said, glancing at both. "Gentlemen, if there will be no more secrets, I *demand* reciprocity! For you do not know how the knowledge that I'm about to share will change your lives. If you did, you might well recall your demand and be grateful that you were spared what *we* have not been spared!"

Daniela stood, focusing dead on Logan.

"Tell him."

At her movement, Logan saw how truly, stunningly beautiful she was. She was both athletic and darkly sensuous, but it was a veneer over a consuming hate wrapped around a mind and will that was anything but beautiful.

Canaan was angry, but he did not look at her again. Then Logan walked over to the desk where Webster stood and poured two drinks. He handed one to Canaan and stood in the middle of the room. It was meant as something of a peace offering, which is how Canaan took it. He sat heavily, suddenly seeming very old and tired. He stared into his glass a long moment, then sighed, nodded.

"When a deed is dark enough," he began, with a solemn sip, "a justice beyond the law of man can be required by God."

The room was still.

Logan knew that he didn't have to press anymore. The general was going to talk, and what would happen now would probably change all their lives. He took a sip—a heavy one.

"Whom?" Canaan continued gravely, as if the statement were long overdue. "Whom did Silman serve?" he asked. "That is the question which must be answered."

Logan's eyes narrowed. "Silman served himself."

"No," the general shook his head, smiled sadly. "Here, your great detective skills fail you, Agent Logan. No man can serve himself and rise to Silman's position of power. They may eventually break from those whom they served. But they did, once, serve someone. So the question remains; whom did Silman once serve?"

"I haven't the foggiest." Logan answered honestly.

"Of course you don't. Nor is it to your shame, for you have only been hunting this man three days. We have hunted him for twenty years, and even we do not know. But..." The pause stretched until Logan thought the general was finished, "...we *do* have a suspicion as to *how* it began. And that is why we are willing to violate American law—*any* law—to hunt this man down. And kill him."

It was best, thought Logan, to let the general say the rest without commentary.

"Do you know, Special Agent Logan, how much gold and art and precious stones were stolen from the Jewish people during World World II?"

For some reason, Logan wished he did.

"No," he said.

"Strange, is it not," proceeded Canaan, "that Hitler took so much treasure from those he considered to be so inferior? Perhaps Israel was not so inferior, after all, in the mind of the monster."

Logan knew there was nothing he could say to make the atmosphere more comfortable. But he noticed that Webster was finally beginning to relax even though his face was more somber, darker. He suspected it was because Webster, like him, was realizing that Canaan withheld no more cards—this was the last.

"When we first investigated Silman after the death of Justinian Falken, we discovered a great deal about his early activities." Canaan's voice was without stress; a man speaking plainly, simply. "We discovered that much of the gold he had smuggled had been smelted in a form that concealed its origin. But he could not hide the origin of the art—the paintings, the sculptures—that he also smuggled."

Anger entered Canaan's face. "In the art, we found the first faint trace of where Silman's empire began." He smiled. "Yes, during a search that was sometimes postponed for years, because my country had other campaigns to fight, we managed to discover when Silman's art had been collected."

"The Holocaust," said Logan, for some reason choosing to take the burden off the general. He didn't know, exactly, why he was not surprised by the revelation. Perhaps because the Holocaust was the only logical explanation for Canaan's intense passion.

"Silman will die for what he has done," said Daniela, and Canaan smiled at her words.

"Daniela is passionate," he added, and then the smile faded. "Her grandparents, the parents of her mother, died at Dachau. Her mother, herself only a child, was used by Joseph Mengele in a medical experiment, which she miraculously survived. Her eyes were injected with an acid meant to change their color. As a consequence, she was blinded and lived the rest of her life in agonizing pain until she died not long ago. Daniela's father, also, was in a camp. But he survived because he was a strong, quiet boy, and managed to resist detection." Canaan did not move and his next words froze everyone else even more. "Her husband was killed while serving his term in the army. And Daniela, hunting Silman, has lost her most precious blood. Yes, gentlemen...Her little one was taken from her by Charon, as a warning."

Logan bowed his head: So, Charon had killed her child. After a moment, he sighed heavily, and purposefully didn't look at Daniela's frozen form. He resolved to keep his concentration from being swayed by the impact of what was being said. He couldn't allow compassion to upset his focus.

"So you discovered Silman was smuggling art stolen from the Jews during World War II," he continued. "I'm sorry, general, but I'm not familiar with who obtained the art after the war."

"No one *officially* obtained it," Canaan said forthrightly. "The gold and art of Israel was apparently destroyed."

"Apparently not."

"No," Canaan smiled bitterly. "Apparently not."

"All right: Who would have used Silman to see the gold and art on the black market?"

"We do not know," Canaan answered.

Then, slowly, he reached beneath his coat to withdraw a Luger—a World War II-era pistol with a Nazi SS Swastika boldly stamped into the black steel.

"But when I find Silman..." He pensively studied the Nazi Swastika, "I shall kill him with this. Then I shall leave it on his body—a message to his friends that we shall find them all, and they shall all die, in the end."

Jonathan and Blackfoot were half asleep when Logan turned the key. Wisely, Jonathan had left the overhead lights on all night and was already on his feet with the shotgun aimed at the door when Logan entered.

"Turn off the light," Logan said as he set pizza and drinks on the desk.

Jonathan turned it off. "Did you see Webster?"

"Webster and then some."

"What happened?"

"I'll tell you about it later."

Logan sat down heavily, his face sweat-streaked or rain-streaked, and he seemed depressed and fatigued. He rested with his forearms on knees, still holding the semiautomatic.

"What'd you boys get?" he asked, eyes flat and sullen. "For your own health and well-being, boys, don't tell me you don't have anything for me. That's all I've got to say."

Blackfoot grinned, "Fincher made contact with someone. I think it was Phantom."

Logan was skeptical. "How do you know it was Phantom? That's *our* code name. Not theirs."

"Fincher sent a coded transmission to World Finance but this time he used an encryption disk."

"NSA?"

"CIA."

"How can you tell for sure?"

Blackfoot shrugged. "It's philosophical. Each agency's Black Light guys operate from a family mind-set. Once you've seen enough codes, you can read their personalities." He paused. "It's kinda like literature. After you've read enough authors, you can sort of guess who wrote something without looking at the cover."

Logan grunted, "So what'd it say?"

"I think it told us where Phantom's hiding."

Suddenly Logan had a wild image of dragging Phantom from his rich-man's bed in the middle of the night and throwing him into the sights of the Mossad. But he hadn't heard anything yet to convince him that was the destination of the telefax. He reached out: "Let me see what it is."

Blackfoot handed over the printout. "I told you they'd trace my invasions of World Finance and BCCI."

Withdrawing a penlight from his shirt pocket, Logan shone the light down on the page. He read with a slow smile crossing his face: "Unauthorized and illegal intrusion of World Finance Account confirmed. Suggest indefinite hold at London safe-house for Omega until sanitation procedures are complete."

Logan laughed out loud. "We got him now, boys." He studied the top of the page, searching for a sending and receiving code but there was nothing. He looked sharply at Blackfoot. "Did you get the—"

"Yeah," the Sioux answered. "It was sent through World Finance, sort of like a South Central Bell connection to put in another firewall, then wired overseas."

"A lending house?"

"A bank. A big one."

"You're sure it's London?"

"Consolidated Bank of England. But the message didn't go out again from there. So we think it was probably taken by physical courier from the lending house to where Phantom is holed up." Blackfoot revealed exhaustion for the first time. "I agree with Jonathan," he added. "I don't think Phantom's going to be receiving electronic messages where he's staying. He doesn't want tracks."

Logan was nodding. "Well, he left some tracks tonight." He stood. "All right, boys, eat up and we'll get out to the airport. We're going to England."

Frazier took the sheet of paper from the courier's hand. A red sky of morning—*sailor take warning*—hazed the horizon as he closed the door and re-entered the castle located in the oldest district of Waltham Forest, northeast of London.

Dressed in brown corduroy pants with the sleeves of his dark blue sailing shirt rolled to the elbows, he moved back through the 117-room mansion to observe Lazarus Dumont casually pacing the floor, smoking one of his thin black cigars.

Dumont turned as he entered: "Yes, Frazier?"

"They have done something we did not expect." Frazier handed the note and waited patiently for Dumont to read. Shaking his head, Dumont laid it down.

"The fool," he muttered, moving before the fire in a brief flash of uncharacteristic emotion before, just as suddenly, the emotion was gone. "Contacting me was exactly what they wanted him to do." He sighed. "It is sometimes difficult to endure such cretins. Even though I am accustomed to it, it does not become easier."

Frazier waited in silence.

"Contact Charon and discover if he has been successful," Dumont continued. "If he has not, advise him to return. And tell him I wish to speak with him as soon as he arrives."

"It is not yet morning in America," Frazier replied. "Until then, he will hunt. It would be best to wait until dawn to make contact at the safehouse.

Dumont considered a moment. "Yes...Of course, you're correct." He paced before the hearth, cupping his chin, one hand on his hip. "So what do we do from here?"

"We have several options."

"Continue."

"First, we post men on Bond Street and Park Lane to watch the American Embassy. We will have all the entrances covered, should Logan's team contact the FBI Legat."

"But Woodard is dead."

"Webster ordered a replacement—Mark Hooper, the agent in charge of Strike Six."

Dumont laughed. "Webster is so very cunning. He knows that Hooper is a lamentably honest FBI agent. Just as he knows Strike Six is crippled. And he knows that, in England, Hooper might be able to damage us." He seemed to meditate on the thin ribbon of smoke spiraling up from the cigar. "Does Webster know yet that Logan and his men are coming to England?"

"I don't know," Frazier rumbled. "They are using precautions. But Webster will know before they leave the country."

"Yes...yes. Webster is a worthy adversary. It has been a while since I dealt with anyone who approached my equal."

"There is also Logan."

"I have not forgotten."

"He is dangerous, Mr. Dumont. More dangerous than you might realize."

"I realize everything, Frazier. That is how I survived these years. I know that Logan has wisely played every move. But there are many more moves to make, and he shall not finish this game. Neither Webster, nor Logan, nor the rest of his team. If Charon cannot complete the task, then *you* shall complete it. But Logan shall soon be removed from the board." He refilled his glass. "Next option."

"We will try and pick up Logan and his men up at the Embassy and follow them. That should make Charon's job easier."

A wave. "Charon works alone, Frazier. You know that. He is somewhat unbalanced in that respect...among other things." He studied the mantle. "What is the best option for terminating this entire investigation?"

"A sacrifice," Frazier said dully. "We can throw the Justice Department a bone that they can use to satisfy public outrage. We can give them convictions with World Finance and instruct our man in Treasury to contain it. It is doable. The Senate will not allow the situation to progress beyond the initial prosecution of the company. There will be little collateral damage."

"Yes, that is an option." Dumont inhaled deeply on the cigar. "But I think it will be necessary to satisfy the American press with a larger catch than my vassals at World Finance."

Frazier said nothing.

"Contact our friends in the Justice Department," Dumont said finally. "Inform them to tell this...I'm sorry, Frazier, what is the name of this FBI team?"

"Strike Six."

"Yes," Dumont nodded, "Strike Six. Tell Justice to leak documents to Strike Six that give credence to suspicions warranting an information search that will confirm that World Finance has no money in BCCI. Inform our New York judicial people to authorize a search of World Finance's account. It is no longer a secret, so we must use it to our advantage. Inform Justice we are willing to sacrifice BCCI. But only for their continued protection. They must insure that the situation will be contained."

"I'm sure they will agree," Frazier rumbled. "But once BCCI is implicated, we cannot be certain what will happen. Success breeds success. And there are enemies in Congress that we cannot control. There is a chance that an implication of BCCI's participation will lead to further complications. There is even a chance that someone will discover BCCI is ultimately owned by our friends in the Middle East. Then the American people will discover that the largest, most powerful bank in America has foreign ownership, violating American law. And if that happens, Mr. Dumont, we will be forced to buy our way out of prosecution. It may cost us several hundred million dollars. Maybe even a billion."

Dumont waved vaguely. "A billion dollars isn't what it used to be, Frazier. It is merely a sacrifice we can make to protect our greater resources." He was contemplative. "Contact Agansi Agnossi in Saudi Arabia. Inform him that the situation with BCCI is rapidly deteriorating and that he may be forced to take ultimate responsibility for the foreign ownership. Advise him that the fines and penalties shall not exceed one billion dollars. But if they do, we will pay them."

"It will be done."

Frazier inwardly cursed his treacherous mind. For so long, he had been able to avoid these situations and decisions, which preyed on his thoughts at night. He would reflect on the nature of good and evil. If only it were so black and white. The government was corrupt, so he felt no remorse helping Dumont cheat the system, and Dumont did what he had to in order to survive. Life came to him in shades of gray. He wished he had the faith and convictions of Justinian. He hadn't thought of his old friend in so long, preferring not to relive the past, but lately he had been thinking about his old friend often. Justinian had chosen the other path, and sometimes Frazier wondered if he had made the wrong choice, regardless of the consequences.

"Good." There was a studious silence. "Contact Justice... no, wait. Contact our people in the White House and tell them to closely utilize resources to oversee this affair. Tell them to make the requisite careful appointments. Inform them that fines for BCCI are not to exceed one billion. Then leak information to the American press that BCCI is involved in covert but legal CIA activities. The American press will leap upon it and their first conclusions will lead them—it is too easy to lead them by their herd mentality."

"A good decision, Mr. Dumont. It is better to sacrifice World Finance and BCCI than to compromise your anonymity. There are those who seek regress."

"There always will be, Frazier."

"And Charon?"

"Charon is not finished. I believe he will have the advantage in London. It is the ground he knows best."

"But if he fails?"

Dumont laughed, tossing his cigar into the fire.

"There is no danger, Frazier. The Americans will never drag me into the daylight." He smiled into flames. "What they have done in the dark is far too dangerous to ever see the light of day."

※ ❋ ※

It was almost six o'clock when Webster returned Logan's page at the airport. They were studiously avoiding cell phones, which could be targeted or taped. The rule was to use only landlines set up by pagers.

"Is this a secure line?" Logan asked. He had one hour to catch their flight. Webster had returned to Washington to endure a long line of wrath and buy them some time.

"It's secure for the *moment*." Webster's voice was hoarse, as if he'd been shouting. "But it's getting out of hand, Logan. I guess you've noticed gas prices skyrocketing."

"I passed a newsstand."

"So you heard that over five billion in Fannie Mae bonds are endangered again, consequently threatening about thirty million mom-and-pop retirement villages that live off the tax-free interest."

"Yeah, I heard."

Webster grunted. "Then I guess you know your picture is being plastered all over creation, too."

"Uh huh."

"But you're not worried about it."

"Nah," Logan drawled. "People don't pay attention to pictures unless it's right in front of them when you walk by. And this guy is gonna keep demolishing American companies and bonds and the gold market and whatever else until we either leave him alone or kill him. That's what it's come to."

"So what'd you decide?"

"London."

Webster didn't reveal any surprise. "I had a feeling this shebang might end in London. I assigned Hooper to the Legat post until a permanent SAC officer can be appointed."

"Good move. I'll call Hooper tonight with a progress report. And we'll need serious weapons. Get in touch with our Israeli friends and have one of them meet us on Delta 456, landing at Heathrow. Tell them to be discreet. We'll need a safehouse where we can get weapons, food, and some rest."

"I'll take care of it." Webster's voice intensified. "Logan, listen to me. The director called me last night and said they've been tracing your withdrawals on the operational account. They know every place you've been. They're one step behind you."

"I figured on that. But I don't care if they know where I've been. I just don't want them to know where I'm going." Logan was struck by a sudden thought. "Are you in any trouble because of the shootout at the impound lot?"

"I'll handle that. You have bigger problems. The director had to agree on a time period with your team."

"A time period?"

"Yeah," Webster was talking quickly, as if he knew he could never explain all the complications. "He agreed that you and your men could stay active 'til tomorrow night. He defended it on grounds of agent safety. The president didn't like it but he didn't have a choice. So as of this moment you've got less than twenty-four hours."

Logan leaned his forehead against the phone: *from bad to worse.* "What else?"

"There's a dispute over the operational fund for your team and it's seriously complicating things. I think that by midday tomorrow Justice will shut down the account."

"Shut down my account?" Logan couldn't believe it. "On what grounds? They're giving me until tomorrow night to finish the investigation! How can they shut down the account before then?"

"It's a crock. But Justice is claiming the money wasn't taken from the director's discretionary fund. They're claiming it was wrongfully withdrawn from the equipment budget and that it's going to take five to six days to straighten it out."

"We'll be dead in *two* days."

"They know that."

Logan was silent, then, "This means I'm close."

"Yeah, it means you're close! So find him!"

"Is CI-3 still on standby?"

"Yes."

"Who's got authorization to activate them?"

"I do."

"*You* do? You don't have to clear it with the director?"

"Fletcher issued an edict yesterday that granted me Extraordinary Power to scramble the unit if I corroborated a cause of international provocation jeopardizing American financial security. Quote, unquote." Webster paused, mumbling, "Both sides are pulling out the heavy artillery. Winner take all, no prisoners, no mercy."

That was all that needed to be said.

"Fire 'em up," said Logan.

Using every lie and implied threat he could conjure or suggest, Logan managed to withdraw three hundred thousand dollars in bonds from a bank inside JFK and quickly returned to Jonathan and Blackfoot.

They were hanging close because they had ditched their weapons in the Hudson. Their plan was to avoid a conflict by stealth, speed, and strength of numbers.

"All right," Logan slid into a booth, "after we land in London we'll be armed. Then we're going to hit this guy."

"How are we going to get weapons?" Jonathan asked.

"We've got friends," was all Logan said before looking at Blackfoot. "You got everything you need?"

"Yeah."

The second flight call.

"I'm separated from you boys on the flight," Logan said curtly. "But I want one of you awake at all times. When we get to London we'll pick up some weapons and bed down for the night before we get into this thing neck-deep tomorrow."

"How long is the flight?" Blackfoot asked. His words were a little slurred, and Jonathan remembered that the Sioux had probably been working nonstop for almost three days.

"Seven hours," Logan said. "If you feel yourself going out, let Jonathan know. I don't want to get to London to find both of you dead in your seats."

"Charon won't be on this flight," said Jonathan. "He'll have his own means of traveling."

"No kidding," Logan looked around. "Probably a coffin filled with dirt."

The last call.

Logan stood.

"Showtime, boys."

Matsumo found the American Embassy in London before midday. He stood in the fifty-acre park across the street and stared over the building, knowing that others were probably staring back. But the park bustled with activity, and he had done nothing illegal or even suspicious.

Before he left the FBI Academy in Quantico he had discovered where the FBI entered the building and he could see the entrance, located on the far north side. He was hoping that, if Jonathan were in London, he would have to make contact sooner or later with the resident FBI legal attaché—a desperate move, the only move.

Seated at the pond teeming with golden trout, Matsumo began feeding the fish while straining his eyes to observe the entrance, scouting for Jonathan's outline.

Matsumo wasn't afraid of his own death. He had made peace with God long ago. Even though he was able to bring his body under subjection—he was a warrior—there was something missing. Until that day soon after he moved to America when, vaguely homesick, he went to a Japanese church to hear his native language. At least, that's what he thought drew him in. Really, he never could say what made him slip into the back pew. Then he heard the preacher speak on peace, the one thing he had strived for, in all his fighting. As he told Jonathan, a death must be right—but in that moment, he knew it wasn't the physical death that mattered, but the state of the soul when it happened.

He tried to ignore the slow, gathering November wind that crept over him with a strange dread—not dread for his own life, to be sure. But dread of something else—something he could not identify.

He had no weapon, since he could not bring one through Customs without a Writ of Appeal from the State Department. But it did not matter, he thought, as he caught a glimpse of his brooding, hulking image in the dark surface of the pond.

His right hand clenched into a fist.

No, he had no weapon.

He did not need one.

As the jet climbed steeply above the storm, Jonathan watched winter swallow the city, the world. Then the plane was level and people began moving and he heard Blackfoot speak, a faintly nervous timbre in his words. "What are our chances?"

Jonathan didn't look. "I don't know. But Charon isn't more than one step behind us, I guarantee you that."

"I didn't think there were really people like him in this

world," Blackfoot said quietly. "He's like Death, man. The Grim Reaper. A walking skeleton or something. You think someone will call him off?"

There was no hesitation in Jonathan's reply. "The only way we'll get to Phantom is over Charon's dead body."

Blackfoot didn't take that very well. "Well, just how good do you think he really is? I mean, there's three of us and only one of him. That makes a difference, right?"

"No," Jonathan frowned. "Charon is a master at this. If we're together, he'll separate us. Or he'll hit us from a distance, a sniper attack if he has to. But he'll save me for last."

"Is he that much better than you?" Blackfoot asked the question as if he knew more than he would reveal. Jonathan turned, not knowing what was truly meant.

"I don't know," he said, surprised by his next comment. "He's beat me before. When I was at the top of my game."

Blackfoot said nothing, then looked at the carry-on at his feet. Inside, the lightning-fast laptop computer was stashed. And it was as if they both understood something else.

There was a silence like the silence that precludes the creation of a world and Jonathan knew everything was leading him in this direction—London, Charon, vengeance, rage. It had been a long time since he had played a game of chess, a game of death. And he had a game of death to finish.

"Does that thing have a chess program in it?"

"Yeah," Blackfoot replied. "Grandmaster. I downloaded it after we talked about chess." He paused. "They say it's unbeatable."

Jonathan frowned.

"Let's see."

Chapter Fourteen

Jonathan was bone-tired and hungover as he climbed the steps of the safehouse, located in the Soho district of North London. Guarding the rear, he was behind Blackfoot as Logan knocked on the door.

His accumulated wounds were nagging him constantly, now. The painkillers were keeping the edge down, but the codeine was making him jumpy. He was grateful the flight had been dull and uneventful. But at Customs it had been an electrifying moment when a man approached fast, slipping Logan a note.

Immediately the man moved past them and Logan glanced down. Then he turned to them and nodded and Jonathan knew the Mossad had made contact.

The streets of Soho teemed with every nationality but British, the perfect place for a Mossad safehouse. The architecture, however, resembled older sections of New York: faintly gothic, old and new worlds combined and sturdy. Jonathan tried to remember how Logan had explained how the team would be safer working *with* these people than against them. And, though he did sound convincing, the words gave him little personal comfort. These were some very dangerous people and he was, even now, unconvinced of their agendas. Or vendettas.

A gray-haired man, two agents, and a stunningly beautiful woman immediately answered the door. The woman had a cut-down Desert Eagle on her right hip and a long, slender fighting knife in a sheath beneath her left shoulder. She also wore a row of anti-personnel grenades on her belt—heavy hardware when you're not in a combat situation. But she had an atmosphere of unending combat.

Her face, perfectly framed by raven-black hair, was stoic and concentrated. The only hint in her, at all, of emotion, was a cold anger burning deep in her dark eyes. Jonathan could imagine that anger burning even when she slept.

They moved to a room stacked with counterintelligence equipment—laser microphones, pistols, radios, Galil sniper rifles, Uzis, and ultra-generation night-vision goggles the size of Raybans. There were anti-personnel and stun grenades, tear gas and gas masks, and a row of kevlar vests. General Ariel Ben Canaan gestured generously: "Take whatever you need."

Logan picked up a SIG Sauer 226, the same gun he had used in New York before tossing it—with the solemnity of interring an old friend—into the Hudson River.

Jonathan also selected a SIG. He racked the slide, then tore it down to examine the frame and guide rod and spring. In seconds, feeling the strange focus of the woman, he reassembled it in a lightning-fast series of clicks to slide it unceremoniously in the belt of his pants behind his right kidney.

Blackfoot shoved a .38 in his belt and a handful of rounds in his pocket. Then he picked up a small, concealable five-shot shotgun. "A witness protection shotgun," he said as he looked at Jonathan. "The Marshals use this thing. Real effective."

"Take whatever you desire," Canaan nodded. "We are all soldiers, here. And I know that soldiers, from superstition, prefer weapons they have used before."

"From reflex," grunted Jonathan.

Canaan smiled. "Yes; there is that, also."

Jonathan gathered six magazines and two boxes of ammo and turned to leave, but couldn't help casting a glance at the woman. She had not moved from her position beside the door.

For some reason, he was attracted to her. But he knew it was just her beauty, because she was cold as ice. Then Blackfoot shoved a full box of 12-gauge rounds into the pocket of his oversized plaid shirt, standing back.

Canaan asked, "Would you like to rest first? Or talk?"

"I'm too tired to care," Logan mumbled, rubbed his eyes. "What do you boys say?"

Jonathan shrugged. Blackfoot was staring at the wall. "My feet hurt," he said numbly.

"That does it." Logan shook his head impatiently. "Poor ol' Blackfoot's so wasted he can't even answer a *direct* question. Where can we lay down?"

"Anywhere you choose," Canaan gestured. "There are two bedrooms on the bottom floor and three upstairs. And as I said, we shall remain on guard until you awaken."

"When did your people sleep?" Logan asked.

"We have our own jet. We slept on the flight."

Logan gave a wistful sigh, then, "You two pick a couple of bedrooms downstairs. I'm gonna bed down up top. You can do what you want, but I'm gonna eat when I wake up."

"Whatever," Blackfoot said, and moved toward the back. He didn't even close the door as he went into a room and Jonathan heard him collapse on the bed. Jonathan turned to the general, blinking against overpowering fatigue.

"Do you mind if I look around?" He was using anger to keep his edge over the pain and drugs, but he was losing the battle. There was simply too much fatigue, too many nights without sleep. He couldn't keep it up much longer.

"Of course," Canaan nodded. "Take whatever security precautions you deem necessary." He gestured to the woman. "I only ask that you allow Daniela to accompany you. There are some parts of the premises that are rigged to prevent attack. Mercury switches with C-4 on the windows, so forth. Nothing someone with your credentials would fail to understand, but you are tired. An imprudent step could result in injury, even death." His smile was becoming.

"I'll be careful." Jonathan turned to Daniela with an equal measure of coldness. "You ready?"

She stood away from the wall, utterly efficient and disciplined and nothing else. But her eyes focused on Jonathan with a barely perceptible measure of what seemed like respect.

"I'm ready."

◉ ◉ ◉

Webster stopped at the door of his office, staring at his assistant. He knew disaster when it saw it.

The phone was blinking constantly and he realized she'd turned off the ringer. Calls were stacking up, but she didn't look like she'd be answering any of them too soon. Her mouth opened to say something.

"I know." Webster continued forward. "The director's been paging me for an hour. Get me a secure line."

"That's not all," she muttered, reaching for the phone. "The NSA has called eight times. And certain *persons* have been harassing me from their outhouse on the Hill. I told them you'd died." She smiled sweetly. "You don't want to know what they said. But don't expect flowers."

"Don't worry."

Webster went through the door and immediately the phone rang. Without sitting down he picked it up to hear FBI

Director Conrad Fletcher's voice once more. "Richard, do you know what kind of pressure I'm under?"

"Yes, sir," Webster responded calmly, "I appreciate what kind of pressure you're under."

"Did you find Logan?"

"Yes, sir."

There was a remarkable pause. *"And?"*

"Logan is close, sir. But he needs two days."

Webster heard Fletcher stand to his feet. He imagined that the director was gesticulating dramatically; a shame the theatrics were wasted without an audience.

"That's impossible! I've tried to play the scenario of agent survival to buy time but the pressure is incredible! Incredible! I..." Webster heard him say something harsh to his assistant. "Oh my God," he whispered as he came back, "this maniac just shut down oil production from the Sultan of Brunea! He's...he's done *what*? Stock of half the fortune five hundred just went through the floor?" He paused. "That's *my* stock! Is that possible? I'll kill this maniac *myself!*"

Webster nodded though no one was in the room. "He's not done yet, sir. Only one of us is walking away from this. He's going to destroy our economy or we're going to take him down."

The words didn't seem to register with Fletcher. "This place has gone insane," he muttered. "Richard, listen closely. They've agreed to give Logan until tomorrow night. But the president wants me back on the Hill."

"For what, sir?"

"Like I would know!" Fletcher erupted, then paused, apparently to calm. "Stay in touch, Richard."

Webster sensed an idea even though there was no time to develop it. He hesitated to say anything only because he didn't like to speak before he had examined the complications of a potentially serious decision, but there was no time for contemplation. Sometimes, when things are bad enough, you have to choose instinct over reason.

"Webster?" came Fletcher's voice. "Did you hear me? I said stay close because we're going to—"

"Director Fletcher," Webster broke in, "does the president know you've given me Extraordinary Power to activate CI-3?"

A subdued pause.

"No. He does not. By policy only I can activate CI-3. I granted you Extraordinary Power because of the covert conditions of this operation. Nor do I think the powers-that-be should know of it."

"If you have to make promises," Webster said, feeling sweat on his palms, "don't tell them CI-3 won't be activated. Just tell them that you yourself will, under no conditions, activate the team. Then tell them that Logan can't be called off for another day because he won't be making contact with us until then. Buy us *one day*, sir."

The silence on the far end of the line stretched so long that Webster thought he'd overstepped the bounds of their relationship, at last. He felt perspiration chill on his forehead and neck.

"That's a dangerous gambit," Fletcher said finally. "The president realizes that CI-3 is a tactical team more dangerous than Delta. And he has legitimate concern over how they are utilized."

Webster went for broke. "Director Fletcher, three of our men have been pushed into traffic as far out as they can go. We cannot, we *must* not, leave them. We will find this man and shut down what's he doing, but the FBI has *never* left an agent in the field! I'll take full responsibility for anything that happens. I'll put it in writing and it'll be on your desk in an hour."

Nothing was said, though Webster heard the assistant's voice in the background and Fletcher responding angrily. Finally he came back to the phone, but his voice was calmer.

"Don't worry about the memo, Richard. I'll stand behind whatever you do. I just don't know what the president is going to do."

Webster closed his eyes, leaning with one hand on the desk. He didn't even want to hear his own question, much less the answer from the other end. "What are you going to do?" he asked.

There was a grunt, heavy with contempt. "Well," Fletcher said slowly, "I don't know how we can call someone off if we can't find them." There was a background of colliding voices. "This is what I'm going to do, Richard. And this is my last card because none of us can take much more of this. I'm going to tell the president that this is an internal FBI situation and that the FBI cannot be ordered to violate *legal* and *binding* policies and procedures by abandoning agents in life-threatening situations. I'm going to tell him that if he *insists* on terminating the team before tomorrow night I will have this staggeringly mismanaged fiasco brought before an open meeting of the Senate Intelligence Subcommittee. I think he'll understand that it can't get worse than that."

"Do you think that'll keep Logan's team operational until tomorrow night?"

"I don't know." Fletcher answered. "I'll be throwing a lot of weight around and burning a lot of favors. I believe that I can pull it off, but I've got a feeling Logan and his men are about to find themselves in a very bad place to be."

"What about CI-3?" Webster pressed.

Ponderous silence.

"Until tomorrow night, Webster."

Hooper settled into London's Kensington office of the FBI and sat down, lighting another cigarette. He was waiting for Logan to make contact. He glanced at his watch—five more hours.

Too long and then some.

Cigarette burning in his fingers, Hooper chewed at a row of sores on the inside of his lip. He was as agitated as he could remember and he had almost turned down this assignment. But then loyalty for his friend had taken over and, in a perverse way, Hooper was glad because he only had six months to go and he didn't want to end it on a coward's note.

A Bureau agent came into the office and Hooper looked up morosely. He had no intentions of revealing anything or even *saying* anything unless he was forced. He was here for one reason—to back up an old friend.

He didn't even plan to be here long enough to get acquainted with any of the men. And when Logan ran this mystery man to ground, he'd catch the first flight home. He'd cite health reasons, debilitation. And as a mucus-cracking, coughing spasm lifted his chest, he knew no one would question it.

"You need anything Mr. Hooper?" the agent asked finally.

"Did Logan call?"

"No, sir, but we're keeping a line clear for him."

"Good man." Hooper took another drag. He spoke through a cloud of smoke. "Keep an eye on it. He's supposed to call at midnight but you can't count on that when people are in the field. They call when they have to or when they can."

"Yes, sir. Anything else?"

"Just keep two men on the horn. Let me know as soon as the call comes in. And if Logan makes contact and somebody neglects to route the call to me immediately, you tell them they're going to be stranded in a shark-infested sea of gloom, doom, and despair."

"Yes, sir."

Hooper nodded. "Get on that line."

Taking the SIG out of the holster, Jonathan entered the bedroom closest to Blackfoot. He had looked in on the Sioux to see him stretched on the bed, feet dangling off the end. The riot shotgun had been leaned against the wall.

With Daniela behind him, Jonathan checked the windows in his room just as he'd checked the others. It was secured with the same set-up; a continuous circuit connector with a mercury-switch backup that would detonate a block of C-4 above the frame.

Architecturally, the house was badly designed for a gunfight. There were too many hallways, doors, connecting passages. If they were hit in this place and it disintegrated to a room-to-room, it would be reflex and speed that determined the winner because there was no way to accurately anticipate movement. But he'd had studied the structure, it was all he could do.

Daniela stood in the doorway of the bedroom.

Jonathan ignored her, but couldn't turn his mind from her, either. It was as if they were two of a kind, each burning with a silent rage that sensed a kindred spirit. Unbuttoning his shirt, he didn't look at her, but he knew she was about to say something. When she spoke, her voice was not angry, as he expected, but quiet, and sad.

"He took something precious from me."

Her voice was not as beautiful as her body. It seemed ravaged and shell-shocked, hinting at a hard price paid for her country. Frowning, Jonathan said nothing. He loosened his shoulder with a painful grimace and he saw her focus on his bandages, the cuts and bruises that discolored his upper body. Some of the contusions had already faded from red-yellow to black, blood dry beneath skin.

"I'm sorry," Jonathan said at last. "I'll try and...make things right."

"Will you arrest him? Or will you kill him?"

Jonathan studied her hauntingly beautiful eyes. He looked down, evading thought. "Do you have a medical kit?"

She hesitated. "I will get it."

In a moment she returned with a medium-sized piece of red luggage. When she opened the top, Jonathan was impressed at the full-blown trauma kit complete with morphine and antibiotics and steroids and enough syringes and medical instruments to stock a small emergency room cabinet.

"I will do this," she said, businesslike.

Quickly—so quickly, in fact—that Jonathan realized she must have been trained as a medic, she taped a fresh bandage to his side. Then she replaced the tape and unused gauze in the bag. "Do you need anything for pain?" she asked mechanically.

"No."

She walked out, but hesitated at the door. For the briefest moment she seemed vulnerable.

"They say you are the only man who can kill Charon."

Jonathan didn't look up.

"He must die."

"Why do you feel so strongly?"

"He is an enemy of Israel and an enemy of mine," she

began. "He stole...everything from me. My faith. The most precious thing." A long pause. "He killed..."

Jonathan turned his face, watching her. She hesitated longer. Her mouth closed tight. "He has escaped me many times."

He looked down.

"I'll kill him for you...For me."

A moment more, she stood poised in the doorway. It was as if she wanted to say something else, then turned away. Watching her leave, Jonathan felt something he hadn't felt in a long time, if ever.

He knew that in situations of extreme peril people tended to develop emotional attachments that they wouldn't develop normally. It was something that happened because every nerve was raw and easily touched. But he couldn't allow himself to be touched, not even by compassion. Not now. He had a job to do: A man to kill.

Lying back, he remembered the flight from New York, how he'd studied the computer's chessboard a long time, wondering how to open. Then he remembered his father and their games and the nights beside the fireplace, the game before them.

Finally he opened with queen's pawn-three, and the computer reacted with queen's knight. He idiotically covered his pawn with his queen's knight and the computer attacked with a king's bishop to immediately pin the knight. From there, it was all downhill and he lost quickly.

He lost the first three games, underestimating complications and failing to see traps, playing too conservatively. Then he got angry, and on the fourth game he opened by fachetting the white king's bishop, controlling the middle from the side. Then he castled early through the king's rook and launched a full-scale attack with all his men, intending to win by attrition.

He won the fourth game, becoming more cunning and concentrated until he absolutely forgot Blackfoot, the plane, white sky beside him, and everything else. In the fifth game he became even more concentrated, laying traps, baiting the computer to open a line in its defense.

In Jonathan's soul an almost evil determination arose, the strength of cold-blooded rage beneath an equally cold, calculating mind. And he slowly began to relish the war, anticipating every move and knowing his own moves long before he changed the game plan with every heartbeat to rise to the war. Because that's what the game truly was—war. And at its best it was more than a game. It was the merciless and total annihilation of the enemy.

Jonathan didn't lose again. And, closing his eyes as the plane descended, he saw Charon coming for him again, grinning.

Black king...

"Soon," Jonathan whispered at the skeletal image.

"Soon..."

Leaning against the mantle, gazing into the fire with a rose-colored glass of sherry in his hand, Lazarus Dumont seemed a man a hundred years out of time.

His immaculate smoking jacket was bloodred and carefully tailored. His pants were black and perfectly creased to gently touch polished lace-up shoes. Seeming to stand well within nineteenth century England, he was cultured without seeming so, dignified without effort, and nonassuming though his very essence spoke quite plainly of aquiline superiority.

He held a slender black cigar and occasionally glanced at a huge, curving stairway that led to the second floor of the castle. But there was the faintest hint of nervousness as he spoke to Frazier, who stood stoically to the side, absently holding a glass of wine.

"How long before Charon arrives?"

Frazier frowned into his untouched glass.

Dumont was amused. "You are quite calm, Frazier. I do not know why Charon has always disturbed me so. Perhaps because I never know when I might become his next—"

"*Victim*?" Charon intoned from the stairway.

Dumont spilled his drink as he spun, though his face remained expressionless. He glared for a moment at the black figure perched on the stairway like a supernatural bird of prey.

Implacable, Frazier did not move.

Descending the stairs, Charon swept forward. But as he passed Frazier, he hesitated, leaning close to the big man. Frazier gazed somberly across the room.

"*Frazier,*" Charon whispered.

Dead calm, Frazier took a sip of wine. "You're late."

Charon laughed and walked to the fireplace, stopping several feet from the flames. "Why did you summon me? Logan is hiding in London. I have much to do."

Dumont had regained his composure. "I summoned you to discuss this situation, and inform you that Logan will be calling the FBI office in Kensington at midnight. We have a man in the office that will trace the call. Perhaps Hooper will even schedule a meeting with Logan."

Charon smiled. "Very good."

"There must be no mistakes, Charon." Dumont's attitude was suddenly edged. "I have already been forced to sacrifice

BCCI and World Finance—a sacrifice I can survive. But you *must* kill Logan before he finds me."

"Logan and his men have been dead for many days," Charon answered. "They simply do not know it."

"Do you need Frazier to assist you?"

Charon's waved with contempt. "Frazier has compulsions against killing children."

"I do not kill needlessly," Frazier said softly, the tone of warning evident.

As if he were forced to again umpire a dispute between warring relatives, Dumont walked away from the mantle.

"Frazier has his own rules, Charon. No, he will not kill women or children. But this does not involve children. There is only Logan and his men. And we must find them before they find us. I will tolerate no more delays."

Charon was unaffected. "I will do this alone."

"Very well. You have until tomorrow night. But finish them, Charon. I want to make that perfectly clear. Face to face. Do not disappoint me again."

Charon swept into Dumont. "Do not *ever* threaten me again," he whispered. "It was Frazier's light, I still believe, that prevented me from killing the child that night!"

Dumont was unfazed by the proximity. "Frazier has demonstrated his loyalty many times since that night, Charon. I have no questions about his allegiance."

There was nothing of agreement or disagreement from Charon as he moved away. He halted beside Frazier, who matched the hostile stare with a flat, dead gaze.

"Soon there will be only one of us," he whispered.

Frazier looked bored. Took a sip of wine.

Charon ascended the stairs, into silence. It was a long time after he departed that Dumont finally moved.

"Is he gone?"

"Yes," Frazier rumbled. "He's gone."

There was an indiscriminate sound of doubt. "How can anyone be certain with Charon?"

Frazier grunted, "He must feast."

The utter calm provoked Dumont into a rare laugh. "You speak without fear, Frazier, though I sometimes wonder if you are not truly as afraid of Charon as the rest of us." He paused a long time. "Tell me, Frazier: Are you afraid?"

Frazier eyes were chilling.

"Yeah," he growled. "I'm afraid."

The smile that crossed Dumont's face revealed the highest amusement. "No," he laughed, "I did not think that you were."

"What do you want me to do, Mr. Dumont?"

"Charon insists on working alone," Dumont replied. "Insure the ultimate containment plan and implant a redundant factor to terminate Logan and his men. If Charon reaches them first, so be it. If you reach them first, so be it. But I want them to be eliminated before they find me. That is all."

"I will double the guards surrounding the estate." Frazier set down his glass. "I will pick up Hooper when he leaves to meet Logan in the field."

"Are you certain Hooper will be meeting Logan?"

"Hooper is afraid. Fear makes a man seek the companionship of stronger men. Hooper believes he will feel safer with Logan at his side."

Dumont nodded as he smoothly slid one hand into the pocket of his smoking jacket. "Then go, my friend. And bring an ending to this. Kill Logan. Kill them all...Kill them tonight."

Webster leaned back in his chair, staring at the early afternoon sunlight reflecting off Pennsylvania Avenue outside the J. Edgar Hoover Building. He glanced down as the phone rang, right on time. With a sigh he reached out and answered, prepared for the worst.

"This is Webster."

It was Fletcher.

"Meet me in my office."

Webster had held an office in the J. Edgar Hoover building for ten years, and he was amazed that he could still get lost in it. He had no trouble locating the director's office; he had been there a thousand times. But because of the building's truly bizarre architecture, he constantly found himself wandering through strange and disturbing maze-like sections that, as far as he could determine, led nowhere.

The two and a half million square foot headquarters building was, in truth, a practical warning against overly creative design. Located on Pennsylvania Avenue between Ninth and Tenth, it included a nine-story section and an eleven-story section joined in such a way that the building seemed to lean maliciously over the street. Also, it held the regrettable fame of being the ugliest federal building in the nation.

And Webster knew he was not alone in his confusion. The building was packed with seventy-five hundred regularly confused Justice Department personnel, of which there weren't more than a hundred that could find their way from one end of the building to the other.

With a light laugh, Webster remembered an incident several years go when he and Logan had become lost together inside the catacomb-like sixth floor and Logan had effortlessly found the way out. Afterward Webster inquired about his method for selecting passages and Logan replied blandly, "When you're dealing with J. Edgar, always pick the way that seems wrong. You'll generally be right."

From his office on the fifth floor, Webster took the elevator to the eleventh. With a curt knock he paused at the director's door. "Come in," called Fletcher.

Fletcher stood with his hands on his desk as Webster entered, calmly closing the door behind him. Almost immediately, he noted Fletcher's disturbed expression. His eyes were narrow, distantly focused, and his long, severe face was haggard. Although his hands were still, Webster sensed they'd been trembling.

"We need to do this in the conference room." Fletcher motioned, and moved through the back of his office into a shielded room supplied with a secure red phone to the Oval Office, a couch, two chairs, and a small table with a bottle of Scotch and two glasses.

Webster had mostly seen the room during Friday afternoon debriefings when senior agents would gather to discuss sensitive investigations and debate current playoff games. Frowning, Fletcher poured himself a drink. "Would you like one, Richard?"

"No thank you, sir."

"Well, I would," Fletcher continued firmly. "I believe it's late enough." Webster waited until Fletcher took a sip, swallowing like a man who fully intended to have another.

"How did it go on the Hill, sir?"

"As you were afraid it would go," Fletcher mumbled, a heavy atmosphere settling. "I told the president that I wouldn't order Logan to stand down before tomorrow night because it would place them in unnecessary danger."

"How did he respond?"

Another sip; a big one. "He said Logan's investigation was no longer required. He said evidence had been uncovered that revealed World Finance has been involved in the suppression of evidence of bank fraud and violation of the RICO Act. He said that BCCI had been heavily implicated with American Finance and that he'd like this terminated before we're all forced to eat dirt. His last estimation indicated that our national debt had just tripled. Oh, and by the way, Delta and American Airlines are in the process of canceling five thousand flights. Fuel shortage. Hit particularly hard were UPS and Fed-Ex and medical supply transports. Now people are going to be dying in droves because pharmacies will be shut down." He sipped again, wiped his forehead. "Good Lord...It's like the end of the world."

Despite Fletcher's shell-shocked thinking, Webster managed to keep focused. "What is American Finance?" he asked.

"It's an American financial house owned by a Saudi named Sheik Agansi Agnossi."

"That's..." Webster closed his eyes, understanding a masterful move, "that's a spectacular catch for Justice, sir. They've nailed Agnossi for violating federal laws prohibiting foreign ownership of an American bank. It almost makes them look serious."

"Yes," Fletcher replied grimly. "The president said all sources inside Justice confirm that Agnossi is the man behind the banking takeover. And early conjecture is that the American owners of BCCI didn't know that Agnossi was ultimately the owner of American Finance. He said that the American officers of BCCI are...uh, *innocent*. Then he added that Justice had confirmed that Agnossi is Phantom and that whomever

Logan is chasing in England is the wrong man—an innocent man. He wanted Logan called off *now.*"

Webster massaged his temple, debated the Scotch.

"What'd you tell him?"

"I told him we were not convinced that Agnossi is ultimately responsible for BCCI." Fletcher stared into his glass. "I told him Logan might be on the trail of the man who, in truth, set up Agnossi. Then I said this was ultimately a Bureau situation and that until the Bureau was satisfied, we would not terminate Endgame."

"And?"

Fletcher paused a long time. "Logan and his men remain in the field until tomorrow at midnight. But not a moment longer. He ordered London's CIA team to place Logan under surveillance, if they can find him."

Webster stared. "Now the CIA is hunting Logan, too?"

"Pretty much everyone in the *world* is hunting Logan!" Fletcher shouted. He gestured high with the glass. "I'll even bet the Russians are hunting Logan and those commies don't have anything to do with this!"

Webster realized he was staring at a bare white wall, though he could hear the director speaking. Then a suspicion came to him, something he didn't like at all—something Ariel Ben Canaan had said. The feel, the magic of *misdirection, too many tracks, too many facts, too much evidence.*

It was vague, but solidified fast.

He saw Phantom connected to the FBI, connected to Secret Service, to Scotland Yard, Treasury, Justice, State, the White House, everybody in the world.

Or *almost* everybody...

And he knew: Too man tracks...The man had been too careful. His only mistake.

Fletcher was speaking again. "Richard? Do you fully understand what I am saying? We *must* find Logan!"

There was a moment of silence and the director sat tiredly into a plush chair. "Did I ever tell you, Richard, that I was once the Assistant Legal Attaché in Charge of London?" He spoke so slowly that Webster knew yet another revelation was coming.

"I was aware of that, sir."

Fletcher was motionless. Then he spoke, his voice so soft Webster could barely hear it. "I am...the man...who gave you the file on Jonathan Malone," he said.

"Yes, sir. I'm aware of that."

"I know you are." He swallowed a mouthful of Scotch. "But you do not know this: I gave you the file on Jonathan Malone because I am the only man who has ever seen that file."

There was a moment of slow shock settling. Webster didn't like the words at all. He didn't like the implications even more. "What are you telling me, sir?"

"What I am telling you is," Director Conrad Fletcher explained slowly, "I am the man who hid Jonathan Malone's file from any classified criteria, Richard. What I am telling you is that I am the man who relocated Malone, or Jonathan Falken, in the United States over twenty years ago."

Webster took a step forward.

"Yes," Fletcher smiled, "as you can see, all of our secrets are being exposed." The smile waned. "I have always known more about his man, Phantom, than I revealed. And further, so do many high-ranking members of this Administration. Silman's empire is an inherited dynasty of horror that reaches back through the history of this nation in ways you cannot begin to fathom."

"What do you mean?" Webster asked.

Fletcher grimaced, as if in physical pain. "I mean that this man, Silman, has owned every administration of this country for the past twenty years. Because the single, great secret that Silman holds is too dark to *ever* see the light of day. Ever! The *secret* is his failsafe! His blackmail!

"Even if we *do* find him, despite all this economic chaos he has plunged us in up to our neck, he can never be exposed! No measure of law will *ever* override the card he holds!"

Webster remembered what Canaan told him about the gold and art treasures recovered after World War II by senior members of the OSS and MI6. It was something he had not yet confided to Fletcher. "What secret would that be, sir?"

Fletcher blinked at the interruption to his tirade. "Honestly? I do not know, Richard. But I have been formally *instructed* that if Silman is found, Justice has no intention to prosecute him because he is a government informant who protects the highest interests of this nation."

Dead still, Webster imagined the scope of that.

Fletcher's head bent; he raised it to reply. "Webster, let me tell you a story. A story that began twenty years ago in England. It began when I was contacted by a man who worked with Silman. A man who, to this day, I cannot identify because all our communications took place in dark parking lots or hallways.

"I only saw his profile in shadow. But he was a big man—a dangerous man. And it was this man, twenty years ago, who told me who murdered Falken because Falken had alerted Israel to an invasion by Egypt and Syria. He also told me that Falken's son had escaped the attack, but remained in danger. Having no one else to trust, he asked me to help him hide the boy. And with the help of Admiral Haitfield in

MI6, I agreed to do so. But I also demanded something in return."

Webster wasn't disappointed. Somehow, he had passed that. "What did you demand?"

"Information," said Fletcher. "Information that would convict some of Silman's cohorts. I was willing to help, I said. But I wanted something for my services. And that was my price."

"And this man cooperated with you?"

"Oh, yes. He delivered more than enough information to bring down a significant part of Silman's empire. We closed down a smuggling network that stretched from Libya to Brussels. Not the entire network, mind you, but enough. So I relocated Malone in America. I managed to get him American citizenship. And I never heard from the man again. He vanished as mysteriously as he came." He paused, half turning away. "I had almost forgotten him...Until this."

"So you knew," Webster stepped forward. "You knew Malone would be personally targeted in this."

"No." Fletcher was unfailingly honest now, raising a hand at Webster. "No. I did *not* know the Israelis would use Malone was a target to draw Charon out of the shadows. But when you told me the information delivered by Canaan, I realized that Malone's past reached into the very heart of this thing."

Webster was close, now. "But by yesterday you understood Malone was being used as bait." Utter calm made his tone all the more terrible. "And you didn't do anything."

A justice beyond both of them settled over the room. It was as if there was nothing to be said, after this. But Webster knew this meteorite had just entered Earth's atmosphere and was burning up fast as it descended with three men fighting to survive the holocaust. And he knew with grim finality where he was going to stand.

"I'm going to London," he said, staring down over Conrad Fletcher, who hung his head. "Don't try to stop me."

"The president will attempt to stop you," Fletcher said wearily. "All of them will try to stop you, Richard."

"Stall them."

"Impossible."

Webster let his words stand. Finally, Fletcher looked up. "Don't you understand, Richard?" he asked, plaintive. "Don't you understand what is happening?"

"No. Explain it to me."

"Silman will *not* be prosecuted. The president will explain that he is a valuable source of top secret information. This entire incident will be classified so heavily it will never see daylight. Silman will *never* see a prison. *That* is why Canaan requested Malone. He anticipated that Logan would uncover Silman's hiding place, and then Malone would take it from there for *vengeance!* It was a desperate gambit, but the Mossad played their cards perfectly!"

"Who knows about this?" Webster waited in defiant silence as Fletcher stared aside, somber.

"I don't know," he answered finally. "There are too many secrets, Richard. Just...too many secrets."

"These are my men!" Webster shouted. "I do *not* send my men into the field to be sacrificed! I am *not* going to let Malone be used as some kind of *loose cannon* to take this man down!"

Fletcher was silent.

Webster's frown was threatening. "I'm going to London."

Fletcher shook his head. "Our leaders are in league with the devil, Webster. Believe me, I know. And they *will* try to stop you from finding Phantom."

"Stall them."

Silence.

"I'll try," said Fletcher tiredly. "But whatever you are going to do, do it quickly. And tell me nothing more." He tried to reassume an air of authority. "If any more of our people are killed, I am terminating the exercise. Make no mistake about that. I have enough on my conscience; I want no more."

"Do you still have contact with Silman's man?"

Surprise.

"I...I attempted to when this began. I was not certain what to tell him, but I told him about Malone. I never heard back from him. I don't even know if the drop is still active."

"Contact him. Demand a location for Silman. Tell him that things are too out of hand for anything else. Tell him that we'll protect him, put him in witness protection, whatever. But we have to know where Silman is located, and we have to know *now.*"

Fletcher was defeated. "Very well. I'll try."

Webster walked away.

"Webster?"

He turned in the doorway, staring back to see Fletcher holding a half-empty glass of Scotch. His voice was haunted. "It's a game, Webster. And Phantom is the best player in this world."

"No," Webster frowned. "That would be Logan."

As Webster reentered his office he lifted the phone to dial a top-secret code that caused a bar to lay across another line deep inside the South Central Bell office in Washington, connecting. Ten seconds later he heard a thin drone and a voice answered.

Webster gave a classified cryptonym and number.

THE SCAM

"Yes, sir?"

Hesitating, Webster stared at his desk.
It was too late to turn back.
"Scramble CI-3," he said.

Chapter Fifteen

Shadowed and silent, Matsumo stood unmoving beneath darkened trees. He could not be seen with the naked eye, but he was not certain about night vision equipment.

He tried to use the trees for cover but he knew that there was no way to watch without also being watched. If someone were suspicious of him, they could find him.

He had not eaten all day and was beginning to wonder if he were not wasting time when a black four-door Mercedes with tinted windows veered to the curb, not so far away. No one exited and Matsumo faded further into shadow, using a tree for solid cover. He made no sound, allowed no more movement.

A long time the car idled at the curb, the engine clicking, cooling. Passersby did not cast it a glance, and Matsumo could detect no movement within. But ten years of teaching survival had honed his instincts to an edge keen and alert. He knew something was here that he could use—something that was not ordinary, which made it important.

Eyes narrowing, Matsumo held his place.

His hands formed fists, hard as stone.

Waiting.

⊙ ⊙ ⊙

"We've got surveillance," said Daniela, appearing in the doorway of the kitchen where they were finishing off coffee and pizza. Her voice was calm, but her stance was tense.

"Who is it?" Canaan asked as he walked forward.

"Their methods seem American."

Logan and Jonathan followed the general to the front room as he gazed through a corner of the curtains. Daniela added, "The brown van down the street. We cannot see movement, but it is occupied. And further up the street, two men occupy another vehicle. They have coffee and food."

"Is anyone at the garage entrance?" Canaan asked.

"Two cars block each end of the alley."

The General grimaced. "This is unfortunate." He looked at Logan. "Who are they?"

"Who knows you're here?"

"Just our people."

"I beg to differ." Logan moved to the window to risk a narrow glance. He didn't move the curtain. "Do you have a vehicle in the garage?"

"Yes."

"What is it?"

"An Audi and a Ford Explorer."

"It's enough." Logan turned to Jonathan and Blackfoot. "You boys ready?"

Blackfoot racked a round in the shotgun. The Sioux seemed as comfortable with a weapon as he was with a computer. "What do you want us to do?"

"Get the equipment and put on your vests," Logan focused on Jonathan: "Do your thing, kid. Take care of the guys blocking the alley." He turned to Canaan. "I have a feeling these guys are CIA because they're the only other agency that might know the location of your safehouse. I don't intend to hurt any of our people, no matter what they've been ordered to do."

"We will simply detain them."

Jonathan moved for the back door. "I'll clear the car out of the south end of the alley. Five minutes."

"I'm going with you," Daniela said.

She picked up a heavily laden belt of clips, quickly fastening it around her waist. She put on a light black coat that concealed the Uzi, extra magazines, and four grenades attached to her vest. She was a walking arsenal, but when she closed her coat, she appeared harmless.

Jonathan hesitated; this woman was deadly. "You follow my lead," he said, leaning close to her. She did not blink. "Do *not* kill anyone unless I give you the word."

She said nothing, but Jonathan knew she wouldn't kill unless he gave the word. Just as he knew that, if things went bad, she would be more than capable of handling it.

"Five minutes," he said to Logan and moving out the door as Logan heated up: "Okay, boys, showtime. We take the Audi and then ditch it and steal something. Let's go."

Jonathan moved down an ivy-covered fence for the length of seven homes, coming up next to the vehicle. Staring quietly between planks, he saw two men seated in the front of a Cavalier. Both of them were dressed in casual clothing and held bland, tired expressions. The window on the driver's side was rolled down.

Raising two fingers, Jonathan turned back to Daniela, who knelt without emotion, the Uzi clutched in both hands. She nodded coldly at the sign and came forward to the fence, taking a place so she could see through the slats. Jonathan whispered, "Only if I get in trouble."

She didn't take her eyes off the vehicle. Nodded.

Without another word Jonathan moved down the far side of the fence, the side facing a connecting street, and vaulted over it to land on the sidewalk. Then he walked toward the alley and rounded the corner to come up the rear of the vehicle fast.

He didn't really have a plan. He only knew he had to use sufficient force to shock them. And he thought he could carry it off if he hit quick to put them in fear, not giving them a chance to think. He took the SIG out, holding it behind his right thigh. He resisted the temptation to think that nothing he did now would ever see the light of day.

The man reached into his coat as Jonathan came around the corner and Jonathan placed the barrel of the SIG against his neck. "Move and I'll kill you."

He purposefully spoke softly because he'd learned that it was far more frightening to face someone who was coldly in control than someone emotional and unprofessional.

Instantly the driver's hands were in the air but the second man hesitated, hand under his coat. Jonathan looked him in the eye. "He dies first and you're next. Show your hands."

His hands came up empty.

The driver stammered, "Okay, okay...Listen, Malone. We're CIA. We're here to protect you and that's it, man. We're not—"

"Shut up!" Jonathan shouted, pressing harder with the barrel. "Get out of the car! You first!"

Jonathan opened the door and pulled the driver out, shoving him against the car to search for a backup weapon, found none. Then a car engine roar to life at the safehouse. Instantly a car screeched from the garage and into the alley, coming at them hard.

Fired by adrenaline, he saw Logan at the wheel, Blackfoot riding shotgun. "Time to go!" Jonathan said to the second man. "Move this thing out of the alley! Now!"

Jonathan hurled the driver of the Cavalier to the fence and then the passenger slid over. He backed into the street as Logan skidded past them to stop the Mossad car.

"Daniela!" Jonathan shouted, holding a cold aim on the CIA man behind the wheel of the Cavalier. "Let's go!"

She rounded the fence as the CIA car at the far end of the alley came barreling forward. But at the last second the Explorer exploded from the safehouse, slamming into its side to send them both into a dumpster.

"Daniela!" Jonathan shouted. "Get in the car!"

Daniela dove into Logan's car in front of Jonathan, who spun to see General Ariel Ben Canaan exiting the Explorer, shouting at the CIA driver. The general stood in the alley, shaking his fist and cursing in Hebrew.

For a second Jonathan felt like laughing and then he heard tires skid a block away—the secondary vehicles had been alerted.

Logan floored it and they skidded out of a hard right and another then right to send them hurtling back down the very street in front of the safehouse, traveling in the other direction. Twenty minutes later Logan threw the car into park beneath a bridge and they hailed two taxis, weapons hidden beneath their coats.

"Where we going?" Jonathan asked, drenched in sweat and moving, out of a strangely protective impulse, to get into the taxi with Daniela. Scowling, Logan glanced around, as if he could read the terrain beyond the buildings.

"The nearest train station," he said. "I've got a call to make."

"To who?"

"To the only person we've got over here."

A graveled voice answered the phone and Logan spoke fast, glancing at the gathering storm clouds above Eustus Train Station. "What do you have, Mark?"

"Logan!" Hooper shouted. "What are you doing?" He instantly regretted the question. "Wait! Forget that! Listen, man, we got barbarians at the gate."

"I figured. How's Webster doing?"

"Holding his own. But Fletcher in a fiasco with the White House. No matter how this ends, I think we're all gonna be running a hot dog stand."

"Fine with me. Anything useful?"

"Webster's on his way. He'll be groundside in five hours and he's, uh...bringing friends."

"Friends?"

"Mean ones."

"Good. What else?"

"Webster faxed something from the jet about fifteen minutes ago." Hooper spoke in a hushed tone. "It doesn't make sense to me, but maybe you'll be able to understand it."

"What does it say?"

Logan glanced around to see Jonathan watching the crowds going in and out of the train depot. It was one of the most heavily walked areas in London and would bustle with activity until early morning with trains leaving and arriving until almost five a.m. It was a good place to be if the call was somehow traced. Disappearing into this crowd would be easy to do.

"You ready?" Hooper asked.

"Yeah."

"All right, Webster says: Too many tracks. What you're looking for isn't there. Silman was too careful."

Logan scowled. "That's it?"

"That's it. It doesn't make any sense to me, either. Webster obviously thought you'd understand."

Logan's eyes narrowed. "If Webster calls, tell him I got the message. But I've got to get moving. Is there anything else we need to know?"

"I want to hook up with you," Hooper said.

"Too dangerous."

"C'mon, Logan, this mystery man has ruined my career. I deserve to be there when you kick his door in. You need some backup, anyway."

There was a long pause. "All right. Meet us at Eustus Station. A half-hour."

"Twenty minutes."

Logan hung up and walked slowly to Jonathan, who was still scanning the street with his back to a wide, three-story building opposite the station.

Eustus Road was bustling with activity and small congregations of punk rockers and androgynous clones. Logan ignored them. He leaned back against the wall, hand casually closing over the SIG beneath his coat. Jonathan didn't look at him: "And?"

"Webster's coming in." Logan centered his gaze on Blackfoot and Daniela, who were standing on the opposite side of the street.

Daniela appeared innocent but Logan knew she had the Uzi under her coat, finger curled around the trigger. He couldn't keep himself from muttering, in a North Carolina drawl, "You know what, boy? That woman right yonder is absolutely dangerous."

Jonathan laughed, "Yeah. So what else did Hooper say?"

"He gave me a message."

"What was it?"

"Webster said what we're looking for isn't there. He said there's too many tracks. Said Silman's been too careful." He thoughtfully chewed on a matchstick. "I think he means that... Well, to tell you the truth: I have no idea what he means."

Jonathan looked away. "...too many tracks."

After a moment of silence Logan seemed to settle into it, slightly piqued. "All right, Hooper's on his way, so let's look at it for a minute. Webster said there's too many tracks. Meaning that Silman's been too careful, and that was his mistake. So what kind of tracks is Webster talking about?"

"Tracks to intelligence agencies."

"Right; tracks that lead to intelligence agencies. But Webster said what we're looking for isn't there. And that's the key to unlocking this thing, so..." Logan became even more concentrated, "Let's look at what *is* there. Silman is a popular informant. He's worked for almost every intelligence agency in the world and..." He stopped for a long minute, expressionless. Then, "Wait...If it's not there, then it's a process of elimination."

"Yeah," Jonathan agreed. "But what's not there?"

Staring off into the distance, Logan muttered, "Silman has worked for Scotland Yard, the FBI, the Secret Service, Treasury, Justice, the Canadian Secret Police, almost everybody in..." Logan's jaw dropped as he came off the wall, unable to contain his excitement. *"Almost everyone!"*

"What is it?" Jonathan asked before he glimpsed Daniela and Blackfoot stepping forward. They stopped as Jonathan sharply shook his head. "What is it, Logan?"

Logan rubbed his eyes for a minute, as if he couldn't believe it was so simple. *"Almost everyone.* That was Silman's mistake! He was too careful!"

"Could you explain this to me?"

"Yeah, yeah," Logan almost laughed. "Silman has worked for *almost* everyone, right? He's laid tracks to a dozen intelligence all over the world from the FBI to the Secret Service to Scotland Yard. He's worked for American embassies and foreign embassies, the American Mafia and the British Mafia. Drug runners, arm smugglers. He's worked for *almost* everybody. But what are the only agencies he never claimed any affiliation with? What are the only agencies he never claimed to work for?"

Jonathan didn't move. "Who?"

"MI6," Logan said solidly. "MI6 and CIA. Those are the only two agencies that Silman never claimed any association with. And I'll guarantee you those are the only two agencies he ever *did* actually work for. Webster was right. Silman was too careful. That was his mistake. He never laid tracks in the one direction that held the truth. He laid too many lies and made the truth obvious by too much deception. It even backs up Canaan's theory of the gold and art taken from the Nazis after World War II. Only MI6 and the CIA could have done that."

"But the CIA didn't *exist* until after World War II, Logan. The CIA wasn't created until 1947."

It didn't slow Logan. "That has to be it. MI6 and CIA are the only groups that could have made it look like Silman worked for Scotland Yard. MI6 is the only group that could have provided him with police documents to impress the Krays. MI6 probably even arranged for Silman to get married to a British citizen after he was released from an American military prison so he could obtain a British citizenship."

Jonathan asked, "But why would the CIA have to be involved? It could just be MI6."

"No." Logan was certain. "The CIA has to be involved because MI6 couldn't have pulled this off by themselves. Only the CIA could have created so many ties to American intelligence agencies for BCCI. The FBI or Secret Service couldn't have networked three thousand underworld figures. But Central Intelligence could do that because the CIA is all over that world." He grimaced. "That has to be it!"

Breathless, Jonathan paced a short path in front of Logan. Something still didn't make sense to him. "Logan, listen to me. Something's not adding up. There's no way MI6 could have reached Silman in an army prison in Germany and trained him. Why would they do that anyway? Why would MI6 care to recruit an American military convict out of an American prison? That's...that's *wild*."

"I know I'm right." Logan crossed his arms. "All of it doesn't add up, but I know I'm right. If it wasn't the CIA working with MI6, then it was the forerunner of the CIA."

"Like what?"

"Like the Office of Strategic Services, which largely *became* the CIA after the war. Most of those guys in the OSS during the war instantly became the most senior, and most powerful, agents of the CIA when it was chartered in 1947."

"Why do you think MI6 recruited Silman?" Jonathan asked.

"I don't know, kid. But I'm gonna find out."

A pause.

"I think," Jonathan added, "that I know where we can find some answers."

"Where?"

"An old friend."

Logan knew that it had finally come home to Jonathan, realized why the kid had been the key all along. He added, "I don't think this admiral friend of yours is going to talk, Jonathan. Especially if he was involved."

"He'll talk," Jonathan whispered as Hooper arrived in a LTD.

Jonathan's fist closed as a light rain descended over them, dark and glistening. *"Especially* if he was involved."

Charon watched as Jonathan and Logan climbed into Hooper's LTD. His gloved hands tightened on the steering wheel and he felt the black rush in his soul. He waited patiently until Hooper pulled back into traffic and made a sharp right, traveling east. Then in moments they were in the chaotic flow of the night, moving toward Westminster.

Charon laughed.

"Professionals," he whispered, "...so predictable."

Careful to use every skill he possessed, Matsumo remained far to the rear of the Mercedes. He knew somehow in this soul, as the man had exited the FBI office in a rush and the Mercedes began following, that something was amiss.

Quickly climbing into his rented car, Matsumo followed the Mercedes, knowing that whoever was in the car would also be careful to watch for a tail. Almost, on two separate occasions, Matsumo lost the car in the night and the rain and the heavy traffic.

It was only by luck that he picked the Mercedes up again, moving northward. It still drove slowly and he knew that the FBI agent was failing to use sanitation procedures. He was in a hurry to get to where he was going, making a direct line.

"Fool," Matsumo rumbled.

He wished he had brought a gun, but that had been impossible. If he had been caught, he would have been jailed until questions were answered, and he could lose no time. He would have to rely upon his own strength—the strength of his hands, as in the old days—and pray that God was on his side.

The storm hit full force as they entered Westminster.

Shrouded by dark rain and heavy fog, Jonathan led them toward the mansion of Admiral Benson Haitfield.

It had taken an hour because Jonathan's memory was vague. But then he saw the distinctive southern outline of majestic Westminster Cathedral from the West end of Vauxhall Bridge Road, a landmark. He told Hooper to park alongside the curb.

After walking the street for ten minutes, Jonathan finally found the house. It was smaller and less impressive than he remembered, but the iron gate still barred entrance to the formidable manor set distantly from the road.

Sirens surrounded them, moving in every direction, and Jonathan thought vaguely that he had never been in a town that echoed with so many sirens. He turned to Blackfoot. "That's it."

Blackfoot studied the gate. "An index card-lock. I can bypass it, but it'll take a few minutes; we might attract attention. But we're gonna attract attention anyway, standing in the rain."

Jonathan waved to Logan and Hooper and in moments they stood together. Logan studied the house, unimpressed. "Is the old guy home?"

"No way to know. But I don't think he travels a lot."

"Let's go around back," Logan said, and looked at them. "If something goes down, try not to shoot *me*."

They moved into the darkness on the east side of the sprawling, two-story gothic manor, walking quietly in single file. Jonathan was in the lead with Logan guarding the rear.

Blackfoot was second with Daniela and Hooper following.

"Jonathan," Blackfoot whispered, "I can't see anything. Can you see anything?"

"Blackfoot, how am I supposed to see anything when you can't see anything?"

Logan hissed, *"Neither* of you are gonna see anything if that German blows your brains out! *Shut up!"*

Standing grave and silent and unmoving, Charon felt an impulse to reach out with his black-gloved hand to touch the dark, dark hair of the woman as she walked past him, eyes wide and staring. She even stared directly at him, so close, but she could not see.

As he could.

Charon knew they were his, now. But he did not wish to end it here. There was another place, a more important place, for the final conflict. So he allowed them to walk slowly past and, still, he did not move for another moment.

Wind rushing high and harsh through the trees almost covered the sound of their advance through ivy and bush, the ground wet enough to absorb their steps in something akin to silence. Then they were gone and Charon moved patiently and calmly in their wake, hands empty, knowing they were easy prey in this arena of night.

Matsumo smashed an elbow through the window of the dark man's Mercedes. He knew the man had already left the vehicle; he did it to leave a message.

He had lost the man as he exited the vehicle, the man moving so quickly; a shadow that took a dozen strides to the side before he vanished into rain and darkness like a living darkness.

Matsumo could not conceive defeat. He knew that there *must* be a way to find Jonathan. He walked the sidewalks, using the passing headlights for much-needed illumination until he spotted the FBI agent's abandoned LTD. But there was no one inside, and where they were going, they had already gone.

Matsumo glanced at the long, majestic black profiles of manors that lined the street—they could be inside any one of them. Or none of them. It would be the wildest guess to begin a blind search and might alert guard dogs, which would bring police.

Backing into an alley, cold now in the rain that fell more heavily, Matsumo waited beside the LTD. He knew that whatever would happen would happen quickly. He breathed a prayer and tried to resist a fear he felt in his soul, a fear he felt when he saw the tall, thin man vanish into the darkness as if he owned it.

Breathless curses emanated through the darkness and rain as Logan and Hooper struggled to climb the back fence.

The spiked iron bars were almost ten feet high and presented a formidable obstacle even for Blackfoot, though Jonathan and Daniela made it over quickly and easily. Finally, breathing heavily, Hooper and Logan stood inside the yard.

Hooper held his chest. "Good grief," he whispered.

Logan caught his breath. "Come on."

In a moment they were at the back of the manor. Blackfoot bent over a box positioned near the door, removing the screws with a leatherman pocket tool. He left two wires twisted together. "That's it," he said simply.

Logan was staring down. "That's it?"

"That's it."

Together, they stared at the door.

"I've never seen a lock like this," muttered Logan. "Is anybody good at picking locks? I'd hate to have to bust this old geezer's door down in the middle of the night."

"Well, we *could* knock," Blackfoot offered.

Logan straightened. "Sounds reasonable, Blackfoot. When the old guy answers the door, tell him we're him here to find out if he worked with Silman to launder Nazi gold. Tell him the Mossad is here, too, and she's lookin' to kill anybody who was involved."

Blackfoot gazed at the lock.

"I can do this," said Daniela.

She reached down to her ankle and removed a long black pick from the outside seam of her pants over her right boot. Then she pulled another pick from the seam and inserted both of them in the lock of the knob, one above the other.

Standing in a silence, they watched.

Sweating. Soaking. Waiting.

Daniela's concentration was almost hypnotic and her dark face glistened with pale light cast from the distant alley behind them. Two minutes passed before she began working on the deadbolt and Jonathan knew they were halfway home.

Finally she twisted the lock and they heard the bolt snap. She placed the picks in her mouth as she delicately twisted the knob and the door opened. She nodded to Jonathan.

In seconds they were moving through the lower level, exceedingly careful, each carrying weapons in plain sight for fast use. They went through the back of the manor and started to ascend the stairwell when Jonathan froze, staring hard at light flickering in a front room. He squared his shoulders and moved into the room, something dangerous reflecting in his eyes.

"Jonathan," whispered Logan, but Jonathan was moving with a purpose. He knew somehow, knew in his heart, what awaited him. He lowered the SIG as he walked slowly and quietly into the front room, the rest of them trailing cautiously, nervously.

Seated alone before roaring flames, Admiral Benson Haitfield wore a voluminous red robe. Upon the table were loose photographs and a half-empty bottle of Glenlivet.

"Good evening, Jonathan," the admiral whispered.

Jonathan glanced at the Scotch, focused on the admiral. "Does it make you forget, Admiral?"

Haitfield laughed tragically.

"I have drunk enough Scotch to send an entire battalion staggering, child, but I am cold sober. Because I knew that you, Jonathan, were coming home."

❂ ❂ ❂

President Stanford glared at the documents placed in front of him. Beside him stood three men who held the coveted post of senior advisors. All of them were dressed in dark suits with varying ties of dark red, green, and blue. They waited patiently.

Another man stood in the corner, hands casually in the pockets of his pinstriped suit. The president's voice cut angrily through the gloom of the room. "What has Webster done?" he asked, unable to keep himself from repeating, "What has Webster *done*?"

"He activated CI-3," said the man who stood in the corner. "He's flying to London to cover Endgame."

"How close is Endgame to finding Silman?"

"We don't know," the man replied. "Logan communicated with another FBI agent at the American Embassy, but didn't say anything important."

"I *ordered* the CIA to find Logan!" said the president of the United States.

"The CIA *did* find Logan. But Logan threw 'em off. Malone, the young FBI agent—"

"I *know* who Malone is! Malone is the primary reason for shutting this operation down! If Malone discovers...if he discovers..." Stanford shook his head. "What a disaster!"

"We have people who can handle contingencies."

"And we will most assuredly need them," Stanford replied, leaning wearily on the desk. "Very well. Let us make an intelligent decision, if we *can*. What is the best course of action?"

"Find Logan and his team and bring them in."

"Can't the CIA reacquire them? Doesn't the CIA have people who do that sort of thing? I mean, isn't that what we train them for?"

The man laughed. "It's not that simple, Mr. President. Logan isn't telling anyone his moves and he's moving fast." He blinked with reluctant respect. "He's smart."

Stanford cursed in a sharp proficiency of usage that permeated the room with a noxious, obscene air. Then, "How could this situation get so out of control?"

"We underestimated Logan," said the man. "We underestimated Webster. And Israel was cunning. But Blackfoot..." The man sighed. "He was the one who broke the Encryptions and frontline defenses at the NSA and BCCI. Even the Bureau, itself."

Rage undercut the president's words. "Find Logan," he said quietly. "I don't care what you have to do. I don't care how many men you have to use. I don't care who you have to kill. Tell the CIA that I want Logan *found!*"

"Of course. Is there anything else?"

"Can we take CI-3 out of Webster's control without the support of Director Fletcher and without raising questions of misconduct? Is there any way we can justifiably circumvent the authority of the FBI and shift command of CI-3 to Central Intelligence?"

There was an uneasy exchange of glances.

"It's possible," said the man from the corner. "We can order the realignment of CI-3 to the CIA because Webster is operating in international territory without a jurisdictional Order of Rebate from the State Department. At this moment, Webster really doesn't have authority to go tactical in a foreign country."

"Do it," said President Stanford. "Do whatever it takes. But take this infernal hit squad out of Webster's control!"

Without hesitation two of the aides left the room. As they went out of the door, they closed it quietly, leaving the president and the man in the corner in commune.

"This situation has been badly managed," the man said from darkness.

Stanford was still. "How do you think this will affect my reelection?"

The man laughed. "Your aides pride themselves in reinventing you. I'm sure they'll tell everyone they've 'reinvented' you above this. Then they'll publicly congratulate each other for their cunning so that the media will know how smart they are."

The president turned. "You think my aides are fools."

"Yes."

"So what am I?"

Another laugh. "You're a man sworn to protect your government's interests and your own interests. And you shall."

A long moment passed.

"Webster and Logan," the president frowned. "They don't even have the brains to be bought."

⊙⊙⊙

"I suppose you are here for my confession?"

The admiral's voice was so world-weary and old that Jonathan felt a measure of compassion. Then Haitfield added without concern, "Or are you here to kill me?"

Jonathan frowned, shook his head. "You're dead, already."

"Yes, child...That is true."

The admiral grimaced in an unknown, deep pain. His words came with difficulty. "Confessions, Jonathan. Confessions...are the life of an old man. Repentance for what cannot be repented. An absolution that will never be found...Long stories...that have no listeners."

Silence.

"I'm listening," said Jonathan.

Logan moved up behind them, and the admiral raised his head to see him standing so close to Jonathan, staring down as if he were angry at even being here.

"Ah," laughed the admiral, "you have not come alone—a good tactical decision, Jonathan. But, then, you were always skilled at tactics. At least with the game."

"I'm playing again," Jonathan replied, and the admiral's face lifted with a light. "My last game."

"You were such a loss, my boy," the admiral mused. "You were truly...*truly* the greatest to ever play the game. Greater than Reschevsky. Greater than Evans or Karpov, or even Fischer. Because no one before you ever played with such fierceness! None of them!" He bowed his head. "You were truly your father's son, Jonathan. Pure. Intense. Single-minded. Nothing could distract you from defeating your enemy."

Jonathan blinked. "People change."

"Not you," the admiral laughed. "Your father knew you were destined for greatness. He told me so many times, his pride shining in his face. And he loved you so! Nor can you change what you are. Not by remorse, or wine or the weight of age. You are what you are. You always have been, and you always will be, a player. And that is why I knew you would return to me one day...to win the game you lost as a child. Against your greatest enemy."

Daniela had moved across the room to face the admiral. Her face was a mask of cold duty as she lifted the Uzi. Implacable, she held unwavering aim on the admiral's chest. He did not seem to mind.

"So...Israel has her defender, also." He smiled at her. "Yes, someone who kills with passion...As you should."

Jonathan stated, "I want answers."

"And you deserve them, Jonathan. Yes, just as I deserve that my sins should be disinterred." Haitfield looked at the fire with sadness. "Oh...how I envy you children. You challenge a giant, the devil incarnate, and you have no fear of the consequences. But I understand—you do not know your enemy, so you are not afraid. Your lack of knowledge is your strength. For if you knew more—if you knew how your adversary has gained control not only of the world banking system but the world intelligence community as well, then you would be as I am, broken and defeated."

"Why was my father murdered?" Jonathan asked as Logan turned to Hooper in a low voice: "Go watch the back door, Mark. Make sure we're covered and keep an eye out for that German. Remember, he can see in the dark."

"I'm on it," said Hooper, walking away with his gun in hand. "That Nazi ain't gonna take me like he took Woodard."

And then he was gone, checking every corner with the semi-automatic held close.

Blackfoot moved to the front door, still in view of the room, gazing up the stairway. Logan subtly backed away until Jonathan and the admiral held their own space.

"It's time to talk," Jonathan said quietly.

"Yes, Jonathan, it is time to talk. And what do you wish to talk about? Your father and mother?" He closed his eyes. "Yes, your father and mother. I suppose that is the place to begin. Death is the beginning for all of this.

"It was Justinian who first uncovered the conspiracy," Haitfield nodded, every year of his life in his voice. "But when he discovered it, it was already beyond remedy." A pause. "Yes, it was far, far too late. And I told him it was too late, but he would not listen. He thought of your mother and her people." He glanced at Daniela. "*Your* people, my dear, because it all began with them."

"How?" asked Logan.

"Simply enough." The admiral seemed amused, but not with amusing thoughts. "You see, World War II ended as all wars end. In chaos. In confusion." He waved with fatigue. "Stalin suppressed information from us, so we suppressed information from Stalin. The OSS was spread thin—at least, those that had survived. MI6 was busily eliminating their own people who had been double agents for the Nazis. The Army was attempting to find Hitler's hierarchy. But *everyone* was searching for the treasures and the art that Hitler had taken from the Jews."

"The artifacts that Silman smuggled," said Jonathan.

"Yes, Jonathan. Those very artifacts—the gold, the bracelets, family heirlooms and treasures, some as old as recorded history. Over thirty thousand tons of gold, all secretly stored and hidden in an abandoned railroad tunnel at Rostack, near the Swiss border. And with all that gold were the priceless works of art confiscated during the Holocaust—the paintings of Fabriano, Raphael, Mantegna, Picasso, Parmigianino, Giorgioni, da Vinci, Michelangelo. There was enough wealth in that tunnel to build a nation." His voice fell to a whisper. "And it was in that terrible darkness, in that underworld where secrets can never be spoken, that the conspiracy was born."

The admiral coughed spasmodically, taking a minute to draw a breath. "Yes, that is where it began," he continued. "After the war, you see, not all of Hitler's highest aides escaped. They were captured in Austria by the OSS and MI6."

Logan broke in, "Who from American intelligence captured Hitler's henchmen?"

"Donovan's people," the admiral said, referring to "Wild Bill" Donovan, who led the OSS during World War II. "Donovan's people captured Mengele. And certain high-ranking officers of MI6 were also present."

Logan grunted, "And nobody talked."

The admiral seemed amazed. "We were not fools, sir. Yes, Mengele and those with him very wisely used their knowledge of the gold. They traded the location of the treasure for their freedoom and safe passage to South America. Really, there was nothing else they could do. They gave all they had in exchange for their lives—a lesson from the Old Testament, is it not? Flesh for flesh."

"So MI6 released them," Jonathan stated.

"Even more," the admiral shook his head, as if in disbelief, "we *protected* them." He paused. "Yes, with the assistance of our American friends, we relocated them all, some in South American, some in America, some in England."

"How did my father discover this?"

A frown darkened the admiral's face. "That is a question I have never been able to answer. But Justinian did, indeed, discover that the Nazis had bought their freedom with the gold." He leaned forward, folding fingers. "Your father was English, but his heart was Jewish. His love for Israel, though it was not yet a country, was great. He knew Israel would return, and he was enraged that this move had delayed Zion. Had endangered the dream of a nation, for he believed that God had, indeed, given to them the Promised Land, as in the days of old. And, so, he was planning to share his newfound knowledge with an official from the Israeli Embassy, bypassing our security."

Jonathan took a slow step forward. "You knew my father had been targeted for assassination?"

"I knew," the old man replied, "that Justinian had been targeted by Charon. But there was nothing I could do about it, Jonathan. Charon was both the servant and master of men who had sold their souls to the devil. And I was one of them. Because I was there, the night, when Mengele and his colleagues were apprehended in Austria."

"Who's behind this now?" asked Logan. "Most of those guys are dead."

"Ah," said the admiral, "that would be the notorious Simon Silman." He coughed thickly. "Silman was, and is, a monstrous criminal genius. He was recruited out of the American Army prison in Germany in the years following the war for the sole purpose of smuggling the gold and paintings. And he was the proper man for the job, I believed. A soulless thief. A mercenary of ruthless but keen intelligence. And yet he was utterly predictable because his corruption was so utterly complete.

"After the confusion of the war died and the rumors of

the gold faded to legend, Silman was trained to convert it into money. We gave him an international network of underworld contacts forged during the war to facilitate the task. And this explains how a simple thief could emerge from an American military prison with an international network of underworld connections."

"You haven't answered my question, Admiral," Logan interrupted. "Silman plays his own game, now. Who's in charge of the gold?"

Haitfield's smile was bitter. "That would be the descendants of those who launched the initial conspiracy." He laughed tragically. "Did you never wonder, Mr. Logan, how such enormous, modern wealth came to be focused among so few East Coast and European families in the years following World War II?"

"Plenty of times," said Logan. "How did you know my name?"

"Mr. Logan, I am old, but I am still capable of discovering what concerns me."

Logan took a more precise tactic. "Who, exactly, in American intelligence cooperated with MI6?"

The admiral's laugh mingled with flame. "Children, if you wish to play with adults, you must understand history. Donovan's OSS was not 'abolished' after the war. The OSS was merely 'relocated' under American military supervision and given a new title. It was known as The Strategic Services Division."

"The official counterintelligence division of the United States Army," said Jonathan. "That's how the OSS gained access to Silman when he was incarcerated in an American Army prison."

"Yes."

"But that doesn't make sense," Logan muttered. "If these guys were in Strategic Services, they were taking orders from the Pentagon. They wouldn't be working with MI6."

"No, no, Mr. Logan," the old man said steadily. "You do not understand because you do not know the nature of counterintelligence. You are talking about senior officers of OSS who happened to be reassigned to the United States Army. These were not soldiers. They were spymasters. All of them. And they were loyal to the infamous Colonel Wild Bill, not the army. So, despite any *official* station, they continued to work with those of us in MI6 for the proper man to market the gold and stolen paintings."

He coughed, continued, "Now, despite an extensive search among London's criminal element, MI6 was unsuccessful. The OSS, however, or the SSU as it was then known, located Silman while he was incarcerated in prison in Germany.

"It was agreed among both parties," he proceeded, "that Silman was perfect for the job. A genius. A madman. A man who knew no remorse, or pity, or conscience. So MI6 worked with the SSU to train him in the secrets of moving and hiding money. We provided the network that would enable him to smuggle and sell what we had recovered in that railroad tunnel in Rostack. Then, when Silman was released from prison, he began marketing the gold in Europe and the Middle East and America, profits of which were then disseminated among dynasties of the spymasters who conceived the plan."

"So all of this was a conspiracy between high-ranking members of MI6 and OSS," Logan said. "How come these two organizations were so trusting of each other. That's a lot of money, and money makes people untrustworthy."

"You are talking about *personal* relationships, Mr. Logan," the old man said. "During World War II, certain members of

Donovan's group and certain members of MI6 worked closely on a number of dangerous missions. Perhaps, even, too closely. And by necessity they became consummate liars. Men who knew how to make a lie consistent not only with the truth but with all other lies—men who knew how to keep secrets from the enemy as well as their own governments.

"Taciturnity was an art. Indeed, to speak at all was tantamount to treason. And personal relationships formed in that intelligence world shall, quite probably, never be equaled, primarily because today's enemy is diminished by obscurity." He laughed. "Not a problem we possessed during the war. We enjoyed the luxury of clarity—we knew the enemy was not one of *us*."

He faintly waved his hand in dismissal. "Yes, of course, there was Philby and The Five, who were never fully discovered. But on the side of clarity there was Hitler and Hoover, who fought our relationships at every turn. So during the later years of the war we came to understand that the enemy was anyone who did not share our personal alliances, governments notwithstanding. And our secrets, within and without, were the essence of our survival."

"And my father?" asked Jonathan.

"Justinian..." the admiral began, and averted his eyes, "was not a visionary, Jonathan. He was loyal to God and country, in that order. A man of integrity. Of moral ethos. A man who would have sacrificed his own life to help someone he did not know. A man...I loved."

Smoldering, Jonathan glared and his fist locked hard around the gun. His voice was so quiet it seemed to come from the air. "So you killed him," he said.

"No," the admiral replied, exhausted now, "but I knew he would be killed. And, at great risk, I tried to tell him that it was foolish to go to the Jews." He shook his head again. "Even today, I remember the meeting. We held it beside the round pond in Kensington. It was dark, through it was hours before dusk. I had a foreboding of doom. I openly warned him not to interfere. But he would not listen to my remonstrance. He insisted on taking what he knew to others because he knew he could not appeal to his own. So he took it to the Mossad and... and when he did that, I knew it would not be long."

The admiral closed his eyes. "And so Charon killed your father. Charon killed your mother." He released a breath. "Charon—he was the pride of Hitler's breeding program. No one knows when he was born, but it was before the war ended. Indeed, he was still young when he killed your father, though he had already killed a hundred men.

"At birth, he was considered a failure because he appeared to be less than the perfect, blue-eyed Aryan warrior. But that was only before the Nazis realized his unique abilities. Photosensitive, they said. A man who could see in the dark as easily as another man could see in the day. A man so completely cold, so perfect in killing, that he was considered a monster even as a child. He was hidden in South America following the war, protected by surviving members of the Reich, and trained in all the skills of murder. Then, eventually, he went to work for those passionate few who survived the witchhunt— those smuggled to South America or who hid in Switzerland. He became their protector. Their avenger." A reluctant pause of respect. "Yes, the best of his kind."

The admiral grimaced as he poured himself another glass of wine. "Do you understand Charon's perfection, Jonathan?" He waited for a moment for a response and, when none was forthcoming, continued. "I will tell you. It is because he has killed hundreds, Jonathan, removing himself from the guilt and anguish of those who merely kill one, or two, or twenty. What is the difference, you ask, between killing one man and a hundred? I'll tell you. It is conscious. To kill a single man brings guilt and remorse. To kill a hundred...brings power. It transforms you from a murderer...into a conqueror."

Expressionless, Jonathan thumbed back the hammer of the SIG.

"Don't kill him," said Logan, stepping forward. "I mean it, kid; we need him."

"It's over," Jonathan said. "You're going to tell everything you know."

"Yes, it is, indeed, over." The admiral bent his head. "More than you know, Jonathan. Because Hitler left...his legacy."

Suddenly the lights went dead.

Darkness.

Logan spun and raised the radio. "Mark! Can you hear me?"

"*Yeah!*"

"What happened?"

"I don't know!" Hooper's voice was shrill with fear. "I don't see anything!"

"Get back in here!" Logan shouted. "And use your Maglight!"

"On my way."

Logan moved forward. "Admiral," he said quickly, "you're coming with us."

"No, detective," said the old man, and raised his face to encompassing shadows. "I doubt very much that any of us are going anywhere at all."

◉ ◉ ◉

"Commander Webster?"

Webster raised his face from a review of Federal policies

regulating the actions of FBI Special Agents in foreign countries. "Yeah?"

"You're needed up front."

Webster muttered as he laid down the book and stood. He'd been dreading the pilot coming back to him with those very words.

They were flying at 37,000 feet—at the Lear's top sustainable speed of 450 miles per hour. Behind Webster were ten men in civilian clothes, men who could be salesmen or schoolteachers or lawyers. Except school teachers and salesmen wouldn't have dead-flat eyes that stared through people instead of at them. Nor would they have a cache of high-tech weapons stored in the cargo space of the plane.

"Yeah?" mumbled Webster at the cockpit.

"We've got the director on the line, sir. He wants to talk to you."

Webster picked up a headset. "This is Webster."

"The president knows that you've activated our friends, Richard." Fletcher's voice was tiny and static. "There's a reception awaiting you in London."

"Our people?"

"No."

"Family?"

"Yes."

Webster debated what to say next, knowing there was no way to insure the line was totally secure. Also, he didn't want the pilots knowing any more than they had to. Finally he just asked, "How do you want me to handle it?"

"I think it might be best to cooperate."

He paused. "Understood."

Fletcher added, "The president is saying that the reception will have jurisdiction over our friends when you arrive.

They are going to assist, and you yourself will not have the authority or legal sanction to order the unit into the field."

Webster's face twisted. "Understood."

"Good luck, Richard." Fletcher's voice was tired, as if he'd reached the end of his line only to find that there was nothing below him. "I'll stand behind you in whatever you do."

"Yes, sir. Out."

Webster walked into the cabin and stood evenly in the middle of the isle, staring. Immediately every eye centered on him. Webster realized these men didn't need many words; they were professionals and were surprised at nothing.

"Gentlemen," he began, "when this bird lands, there will be a party of CIA who want to take authority over you." He let that settle to hostile gazes. "That comes from the Hill."

"Well, *we* ain't CIA," mumbled a lean, thirty-something black man seated beside a window. Webster didn't know him. He only knew that the others called him "Rabbit."

"I know," Webster acknowledged, "but it's not my call. I only want you to remember one thing. This situation remains in flux. We do not yet know who has the authority to control you. So, for right now, we're going to cooperate with the CIA case officer."

Webster focused on a big, bald man who sported a Wyatt Earp mustache. The man was heavily built, like a professional wrestler, and commanded the front seat of the jet opposite Webster himself. "Agent Reibling?" Webster asked, "tell me how you'll be ordering your men when we set down in London."

Reibling seemed to study the wall. "I'll order them to cooperate with Central Intelligence, Commander." He pursed his lips. "Until it's time not to cooperate."

"Listen to me," Webster suddenly commanded the plane and passengers with a power that he had obviously earned and knew all too well how to wield. "I expect you to cooperate *fully* with the Central Intelligence Agency. That is not a request, gentlemen. We have no sanction whatsoever to usurp the CIA's international charter. And if and when a decision of that gravity should be made, it shall be made by me and me alone. Is that understood?" Webster glared down the aisle. "Tell me right now, gentlemen, if you have any objections. I can relieve you of duty and personally place you on the first civilian flight back to the states."

There was resentful silence.

"Yes, sir," said Reibling, staring back. "We understand you perfectly. But let me say for the record that I formally protest the action of the Executive Office to surrender authority of this highly classified team to the CIA. It is outside parameters of the program and in contradiction of separate Enactments that regiment the coordination of American civilian forces. It may be a legal action, sir, but it is not secure and compromises the tactical counterintelligence ability of the Bureau. It may also endanger our men in the field."

Webster frowned, looked down, tired.

"I know."

Chapter Sixteen

Daniela opened the bolt in the Uzi and spun, placing her back to the wall. She stood in clear view, using nothing for cover, inviting the intruder to take a shot that she was more than willing to give back.

Jonathan reached Blackfoot and pointed to the large oak door behind the Sioux. "Watch the stairway and converging hallways," he said. "Don't move from this spot. Don't investigate anything. Shine your flashlight so that it angles off the ceiling and illuminates this entire section. Take that shotgun off safety."

"It's already off," Blackfoot said, long black hair framing his dark face. "I don't like this, Jonathan."

"Don't worry, man, we're making tracks." Jonathan turned and walked up to the admiral. "Get up."

"He is playing the game, Jonathan."

"So am I: *Get up!*"

"He would be surprised if you could kill him."

"It's gonna be the last surprise of his life." Jonathan grabbed the old man's arm as Logan lifted the radio, nervousness quickening his words. "Mark, what are you doing?"

Logan stared into the darkness. "Mark! Get back in here! Can you copy?" There was no reply. "Mark!" Logan was becoming more alarmed. "Mark!"

A soft voice came over the radio and for a second Jonathan was afraid it was Charon. But it was Hooper, his words so faint they were almost indiscernible: "Logan. I can see him. I think I can get an angle on him. He's between us."

"Mark!" Logan shouted. "Don't go after him! Do you hear me?" No response. "*Mark*! Do you hear me!"

Silence.

Immediately Jonathan and Daniela were moving toward the back of the house, coordinated by a warrior sense that compelled them to put themselves on the line. Somehow, in a collision of passion, they wordlessly chose to work as a team, a decision seemingly made from trust in the other's courage and ability. But Jonathan knew it was more. He looked at Logan; "We'll get Hooper."

"Hurry, kid."

Jonathan turned to Daniela. "Two by two, standard entry on doors on three. You're high on crossovers, low forward in hallways. Take stairways with opposite walls."

She nodded, hands melding solidly and with practiced control to the Uzi. Although she was sweating, her face contained far more rage than fear, and Jonathan knew she was experienced at full-contact—no rules, no second place. And for a split-second he wondered how many men she'd killed.

Too many...

With Logan watching the admiral, they moved into the darkness. Both of them used Mag-lights, and the 250,000 candlepower was comforting. For a long three minutes they advanced, careful and coordinated. Jonathan called out loud for Hooper but Hooper didn't respond.

Then, strangely at the same time, Daniela and Jonathan paused in the hallway. She cast him a glance. It was clear—she didn't understand what she'd sensed. Jonathan shook his head once; he'd felt something, but he didn't know either.

Cautious, dropping to one knee, Daniela crept to an open

doorway. She moved in almost perfect silence although the light revealed her position. One hand flat against the wall, she leaned to get a narrow peek into the room.

Behind her, Jonathan took the higher position, the SIG raised slightly lower than his shoulder. With both eyes he scanned the darkness, but there was nothing there. Just an empty hall and doors leading from the side, the most dangerous part of the approach.

It was a good place to be ambushed, so he decided they'd close doors as they passed them. If they used that method, Charon would be forced to open a door to ambush them from behind; it would give them another second to react.

"Daniela," he whispered. "Close the door and—"

Charon emerged from the door frame.

"*Get down!*" Jonathan screamed and Daniela instantly dropped to roll through a doorway as Jonathan fired a half-dozen rounds at Charon with a white strobe in the darkness before Jonathan knew that the hit man was gone.

Sensing what was about to happen, Jonathan rose to his feet to shout, "Hooper! Stay where you're at—*just stay where you're at!*"

Hooper ran toward the gunfire when he glimpsed something and whirled; the German was leaping toward him from a doorway and Hooper fired from the hip to see...

A mirror shattering glass breaking not—

Hooper tried to spin as a black arm came around his neck and he glimpsed a geyser of blackness spiraling into the ceiling from his collarbone. He knew pain driving again and again into him but he was too enraged to feel fear.

The arm wrenched his head back, controlling his body, and Hooper heard gurgling only to realize with horror that it was him and then he was being dragged backward into the doorway within a storm of screaming, screaming, pain screaming, pain and fear.

Hooper surged hysterically but whatever had seized him—he had a vision of a spider springing from its trapdoor to pounce horribly upon its prey with encircling legs dragging him back with it into its lair.

He saw something flash down again.

An ice pick?

No, no, ice pick and rain...

Red rain...

"Hooper!" Jonathan shouted as he heard screaming in the back of the house.

He was instantly running, dropping the half-used clip from the SIG to slam in a fresh fifteen-round magazine. He collided with a table in the dark, reached down and sent it pinwheeling to the side. He didn't check all the doorways, didn't care about silence. Hooper was under attack and the only choice they had was speed.

No more tactics.

Daniela was close behind him and he knew she understood just what he understood and accepted it. It would be pure speed and skill to identify the target and kill or be killed and everybody was going to be wounded or dead.

As Jonathan came into the back he saw glass littering the floor of the hallway, the strong smell of gunpowder clouding the air then he heard another scream from Hooper. Raising her face to the ceiling, Daniela spoke with remarkable control, as if she'd been in this situation many times before: "He is torturing him."

Enraged, Jonathan whirled to an open doorway and

glimpsed a stairway that led to the second floor. Then Hooper's screaming reached a high-pitched, pleading whine—the screams of a man in the grip of a torturous, horrifying death.

"*Charon!*" Jonathan screamed at the ceiling. He leaped into the stairway. "Come on!"

"Wait!" Daniela grabbed Jonathan's arm.

Livid with rage, he glared down as she said with incredible control, "It's a trap!"

Jonathan grimaced, "Stay here or go back to Logan! I'm going after Hooper!"

Hooper's screams were rhythmic, as if his assailant were sawing off portions of his body. Daniela shifted her burning gaze to the stairway, concentrated. With a grimace she clutched the Uzi once more, tight and controlled. "Let's go."

Moving quickly, Jonathan went up the stairway. He knew that if Charon tried an attack he would fire the SIG, no matter how badly he was hit. Just as he knew that he would probably be killed on the first round but he wouldn't die for a few seconds and, as surely as there is a God in heaven, he would fire a full clip in return. Just as he knew Daniela would instantly cut loose with a fully automatic burst from the Uzi.

Hooper's screaming diminished in crescendo, becoming more plaintive. It was a sound weak and instinctive, like the death moan of someone who knew he was dead but was simply too shocked to believe it—as if Hooper's mind were trying to conceive the separation of his soul from his body.

Together, Daniela and Jonathan came to the second floor. They could hear Hooper in a nearby room, moaning now, almost silent, and they moved back to back, scanning everything. Jonathan went first into the room spinning, searching and constantly glancing down to check for tripwires.

Refusing to pay attention to Hooper until they secured the room, Jonathan moved instantly to the far side and kicked the door shut so the hit man couldn't step into the room. Then he bent compassionately over the senior FBI agent, shining the flashlight.

Hooper no longer resembled a human being.

Shocked, Jonathan stared over the carnage. He shook his head, gripping Hooper's blood-drenched shoulder. "Hooper..." he whispered, knowing it was far, far too late. "Take it easy, man. We're going to get you an ambulance."

Gurgling, Hooper tried to respond.

Shaking his head again, Jonathan glanced up at Daniela. She wasn't looking down. She stood in the only open doorway, her emotions as cold and controlled as human emotion could be, though from her frown, Jonathan knew she was enraged. Her hands were tight on her weapon and she held a solid stance, prepared to hold the doorway against one man or a thousand.

Gunshots exploded downstairs and Jonathan was through the door, on the stairway and descending the flight with four huge strides to hit the lower hallway. He shattered the plaster in the hallway as he hit the wall and spun, instantly running.

Behind him he heard Daniela close but unable to keep up with his descent and he almost hesitated for her but knew she'd stay close enough for him to cover. More gunshots burst out and as Jonathan hurtled out of the hall and glimpsed something happening in the front room beside the stairway.

Logan was on the floor. The admiral was slumped in his chair, the wall behind him splattered with blood and brain and skull fragments from a bullet that had entered his forehead.

Jonathan spun. *"Blackfoot!"*

A savage struggle, the collision of bodies shattering furniture in a ferocious fight echoed in the dining room adjacent to the gigantic front entry and Jonathan exited the den to see a black cloaked figure holding Blackfoot as a shield.

Charon controlled Blackfoot with an arm around his neck. The hit man had a large black semiautomatic in his right hand, the silenced barrel placed firmly against Blackfoot's temple. Although Blackfoot was strong, Charon had the advantage of leverage, and Jonathan realized the hit man was highly skilled in Aikido or something else. Even outweighed, he easily controlled the Sioux.

"Kill him, Jonathan!" Blackfoot screamed.

Jonathan met Charon's eyes.

The assassin smiled. "We meet again, Master Jonathan." He pulled Blackfoot closer. "Shall we finish the game?"

Daniela fell to a knee and extended the shoulder stock for the Uzi, raising the weapon for eye-sight alignment. Without hesitation she locked aim on what could be seen of the German's forehead.

Jonathan gestured for her to hold fire and Charon seemed to take pleasure in what he observed.

"So you understand each other," he murmured. "That is good, is it not, Jonathan? To be understood? Especially since you are all alone, now, with no family to comfort you."

"You're not getting out of here alive," Jonathan said.

Charon laughed. "Put down your gun."

"No."

"I have a hostage."

"Tonight you're not taking hostages." Jonathan thumbed back the hammer. "I'm not taking prisoners."

Charon thumbed back the hammer of the semiautomatic. "Then be prepared to join him in hell. Because I will kill him and use his dead body for a shield while I kill both of you."

Eyes narrowing, Jonathan studied the space separating Charon from Blackfoot. Both of them were the same height and Charon was effectively using the Sioux. There was less than an inch of separation between Blackfoot's forehead and Charon's skeletal face; a one-inch shot at fifteen feet. He took it.

Jonathan fired before the gun was even level and Blackfoot screamed as he fell back with Charon roaring—shocked—rolling into darkness and then Jonathan and Daniela were simultaneously firing, firing all they had in a firestorm of flame that shredded the plaster wall above Blackfoot's prone body, demolishing the house and shattering the sheetrock and wood and doorway in a continuos streaming rage of fire that blazed across the air.

Inside thirty seconds Jonathan changed three clips and Daniela dropped four, efficiently throwing three hundred rounds in an eight-figure pattern that demolished the wall and everything on the other side in a carpet of lead. As Daniela calmly dropped her fifth clip and expertly slammed in a sixth, Jonathan raised his hand.

Not glancing at the gesture, she held a dead-steady aim on the smoking doorway. Her face was patient and cold; watching. Smoke filled the air and spiraled from overheated gun barrels. The atmosphere was warmed and the white wood wall where Charon had rolled was on fire.

"Blackfoot!" Jonathan shouted into the cloud of heated smoke. "Are you okay?"

No response.

"*Blackfoot*! Are you okay!"

Gingerly, Blackfoot shifted. Slowly, he pushed a dusty

sheet of ravaged plaster off his shoulders. Barely, he lifted his head to glance cautiously at the demolished wall.

He was all right.

Jonathan moved around one end of a table and Daniela crept around the opposite. She held the Uzi at arm's length, both hands locked. Jonathan went through first with Daniela coming across, instantly crouching, Uzi shoulder-high.

Nothing.

As soon as he saw the empty, demolished room, Jonathan knew Charon would not be found anywhere in the house. Incredibly, the German had escaped.

Again.

Jonathan backed out of the exit and re-entered the dining room to see Blackfoot rising from the floor, clutching the lost shotgun in his hands. Shaken, they exchanged glances. Blackfoot shook his head, "Man, I didn't think that I was going to—"

A thunderous impact split the huge front door in half and they whirled raising aim at a roaring, hulking giant that swept out a tree-trunk arm, blasting aside the oak slabs like paper. Despising the strength of wood and stone alike, the beast came down challenging everything, crouching and snarling, fingers curled like talons to crush and kill.

Almost instantly the man saw them. He hesitated a split-second, rose from his crouch. Jonathan reached out and gently touched Daniela's hand, lowering her aim.

She gazed at him, eyes wide and somehow...vulnerable, as if she had never truly allowed anyone to touch her. Jonathan smiled with affection, and she finally lowered the weapon to her side. She stood beside him.

Standing in the shattered doorway, Matsumo turned his head to see Logan lying in the living room, the form of the admiral slumped in death. And with a measure of calm that told them Matsumo had seen far, far more of life than he would ever reveal, he gazed over them.

Sirens were approaching.

"The back door is our only means of escape," he said.

Webster was reluctantly impressed by the reception of moderately dressed CIA case officers and, near the outskirts of the tarmac, a host of uniformed SAS.

Obviously the British government was cooperating with whatever President William Stanford requested. But Webster ignored the intimidation and moved away boldly from the jet, walking up to a man who extended his hand, cordial and without threat.

"Kyle Chapel," the man said. "I'm the Senior Case Officer for the London office."

"Richard Webster."

"Welcome to London."

Chapel glanced at the jet to see CI-3 soldiers in the exit. Webster saw the SAS soldiers shift nervously. "I think that we should leave the airport," Chapel continued. "Please instruct your men that they should leave their weapons in the jet. They won't be needing them."

Webster doubted that that would fly with CI-3, and he was right. Reibling, calm as he could be until he was told that they would be required to leave their weapons on the plane, responded that they would not, under any circumstances whatsoever, be doing so.

Returning to Chapel, Webster said, "It seems we've got a situation, Agent Chapel. These men are under federal license and, in fact, under American policy, to never surrender their weapons."

Chapel was clearly disturbed. "They can't go without weapons? Why not?"

"Because these men are part of a classified field unit that has repeatedly engaged terrorist forces, and each one of them has a bounty on his head." Webster was firm, calm. "Officer safety is the Bureau's tantamount concern in this matter, Mr. Chapel. We will not allow these men to go unarmed in this or any other country."

"Well, then, they'll have to return to America," said Chapel, a sad shake of his head. "I'm under orders not to let them into the country with their weapons. That comes from Langley."

"These men don't answer to the CIA, Chapel." Webster was becoming more comfortable with the situation as it developed, and he knew his position was good. "At the most, they must coordinate their actions with CIA tactical forces to prevent collateral damage in the field."

"But, sir, these men can't go into the field unless they are issued a sanction. Those are the president's orders."

"The president's legal right to recall these men is limited," Webster said plainly, "to peacetime operations. He has no right whatsoever to recall these men without my recommendation or approval in a tactical situation." Webster stared a moment, letting that settle. "What is the CIA's rationalization for defaulting my full authority and command to the Central Intelligence Agency?"

"Because your unit hasn't yet acquired an Order of Rebate from the State Department to operate in England," said Chapel, exasperation revealed in his tone. "They are legally required to submit themselves to the governing American authority on this soil."

"Fine," Webster said. "Then they can stay on the plane. They won't be on international soil until they disembark."

Reibling laughed from the door of the jet.

Not glancing at him, Chapel focused hard on Webster, as if he had expected this CIA-FBI clash over territory and authority, "Mr. Webster, clearly this is a difficult situation. For all of us. And I have no wish to interfere. But I was told specifically that CI-3 could not disembark onto British territory with weapons in hand."

Webster turned back to the Lear. "Reibling! Make your men comfortable on the plane. Order food and whatever else you need and charge it to the Bureau. I'm going to the embassy to check on the status of the team."

"Yes, sir."

Webster focused on the CIA man. "As an Assistant Director in the Federal Bureau of Investigations it is my privilege under Senate Intelligence Subcommittee Finding 240 to, at any and all times, insure the security of FBI classified operations and the welfare of internationally-stationed agents, non-exclusive of competing or alternate American Intelligence Agency jurisdiction. Do you have any argument with that, Chapel?"

"I'm not familiar with that finding."

"Look it up," Webster responded. "I had to. And in case you don't know it, Chapel, the CIA has no international police, subpoena, or law-enforcement powers whatsoever to restrict me."

"I certainly know that, sir."

Webster glanced at the soldiers. "Good. Then you'll understand me saying that if those SAS are still surrounding my team in one hour, or if *any* of my agents are in any danger, I will be on the phone with the director immediately. And by tomorrow there will be an emergency Senate Intelligence Subcommittee meeting on the supra-jurisdictional efforts of the CIA to restrict a legal action of the Federal Bureau of Investigations. An action meant to insure the safety of special agents caught in an immediate life-threatening situation. Is there anything about that statement that you don't understand, Chapel?"

Chapel took a step back. "Uh...well, no, sir. I understand you perfectly."

"Good," Webster's gaze was frightening. "Now I need a man to escort me through customs so I can do my job."

Motioning to a man behind him, Chapel said quickly, "Escort the AD to the Embassy. Insure that he arrives safely and—"

"He'd better," said Reibling from the stairway.

"I..." Chapel hesitated, "and, uh, and insure that he makes contact with his men."

"I'll see to that myself," Webster replied, moving face to face with the CIA case officer. "We've already wasted too much time. And let me tell you something else, Chapel. If it weren't for this type of in-fighting between the FBI and CIA, we'd probably be able to accomplish anything we wanted in American intelligence."

⊙ ⊙ ⊙

Logan groaned as they rolled him onto his back. His forehead was badly bruised and cut. Instinctively he lifted a hand to touch it, saw the smeared blood, cursed.

Sirens closed on the manor.

Blackfoot spoke quickly, "I heard Logan shooting, and I ran into the room just as he went down. I saw Charon in the doorway, and I dove as he fired. Then, I guess, he killed the old man. After that, there was this weird gunfight in the dark and we ran into each other. That's when you showed up."

Outside, the sirens thickened. But none of them approached the house, as if they weren't in a big hurry to do battle with whatever forces had collided.

Matsumo raised his face to the night as if he had learned, from experience, how long they had. "They will wait for an armed response unit to arrive. We have twenty minutes, at most."

"The back will be covered," Jonathan said.

"I will deal with it," Matsumo said, and Jonathan thought he read something ominous in the tone. They went together out the back door and in minutes were at the fence.

On the other side, Jonathan saw through the slats two cars were guarding the alley. Four uniformed bobbies, nightsticks in hand, stood ready. And although English common law didn't allow police to carry firearms, Jonathan knew the fearless street cops were tough as bulldogs and could give more than a fight.

"Stay here," said Matsumo, and vaulted the fence.

Before Jonathan could object, the big Japanese landed on the other side of the ivy and a stunning battle erupted without spoken challenge. He heard men scuffling and striking only to be brutally knocked down to rise again, knocked down, rising, cursing. The conflict continued for thirty seconds, a cacophony of blows and fierce collisions before an ominous silence fell like a thunderclap.

"Come!" Matsumo shouted.

Daniela climbed as easily as Jonathan though Blackfoot continued to have trouble. Logan was last, sweating and grimacing at the effort to scale the barrier, but then they were over it to see four London police officers sprawled unconscious in the gravel. Three of their unbreakable nightsticks were broken.

"They are not injured," Matsumo rumbled.

They moved to a car.

Jonathan didn't ask any questions as he took Blackfoot's shotgun and Matsumo climbed into the driver's seat, instantly revving the engine. They backed out of the alley without lights as the radio blared; a detective asking for a status at the back of the residence.

Remembering time as a street officer, Jonathan picked up the microphone and turned up the squelch, knowing that the sergeant on the other end would be cursing the inadequate radio equipment that he was *still* forced to work with in emergency situations. Speaking just enough beneath the squelch to sneak a word every two or three seconds, Jonathan kept up the transmission until they were on the street and Matsumo was driving away.

The Japanese filled half the front seat, scowling as he drove without lights. Then they hit an intersection and Jonathan began giving terse directions that Matsumo obeyed without blinking. In moments they were moving across Lambeth Bridge.

No one was following; they were almost safe. And in minutes they were in a heavily roaded section of Waterloo where they could lose themselves easily from a pursuit. Jonathan dropped the radio, knowing they didn't need it any more.

Logan was groaning. The bullet that grazed his head left an ugly contusion.

"Where do we go?" asked Matsumo. "We cannot keep this patrol car."

"Drive parallel to the river," said Jonathan. "We'll ditch this at Blackfriar's Bridge. Then we'll move across it into Holborn and find a place to hole up. We'll have to find a warehouse, something abandoned. It'll be safe enough for tonight."

For a moment Jonathan wanted to ask Matsumo how he had found them but it wasn't the time. They were shell-shocked and Jonathan still felt a terrific adrenaline rush from the frantic search for Hooper and the gunfight in the dining room.

He didn't even care anymore, somehow, that he had missed Charon. But he knew it was just fatigue. As soon as the trembling stopped and his mind returned, he would find and kill the German.

Matsumo reached the bridge and Jonathan cast a glance to Daniela; she was leaning her head back against the seat. Her eyes were painfully closed, and her brow was furrowed like a woman remembering far, far too much pain.

"Ditch this thing, Matsumo. They've got to be on us by now."

Immediately Matsumo angled behind a building and in five minutes they were walking across the lower tier of the bridge, out of sight of passing cars. Then they were in Holborn and Jonathan found an abandoned building. He kicked in the back door and they entered.

Daniela did what she could for Logan, who sprawled onto a mattress, unconscious. Silence settled as she worked, and they tried to find places to rest. Then she turned to Jonathan in the faint half-light and, for a strange moment, Jonathan saw her anew.

She was, he saw, a woman tired of fighting, so tired of it, but driven to it because of whatever dark cause burned in her heart; a woman who had become what she was because life had demanded it from her. And if she could have had it another way, she would have.

"Is Logan going to make it?" he asked quietly.

She looked back at Logan, softly touched his head. "He needs rest," she whispered. "He has a fever. He's going to need medical attention if it continues."

"Why?"

"Because that will mean that the meninges, the membrane surrounding the brain, is bruised." She placed a palm fully over his forehead. "It will mean that his head is accumulating fluid, placing pressure on his brain."

Jonathan grimaced, trying to rise to the challenge. Because he knew that, now, he was in charge. "It's only three hours until morning," he said. "We need some sleep. If Logan's fever hasn't broken by then, we'll call the Embassy or an ambulance or...something. But we'll give him until morning."

With a frown, Daniela left her hand on his head for a moment before standing, staring down for the briefest second before she turned away from Jonathan without words.

He watched her as she walked to a small pile of mattresses—this was obviously an abandoned warehouse—to tiredly remove her coat. But before she lay back, she looked at him.

Her face was soft and transparent.

It was a moment between them, and then she painfully closed her eyes. She lay back carefully, wakefully, still wearing her combat gear. And Jonathan turned to Blackfoot and Matsumo. For the first time, he felt like he could ask, "How'd you find us?"

The Japanese was somber. He looked at them as if he were a long overdue father, a father inured to this world far more than they, and he was grieved that he had come so late. But now he was here to protect them, and things had now and forever changed.

"Does it matter?" he smiled, mountainous in the gloom. "All of you are safe, now."

Jonathan looked across, at Daniela.

With ponderous strides Matsumo moved to the window, glancing both directions. "I will watch. The rest of you can get some rest. I will wake you when it is time."

It was still dark when Jonathan awoke and moved quietly to the window of the warehouse. He held the SIG in his hand as he searched. Then he felt eyes upon him and turned, saying nothing.

Daniela gazed up at him, so close. Even her breath seemed like thunder, and Jonathan was struck by the softness of her eyes. She did not move.

He smiled, "You need to sleep." But he knew that, like him, she never truly slept. She continued to gaze up, saying nothing.

Gently, Jonathan moved to her. He wanted to say so much, but only one thought came. And although he knew she had heard it a thousand times, he trusted his soul, hoping she had never heard it as he meant it. "You're beautiful," he said.

Daniela blinked, vulnerable now, and sad. "In Israel, they say you must be smart because everyone is beautiful." Her smile held even deeper sadness. "It is a place where beauty means nothing."

Jonathan frowned. "Why do you do this?"

"Revenge," she murmured.

He said nothing.

"I don't need to tell you," she added, after a time, "what this monster did to me. And my mother."

"No."

"There's more," she continued, but paused an even longer time. "I had a child, Jonathan."

Jonathan didn't move—not even his eyes.

"Her name was Sulieka; she was my life." Her eyes shone with glowing love. "Silman...He kills everyone close to you if he cannot kill you. He destroys you by killing everyone you love." She closed her eyes. "I almost..."

She took a deep breath. "I used to have faith. I believed

God was watching out for Israel. I had a good life. I served my country. And in one moment, everything was ripped from me. How can I forgive? Not until this is finished."

Jonathan stared down, immobile. What passed beyond his eyes was also beyond this world. Jonathan recognized himself in her words. Again, he remembered a time...before. Playing chess with his father before the fire. Bedtime prayers. Celebrating Shabbat. Being safe and loved.

"He thought that her death would destroy me. And it did, I suppose. I feel nothing. I can't remember when I felt anything. God has given me the strength to live for just one reason. To kill Charon." Her breath was heavier. "I must kill Charon...for what he did to my little girl."

Jonathan released a heavy breath. With an effort, he collected himself, then gently pulled a blanket to her shoulders. Her eyes were closed again, but she was not asleep.

"Sleep," he said.

She said nothing, and he knew she would not sleep.

He lay beside her, and she lifted her arm, her head settling tightly upon his chest. As lovers, he held her, inhaling her scent, her pain, her soul. Her voice was life to him; "Why do you fight?"

Jonathan stared into the darkness, watching the curve of her body as she breathed. "To be free."

"Jonathan..."

"Yes?"

"How can people like us ever be free?"

"We'll be free," Jonathan tightened his arm around her. "Both of us...I promise."

A surrendering, a relaxing that was total and at once, occurred down the length of her body. Her face was pressed against his chest and he knew she could hear his heartbeat, prayed she knew it was for her. She whispered, "I felt dead... until I met you."

He understood. Neither of them were alone, now, but it was more. It was a kind of understanding and unity that came from something far stronger than words or actions.

Her words so quiet that he barely heard.

"Finish it, Jonathan...Kill him."

And he knew she spoke of more than this fight. She was asking him to finish this nightmare that had burned up both of their lives for too long, because each of them wanted to live again.

"I'll finish it," he frowned, blinked to clear his moist eyes.

"For both of us."

His teeth clenched, though Jonathan said nothing. His arm closed on her so that he reminded himself of his strength, not to hurt her, and relaxed. Her fingers curled on his chest; *yes, hold me...*

She whispered, "Tell me what life would be like without war, Jonathan. Tell me what...we...might be like."

Jonathan reached up and touched her face, moving a finger to her eye, where a tear gleamed.

"It will be peaceful," he said, as quiet. "It will be a place where our children will be safe, and where we'll be safe. It will be a time when we can worship our God in peace instead of visiting His wrath on the enemies of Israel. A place where God will return to us what was stolen. Where no one can take from us what we love...Never again."

After a while, Jonathan saw her back lifting in heavier breaths, and he knew she was asleep. He caressed her face gently as she moved her face closer to his, so soft, and then he slept as well.

The warehouse was indiscriminate enough to be lost in the bland haze of warehouses surrounding the river. It was not special in any way, neither in architecture or oldness or newness. There was nothing to make it more noticeable than another warehouse.

Yes, Jonathan had made a good choice. They would not be disturbed here.

The man left the deep harbor of shadow and crept soundlessly down the fence line. He studied a patch of ground that lay in complete darkness a long time before stepping onto it, moving his feet slowly and close to the ground. If there had been a can or bottle before him, he would have felt it soon enough to avoid.

It took him thirty minutes to move a hundred feet, and then he walked up the side of the warehouse, taking his time. He was not impatient—impatience was a mistake of amateurs. Even when he reached the front of the warehouse, he did not move for the door. He stood unmoving in the shadows, and patiently watched the windows, but he did not watch for a face or body.

He watched for shades of shadow that might shift the slightest degree. He watched for movement akin to what a man sensed when a shadow moved upon the face of the ocean. It could have been a cloud; it could have been a shark. Patience...

Patience...

Chapter Seventeen

S trange, isn't it, that men seek truth?" Dumont remarked to Frazier. "Truth is such a cruel, ugly thing that ruins happiness. How insane that some men prefer it to a lie."

Frazier said nothing.

"Have you never thought," Dumont continued, "that almost everything we say and do is a lie? We say things that are not true because we do not want to injure. We play charades so that those around us will be happy, and truth has no place in it. Except the truth of our intentions." He turned to the morning. "Yes, I find it amazing that men would prefer the heartless tyranny of truth over the protective kindness of lies."

Frazier turned his stony gaze to the fire.

"No matter," Dumont sighed. "Some men are too...too *intellectual* for such reasoning. They cannot be persuaded of something so simple. So we must deal with them in kind, delivering to them what they would deliver to us. A tragedy and..."

"Truth?" finished Frazier.

Dumont turned to him. "Yes, my friend. A tragedy and a truth." He added after a moment, "Is everything in place?"

"Yes."

"Will Charon return here?"

"Yes."

"When?"

Frazier tilted his head toward a doorway.

"To rest?" Dumont asked.

"No," said Charon, emerging from the doorway. "I will not rest today."

Dumont revealed neither surprise nor alarm, as he had the day before. "And why not, Charon?" he turned to the black-clad figure. "You always rest during the day."

Turning to frown at Frazier, Charon answered. "I will not rest until the child's blood is finally mine. Any argument with me, Frazier?"

Frazier held the Iceman's gaze.

"No words," Charon whispered. "How appropriate." He stepped directly in front of the bear-like form. "The time is close for truth, my friend. All games must end."

Frazier appeared bored.

Charon pressed, beginning to circle. "I know it was you who saved the child that night! Why?"

"Charon!" Dumont shouted. "It's *enough*! We've been down this road before!"

"This is the last!" Charon twisted. "I *demand* Frazier's head on a pike before—"

Frazier hit—quick, no warning—a bear leaping from ambush to strike its prey to the ground. His fist sank into Charon's chest, bending him double. His other hand locked on Charon's white hair and the fist struck again—no words, no hesitation, no emotion—and Charon fell at the impact of a meat-cleaver.

With a curse Charon rose, reaching for his pistol.

Frazier's .45 touched the skeletal forehead. As he thumbed back the hammer, his eyes were cold and impassive—a machine pulling a trigger to hit a paper target, nothing more.

Charon froze; his empty hand fell slowly to his side. Frazier lowered the hammer on the .45, lowered the gun to his side. He rumbled, "Be careful what you ask for."

With a silent snarl, Charon backed slowly away. When he was at the edge of darkness, he turned and was gone. After a still moment, Frazier holstered the .45, looked at Dumont.

With incredible calm, Dumont sighed.

"Soon," he said.

Thoroughly impatient, Webster moved through the doorway of the FBI headquarters at Kensington. Two sleepy agents cast him curious glances as he came in and then one of them leaped energetically to his feet, recognizing.

"Good morning, sir!"

"Get Hooper at his hotel." Webster didn't raise his voice; he didn't have to. He moved to Hooper's office. "Tell him to get back in here. And page the rest of the team."

"*All* of them?"

"If they wanna keep their credentials, they better be here in an hour."

"But Hooper's not at the hotel, sir." The second agent was steadier. "He left early last night to meet someone. We tried to page him and phone him in his room but there's no answer."

Webster didn't like it. "Send two men to Hooper's hotel. Find out whether he's there or not. And keep paging him. If that doesn't work put out a BOLO with London police. Tell them to keep it quiet, but tell them we've got an agent missing. Get on it."

"We're on it." They were both on their feet. "Is there anything else, sir?"

"Start a pot of fresh coffee and get me secure lines to the duty officers at Interpol, Scotland Yard, MI5, the CIA, the London police, and the director's office in Washington. Advise the Embassy operator to keep six lines open at all times. If Logan calls—"

"We'll put him through to you immediately, sir."

"Good. Get to work."

Opening his eyes with an effort, Jonathan tried to bring himself to consciousness. He anticipated that it would be difficult to awaken, but it was easier than he expected, probably because he had already gone so long without sleep.

He knew that, contrary to what many people thought, the less sleep you caught, the easier it was to do without. And nobody could "catch up" on it. When it was lost, it was lost. There was no way to restore the body beyond what could be gained in six to eight hours.

Rising slowly, Jonathan sat up and saw Daniela still asleep on the mattress. And Blackfoot was out solid, lying on a dust-covered couch, clutching the shotgun in his hands. Logan was where they'd left him. But Matsumo was gone.

Jonathan felt a thrill of alarm, rising quietly to his feet with the SIG in his hand. He gazed around the room, the sun beaming bright through dusky clouds. No, Matsumo wasn't here. He had gone, and Jonathan didn't know if—

Paper on the floor.

Blinking, Jonathan focused: a sheet of paper was laid on the floor, just inside the doorway. And he didn't know for a moment what it was that had attracted his attention until he realized the paper was stark white and clean, while everything else in the room was covered in black dust and grime. It'd been left some time this morning.

Jonathan didn't know why he didn't alarm the others. Perhaps it was because he was just tired enough to doubt his own judgment. But then he heard Daniela moan and sit up.

When he glanced at her, she appeared fully awake. Her face was pale but she seemed to come back immediately to full alertness. She was conditioned to brief snatches of sleep in perilous situations.

Jonathan couldn't keep himself from smiling, and she returned it, a smile that spoke of another time and another place. Then she rose and, as she stood motionless, he saw her slowly switch to a violent warrior-mind. It was a change solid as an eclipse, casting a bitter light from her dark eyes. Where there had been softness, now there was only danger. Her frown said it for her: *It's time to kill these people...*

Jonathan nodded, then turned to the paper, not visible from her vantage. As if he were approaching a trap, he checked the angles of the windows, walking forward.

He took out his pocketknife, a specially designed switchblade manufactured for Special Force soldiers. It had a rayon handle with a grainy gray surface that provided a secure grip. Then he hit the button and blade cleared the handle, the edge serrated to facilitate sawing through tangled parachute cord.

He lifted a corner of the sheet. It couldn't be a bomb, but he didn't know what might be coated on the surface. He flipped it over with the blade and gazed down. Printed in bold letters: *GO HOME!*

"What is it?" Daniela asked.

"A message."

"From who?"

"I don't know."

She came forward, glancing at the windows, also checking for snipers. "It's from an enemy, Jonathan."

"What makes you say that?"

"Only an enemy would leave a message without awakening us." Her voice was toneless, as it was always toneless when she spoke of tactics and fighting and killing and war. "If it was a friend, he would have done more than warn us."

"That doesn't make sense, Daniela. It would have to be someone who followed us from the admiral's house. Somebody we didn't shake. But we shook the police."

Logan and Blackfoot stirred, both rising. Jonathan and Daniela turned, staring. After a moment Logan rubbed his head. "I have..." he muttered, "...a headache."

"You got hit by Charon." Jonathan walked to him. "You took a round off your skull. It was a miracle you survived. You were pretty punchy last night after you went down, so you might not remember what happened."

"I don't," Logan said. He didn't seem all that thrilled be alive, and Jonathan realized it was the typical reaction for a man who'd been shot, starved, hunted for two days, and thrown unconscious on a dirty mattress in a dirty warehouse only to wake up and find himself in the same miserable condition. Logan looked around the room for a long count. "Hooper?" he asked.

Jonathan shook his head.

Slowly, Logan bowed his head. "I thought so," he said. "I wasn't sure if was a dream or not." He paused, looked suddenly alarmed. "Where's Matsumo?"

"He's gone."

"Gone *where*?"

"I don't know. He was gone when I woke up."

They pivoted together, drawing weapons, as Matsumo came through the door, three enormous paper sacks beneath an arm. He nodded to all of them, unaffected by the armed response. Instantly he began removing hot coffee, bagels, bottles of water, and the entire menu of McDonald's breakfast meals.

"It is the best I could do," he rumbled. "But it is sufficient to restore our strength."

There were no complaints.

Scotland Yard returned Webster's call as sunrise cast a dark green glow over Baker Street, directly across from the embassy. Webster was standing at the bulletproof window, wondering how it would all end, when he heard an agent behind him.

He picked up the phone. "Yes."

"Assistant Director Richard Webster?"

"Yes."

"This is Wilfred Johnson with the Domestic Intelligence Division of Scotland Yard. I am returning your call, sir, and I will save you the trouble of explaining the situation. I know already and can meet with you immediately. I am at your service and will do whatever is in my power to assist you."

Webster was relieved to hear the voice of someone who stood with him. "Can you meet me here at the Embassy, Mr. Johnson? I've got calls waiting at Interpol. I want to search their files for a man once known as Simon Silman."

A cautious hesitation. Webster could almost hear Johnson glancing over his shoulder. "Interpol will provide nothing useful, sir. We are familiar with their files. Remember, Interpol functions simply as a storing house for information. They have no agents, no police power. If they know anything, and I can assure you they do not, you are wasting your time awaiting their call."

"What about MI5 or MI6?"

"MI5 possesses supervision," Johnson replied. "The rest cannot be classified in the same category." Webster knew that was a way of saying MI6 was compromised.

"All right," he agreed. "When can we meet?"

"I await you on Baker Street," said Johnson.

"Go home?"

Logan stared at the anonymous note like it was a speeding ticket from the Indianapolis 500. He ignoring warnings that it might be poisoned.

"I *wish*," he mumbled as he held it in his hands. "Go home? What does that *mean*? Go back to America? Get out of my country?" He sighed. "I have just about had it with these maniacs."

"It's a warning," said Jonathan.

"Obviously, Jonathan. The question is, who would leave us a warning?"

"The CIA."

"No, son, not the CIA. If the CIA knew we were here, they'd have shot us."

Blackfoot gaped, "The CIA would have shot us?" He was truly amazed. "Are you serious?"

"Yep."

Logan's utter stoicism could be unsettling—much more so than his anger, which came quickly and went quickly and meant nothing. And Blackfoot was particularly unsettled by it, having somehow come to rely on Logan more than Jonathan.

"B-But..." the Sioux struggled, "but, I mean, are you sure they're in on this?"

"Uh-huh."

Blackfoot was near his limit. "*Why?*"

Slowly, Logan lit a cigarette, exhaled in a mean mood. "Because, Blackfoot, this thing began in 1945. But Silman was working through the fifties and sixties and seventies and right on up to now. So the CIA, or all those guys who survived OSS and, uh, the..."

"Strategic Service Unit," said Jonathan.

"Right. Those goons from SSU who went into the CIA

have been cashing in on Silman since World War II." He became morose. "Last night was a kick in the gut, boys. I never expected us to get what we got. Never expected the old guy to spill his guts like that. But this still isn't coming together like it should."

"What do you mean?" Jonathan asked.

"Like, why did that old admiral talk to us, Jonathan?" Logan lowered the paper to his side. "What part did Haitfield play in protecting you after Charon murdered your parents? And how does Silman go from organized gold smuggling for a bunch of OSS and MI6 spymasters to laundering drug money for cartels? How did BCCI get involved in all of this? Was BCCI Silman's exclusive enterprise or was it CIA? Or MI6? And if it was CIA, then why were they laundering drug money and other funds for two thousand of the world's biggest criminals and terrorists? There's still too much spiraling out from this octopus that doesn't tie in. I was going to ask the admiral about it before Charon killed him." He paused. "No way to do that, now."

Blackfoot took a sip of coffee. "Maybe it doesn't have to all tie together, Logan. Maybe it's just a mess."

"I've considered that, son." Logan expelled smoke slowly. "I've considered that maybe this was all just a major fiasco since Silman went renegade, and now everyone is just scrambling to save their worthless lives. But that doesn't add up, either."

He grimaced, took a drag. "All right. Let's look at it. Silman is recruited by a secret coalition of MI6 and OSS agents to smuggle Nazi gold. A bunch of Yale and Harvard geeks get rich. MI6 gets rich. That's how Silman got rich so fast after being released from the Army prison.

"The OSS gave him the same international network they

developed during the war, and that's how he laid ties to all these different intelligence agencies, using intelligence ties to cover his covert activities in smuggling." He took another drag. "Now, though, it begins to get complicated. Silman has the money to do whatever he wants. He doesn't need OSS or MI6 anymore. So he goes renegade. And nobody kills him because he knows too much, has too many connections. It's better to protect him."

"Insurance?" Jonathan asked.

"Yeah," Logan answered. "Silman knows secrets that neither America nor England could survive."

"Is it that big?"

"Yeah, Jonathan, it is. Those guys got rich off the blood of six million murdered Jews. *Six million*. Then he tried to destroy Israel *after* the war. And America's interests are directly tied to Israel. Without a power base in the Middle East, we have no way to insure oil. And without oil this country would crash. But Silman doesn't worry about that because he's got the Saudis in his pocket."

He looked at the window, "No, kid, neither country can afford to let that kind of information get loose. Not then, not now, and Silman knows it. Knows how to use it. So he covers himself by telling CIA and MI6 that if anything happens to him, secrets will rise from the dead. He's probably got documents and names and dates and everything else he needs to bring down both the United States and English intelligence agencies at the same time."

"You're good at this," Jonathan muttered.

"I'm just warmin' up, kid." Logan squinted through smoke. "So Silman goes renegade with the bright idea of making money off loan scams which, if anyone remembers, is how all this got *started*. He leaves the gold operation in the past."

Blackfoot interjected, "They probably didn't have any gold left, anyway, Logan. Silman smuggled the stuff for twenty years. I mean, I know there was a lot of it, but twenty years is a long time. It was probably gone."

"Whatever," Logan waved. "The crux is that Silman had gained the reputation of being a solid independent operator who could get things done. He was connected. So he sets up the loan operation to scam Americans and American businesses out of more money. But he starts crossing lanes, making himself noticeable. He gets the attention of the FBI and the Secret Service. Federal investigations get started and then Silman has to start scrambling. He finds out that his old buddies in OSS can't cover him any more. He's gone off the reservation and things are too messy. So Silman's on his own, except for his insurance."

Jonathan digested it. "Is that when we come in?"

"No," Logan answered, not missing a beat. "This is where it gets dark. I can't...can't really see it. But there was something mysterious going on here for about ten years."

"What do you mean?"

"Look at it this way." Logan flinched, as if his headache had suddenly intensified. "Silman breaks from the OSS and MI6 guys who started him. He starts World Finance, founds BCCI. But somebody in our government—and believe me on this, boys—*somebody* knows who he is and what he's done—decides to let him get away with it. Despite the fact that they know Silman is crooked to the bone, they let him get by with his crimes, even protect him."

There was silence.

"So?" said Blackfoot, a bit dazed.

"*So?*" Logan looked at him. "*So,* Blackfoot, why did people inside the American government refuse to stop Silman from doing what he was doing? They may not have stopped him from smuggling the stolen gold because that secret was a significant threat. But when Silman started stepping on feet with his own operations somebody had to make a decision to leave him alone. Somebody had to say that he was not to be touched. And they didn't do it because they wanted to protect America, either. These people wouldn't have done it for free."

Together they were staring at him, and Logan leaned forward, gesturing with his hands. "Let me put it this way, boys. Because it always, *always* comes down to this: Who, I ask you, made money when Silman was working his own schemes in America?" He paused. "We know who made money off his gold smuggling. But Silman was working in America for over ten years before the FBI or any other agency really began cracking down on him. And why was that? Who did Silman own who could cripple so many investigations? Who in the State Department protected him?"

"Stanford," said Blackfoot.

"No," Logan answered, rubbing his head. "Stanford's too lightweight for this. He's somewhere in the floor plan but there has to be somebody else." He paused, grim. "But, then again, what if it wasn't somebody in the White House? What if it was somebody in the FBI or Justice? What if it was *all* of them? What if it was just a load of ex-presidents and secretaries of state and ambassadors and CIA directors and everything else? And that's where the *real* fiasco came in. And that is answered, boys, by: Who made the money?"

Together, they stared.

"*Well?*" Blackfoot blurted.

Logan smiled faintly. "The worst mistake you can make, Blackfoot, is to assume that every question has an answer or that everything has a solution." He became strangely pensive.

"You have to be realistic, boys. The people who have profited from this will never be tied to it. Most of these guys are dead, anyway, and the money is old money by now. It's spread across this nation like the drug money, just sauce lost in sauce. And journalists and FBI guys that run around trying to find all the arms of this octopus end up dead in a bathtub or blow their brains out before it's over."

There was a sense of ultimate justice to Logan's words. "Hear me out; we can't find all of them. But we can find this man. And this man is the one who made it work. Killed a lot of good people, ruined a lot of good families, threatened the existence of Israel. And he's not going to stop.

"You can't get justice for the whole world, but we *can* get justice." He paused; his words were certain. "We're gonna take this guy down. For Woodard. For Jonathan's parents...For Daniela—"

"And my daughter," said Daniela.

Logan nodded. "You bet."

He looked at all of them in turn. "People, we are going to kill this man graveyard dead and the Nazi, too. If he ain't gonna answer to justice in this world, he can answer in the next."

"It is right," Matsumo rumbled.

"It is justice," said Daniela.

Jonathan said nothing. His eyes were deadly.

"What about everyone trying to stop us?" asked Blackfoot.

As if he were insulted at such a question, Logan released a stream of smoke. "Blackfoot, these people can't outpolitick me, son." He winked. "I've got a plan."

Jonathan and Blackfoot smiled at each other while Matsumo stood behind them, poised and dangerous...and smiling. Then Jonathan looked at Daniela and couldn't keep himself from instantly reaching out and pulling her close and tight.

She was smiling, too.

Surrounded by Scotland Yard bodyguards, Webster eased into the back seat of a black four-door BMW beside Wilfred Johnson. Webster had seen a few investigators from Scotland Yard, but he had never seen one of them who fulfilled the title better than Johnson.

A Wyatt Earp mustache curled upward on either side of his mouth beneath a long, broad nose. He was almost completely bald, and he appeared to be in robust physical condition despite the English worsted that concealed his frame.

In a large sense, his hands spoke for him. They were broad, not deeply tanned, and obviously strong. They were hands that seemed ultimately suited to police work—capable of tirelessly writing reports or mercilessly manhandling the meanest thug. Overall, the inspector reminded Webster of a farmer, a man who was strong because his life demanded it, but who was also naturally gifted for the task.

The inspector made a gesture to the driver and he turned right, moving past the Embassy toward Buckingham Palace. Then Johnson pushed a button on his door and a window lifted to isolate them from the front. The driver did not seem to notice.

Settling in, he turned, and Webster saw the clear, concentrated gaze of a man utterly relaxed with secrets and intrigue and tragedy. His first words confirmed it. "I think," said Johnson gravely, "that one of your men is dead, Director Webster."

Webster opened his mouth but didn't say anything. He figured it was Hooper and then it was confirmed as Johnson continued, "We discovered the body of Special Agent Mark Hooper this morning."

Webster glanced out the window. He tried not to show emotion, but the rage he felt couldn't be denied.

"Did you find anybody else?" he asked.

"Yes," Johnson replied, prepared. "We found the body of Admiral Benson Haitfield, formerly a senior member of MI6. He was shot in his house on Vauxhall Bridge Road—a tidy assassination. But your man, Hooper, was stabbed to death in an upstairs bedroom. We believe he was tortured. Very unprofessional, of course, unless the professional was attempting to make him talk."

"When did your people find this?"

"At four o'clock this morning."

"Why didn't you inform the Embassy?"

Johnson clearly considered his reply, apparently judging that truth was best. "Because we knew that you were flying in from America. And we were informed by...friends...that you would be the proper man to handle the situation. We were also informed that the FBI office at the Embassy was electronically compromised. Plus, our Intelligence Division suggested that you would have a difficult time if knowledge of this event were leaked to other sources."

Webster asked, "When did General Ben Canaan contact you?"

Smiling faintly, the inspector replied, "This morning. And there is more."

"What?"

"Logan's team is currently sought under a warrant for conspiracy to commit murder by three agencies—your CIA, MI6, and Interpol. We can assume Silman knows of this, and perhaps orchestrated it."

"You know about Silman?"

"All too well," replied Johnson somberly. "We have known about Silman since the Krays. The Yard knew at that time that Silman had claws somewhere in Whitehall, but we could prove nothing. The evidence was not there. So we were forced to release him, and we continued to follow him through the years until we lost him to your Witness Protection program. We have been seeking him since, waiting for him to make a mistake."

Webster decided his men were more important than Silman. "What about Logan and the team? What's their status?"

"They were apparently heavily involved in the row at Admiral Haitfield's residence," Johnson answered. "All except Hooper seem to have survived, but we cannot be certain." He glanced out the window. "I must say that I was actually astonished by the carnage of the crime scene. If your men survived, sir, it is only because they responded with a bloody serious counterattack."

"How many people are dead?"

"Just the admiral and Agent Hooper. But this is far from over. Our Israeli friend tells me that he has also lost one of his men, or one of his women, rather. She is a highly skilled agent who has teamed with your men to discover the hiding place of this vermin. And they are, at this time, playing a rather desperate game."

"Yeah," Webster mumbled. "A game against time."

"More than that, sir. They are playing a game against both your government and mine. Of that I'm certain. Because not only has your authority been undermined by the detainment of your CI-3 men at the airport, but my position has been laboriously deterred by the intrusion of abstract government priorities."

Webster shook his head. "Seems like both of us have been pushed into traffic."

"Precisely."

Somehow Webster trusted the inspector, perhaps because he seemed so much like a regular cop and not an intelligence agent. Together, they had something in common. They had both survived the street to rise to a position of authority over others who were also on the line. It was ground for common loyalty among all cops of all nations. It's what separated them from their own people and from anyone else. Because they were the ones who had spent time on the line, and the only ones they truly trusted were each other.

Webster spoke without looking. "We have to find Silman, Inspector. We have to finish this."

"Oh, yes," Johnson said, frowning deeply. "Most assuredly."

Frazier revealed nothing as Charon glowered at him. They stood in the lower level of the mansion in Waltham and Charon appeared far worse for wear. His face was even paler than usual and he bore a scarlet crease to the side of his right eye. Also, he moved with a strange stiffness, as if he were injured.

Dumont gazed at both of them. At the last he concentrated on Charon, perhaps because there was so much there to see. "And what is the news?"

"Hooper and Haitfield are as they should be," he replied, intoning a strange depth in the words. His dark glasses seemed to darken even more. "Logan and his team live."

"The female Mossad agent?"

Charon did not move. "I tire of killing Mossad."

"Perhaps," Dumont replied. "But she must be killed, nonetheless. She is obsessed over...what you did to her, and we can leave nothing to chance." He turned to Frazier. "What is your progress?"

"I was forced to detain Webster's special response team," Frazier replied. "They were more dangerous than Logan and Malone combined. To render them impotent, I was forced to coordinate other matters last evening."

"They are returning to America?"

"No. But they cannot disembark the Bureau's jet at the airport, either. They will remain at the airport until they leave. At this moment, Mr. Dumont, it was the best that could be done. But it is a situation that shall remain constant until tonight, when Logan and his team exhaust their sanction."

"That is sufficient," Dumont turned away. "Yes, sufficient. And now we must insure that neither Logan nor any of his men are capable of causing an incident. I want both of you to—"

"I work alone," said Charon flatly.

Dumont snapped, "You will work as I tell you to work or you will work for someone else!" He waited, but Charon said nothing.

Charon glowered in Frazier's general direction and seemed to descend somehow within himself, as if his soul were even deader than his corpselike face revealed and yet, still, the face lowered itself deeper into some inner depth, a condensing darkness.

"So it seems," he said.

"Now," Dumont continued, "Charon, you must search for Logan. Frazier will remain here to guard me. The only messages will be by courier. The Indian has means of penetrating any and all electronic communications."

"The Sioux's equipment was recovered from a raid on the safehouse," said Frazier. "Now they have only their guns."

"Tools of the truly desperate," Dumont remarked, then stared into the low-burning flames. "Very well, make contact with our people in America and insure contingency plans are coordinated. We are entering the endgame, and procedures must be in order, just in case Logan or his people stumble over us."

"I have remedies for every scenario," said Frazier. "But I do not think Logan or his men can defeat our defenses. Even if they find us, I have designed trapdoors."

"Good," Dumont turned away. "It is regrettable that this situation ever became so precarious, Frazier. Our sources inside the State Department had contained any investigations launched against us quite well. Until, of course, Israel used their people to initiate this desperate gambit. They were cunning, true, by going outside established lines of command. But they have always been cunning. Their God has given them that much.

"Now, if we can only curtail Logan and his men and put Israel back in its place, I believe we may survive this intact. But, regardless, you must remain close. If Malone or Logan comes, you are to kill them."

"I will kill them, Mr. Dumont."

"I know you will, old friend."

Logan didn't glance around the intersection. Blackfoot and Daniela watched on the near side of the street, though Matsumo and Jonathan were three miles away, outside the Consolidated Bank of England, the bank that received the message from BCCI.

Logan knew that there was only one way Charon could have found them last night. And that was by knowing, somehow, that Hooper was leaving the Embassy to meet with them.

Somebody, and that meant somebody *inside* the FBI office, had contacted Silman after Logan called. So somebody had turned, and bad. Logan didn't really care who it was. It was unimportant. Silman already owned so many people that there would be no way to nail them all. What he really wanted to do at this moment was find where Silman was hiding, and the best way to do that was by using Silman's people the same way Silman used the FBI.

All the agents in the London office could be replaced, anyway, as soon as this was over. Plus, they would all be kept under tight internal security supervision for the rest of their careers. It was cruel, Logan knew, to the innocent. But the FBI had always been systematically cruel in how it treated its people, especially in the area of transfers and promotions and evaluations.

He glanced at his watch, determined not to stay on the line for more than fifty seconds, leaving a twenty-second safety margin. Then a voice came back over the line: "AD Webster has been paged, Special Agent Logan. We're waiting for him to return the call."

"Hurry it up," said Logan. "I haven't got all day."

"Yes, sir."

Another ten seconds and Logan spoke, "Are you there?"

"Yes, sir."

"Give Webster this message. Tell him we're at the intersection of Kingsland Road and Great Eastern Street in the district of Shoreditch. Tell him to get a carload of agents out here as soon as possible. We're in a deserted parking lot on the northeast corner; a white van with tinted windows. We'll be waiting."

"Yes, sir."

Logan hung up and turned to Blackfoot and Daniela. Both of them appeared unarmed but he knew they were sufficiently armed to take on an army. In addition to weapons, everyone was wearing the bulletproof vests Blackfoot had brought from the safehouse.

"All right," he said to all of them, "this is how it's going to work. If I'm right, somebody is going to send a message to Silman by courier. Jonathan and Matsumo will try and pick him up and follow him to where Silman's gone to earth. Meanwhile, we're going to ambush the German when he tries to hit that van that we stole from the bus station. How does that sound?"

Daniela nodded without words. Clearly, to her, killing the German would not be a traumatic experience.

Blackfoot smiled widely, "Sounds real western, Logan. Just like cowboys and—"

"Don't even say it, Blackfoot."

Chapter Eighteen

There," Matsumo said, instantly raising himself to an even higher level of respect to Jonathan, as men did when they were unconsciously testing one another in the field.

"I've got him," Jonathan answered, studying the slender, dark-haired man who ran from the back door of the Consolidated Bank of England and climbed onto a black BMW motorcycle. The man placed a helmet over his head and within seconds was burning out of the parking lot.

There were dozens of people moving around the bank but none of them had moved with such single-minded purpose, none of them had mounted a motorcycle parked so close to the back door of the bank, and none of them had left seconds after Logan's call.

Reflexively, Jonathan also realized that there were a dozen other factors coming into play, like the fact that the man wasn't dressed for a bank, but the bike had been sitting in the lot all day. Or that it was too early for lunch, too late for breakfast, and that the man carried nothing pertaining to business. He was simply exiting in a hurry, like a man with a mission. Like a courier.

"I'm on him," Jonathan climbed onto the stolen BMW motorcycle, apparently the only bike used in England. "You catch the next. And look quick, man, we only have two shots at this."

"Be careful," Matsumo rumbled. "Keep your distance. We will do the rest together."

Jonathan revved the engine, leaned forward. "Watch your back."

He gunned the bike, weaving a tight pattern through the wildly disorganized London traffic.

In sixty seconds he was moving out Gray's Inn Road to hang a sharp right at the four-lane intersection of Pentonville Lane. Then he moved northeast at alarming speed, revving the bike higher and higher to speed dangerously through intersection after intersection.

Again and again Jonathan was tempted to search for London police but they were moving far too fast. He managed to hang back at about an eighth of a mile, riding behind vans and larger vehicles as he kept a narrow view on the runner. In thirty minutes they cleared the city and entered a section Jonathan didn't recognize. It was wooded and unpopulated except for isolated, strategically placed estates far from the road.

It was some kind of exclusive section for rich landowners who used the ground to insulate themselves from the lesser few—everything was old, dark, rich English forest.

A land fit for a king...

"How long do you think it'll be?"

Logan didn't even look as Blackfoot adjusted his kevlar vest with irritation. He had an abysmal headache from his scalp wound, but he was trying to stay alert. He scanned traffic, ignoring the stiffness in his neck. "No way to tell, son. Might be soon. Might be a while. He'll come when he comes."

Frowning, Blackfoot scanned the increasingly thick rows of cars and vans and trucks. He had the five-round shotgun beneath his coat. Across the street, on a payphone, Daniela stood demurely in the crowd. She was talking excitedly—a natural actress.

Logan watched her for a while, amazed at how she went from one activity to the next, so relaxed, so natural. She seemed utterly at home and friendly and nonthreatening. She could probably stay there all day and acquire a dozen friends, be invited to dinner.

Once, to a shock Logan did *not* need, she engaged a London police officer in friendly conversation, as charming as could be while she held the Uzi under her coat. Sweating profusely, Logan found himself cursing under his breath for ten minutes.

"I can't take this," Logan muttered as the bobbie finally walked off, whistling. "I'm getting too old for this."

Streaked with sweat, Blackfoot said nothing.

"That woman is something else," Logan said later. "Jonathan's going to have his hands full."

"You think they'll get together?"

"Probably." Logan scanned traffic. "They're made for one another."

"Why's that?"

"They're both deadly as sin."

Laughing, Blackfoot also continued to search. "Yeah, I guess." Suddenly he seemed to become more nervous, and tense. "How do you think it's gonna happen?"

"Probably an outright attack," Logan answered, not removing his eyes from the street. "A machine gun through the walls of the van. A rocket. Who knows? But the German will hit hard. He'll try to take us all out in a bang. And then we'll throw down with him. That's why I told you to wear that vest. This'll be a stand-up fight."

Blackfoot studied each car. "It's not gonna be easy to take him, Logan. That guy...he's good. When he had me last night, I couldn't move him. He was like..."

"Like ice?"

He paused. "Yeah. Something like that."

"Don't worry about it, son." Logan lit another cigarette. "Just lay down on him with that twelve-gauge. Unload, load it up, unload again. He won't be walking away."

Silence.

"I was scared last night." The Sioux seemed ashamed to admit it and Logan turned to him with an aspect that was solemnly serious.

"You were scared because you're too smart not to be scared, kid. If you weren't smart enough to be scared, I sure wouldn't be working with you."

Blackfoot seemed to study nothing. "Logan, can I ask you to do something for me?"

"Sure, kid. What you need?"

"Did you know," Blackfoot said slowly, "that the Bureau only hired me because they were scared of me?"

"Had good reason to be. I'd have hired you, too."

"Yeah. But I have a brother. And...and he got into some trouble. I got him out of it, but I've always worried about him, because I made a lot of enemies. If...if anything happens to me, Logan, I want you to make sure that nothing happens to him after I'm gone." The Sioux paused. "Can you do that for me?"

"Ain't nothing gonna happen to you, Blackfoot. You just stick by me. You'll be okay."

"I want your promise, Logan."

Traffic was the only sound.

"You've got it," Logan answered finally. "I promise I won't let anything happen to your brother." He looked at the van again. "You just do what I tell you to do, Blackfoot, and you'll be okay. You hear me?"

"Yeah," the Sioux smiled after a moment. "I hear you."

A massive black iron-grill gate barred entrance to the castle located deeply inside Waltham Forest.

Crouching behind trees, Jonathan was hidden in the nightvale of mossy forest gloom. Watching.

A single side of the wide double doors opened and Jonathan saw a heavy, red-bearded man in the entrance calmly take the note from the courier's hand. And Jonathan waited for something, anything, so he could make a decision.

And it happened.

The courier turned to his bike, gunning the engine and riding out quickly on the circular drive as the red-bearded man, almost as big as Matsumo himself, reached up to touch the door to close it. But then the man paused, head bowed, as if he had heard something.

Jonathan knew the man could not see him—he was far too deeply concealed with the wood line. But the man raised his head, staring straight at him, gazing into the surrounding forest.

And Jonathan knew.

This man was a soldier, and a good one. He was a man whose instincts were finely focused and alive, a man who heard intuition as keenly as most men heard a shout in the dark. And he had somehow sensed that someone, or something, was near.

This was the place, because no one hired soldiers like this unless they had a profound need for protection. Men like this were expensive—prohibitively expensive—and only the most powerful men in the world could afford them. And there was probably only one person outside the royal family in that league.

Jonathan held his breath as the man stared across the land. Then, bowing his head slightly, the man turned and closed the door. Slowly Jonathan stood to his feet, knowing that even then he could not be seen. His face bent toward the castle.

"Endgame..."

"What is it, Frazier?"

"An ending."

Dumont looked up from the desk. His face was calm, though he realized that such a statement didn't come from his bodyguard without sufficient cause.

"Do we have Logan's location?" he asked quietly.

Frazier hesitated, "Yes."

"Where?"

"In Shoreditch."

"Can you get to them?"

"Not before the FBI arrives. Our man in the Embassy could not keep the news from being routed to the appropriate channels." He paused. "We do not own them all."

"What about Charon? He is already in the city."

Without pause Frazier picked up a phone. He spoke so quietly that he could not have been heard two feet away. Then he replaced the receiver on the hook, straightening.

"Charon is already close. He says he can be at the location within minutes. And he knows that time is of the essence. He will strike Logan as soon as he arrives."

Relieved, Dumont leaned back in the red leather chair. He folded his hands before him with an aspect of meditation. "Then everything is good," he said.

"We should not leave it to Charon alone," Frazier rumbled. "His performance in this situation has been less than perfect." He paused. "I think that, perhaps, you are right. Perhaps Charon is too old. Or careless. I think that I should go into the city and insure that the job is performed as we need it to be performed."

Dumont nodded, thoughtful. "Go, then," he said. "Insure that neither Logan nor his team escapes."

Frazier turned.

"It will be done."

◉◉◉

Jonathan hit the highway in a rush, angling the bike low in a shower of gravel and then he straightened, using speed to outrun the approach of an approaching tractor trailer.

He didn't have it in his mind to reach a phone, he only intended to reach Logan because he knew in his heart that this was the place and that a message had been sent. And he wanted to be there for the ensuing battle.

Flatlining the bike, he passed a Jaguar and angled close enough to take off the sideview mirror of another car. Then he was ahead of the Jaguar and screaming into the wind, pushing the machine and his driving skills to the maximum, riding the edge of control.

◉◉◉

In the shadows of the alley, Logan raised his face and his entire stance tightening. He blinked to clear his vision. "On the clock, Blackfoot. Showtime."

Logan looked at Daniela to gain her attention but, as casual as a tourist, she had already hung up the phone and was walking slowly toward the white van. She knew.

The black Mercedes pulled into the parking lot, stopping thirty feet from the passenger side.

Logan started across the street, Blackfoot close. And he kept his hand on the SIG as he walked forward, his finger closing around the trigger as Charon got out of the car, dark glasses shielding his eyes. He held a cut-down MP5.

353

Almost as soon as the hit man's feet hit the ground he straightened, raising the barrel to the side of the van and a silenced thudding terrorized the street.

Even though it was less than a roar, the massacre was obvious to the Londoners who screamed and ran or dropped to the ground as Logan ran across eight lanes of Kingsland Road, stealthily approaching the Mercedes. Charon finished a fifty-round clip, riddling the back of the van. In a heartbeat he inserted another, continuing to fire.

"*Charon!*" Logan shouted, straightening aim over the top of the Mercedes as Blackfoot moved to the front of the vehicle, the shotgun leveled.

The Sioux moved swiftly, standing his ground to kill or be killed and for a split-second Logan felt a paternal instinct and his hand closed on the trigger.

Charon dropped so quickly that Logan's bullet hit the van and somehow Logan *knew* what was about to happen—an instinct-reflex compelling him to whirl and scream, "Blackfoot! *Get down!*"

The explosion was stunning.

Wall of *fire!*

Fire in a volcanic wall blasted Logan through the air to smash him against something he didn't have the impulse to identify. He couldn't catch his breath but he knew he was alive; it was enough.

Enraged, he rose to see Blackfoot rolling to the front of the car, evading the gas tank Charon had ignited with a blaze from the MP5 and Logan gained balance, his gun rising before him.

Charon stood.

The Iceman fired at Blackfoot before the Sioux even cleared the front of the burning Mercedes, and Logan saw the shotgun blast go wide, Blackfoot shouting and falling back, a geyser of blood spiraling from the Sioux's severed neck.

With a vengeful roar Logan fired at Charon's tall black form outlined against flames and Charon smashed into the van, hit in the back by three shots.

Daniela came across the front of the van. But, incredibly, the hit man sensed or heard or glimpsed her approach and even as Daniela was at the headlights he jerked open the bullet-shattered door, rolling inside the back of the vehicle.

Logan saw what was about to happen and he raised the SIG as Charon raised his MP5, aiming at Daniela as she passed the front windshield, the Uzi held high. With pure rage Logan fired a half-dozen shots before the hit man also fired and the glass exploded at the front of the van and Daniela fell shouting.

Running forward with the SIG tight in both hands, Logan lost sight of Charon. Then he was at the van, the gun close, searching frantically, searching, trying to ignore Daniela's writhing form on the concrete before he sensed—

Charon moving from behind the van...

Instantly Logan realized: After hitting Daniela, the hit man had fallen out the side door and run to the front of the van, then back down the driver's side and around the back, coming up behind Logan as he reached the side door.

Logan spun as—

A bullet hit him solidly in the chest.

Logan flew back, firing frantically at the nightmarish shape but in a split-second Charon was over him; a vulture descending from flame, skeletal face enraged.

Charon fired another bullet into Logan's shoulder, a numbing blast that was deflected by the vest but hammered his shoulder to the ground and Logan bellowed. Then the vulture-like black form stepped on his wrist, pointing the silencer point-blank against Logan's right forearm.

Logan twisted.

Charon fired.

Roaring in pain, his face splattered with blood, Logan struggled frantically to draw his backup. Charon placed the barrel against his forehead.

A breathless moment, a moment sweating and grimacing in pain, and Logan laid his head back. He spit, glaring into the stark-white face, the black glasses.

Bending face to face, Charon pressed the silencer hard against Logan's forehead. "Only one thing preserves your life!" the hit man shouted, barely audible above the roaring flames. "Tell Jonathan the game is not over! Tell him to meet me where it began!"

"He'll kill you," Logan spat.

Charon laughed. "Enough banter! I must leave! And I am taking the woman with me." He smiled. "Tell Jonathan to come for her!"

He dragged Daniela to the van, smashing his pistol down across her neck, then pushed her inside.

As the van cleared the parking space Logan rolled away from the unendurable heat of the Mercedes, leaving a wide trail of blood, trying to determine whether his clothes were on fire. He continued to roll until he felt a draft of cool air and then he half-rose, bathed in blood, searching for Blackfoot.

The Sioux was silent on the pavement; his legs were on fire, and Logan knew he was dead.

With a groan he closed his eyes, whispering through pain and fatigue and the roaring of violent, violent flame. Then he heard a motorcycle frantically skid to a stop beside him and an enraged voice shouting his name over and over, coming closer.

Hands on his shoulders as he fell back, Jonathan's face over him before he closed his eyes to darkness sweeping up from the edges of his vision like fire.

"Fire," he whispered. "It's coming..."

○ ○ ○

"It's over," Webster said coldly.

There was an almost funereal silence in the lower level conference chamber of the American Embassy. Webster glanced at Inspector Winfred Johnson of Scotland Yard.

"The director had informed me that the president is turning over the murder of our man to your people, Inspector. He says the situation has become too complicated for FBI intervention. From here, it's Scotland Yard's game."

Jonathan stood at end of the table, Matsumo beside him.

"Blackfoot is dead, sir. Charon is still out there. Daniela is missing. And we still haven't found the man responsible for all of this. We can't let this go."

"There will be no argument, Special Agent Malone." Webster's gaze held the faintest trace of compassion, but implacable authority dominated his demeanor. "We are officially ordered, by the president himself, to return to America where there will be a debriefing with the State Department. The director is holding a press conference within the hour to say that the murder of Blackfoot and the assault of Logan will be taken from here by the London police. There will be no mention of the Mossad agent. Israel and the proper London authorities will be making their own arrangements for her rescue."

Webster paused. "Both of you are officially relieved of duty until a full report can be made of every activity that has transpired since this assignment began. You will travel back to America on the director's jet and debrief in flight."

"We can't do that."

"You *will* do that!" Webster said. "The director has stood behind us though this entire thing, Malone. He has backed you and me and Logan to the wall. But there's nothing more he can do. The CIA will complete this investigation."

"You know I can't," said Jonathan.

There was a moment where Webster seemed to react, but in the space of a breath, he shut it down. He placed both hands on the table and leaned forward, staring at the dark wood.

"Jonathan," he began, "I want you to know that I am truly, truly sorry about Blackfoot. I know he was your friend. And I want you to know how upset I am about Logan. He's a good man. He is *my* friend. And I regret that the Mossad lost their agent. I understand that she was a highly-respected operative."

"There's also Hooper and Woodard," said Jonathan. "And everyone else that Charon has killed. Like my parents. Like Daniela's daughter—a child. How far does this have to go, Mr. Webster? Where does the Holocaust end?" He shook his head. "This killing has to stop."

Webster took a breath. "There is simply too much at stake here for revenge. But this is not over. We still have a few cards left to play, especially with the House." He paused. "All of this is regrettable, Jonathan. But we cannot violate this mandate."

Jonathan didn't move. Matsumo didn't move.

Webster stared down at the table. He spoke with extreme caution. "Jonathan," he began, "I believe I know what you're thinking. I'm warning you, son: Don't do it."

Jonathan reached slowly into his coat, pulling out his FBI credentials. He opened the case, gazing down for a moment. Dropped it on the table. He turned without words and walked to the door, Matsumo following. Inspector Johnson rose to feet as they moved away, staring after them.

"Jonathan!" Webster shouted. "You're doing something you can't undo! If you come back and keep this between us, I'll forget that this happened! But if you walk out that door, you're walking out of the Bureau and you'll be on your own! You'll be subject to the laws of this country just as much as the citizens of this country or anyone else! You can be prosecuted and jailed for whatever you do without diplomatic cover or legal authority!"

Pausing in the doorway, Jonathan gazed back sadly.

"Jonathan, try to hear what I'm saying," Webster leaned forward. "I want Charon dead, too. I understand why you want justice. But if you walk out that door, you're not FBI anymore. You'll have nobody to cover you except Matsumo. And Matsumo will also be operating without sanction or immunity. Both of you will be alone."

With a strange smile, Jonathan nodded.

"Hooper was alone, sir." His eyes clouded, gray and resigned. "Woodard was alone. Blackfoot was alone. My parents were alone. Daniela's daughter was alone. We might as well be alone, too."

Chapter Nineteen

Black rain fell on hallowed ground. A lordly tomb rose monolithic in this thunderous storm, brooding before Jonathan as he stood in the meaningless night. Darkness was only illusion, he knew, for what waited for him inside the stones did not know darkness.

His father's manor, a grave now, was silent and black and somber, and Jonathan moved into the past as he stared over it. It had been two decades since he last walked this ground on winter's dead leaves. And within those walls, then, death had come for him.

And, now, had come for him again.

Matsumo's voice was quiet. "Are there means of illuminating the house?"

"No."

There was no true silence because the night contained no silence. The wind cried through overhanging bushes and limbs that reached down with skeletal tendrils, coldly grasping. The ground was dead and wet and moldy, hushfully enveloping their steps. Jonathan gazed at the spired stone walls etched against a moonless, starless sky.

"How do you know he is inside?" rumbled Matsumo, squinting fearlessly at the structure. He seemed far, far different than Jonathan had ever known him. There was anger in the set of his jaw, and although his hands were open, they seemed far more hardened, as if he had awoken an inner strength. His fearlessness, masterful and menacing and unmerciful, was comforting.

"He's inside," Jonathan said. "He killed my parents here, but he didn't kill me. He wants to finish the game."

Matsumo gazed at him. "And how shall we play this game?"

Jonathan searched every blackened corner. "There's no good way to do it. He's had all day to prepare."

"We could wait for daylight."

"No. Before they carried Logan to the hospital he told me Daniela was hit. I can't wait for daylight."

"How will we get inside?"

"We'll go through the upstairs window." Jonathan pointed to a wall that was climbable to the roof. "He'll probably have the doors wired. So we can't take a chance with the lower level entrances. But it would have taken him a week to wire the entire house."

Taking a step forward, Matsumo paused, turned back. "What are you waiting for? There is battle, here."

Without moving Jonathan continued to stare at the structure. His face was faintly tense, anticipatory. It seemed as if he were watching something pass before him—faces, or memories.

But it was a ghostly parade he saw—a remembrance of words, touches, love, affections of a child. He saw his father's face before him, kind and benevolent and wise, loving and pleased as they played their last game before the flames.

Jonathan closed his eyes...*flames*.

He bent his head, and then without expression he took out the SIG, dropping the magazine and tapping it once, seating the rounds to prevent a jam. He gentle inserted the clip again, pushing it home with a soft, lethal click taken by the wind.

He looked at Matsumo. The Japanese nodded once. There was nothing more to be said.

Jonathan's hand tightened on the gun.

He walked forward.

Webster bent over Logan's bed, staring into the pale face. Logan stirred, looking up. He seemed to become angrier and angrier as he began to realize where he was.

"How bad is it?" he groaned, glancing at his forearm, surrounded by a plaster cast from wrist to elbow. His hand was swollen, the fingers thick and unbending, and his chest was bruised. He gently raised his left hand to feel a large contusion on his sternum.

"The shockplate held," Webster said with a faint smile. "But the bullet fragmented and put a few shreds into your neck and arms. Nothing serious. You were lucky."

With a grimace, Logan raised his forearm, studying the bandage. "What about my arm?"

"Not so bad. You took a nine millimeter hardball through and through. And you've got some more bruises and second degree burns on your neck and hands. But you're alive and, believe me, Logan, it could be a lot worse."

"Blackfoot?" Logan asked, hesitant.

Somber, Webster shook his head.

Clenching his teeth, Logan sat upright and turned his mind from it because he had no time. "Where are Jonathan and Matsumo?"

"They were ordered to stand down, Logan. Jonathan turned in his creds. And Matsumo quit, too." Webster paused. "They're gone after Charon."

"Gone? Gone where?"

"I don't know. Jonathan only said that he'd finish it alone.

And he is. Alone, I mean. The Bureau can't protect him any-more, Logan. Jonathan put himself into traffic."

With a snarl of pain, Logan rolled from the bed. He stood, swaying for a moment. "That boy ain't going out there alone! He works for us and, by God, we ain't lettin' him go out there alone!"

Webster glared. "Logan, those orders come from the president! We've been told to pull out! No debate! And there is no way we can violate a direct command like that! Jonathan has turned in his credentials and we can't control him anymore! But you and I have to go by orders!"

With a sore gesture, Logan dropped the hospital garment and walked naked to the closet. There was nothing inside. "Where are my clothes?"

"In a garbage basket in the emergency room," Webster grunted. "They cut them off when you got here."

"I need to find something to wear."

"Logan," Webster said, exasperated, "don't do this to me. I've already got one renegade agent. I don't need two of them."

"A renegade agent who won't cover up this case is the only one who's gonna finish it," Logan said, standing naked and impatient and uncaring in the middle of the room. He was angry, finding strength in it. "I want some clothes, Webster. Help me or don't help me, but I'm hittin' the road."

"They're not going to discharge you."

"That's not their decision. If a man wants to leave a hospi-tal, then he can leave a hospital. They don't have police power to hold anybody. All they can do is detain you if you're under the influence of narcotics."

"You *are* under the influence of narcotics."

Logan roared, "We ain't gonna leave that boy out there!"

He lifted his hand. "Forget the rest of them! The president or the director or Congress or whoever gets in the way! We've got loyalty to each other and that beats any loyalty that we've got toward people who couldn't care less about *us*!" He stared hard. "Besides that, somebody has to pay...Somebody has to pay or there ain't gonna ever be no justice for Jonathan or Woodard or Daniela or any of them. And you know what I'm talking about."

Webster appeared to falter.

With a surprise, Logan had come to a place where it all ended and began again—another life, another chance.

"There ain't no backin' down from this, Richard. There ain't no place to back down to."

Somber resignation solidified in Webster. Cursing silently, he walked to the door.

"I'll get some clothes," he said.

Standing within the dark, Charon stared from the front window of the mansion. He turned to Daniela.

Arms tied behind her back, she leaned forward in a chair. Her right arm was black, glistening with blood. Her dark face glistened with sweat. But her eyes burned and focused with unwavering attention on the tall form before her. Charon smiled.

"He comes for you," he said.

Her mouth tightened in hate.

Tilting his head, Charon walked slowly forward. He gazed down at her with amazement. Then his long, slender hand was raised, the gloved finger gently touching her face beneath a dark-rimmed eye. He raised the finger before his face.

"A tear," he whispered, looking down at her once more. "Strange that a warm thing could fall from such a cold eye."

Daniela closed her eyes, slowly bending her head so that her long dark hair fell over her face. She trembled slightly, tightening, beginning to fight despite her fatigue and blood loss.

"No," said Charon. "Do not move so." His voice was almost nothing. "The bomb wired to your chair is thoroughly unstable. It is...my best work."

Daniela raised her face, teeth clenched.

"No," Charon said quickly. "Before you move to detonate the bomb and, in your mind, kill us both, I will tell you that Jonathan is already within the house. Yes, you will kill me, for certain. But you will also kill Jonathan." He laughed at her expression. "Yes, Daniela, even I know of love. Because I saw his face when he defended you in the house. I saw your eyes when you read his gestures so easily."

Charon's humor ascended. "And now you must leave the game to Jonathan and I, along with the rather ominous bravado that accompanies him. And should Jonathan kill me, which I do not anticipate, then he can attempt to defuse what cannot be defused, and save you. Or die with you."

Blood beaded on Daniela's face.

"You talk a lot about death."

Charon smiled.

"It is all I know."

Webster saw Scotland Yard's Inspector Johnson rise from his seat in the hallway. He walked forward until they were face to face. He didn't know how the inspector was going to accept what he was about to say but Johnson was a street cop—a lot like Logan. They had a common affinity, spoke the same language. And it was the only ground that would bring them together.

"Logan isn't happy here," Webster mumbled.

The inspector couldn't conceal his surprise. "Really?" Johnson replied. "He is...ah, leaving?"

This was the crux.

Webster leaned forward. "I've got some good men on the jet, Inspector. Men who...understand things. There's a chance that jet might develop...*mechanical* problems."

Silent understanding.

"Ah, yes," Johnson nodded, his brow hardening. "Jets are, ah, notorious for all manner of *mechanical* problems. And I can certainly attest, Agent Webster, that you did all that was humanly possible, under my personal supervision, to get your men out of the country, abiding thoroughly by your president's orders."

"Yeah," Webster completed it, "we did. And now I need to ask you something: Do you remember my conversation today with Malone and Matsumo? The conversation we had at the Embassy?"

The confused frown that twisted Johnson's face was genuinely amusing. "I...ah...hmmm. Well, you understand, I wasn't really listening to the, ah..." He cupped his chin, an arm crossed over his chest. "Forgive me, but what was it that you told Malone?"

"I told Jonathan to go *back* into the field and *personally* notify concerned agencies that the FBI was no longer involved in this situation. I told him we were *pulling out*. And without any question whatsoever he *precisely* complied with my instructions."

Johnson nodded vigorously. "Yes, yes, that was the gist of it!" He crossed both arms, emphasizing the pact. "Yes, of course that was it! Thank you for reminding me."

"*However,*" Webster leaned even closer; Johnson froze in concentration—a tape recorder. "I now feel that Malone and

Matsumo might have...*inadvertently*...gotten themselves in a life-threatening situation."

The inspector stared down his prominent nose. "Yes. That would change *everything*, of course."

"Yeah, because we'd have to *rescue* them."

"Oh, yes indeed!" Johnson came alive again. "I agree wholeheartedly! What with the information we have gained, we are certain that Malone and Matsumo may be targeted for ambuscade!" The inspector was utterly British, without the faintest trace of humor. "Be assured, sir; Scotland Yard stands beside you!"

Webster relaxed. "Perhaps Scotland Yard could go to the Bureau's jet when it's disabled." He paused, cleared his throat. "Excuse me, *if* the jet comes into a temporary non-flight status. Then you can insure that my special response team exits the plane to be escorted through customs with their *luggage* to where they're needed."

For the first time since Webster had met him, the inspector from Scotland Yard smiled.

"That's elementary," he said.

A polite, distinctive knock sounded on Logan's door.

"Come in."

Inspector Johnson entered the room to see Logan lying naked on top of the sheets. He scowled as Johnson walked forward with a small stack of casual clothes and sturdy English boots. He had a canvas brogan coat in his hand.

"Permit me to introduce myself," Johnson said, laying the clothes at the foot of the bed. "I'm Winfred Johnson with the Yard, and Mr. Webster asked me to deliver these items. I presume he is going to need your assistance in the field, Agent Logan."

Without a word Logan stood and began dressing. He was glad the morphine was at full-strength because he twisted the swollen fingers mercilessly. He figured he had maybe three hours before the pain was too much to endure, but that was all right. This whole thing was a last-chance power-drive.

"I thought you might also need this," Johnson said as he laid Logan's SIG Sauer P-226 on the bed. He neatly laid five fully loaded magazines beside it. "One never knows what one might encounter...in the dark."

Logan gazed at the SIG, at Johnson.

"Yeah," he said, a grateful nod. "You never know."

Reibling answered the phone and Webster spoke with clear and obvious anger. "You there, Reibling?"

"Yeah," was the sullen reply, "I'm here. Been here. Been here all night. Been here all day. I'm tired of being here."

There was no time for dancing and Webster knew Reibling was too old a warhorse to make a mistake. "It would be a real shame if that jet was temporarily disabled, Reibling. Then your people would have to disembark, with the help of Scotland Yard, to rescue Jonathan and Matsumo. It would be a high-risk assignment. Real dangerous. Somebody would probably get killed."

"Yeah, that would be too bad," Reibling's said without a split second hesitation. "Cause I just heard this bird is grounded. Electrical problems."

"I hope it's not too serious."

"Nah, but we're going to be here for a while."

"How long?"

A contemptuous grunt.

"As long as it takes."

Chapter Twenty

Jonathan stood in the hallway where he last saw the apocalyptic image in the night; Charon emerging from the distant doorway in a black storm, skull-face grinning.

Taking a deep breath, Jonathan raised his face to the ceiling, felt the darkness close and cold about him. His teeth came together, grating, energy building stronger and stronger, overcoming. His fist was tight on the SIG, hot sweat melding steel and flesh. He raised his hands, extending them high into the air.

"*Chaaaaaaron!*" he roared, awakening the dead and darkness together as the thunderous bellow plummeted deep into the house, thrown from a haunted soul to search a haunted house, echoing from dead stone to dead stone, echoing...haunting...

Challenging.

(♀)(♀)(♀)

Charon lifted his head.

"Yes, child...I'm coming."

He reached into his cloak and pulled out a black semiautomatic. He stared down at Daniela. "Your beloved has come."

Daniela spat. "I pray to God he cuts your heart out!" She bared her teeth with each word. "I will kill you a thousand times for what you did to my child!"

"Your child," he intoned, and paused. "That was meant as a warning. You did not accept it."

Daniela's eyes narrowed, her parted lips revealing teeth barred like fangs. With dark hair falling over her face, she was wolfish. "I swear to God: Either Jonathan or I are going to kill you."

"You forget," Charon smiled, "that you die tonight, as surely as him. The device, which is brilliant even if I speak from hubris, will detonate in twenty minutes. Or it will detonate itself, if tampered with. For as I said, it is not defusable. But, as such base herd species such as yourself are prone to philosophize—the two of you will die together. And that is some consolation, is it not?"

Daniela's eyes were dark fire.

"God will not let you escape justice," she rasped. "And if God delivers justice to you, you'll burn in hell...for killing my child. It was *me* you should have warred with! Not my *child!*"

"Hell is the child of conscience," Charon said, becoming one with the dark. "I am beyond such things."

Jonathan swung the mag-light's beam to cut a wide path through the shadows, throwing illumination over the stairway. Dust stirred from their steps, swirling in the beam like ghosts.

He descended, flashlight and gun in hand with Matsumo close and holding his own flashlight. From beneath his coat the Japanese produced the .38 revolver that Jonathan had given him—his backup weapon. It was good for five shots.

Matsumo shifting the flashlight, scanning, searching every shadow with the gun held high. He spoke little, taking cues from Jonathan's quick, subtle hand motions to demonstrate without words that he was adept in this world of silent combat.

As a team they began a cautious reconnaissance of the back of the manor, moving from room to room, searching halls and doors and angling together, crossing over high to low, taking turns at point to give the other a rest. But they found nothing, not—

Matsumo bent sharply, as if he had glimpsed something. Drenched in sweat, Jonathan reflexively threw his back against the other wall. His voice was harsh: "What is it?"

Matsumo squinted. "Steps," he mumbled. "The dust is disturbed, here. He has come this way."

"One set of footprints?"

"Two."

"Where do they go?"

"They go toward the front of the house." Matsumo frowned. "It is a trap."

Jonathan swung his light behind them. "How do you know it's a trap?"

"Charon would not make such a mistake." The Japanese scowled. "He wants us to follow. He is luring us with live bait and a trail too easily followed."

Jonathan felt sweat drop from his nose, his chin. He took a second and wiped hair back from his forehead, slick and drenched beneath his fingers. He rubbed his eyes with a wrist to clear his vision. "What do you suggest?"

"We go forward." Matsumo took a cautious step. "We have no choice."

They went one behind the other through the huge room. Furniture had been covered by large white sheets, some of it faintly glossy beneath a thick layer of dust that overlaid everything with a highlight of white. They reached a doorway and Matsumo shone his light, illuminating the entire room without revealing himself.

Jonathan glanced at the carpet and...and *knew* that something was there...something that disturbed him. He grimaced, thinking; it had been a long time since he had done this, but there was a distinct alarm sounding in his mind. He concentrated; couldn't recall.

"Come," Matsumo rumbled, lifting a foot.

Jonathan remembered.

"Wait!" he grabbed Matsumo's arm and the Japanese instantly halted his movement, foot frozen in the air. "Wait," Jonathan continued, more slowly. "I need to check this."

"What is it?"

Jonathan bent and studied the carpet where it slid into the floorboard. He removed the switchblade and discharged the blade. A second later he had pried up the end of the carpet, finding what he expected. "There it is," he said.

Beneath the carpet, two sheets of metal approximately five inches wide and six inches long were laid, one on top of the other. A thin sheet of tissue paper was placed between them and a single wire led from each plate of steel. Jonathan didn't try to follow the wire.

"Simple," he shook his head.

He holstered the SIG and reached into his pocket. He withdrew a Gerber multi-purpose tool, extending the wirecutter to sever a wire leading from one of the plates. Then he lifted the steel and saw that it had been violently pierced several times with a sharp tool, possibly an ice pick. The ragged edges of the holes were placed down against the tissue, aimed toward the second plate.

"If we had stepped on the top plate," Jonathan said, "the pressure from your foot would have pushed the steel edges through the tissue, making contact with the other metal plate and continuing the circuit. Whatever kind of explosive Charon's using, probably hidden somewhere close, would have been activated by the current."

"Yes," Matsumo rumbled. "A simple trick. But why would he use so simple a trick?"

"Because it doesn't take much time to rig," Jonathan answered. "We've got to watch out for this. If we get to carpet again, leap over the threshold. Don't step on it. These things only go off if you step directly on top of them."

"I understand."

Together they moved deeper into the interior. Then Jonathan sensed something behind them and spun. The SIG rose in his hand as he glimpsed the faintest shadow moving through shadows and he fired even before he had a solid lock on the target, tracking with the strobe-flame as the bullets impacted the door frame and the specter was gone.

"*Charon!*" Jonathan shouted, ignited by the thunder of the SIG and the fleeting black image that vanished in the ringing echo.

Instantly heated, Jonathan took three wide steps and leaped through a wake of fire to come down in the hall—a corridor as wide as the last room. He raised the gun as his feet hit the ground, effectively using the flashlight for illumination.

Even in his speed Jonathan knew that the light was more of a weapon than the gun so he swung it left, right, bathing the room in light but he saw nothing as Matsumo barreled through the door with no questions, gun upraised in a solid two-hand stance. Coming down in a crouch, the Japanese used his light in the same manner, trying to blind the hit man.

Dust and silence.

Charon was gone; Jonathan stifled a curse. Exhausted, he leaned back against the wall. "He's too old to be this fast."

"Not so fast," Matsumo rumbled, undisturbed. "Just smart." He nodded at Jonathan's SIG. "Do not shoot at shadows. Wait until he fires or you clearly see his image."

Jonathan dropped a magazine, inserting another. "That's gonna be harder than you think. He sees in the dark like a bat. Night is like day to him. He'll use it again and again."

"Yes." Matsumo turned his head to the depth of the hallway. "He will use every advantage."

A scream from somewhere near the front of the house made them whirl. "Daniela!" Jonathan shouted.

He ran forward.

"Jonathan!" bellowed Matsumo. "Don't rush!"

Jonathan charged into the dark as fast as he dared, using the mag-light effectively with the gun high and extended. "I know what he's doing! I've seen it before! Stay close!"

Fists clenched, Matsumo thundered behind him.

Watching from inside Johnson's car, Webster wasn't surprised that there was a testy debate between rank members of the Heathrow Police and Johnson as they arrived at the jet.

Challenged, Johnson's expression went from shock that his authority would even be questioned, to anger, to indignation that escalated to outright wrath released in an authoritative stream of profanity—though Webster could hear nothing specific—which resulted in the security officer waving his men off.

In seconds Reibling and his men descended the seven-step doorway to hit the ground and moments later had taken two black bags apiece from the rear cargo hold of the jet. They moved without questions—as if they'd played this game before and knew the bluff could be called any minute—to a row of four cars stationed behind Webster.

Trunks, or "boots" as Johnson called them, were hastily opened and loaded. When they were in traffic, Johnson raised Reibling in the rear car.

Webster said, "Ask him how long he needs to get his team ready." He chose not to use the radio himself because radio transmissions were one of the personal, sanctified dimensions of police work and each nation was reflexively paternal about it. It was a privilege earned from sacrifice and nobody was reluctant to surrender it.

Another Scotland Yard inspector, the one in Reibling's vehicle, answered: "Agent Reibling says his men can be ready two minutes after arrival. He wants to know if we have a site blueprint so that they can form an intelligent attack plan."

Johnson responded that they did not know the site.

There was a pause before the inspector replied: "Agent Reibling says, rather colorfully, that he is not very surprised."

Webster laughed.

Jonathan knew as he hit it.

Tripwire.

He had caught the faintest pressure over his shin and realized it was too late. He instinctively twisted his arm over his face as a wall of fire erupted before him.

A shock-concussion hit him in the chest, blowing him against Matsumo who also threw up his arms. Roaring, wounded by flame and shrapnel, they rolled away, separating instantly. There was no time for anything, not even pain, as Jonathan staggered to his feet. He reoriented by violent reflex, his mind gone. He didn't know whether he could stand until he stood.

He was consciously testing his body with pain and action to determine the extent of his injuries. He knew dimly that stitches had torn in his side and, dazed, he glanced down to see patches of blood on his legs, his shirt smoking, the vest torn. He glared breathlessly to visually confirm that he still held the SIG.

He glared to the side. "Are you—"

A blast tore through the ceiling above them and Matsumo roared as he staggered to the side and Jonathan fell flat to his back, firing into the ceiling in a savage figure-eight pattern. He expended fifteen rounds in three seconds and rolled to come up six feet to the side as the ceiling was shredded with a shotgun blast that vaporized the floor where he'd been—Charon firing downward through the second-level floor.

Jonathan ejected the second clip and fired as fast as he could pull the trigger. He blasted a wild pattern upward and then he threw out the second mag and rolled again as another blast tore a wide hole in the ceiling. Teeth clenched as he rose, Jonathan slammed in another magazine, moving laterally, sighting on the long hallway.

Heard nothing.

He's retreating again...

Jonathan fired down the length of the hall, shooting upward through the ceiling in the direction he anticipated Charon to flee and heard a heavy collapse.

Something hit the floor.

Jonathan ran forward before a primal instinct told him to *move* and he frantically threw himself against the wall with the SIG raised high as a section of the ceiling was blown apart. Charon was firing through the ceiling again—a savage series of blasts; eight, nine, ten rounds that vaporized plaster and wood, ceiling and floor, in a volcanic roar to leave the air white with smoke and dust.

Jonathan didn't know if he was hit—he was too adrenalized to feel anything at all. He lowered his forearm from his face and raised the SIG again, not firing. A combat reflex he didn't even understand held him back; something that told him to play the game...

Lure him in...

Lure him in...Lure him in...

Jonathan raised his hand to Matsumo, who'd begun to rise to his feet. Matsumo froze, his hand wrapped tightly around the .38. Then Jonathan raised his face to the ceiling and held a solid aim, knowing that Charon would not fire again.

No, he wouldn't fire. He was coming down.

Coming down to him.

"Be ready," Jonathan whispered.

Jonathan did a mental check on how much ammo he had remaining. He'd fired three full magazines and part of a fourth. But he had brought six—two more than the HRT guys carried on assignment—so he had thirty rounds remaining, plus a half-clip.

He saw that Matsumo was bleeding heavily from a shoulder. It seemed like the bullet had shattered the flesh slightly beneath his neck, but the Japanese gave no indication of a wound. He was strong, stoic, above pain.

Another minute, then two...

Jonathan crouched in darkness with an almost unearthly stillness, waiting for the slightest shadow to break. Then, he knew, he wouldn't miss. He would lie down on Charon like a cannon, blasting him to shreds in a holocaust. He waited...and sensed.

Something close...

He said nothing and held a centered gaze, leaving peripheral vision to cover opposite ends of the corridor. Darkness was close but there was more than darkness. There was a movement at the far right side, close to the stairway.

As the silent shadow came around the banister Jonathan knew what it was and he spun. His first shot with wide and then he was running forward, howling in a hate that brought the past and present together in a rage that threw everything, even Charon, before it; threw back the world and the pain together.

Jonathan fired his last round as he reached the steps and he angled fast to the right, past the stairway into the room beyond *praying* Charon would make a stand. He made a purposeful pause as he dropped the magazine to insert his last clip, hoping the Iceman would emerge to take a shot. But there was nothing.

Grimacing savagely, Jonathan stalked back into the corridor that held Matsumo. "He's gone!" he yelled, carried beyond quiet. "He's hiding!" He threw back his head.

"C'mon Charon! Let's finish it!"

Matsumo's iron hand settled on his shoulder. "Easy," he said, a controlled gaze. "He's trying to force us to make a mistake."

Jonathan glared into Matsumo's face, taking a deep breath to calm. He knew that he was so close to losing it, was so close to chasing Charon wildly through the house, pushing him to the wall. But there was no hope in that. It was a suicide rush sure to end in his own death and, if he was lucky, the death of Charon.

No, he had to think. He had to outsmart the hit man. That was the only way to beat him.

Gun in hand he walked boldly forward, inviting an attack that he would take and give back tenfold dead or alive. Although he could control his rage to a point, there was also a point where he knew he would lose control—all of it.

There was nothing that would stop him now, he knew, not a bullet through the chest or neck or anything else. He would take a dozen rounds and give everything back, closing the distance on the hit man with every step and there wasn't anything that Charon could do about it. Now, there was no fear.

As he reached the front room he saw Daniela's dark eyes glowing in the gloom. He recognized instantly that she was perilously pale, sweating heavily, almost dead. Her shoulder was black and crusted, but the bleeding had stopped.

"Daniela—"

"Jonathan!" She violently lifted her face at his voice. "Don't come any closer!"

Freezing, Jonathan lifted a hand to Matsumo.

"What's he done?"

She seemed like she was going to faint. Only the violence of her will was keeping her awake. "A bomb!" Her hoarse voice was so ravaged Jonathan could barely understand it. "I don't know what kind! I can't move! You...you need to leave! Finish this thing with Charon somewhere else! It's on a timer!"

Jonathan took a penlight from his pocket, giving Matsumo the mag-light and the SIG.

"Watch our back," he said and crept slowly forward.

He angled the light beneath the wooden chair and saw it: a device the size of a small microwave. It was a mass of wires and intricate switches all leading into a stainless steel canister as thick as a thermos. A large, red, square timer was located prominently on the front, glowing brightly.

A challenge.

Seven minutes, twenty seconds.

Crouching absolutely motionless, Jonathan studied slender threads leading from Daniela's body to the device. They were thin blue wires, thin as fishing line, all disappearing into the bomb itself.

Keeping his distance, Jonathan moved to the back and saw the wires were taped to her forearms, intricately intertwined in the length of white rope holding her wrists. He noticed two more wires wrapped in the ropes holding each of her ankles to the chair legs.

He eased forward, casting a slight glance at Matsumo; the Japanese was crouching to the side of the doorway, shining the light into the darkness, not looking at him.

"Jonathan," Daniela whispered. "Please don't!"

"Shhhh...It's gonna be okay."

He selected a lie even though she knew it was a lie. "I've seen this before. It's not a big deal. A lot of it is a fake. Or a redundancy."

"No, you haven't seen anything like this." She leaned her head back, exhausted. "He said it was...his best work."

Jonathan delicately lay down in front of her. "No, it's nothing special," he whispered. "I've defused a hundred of these in training. Just...just don't move...*Don't move...at all.*"

"Jonathan..."

"Don't move!" Jonathan shouted as one of the wires moved minutely. "Daniela," he whispered, releasing a breath. "Do *not move*, sweetheart. Please; that's all you need to concentrate on."

Six minutes, forty seconds.

Jonathan's heart sank as studied the bomb and realized that it was indeed brilliant—a work of art.

A concert of microwave switches overlaid a continuous electrical circuit. If the circuit were cut anywhere at all, then one or all of the switches would close and set off the explosive. And mercury switches were inset at the bomb-end of the threads attached to Daniela's wrists and ankles, a redundant detonator. If the mercury switches tilted twenty degrees, the mercury would shift and connect another current that would also cause detonation.

Even worse, there was also an electrical current wired into the dual-strand threads that kept the mercury switches level on a parabolic metering system so the mercury could be shifted by either violent movement or an electrical disturbance, whichever came first.

Though he didn't release it, Jonathan felt his breath ascend from him. His face, drenched with sweat, dripped steadily on the floor. With time, he knew, he might defuse this thing. But only if he had a dozen circuit testers and wrap-around current exchangers and battery backups to fool the bomb into thinking that the switches were continuing to function when switch after switch was cut.

And even then it was nothing he would ever choose.

Bombs like this were not disarmed—they were blown. You evacuated the area and stacked sandbags and steel nets around them and set them off with a rifle.

Unless, of course, it was wired to a living human being. In that scenario it became the ultimate nightmare—the mandatory disarming of a bomb that couldn't be disarmed.

A game that couldn't be won.

He looked up at Daniela.

Knew that she knew.

Chapter Twenty-One

E asy, Daniela," Jonathan whispered. "Trust me."

"I am *not* your responsibility." Her head fell back. "It's not your job to do this!"

Jonathan stared at the bomb, trying to discern a weakness, glancing at the clock: *Six minutes.*

"Okay," he whispered, and touched a slender blue wire that held her leg in place. "I'm going to try and disconnect you from this thing. It'll probably be the best way to—"

Gunshots erupted in the doorway and Jonathan was rolling away to see Matsumo firing the .38, charging across the chamber that adjourned the dining room.

"*Matsumo*! No!"

Matsumo dropped to a crouch at the far threshold, whirling back to Jonathan, glaring. "Take care of the woman!" he roared. "I will deal with this!"

Jonathan screamed. "*No!*"

Matsumo disappeared around the distant doorframe like a ghost. He was gone before Jonathan could shout another word and Jonathan dropped to his hands and knees, grimacing.

"Jonathan! You have to *leave!*"

Jonathan glared at the clock: *Five minutes, fifty seconds.* Without hesitation he lay on the floor again and crawled cautiously close to the bomb.

"Jonathan! What are you doing!"

"What I have to!"

She seemed overcome by emotion, resigned to die but not resigned to know he was going to die with her. "What are you going to do?" she pleaded. "I know bombs, Jonathan! Please! I'm an *assassin!* I know some bombs can't be disarmed! You gave me hope. I can die knowing that you'll finish this. Just go."

"I won't leave you."

Jonathan took out his multi-purpose tool and pulled out the Phillips screwdriver. He began unscrewing the explosive canister. He didn't know if it would explode because of static electricity or the pressure of the screws turning in their slots. But he had already made his decision. There was no time for second-guessing.

Two of the screws held wires against the frame and Jonathan guessed that they were a redundancy or grounding the current. He was right. In seconds he freed both the wires and screws, twisting them so they couldn't make contact with the case.

There was no way to be certain that it wouldn't explode when he lifted the lid because it was possible to wire a secondary failsafe for motion-activation. But in reality almost no one did that. For one reason, it was a prohibitively high-risk procedure to place a live electrical current in proximity of the explosive material itself, which was highly susceptible to static charges.

That's why most tampering mechanisms were wired into the switches and timing devices; it was rare that anyone would attempt to defuse a bomb by removal of the explosive material itself. And that, Jonathan knew, is why his idea might actually succeed. It wasn't something Charon wouldn't anticipate.

Use a variation of an expected attack. Something for which the enemy has not prepared a formal defense.

Grimacing, Jonathan took a deep breath; yeah, there was the faintest chance that a suicide move would work, simply because it *was* a suicide move.

Moving with delicate, sweating fingers, Jonathan gently pried open the lid of the thermos-sized cylinder, searching for feed wires on the inside. He angled his pen light through the narrow gap, saw no connections, and in another second removed the lid completely, laying it to the side. There was no time for relief.

He carefully reached inside the lid and found a single bolt the size of his finger at the very bottom of a smooth stainless steel cone; it resembled the top half of a narrow hourglass. Inside the cone, Jonathan knew, was the explosive. He twisted the bolt carefully as then...something made him stop. Immediately.

He concentrated, mind accelerating, trying to understand. He couldn't place it and there was *no time for this!* He resisted the hyperventilating fear, began to twist the bolt again to free the explosive so he could—

A drop of sweat fell from his chin.

His hand froze.

He blew out a slow breath and removed his hand.

Charon *had* expected the move, and he'd wired the cone to prevent it. But the hit man had done it in a cunning, unconventional manner. He had attached a feed wire to the *bolt* at the depression of the cone. And it was the wire's added resistance with the bolt, as Jonathan turned it, that he had felt in his fingertips—something so faint it didn't seem to be there at all.

Drenched in sweat, Jonathan studied the bomb, trying to find a method of removing the explosive substance. He raised up on his elbow, looking at the top the cone. And saw it.

Two wires, barely visible in the mesh of circuitry, led downward through a one-fourth-inch hold drilled into the top of the steel canister and sealed with caulk. One wire was hot; the other wire was the return circuit. If the circuit was broken, going in or coming out, a switch located somewhere else would close and subsequently set off the cone. It was a pure continuous circuit switch.

Rising to a knee, Jonathan was counting seconds in his mind, now, because he knew this would be too, too close. He followed the cone wires in a clarity he had never known, his eyes never losing the red thread in the snake-pit mesh of wiring. With irritation he remembered EOD training where he practiced doing just this—following a single wire through a maze of hundreds.

Most EOD trainees flunked out of the course because it required almost surreal concentration and eye-hand coordination. But that was the specific reason for the drill. It was meant to weed out recruits who simply could not manage the exacting coordination required for extreme defusal situations.

"Jonathan," Daniela whispered, "maybe I can help you. What kind of switch is it?"

"A real complex collapsible circuit," Jonathan mumbled, finally following the wire to the very front of the bomb where it tied into an open switch. Then she was saying something but he wasn't listening. He saw that the tiny device resembled a mousetrap the size of a child's fingernail. But it was held open by an electrical current and would snap shut as the current was removed.

He glanced at the clock: *Four minutes.* For a breath he hesitated, fear and adrenaline causing his hands to tremble. He wondered if he was making the right choice, but there was no choice to make.

He stripped insulation from a section of both wires leading to the cone switch—*thirty seconds*—before he found another hot wire and another ground going into a second switch wired to the clock-standard bomb design. Moving quickly, blinking sweat, he also stripped a small section of them—*thirty more seconds.*

He planned to use the hot wire leading into the clock switch, wiring it directly into the cone switch. Then he would cut the wires leading to the bolt in the cone and remove the bolt. It would probably work, he knew, because there would be more than enough electricity in the clock-switch for both mousetraps. And electricity was like water; it would flow down both wires at once like a river forking in two directions. Against himself Jonathan glanced at the clock; *three minutes, thirty seconds.*

He heard Daniela: "Jonathan, just...just leave me. Let me die alone. That's best for *both* of us."

Jonathan rolled away and snatched a lamp from a table, tearing the wire from the base and wall. In fifteen seconds he cut a six-inch piece of the 16-guage—not big enough to slow down the current—and stripped a small sections. As he made it back to the chair he was already working, trying not to glance again at the clock.

He was sweating so badly his hands were dripping. He wiped them on his pants and continued, making a connection of hot-hot wires and ground-ground. Now the current from the clock should keep the cone-switch open even when he cut the wires leading to the cone itself. Without any hesitation whatsoever, because he was out of time, he reached up to the cone switch.

And cut the wire.

Nothing.

Jonathan closed his eyes, giving himself one second. Then he rolled and was on his chest again, reaching underneath to unscrew the bolt. Moving fast and carefully not create static electricity, he pulled it clear. Then he was watching, dazed, as a white powdery substance spilt free, falling onto the floor like the finest quality cocaine, which is what it was designed to resemble.

"Jonathan...please...please leave," Daniela said quietly and Jonathan saw the mercury switches tilt at her agitation. He raised his head: "Daniela! Don't move! Don't move at all!"

Two minutes, forty seconds.

Jonathan watched the HCH spill from the canister, flooding over the floor. He knew that what he had done was so, *so* desperate, but it was all he could have done. There was no other way around the explosion and he still wasn't sure if this would even work.

"Daniela," he whispered. "I've got to set this off." He raised a hand to her lips as she began to protest. "There's no way to defuse it or stop the clock."

She closed her eyes. Her voice was a plea. "Just leave."

Jonathan smiled. "I don't think so, baby."

She leaned her head back, grimacing like a soldier forced to shoot a wounded comrade to save them from a fate worse than death and Jonathan rose on his knee, holding her tight.

Crying, she leaned her head forward and he held her close, whispering quietly, "Listen, Daniela, I know what I'm doing. This thing is going to off no matter what I do. There's no way to defuse it. I'm trying to remove the explosive material and... and then I've got to let the timer set off the blasting cap inside the cylinder."

"Jonathan..."

"Listen to me!" Jonathan said sternly. "I'm removing the

HCH *itself* so that the blasting cap won't cause an explosion!" He bowed his head against hers. "That's all I can do, Daniela. I can't defuse it! I've got to set it off and...and we've got to hope I've removed enough of the explosive to prevent detonation."

She began to cry, not for herself.

"I'm not going to leave you, Daniela," he whispered and she buried her face in his neck. Jonathan gazed at the timer.

Forty seconds...

Powder poured to the floor...

Matsumo charged up the stairs of the manor and whirled left, right, throwing his back against the wall. He held the .38 close in his right hand, his left hand clenched in a fist.

It had been long, so long, since he was in this world, hunting down predators and beating them into submission only to leave them handcuffed to a fence or park bench so Tokyo police could haul them to jail without a fight. But he was at home with it once more.

He searched and saw nothing but knew in his soul that Charon was close. For he had glimpsed the black, vulturish shadow as it fled into a library at the end of the hallway. Clearly, there was only one way into the room, and only one way out.

Using every skill he possessed, Matsumo went through the door, shining the light before him. He saw instantly that the walls were lined with books, books bound in leather and immaculately positioned, covered with dust. And there was a massive desk, a chair.

The room itself was L-shaped, bending directly in front of him into darkness that the flashlight could not defeat.

"I am here," Matsumo said loudly, knowing that the flashlight gave away his position, so he might as well use it to his advantage. His voice, he knew, would inform the hit man that he was not afraid.

But only silence answered, and Matsumo saw that the mag-light was creating deep shadows all over the room. The sharp, angular architecture of the bookcases, the desk, a series of heavy tables and other furniture cast equally angular zones of black that moved silently with him, across the walls, as he walked forward.

Gun leading, Matsumo went around a corner. He was ready for anything, and his hand was dead calm. He used the flashlight effectively as he searched every nook, disturbingly aware of a chilling sweat on his neck as he narrowed the number of possible hiding places.

Matsumo searched and searched, and still he could not locate the German. He angled the light to the top of the deep bookcases, trying to discern whether the black cloaked figure lay within the deeper blackness at the top. But there was so much shadow...

He moved forward, searching, searching...

Something made Matsumo abruptly pause. Not a sound... No, it was something infinitely faint, infinitely feathery that brushed across his senses with an instinct that made the hairs rise on his forearms, his neck. He did not turn to see what was behind him, but knew that he had already passed the hit man and that Charon was emerging to kill.

The darkness...

He spun, raising the light and gun in a sure two-handed grip to see the hit man rising from a corner, shadow from shadow. But at the blaze of the flashlight Charon screamed in pain and lashed out, a flicker of moonlight striking something that whirled out and hit Matsumo's forehead, cutting deep.

Matsumo's shouted as he fired point-blank and then they collided and twisted in a savage contest of blows thrown and blows received and in the chaos Matsumo dimly realized why his bullet had failed—beneath Charon's coat there was a solid body-vest of steel sheathed underneath by kevlar—armor specially designed and closely fitted to protect him against bullets and knives and fists.

No time to think!

Intertwining of limbs...

Matsumo raised the .38, his hand close to his chest to protect the weapon as Charon shouted and lashed out, striking his face and weapon hand aside with a weapon unknown. The flashlight skidded dead into darkness.

Matsumo's second shot went wide and then Charon was over him in the dark, firing a bullet into Matsumo's arm, his leg as quickly as the hit man could pull the trigger. Matsumo roared at the twin impacts and lashed out again—Charon ducked, firing.

In agony Matsumo fired three bullets in a twisting, savage, grotesque dance with fire erupting from the .38 and Charon's silenced weapon thudding again and again. With a scream Charon twisted frantically...

Firing...

Matsumo kicked—*Missed!*

Charon shot twice—*hit, hit!*

Matsumo spun and struck—*wood shattered!*

Charon staggering—*firing!*

Four!

Five—hit!

Matsumo lashed out—HIT!

Charon hit *falling-firing!*

Six—HIT!

THE SCAM

"Enough!" roared Matsumo as he was hit again and snatched Charon's coat. Twisting with gigantic strength, he violently hurled him across the room where Charon smashed into the bookcase and the hit man shouted in pain, staggering wildly away as Matsumo's sledgehammer fist descended to shatter the shelves.

Charon cursed viciously in German, seemingly shocked at the power of his foe and raised the silenced semiautomatic again but Matsumo leaped into a backhanded blow that struck murderously to send the hit man screaming backward over a desk.

Charon rose almost at once, black cloak spread against white moonlight like some inhuman nightmarish shape. He had lost his gun but drew another from somewhere within his cloak.

Matsumo shouted and kicked to send the desk crashing into the assassin. The huge bulk of timber smashed into Charon's legs, blasting him into the wall where he reeled drunkenly to the side, cursing in rage, before fading again into shadow.

Growling, teeth bared, Matsumo stalked forward.

He was hurt, yes—the bullets had taken three ribs and meat off his forearms and thigh, meat off his left hand. But he would live if he could only hit Charon with a single, solid blow. Then he would shatter that steel armor into shards and drive them deeply into his lungs and heart and the fight would be won. He took three long strides before Charon rose to his side, shadow from shadow.

Charon did not move as Matsumo closed, an ominous rumble beginning in his chest and throat as he bunched his right fist to strike the one blow that remained to be thrown. Then Charon seemed to move one direction, and another and...

Matsumo frowned, blood in his mouth...

Charon was gone.

Darkness...shadow *shadows* moving?

Halting, poised, Matsumo turned only his head to search the darkness—shadows.

Where did he...?

In utter silence Charon bled right and Matsumo understood in a breath that the hit man was attempting to come from behind him. Even with the thought he turned, squarely cutting off Charon's line of retreat. The hit man instantly froze, silhouetted against a window.

His white hair cast a thin, strange halo over his head. His face was darkness. Matsumo turned into him, squaring. They stood five feet apart. Enough for Charon to fire a single shot. Enough for Matsumo to hurl a single blow.

A single blow...

"You are...a formidable foe." Charon's voice was hoarse with pain. He stood slightly bent, rasped, "I have not tasted my own blood in...many years."

Matsumo heard another clip inserted in the semi-auto. The hit man seemed to be waiting for breath. "Do as I say," he whispered, "...and you will live."

A contemptuous growl rumbled from deep inside Matsumo's volcanic chest as he frowned. "I have a better idea, murderer. You have the gun. You kill me...if you can."

Charon smoothly raised the weapon.

"Very well."

Matsumo roared as he leaped with his forearm across his face and the bullet hit there and he claimed another rushing step, head lowered like a rhino and with a powerful twist of his body Matsumo's fist erupted like a cannon to hit Charon dead in the chest.

THE SCAM

At the impact Matsumo's head was lowered still, all his great strength and weight and skill *there in his fist* and he somehow glimpsed Charon's face for a split second at the impact—mouth wide open and eyes wide open in shock *and fear* screaming as he sailed spread-eagle through the huge picture window, hands outstretched to the sky, gun sailing into the light, shards of glass turning, dancing, descending with the assassin as he was enveloped by darkness.

Matsumo collapsed against the shattered framing and rose in the same breath, rising even as he heard the hit man crash into the pavement ten feet below. Leaning heavily against a broken beam, Matsumo gazed down, blinking blood from his eyes, focusing hard to vaguely see Charon rolling, moaning. The assassin crawled in groaning, gasping cries before he finally caught a starved breath.

He rose to one knee, then a foot before crashing headlong with another wounded cry. He tried again, gained both feet, and leaned against a light pole, heaving, He shouted in agony as blood erupted from his mouth, splashing black.

After heaving deep, ragged breaths, Charon finally wiped his mouth and leaned into a shuffling, unbalanced gait like a dead man raised from the dead, unable now to command his body—his arms and legs—because his soul was simply no longer in command.

Matsumo groaned, but not from pain; it was because he could not pursue. His knee was hit, damaged; he was losing blood and strength—the bullets had done their work.

No, he would not die from these wounds. He had been wounded before, and he knew he would not die. But neither could he pursue. He slid to the floor, not bothering to staunch the bleeding—it would staunch itself in a few moments, when his heart slowed and blood loss dropped his pressure and, still, he would live. But he needed a moment to rest, before finding Jonathan.

He did not know if his last blow had killed the fiend, but he had struck true—had felt his fist plunging deep to shatter steel and bone before it, to the end.

Now he needed...just a moment.

Just a moment...to catch his breath...

Just a moment...

Holding Daniela close, her dark hair falling over his neck, Jonathan heard the sounds of gunshots and struggled to contain his rage. It took all his control to remain still, but he could almost see Matsumo fighting savagely with the hit man in a desolate, dark arena.

The shots came from somewhere above, deep inside the manor. But Jonathan couldn't go to them. He had to stay here. He glanced down; *thirty seconds.*

Daniela had become so still that he thought she had fainted. But when he leaned back she raised her face to him, clearly close to unconsciousness but fighting desperately to stay awake.

It would be so easy, Jonathan knew, for her to pass out. She was suffering from shock and blood loss and was perilously dehydrated. Also, if she were unconscious, she would be mercifully unaware as the final seconds ticked down on the bomb. But he knew she would never show herself mercy.

"How much longer?" she asked dully, dark eyes burning with exhaustion and concentration.

"It's over," he said, reaching down to sweep the powdery HCH from beneath the cylinder, knowing it would only detonate if it connected with acid or electricity or fire.

In mere seconds he cleared out the HCH and blew on the wooden floor, dissipating the finest granules from beneath the cone. He hoped that the steel cone was as highly polished on the inside as it was on the outside, so there wouldn't be enough HCH remaining in the chamber to create compression. But there was no way to be certain. This entire operation was a last chance option. And now, as Jonathan looked up again, glancing down at the clock—*twenty seconds*—there was nothing else to do.

Daniela was gazing steadily at him. And there was something in her face that held him. It was a moment, as the last seconds ticked down on the clock, when he could have said anything to her, and meant it. Could have promised and hoped anything, and believed it. He reached up to softly touch her face and she leaned her face into his hand.

"Why did you stay with me?" she asked, so vulnerable.

Jonathan smiled. "Because I love you."

She closed her eyes; a tear fell.

Jonathan touched her face. "And because you'd have done the same."

"Yes..." She opened her eyes. "I would have."

He glanced down: *Five seconds.*

"Time's up," he whispered, raising his face to her, leaning forehead to forehead. Together, they closed their eyes.

Four seconds, three, two, one and the blasting cap exploded inside the cone, louder than Jonathan anticipated to make his heart skip a beat. Daniela flinched and then it was over; the blasting cap blown but the HCH removed so there was no reaction.

Jonathan had gambled, and won.

With the thought he flicked the switchblade, not allowing himself to surrender to emotion, and slashed the rope holding her legs to the chair. Mercury switches tilted at the action but it didn't matter now. There was nothing else the bomb could do. Seconds later he'd freed her and lifted her from the chair. He knew that he had to get her to a hospital as soon as possible.

"You didn't leave me," she mumbled, drifting into unconsciousness, surrendering finally to blood loss. "You love me..."

Jonathan tightening his arms around her, leaned his head closer to her face. "Yes. I love you."

She opened her eyes. "I love you..."

He smiled, kissed her, and her eyes were vulnerable, completely and touchingly. Though her next words were of war, Jonathan knew she spoke for them both: "Finish it..."

He smiled, "Count on it."

Jonathan whirled at a sound, gun leveled.

Matsumo stood in the door. He was almost completely black in light of the distant street. His face glistened with blood. He leaned against the frame, slid slowly to the floor.

Jonathan was at his side. "Matsumo...What happened?"

"I will live," Matsumo rumbled, indifferent to the fact that he appeared already dead. "Men die because they believe... that they will die. Men live because they fight to live: I will *live.*"

"Charon?" Jonathan asked.

"...lives," he grunted. "I wounded him...Perhaps he will die. But he is not dead."

Jonathan frowned, "He will be. Let's go."

No more time for words—they needed an ambulance.

Supporting him, Jonathan lifted Daniela and together they made their way to the front door, together down the sidewalk, and together to the street. Arm in arm, none of them spoke.

They didn't have to.

Falling heavily, Charon struggled to rise.

"Yes..." he groaned, "you...were strong."

He was wounded—wounded so badly that simply remaining on his feet was a supreme challenge. He was amazed that any man could wound him so severely. He had never been wounded so severely, but then the Japanese had not been a man.

The last blow thrown by that god of war had struck with enough force to shatter his steel armor and ribs together, savagely driving steel shards into flesh. Even in the moment, Charon could feel blood congealing in his heart and lungs, death closing.

Two hours, maybe less.

"Long enough," he whispered, staggering from the manor. "Long enough to kill you, Jonathan."

Charon knew where the child that had become a man would go, knew it in his soul. And it would be there, yes, that he would wait for him. Because he did not have the strength to pursue.

Yes, he would wait for the child.

Chapter Twenty-Two

Jonathan raised his face as the ambulance approached. He had carried them to a pay phone, and as the van came closer he gently touched Daniela's face. "They'll take care of you," he said.

Face in sweat, she was barely conscious.

"Be careful, Jonathan..."

Jonathan saw the antipersonnel grenades on her vest, and a stun grenade. Charon had left them there to further amplify the force of the bomb, had it detonated. He reached down and removed the stun grenade, his mind already in the endgame.

Her hand closed softly over his, and she lifted her face. Her dark eyes burned into his. "We can win this..."

Jonthan kissed her. "We will, baby. I promise."

"I love you..."

Jonathan kissed her, brushed her dark, sweat-soaked hair from her face. "I'll see you in a few hours."

She closed her eyes.

In a single stride Jonathan was in the darkness but the darkness belonged to him, now, because he saw the savage final conflict coming with Charon—saw them fighting face to face with everything coming down to the two of them and Jonathan knew his last move—not a move that Charon anticipated.

Not a move thrown with rage and hate and pain.

A move stone-cold and without mercy.

To finish the game.

Holding a report as if it contained invasion plans for D-Day, Inspector Johnson came into the gray office of Scotland Yard where Webster and Logan sat on the same desk.

On the far side of the room, Reibling and his men were gearing up. Their vests, crammed with every conceivable defensive device, were snapped over black BDUs. Each man had a specialized weapon, some working with shotguns, some with MP-5s while two others held sniper rifles mounted with very expensive scopes.

Reibling himself was distinctly intimidating, dressed in full black with his bald head glistening in the florescent light. He had a Colt .45 strapped to his thigh, SAS style, and a SPAS-12 shotgun slung over his back. A bandoleer of extra shotgun shells was looped between his waist and shoulder.

"We've located two of them," Johnson said. "An ambulance just picked up the Mossad agent, Daniela something, and they admitted her in hospital. We've got uniform officers guarding her, and the Israeli Embassy has dispatched a general. There is also the Japanese. He is wounded, but he will live."

"What about Jonathan?" Logan asked.

"Ah, Malone was with them when the ambulance arrived. But he quickly left the scene."

"What scene?"

There was a hefty pause. "Malone was at a payphone near the house of his father. From what I surmise, the battle occurred in his father's manor."

"Is Charon dead?"

"I don't know."

Muttering a curse, Logan stood stiffly. His arm was beginning to hurt like a beast, the morphine thinning in his blood with every moment. "I need to get to the hospital and talk to Daniela," he said, picking up his coat.

"We have a man at the hospital who can question her."

"She won't talk to your people," Logan responded. "She'll only talk to someone she trusts."

"Of course." Johnson started for the door. "I shall have a man take you there immediately."

Another Scotland Yard officer met them in the exit, as if he weren't sure whether he had a legitimate reason to disturb them. He spoke quickly: "Inspector, we have someone of the line who wants to talk to Special Agent Logan."

"Is it Malone?" Logan asked.

"I don't know, sir. It was—"

Logan picked up the phone. "Jonathan?"

A rumbling voice: "I told you to go home."

It took a second for it to register with Logan, and then he remembered the letter. He didn't know who had sent it. But he knew that almost everyone who had knowledge of it was dead. And the ones who *were* still alive hadn't talked to anybody. So by process of elimination the caller had to be who he said he was.

"Yeah," he answered. "But I've still got a man in the field."

"Malone is going to die," the man said. "He doesn't know how to quit...or go home."

Logan knew that the man wouldn't keep the connection more than a minute. "Yeah, we should have gone home but we didn't. So tell me what I need to know or get off the line. Do you know where Jonathan's going?"

"Yes."

No compassion, nothing.

Logan didn't notice the dozen or so stares focused on his

back but he was aware that the room was deathly quiet. His words sounded strangely loud and subdued at the same time, as if he were speaking inside a dark cloud that inhaled his voice from the air.

"Are you going to tell me or not?"

There was a long pause. "Malone is going to 1060 Red Oak Road. Blast through the front gate and come into the house. Charon is waiting for him."

Logan hung up. "How soon can we reach Red Oak Road in Waltham Forest?"

The inspector was electrified. "Thirty minutes with lights and code." Reibling stepped forward: "Is that what we've been waiting for, Webster?"

"This is it," Webster's moved after Logan. "It's time we shut this thing down hard."

◉◉◉

Crouching in the woods outside the castle in Waltham Forest, Jonathan studied two silhouettes beneath the shadow of a willow tree. He had almost missed them, moving intently for the castle, when he caught the scent of a cigarette. At the first sniff he stopped, searching, trying to find the source. It had taken a while.

Gusting wind beneath a black sky made it all the more difficult, but the moon sometimes broke through the cover to illuminate the forest with ghastly white light. Listening carefully beneath the hushed swaying branches, Jonathan caught the sound of subdued conversation. He moved closer, careful and quiet, before pinpointing the small red glow within the leaves.

They were well positioned, and quiet. They were just too relaxed *with a cigarette* for their own good; also a mark of professionals. There would be more, hiding somewhere in the woods.

He saw that the willow branches were so thick that they couldn't look away from the house. Their only vantage was the castle itself, the north side. He figured the other teams were each assigned to cover particular vantages.

He didn't know who they were but he knew they were British so they probably weren't CIA, which left British police or British intelligence; no way to be certain.

With a frown he moved forward, using the wind to cover the sound of his steps. He could generally move four to six paces before the wind fell, allowing a startling stillness to settle that amplified the almost inaudible conversation concealed within the branches.

Surprising even himself with silence, Jonathan came to the edge of the brooding, dark tree without challenge. Then he crouched barely within the leaves, trying to get a clear visual, waiting. He still held the SIG close and tried to formulate a plan.

He couldn't disarm them and set them free because they'd alert the others after he was gone. He couldn't handcuff them to a tree because they'd start screaming as soon as he was gone. No, he would have to keep them under control.

Moving slowly, intently watching their backs, Jonathan took a cautious step.

Too drugged and numb to think, Logan stared through the window of the Ford Taurus—a strange selection for Scotland Yard, it seemed—as they sped up the turnpike, switching highways toward Waltham Forest.

Johnson drove with stalwart British temerity, slashing a fearless path in and out of the heavy freeway traffic to exit onto a wide two-lane. Behind them was a high-speed convoy of cars carrying men prepared for anything.

Logan grabbed the door handle as Johnson threw the Taurus into a sharp bending curve, letting off the gas without touching the brake and hitting the gas again as they straightened out. The inspector gave no expression as the car barely held the road and then they roared away, flat and low. Logan cast him a reluctantly impressed glance; the man drove like a street cop.

"How much longer?" he asked, trying to ignore the breathtaking pain that was beginning to burn again in his shoulder.

"Fifteen minutes." Johnson's reply was quick. "Perhaps longer. It is impossible to tell just yet."

"Have you ever been to this part of London?"

"Several times, yes."

"Do you know where you're going?"

"I cannot envision the particular manor!" The car screeched through a hard turn.

Logan grated, "What kind of people live out here?"

"The aristocratic architects of our nation! Fools!"

Logan stared out the window, at the dark lines of trees racing past—a wall of brown and black and green. It was an old forest, almost impenetrable.

"Tell me," he said, "why do you want Silman so badly?"

"Dumont is the name he is hiding beneath, Agent Logan. Dispatch did a record check of the premises."

"Does Dumont own Consolidated Bank of England?"

"I cannot say. It seems that the man known as Lazarus Dumont has a British passport, but information on him is scant. We are attempting to discover everything we can."

"Dumont is really Simon Silman, an American solder," said Logan. "You're not going to have much of a record. MI6 probably set him up with a British passport in the late eighties. Before that, he didn't exist."

"I presumed," said Johnson. Then the dispatcher summoned him and Johnson lifted the microphone. He listened to an officer on the scene at Falken Manor.

The agent said that police had arrived on the scene with ambulance personnel but had just now completed a search of the manor. There was also a powerful bomb—powerful enough to level the entire mansion, in the lower den. It has been disarmed, but SAS bomb disposal specialists are examining it.

"Secure the manor and summon crime scene personnel," Johnson said as if it did not need saying. "Did you recover any other bodies?"

The answer was negative and Logan bowed his head as he listened. He released a deep sigh, trying to conceal his emotions as much as possible.

"What charges do you have on this man?" Johnson asked, weaving dangerously around a slow-moving truck. "We need an exact crime before we can hold him on remand."

"Murder of a federal agent." Logan stared out the window. His voice was vengeful. "For the murder of *four* federal agents and conspiracy to commit the murder of two more."

"Do you have proof?"

Logan lied. "Yes."

"Very good." Johnson was smiling. "Yes, very, very good."

"We'll deal with the rest of it later," Logan continued. "After an honest task force nails BCCI."

"I hope we are not too late to rescue your man Malone."

Logan remembered the look in Jonathan's eyes after Daniela was taken, as he walked away from Blackfoot's dead body; a glare that coldly said men would die for this.

He stared out the window.

"Malone might not be the one who needs rescuing."

Eyes red with rage, Jonathan closed the final few feet with the slightest whisper of sound and both men whirled, one lifting a radio, the other into his coat but Jonathan was already on them.

Moving with savage speed he struck the man reaching for the radio in the face to blast him back and spun, violently backhanding the second man in the neck. A violent strangling sound burst as the man dropped his gun to raise both hands to his throat and then Jonathan kicked him low, dropping him to the ground. He turned to the first man who was pulling hard for breath.

Intent to demonstrate his superiority, Jonathan half-lifted him from the ground and hit him once, twice, three times. He violently pushed the man as he finished, then searched him to remove a small handgun. Moving quickly, he kicked the fallen radio into the woods and whirled back to the second man.

Gasping, he'd staggered to his knees. He raised a hand for mercy. Jonathan bent and lifted him to his feet only to slam him against the tree. He quickly removed a handgun and dropped the magazine, clearing the chamber to toss it into darkness. Holding the man solidly, he asked, "How many are out here?"

The man was overcome by pain until Jonathan slammed him into the tree again, inspiring his attention. He gasped, "I... ah...my God, I can't breathe...are you *Malone*?"

"How many!"

"Malone..." the man was recovering quickly, "we've got men...Got 'em everywhere! You're outflanked!"

The barrel of Jonathan's SIG was beneath the man's chin and Jonathan let it be known that he would pull the trigger.

James Byron Huggins

"One more time. How many men are watching this side of the house?"

"Four more," he said quickly, searching Jonathan's face for any sign of hesitation, ready to use it to persuade him to back down. Jonathan pictured a standard military pattern of listening posts and figured thirty-two men.

He leaned forward. "You're coming with me! And if anything happens, you're going to be the first dead man to hit the ground! Your friend will be second, and I'll be third but you're not going to like that very much, are you?"

"Malone...be reasonable! It's over! It's—"

Jonathan whirled the man to see the first agent standing on his feet, holding a hand over his injured face. "We're going to the side door and you're both coming inside. Do exactly what I say and you won't be hurt." He frowned. "And know this! If either of you do anything at all to keep me from reaching that place, I swear to God I will blow your brains out without hesitation! Do you understand?"

They nodded together.

"Walk!"

They moved toward the manor.

It was a remarkably short trip, down the sloping hill to the estate and across an open field. Jonathan knew that there was, at this moment, frantic radio communication being hurled from listening post to listening post because they had to see him walking with his gun to the head of this agent. But they reached the door safely and Jonathan smashed out a window to unlock it. Then in another moment they were inside and he quickly cuffed them to an iron grill.

He searched them quickly for a key, found one and tossed it aside. He didn't have time to do a more thorough search but he figured the men weren't cops—they probably wouldn't have backup keys hidden inside their belts or cuffs.

He stood over them. "If you have a backup key and you unlock yourself after I'm gone," he said slowly, "do not...I *repeat...do not* interfere with what I'm about to do. If I see you inside this house again, I *will* kill you. If you get free, go for the woods."

They nodded. Jonathan walked away.

"When this is over, you can do whatever you want."

Johnson smoothly hit the two-lane leading into Waltham. Smothered with intensifying pain, Logan hunched against the door on the far side of the vehicle. Despite the deep aching wound there was something knawing at his mind, something that had been said but didn't make sense. He wondered, glancing at Webster.

Yes, something that—

Understanding with a sudden falling in his heart, Logan painfully closed his eyes, leaning his head back against the seat. His movement, made so obvious because of the pain he was already in, caught the inspector's attention.

"Yes?" Johnson asked.

Shaking his head with a silent curse, Logan peered out the window, feeling sweat on his face, trying to remain calm and concentrated. It was a long time—too long—before he said, "How much longer before we arrive?"

"Five minutes."

Logan was expressionless.

"Logan? Did you hear me?"

"I heard you," he mumbled. "Hey, boss."

Webster's response was slow. "Yeah?"

"I've got a question for you." Logan's voice was dead. "Who do you think it was...that called me on the phone?"

"I have no idea, Logan."

Logan was forced to use all his strength to keep himself from shifting as Johnson took a hard curve. "Well, think about this: Who was the only other person to know that Malone was still in the field?"

Webster was silent.

Turning his head, Logan saw the assistant director staring over the seat, directly at him. Webster's eyes were like gleaming black glass in the sparse light of the interior.

Johnson, sensing something, shifted nervously in his seat. Although he was still driving full-out, he seemed to be listening with the keenest interest. Logan didn't care. He didn't care who knew what, anymore. Didn't care how many secrets were exposed.

"Director Fletcher," Webster said finally. "I called him to tell him that we still had Malone in the field."

"Yeah." said Logan. "Fletcher. And who gave you the file on Jonathan?"

Silence.

"Fletcher."

"And who set up the meeting with Mossad?"

Webster looked away, grim. "Fletcher."

With a grunt Logan shook his head. "Looks like our director has a friend." Silence lasted as the miles sped away beneath them.

"I didn't know until yesterday," said Webster finally.

Logan felt like smiling, though he couldn't understand why. "We fly blind into a suicide mission, and against all odds we pull it off, only to find that the director could have given us the key from day one. But he didn't." He grimaced. "No, he didn't."

It did not seem possible that anything more damning could be said. Then Webster managed to do it. "Justice says they've found the man who owns BCCI. A Saudi. They say that he's Phantom. They say that even if Silman is somehow associated with BCCI, he's not directly guilty of any crimes. They say he's a valuable source of sensitive information. They say he's...a great American."

Logan laughed bitterly.

"I guess," he released a deep breath, "that you just can't ever tell about some people, can you?"

Chapter Twenty-Three

A man with a trim goatee and scarlet smoking jacket was waiting passively for Jonathan when he entered the front room, leading with the SIG. Eyes shifting, Jonathan searched the room, expecting an ambush. Expecting Charon.

But the man was alone, and calm. He held a long black cigar in his right hand, a glass of red wine in his left. He seemed slightly amused, even entertained, by the situation. The lack of surprise told Jonathan that his search was over. Standing in silence, he lowered the SIG.

An interval of stillness joined them.

"So," the man said finally, expelling smoke, "your search has, at long last, ended. I suppose you should feel somewhat satisfied. I certainly did everything possible to frustrate you, short of crashing the international banking system, but you succeeded nonetheless."

Jonathan fingers shifted on the gun as the man glanced at it and smiled faintly. "You will kill me now? Is it not the job of the FBI to arrest their prey?"

"I'm not with the FBI anymore." Jonathan eyes were dead calm. "This is personal."

The man's eyes widened in a flash before it was gone just as quickly. With a contemplative nod he walked to the fireplace, leaned on the mantle. "I suppose you are here because of your father and mother?" he asked. "That was, truthfully, an unfortunate incident. I wish I could have prevented it."

THE SCAM

"Don't waste your time," Jonathan said. "I know everything there is to know. After you were released from prison you worked with MI6 and the OSS to smuggle gold and art captured by Hitler. Then you broke away from them and went private."

Silman seemed to be enjoying it. "And then?"

"Then you created BCCI and used it and a hundred other banks to launder billions in drug money. You smuggled arms to the enemies of Israel. You engineered a worldwide banking takeover worth more than five hundred billion. When we came after you, you ordered Charon to kill Logan and the rest of the team. But Charon failed, and now I'm here. And you're going to die."

It was the calm resignation of Jonathan's voice that seemed to command Silman's attention. He didn't tremble but Jonathan noticed he had become, by the narrowest edge, nervous.

"Jonathan, do you want to know who truly killed your parents?" he asked after a moment. "I can't take it with me, as they say."

Jonathan was grim. "You've got one minute."

Silman took a slow sip of wine, as if to demonstrate time was not an issue. "Your father," he began, "was an exceptional agent for MI6. He was a stalwart man and a true genius at counterintelligence. I admired him greatly. Yes, even when he betrayed me."

"You're a liar."

"No, Jonathan," Silman continued, "I am not a liar. I am deceptive, yes—a manipulator of governments and intelligence agencies and nations. But I am not a liar." His calm was beyond human.

"Your father, Justinian, was my most valuable colleague. The life he had behind him made him virtually invulnerable to accusations or suspicions. He was untouchable in the truest sense. And that, Jonathan, is why I was so disheartened when Justinian told me, just before your ninth birthday, that he was demanding a rather alarming sum of money to insure his continued allegiance."

Jonathan walked forward.

"Do you not want the truth?" Silman stood his ground. "Well, it is this—your father was the best. No one, not even his colleagues—not even Admiral Haitfield—knew that he worked for me." He gestured, the cigar leaving a spiral of smoke. "Nothing sinister, mind you. He gave away no critical information. He did not betray his government in any meaningful way. He merely profited in a few deals that he alone could have brought to pass. Profited handsomely, since assistance such as your father provided was difficult to obtain. But he was also, unfortunately, a fundamentally honest man who simply became caught in the fever that infected us all at the end of the war. And the deception gnawed, somehow, at his soul. And the day finally came, as I feared that it would, when your father decided to break from our secret alliance."

He took another sip of wine, and Jonathan knew Silman had already used his time. He did nothing.

"In any case," Silman continued, "your father wanted a rather exorbitant sum of money for a silent separation—a sum incommensurate with what I could pay. But if I could not pay, then he would expose me and take early retirement under suspicion of mortal sin. Nothing provable, yet it would certainly be a sufficient cloud to force his exit, and sufficient to end my empire, as well. It provided a true dilemma—a dilemma I could not resolve. So I shared the rather alarming situation with certain members of your father's own intelligence agency."

"MI6," said Jonathan.

"Yes, Jonathan. MI6, and older members of the OSS." Silman was supremely relaxed. He was in control of the situation. "They worked with each other more closely than they worked with their own governments, which is what made the network possible in the first place. It was a situation of personal loyalty, as opposed to national ideals. And it was MI6, Jonathan, and not myself, who ordered Justinian's death."

"I don't believe you," said Jonathan, holding a distance of six feet. "My father was a man of honor. He would have never worked for a thug like you."

Silman laughed. "We are *all* men of honor as long as no one knows how we protect that honor."

Jonathan tried to deal with it, but couldn't. "It's over," he said. "I'm not taking you to jail."

Gazing into Jonathan's deadly, unblinking eyes, Silman strangely revealed no fear of death. "You have played an admirable game, Jonathan. You were a worthy opponent. And no, I don't believe you are taking me to jail. Or anywhere else."

Lightning hit Jonathan's shoulder and he spun firing. Then thunder hit him in the chest and with a roar he fell back to blindly fire the magazine before he lost all feeling in his hand and rolled, groaning, realizing that he'd been shot twice, maybe three times.

Struggling, blinking to focus, Jonathan saw the apocalyptic image of Charon as he swept forward, pistol in hand. The hit man was smiling now and in a misty, half-conscious haze Jonathan thought he looked more dead than alive. Knowing the moment, knowing death, Jonathan rolled onto his chest and prepared.

Charon staggered, groaning, as he stood over Jonathan's prone body. He pointed the silenced pistol at Jonathan and

Jonathan saw the hit man's face was slashed and swollen, as if he were dying from some massive, internal injury.

Sirens.

Charon and Silman raised their heads, listening, and Jonathan heard cars approaching. He heard a crash at the front gate; heard the distant shouts of men running.

Reaching down to roughly roll Jonathan onto his back, Charon frowned at the intrusion of his sacred, long-awaited victory. His voice was wet. "You were never my equal, Jonathan. You were destined to lose the game."

Jonathan said nothing as Charon aimed straight for his forehead and then the ghostly white eyes glanced to the side as Jonathan's hand opened to release...a stun grenade.

Light exploded and Charon roared—blinded—straightening as Jonathan ejected the switchblade and twisted to savagely stab up, fully penetrating Charon's steel body armor.

Shrieking, the hit man attempted to retreat but Jonathan held onto the blade and rose snarling, twisting and driving. Charon screamed and Jonathan roared as he twisted his arm again, driving, driving the knife deeper and deeper, plunging his fist flush against Charon's heart to finish the fight, the nightmare, the game.

They stood face to face, eye to eye.

Charon gasped.

"Checkmate!" snarled Jonathan.

With a vengeful twist Jonathan shoved the blade back and Charon screamed as he staggered to hit the glass table and crashed through it to the floor, arms collapsing and extending slowly as the white shards turned through light falling, falling, falling to fall still.

Light exploded from the side of the room, a white eruption of white and Jonathan found himself in the air, searching for a wound knowing he was dead this time and as he came out of the reaction he threw out his arms to land hard against the floor. He didn't know where he was hit but he wasn't unconscious and groped wildly for his pistol before realizing that *he wasn't hit at all*!

Glaring, confused, Jonathan stood.

Silman leaned against the mantle, his smoking jacket reddening far more with a wide circle of blood. His face was the pure portrait of shock, but he wasn't looking at Jonathan. A pistol—a pistol that had been aimed at Jonathan—fell from his hand, clattering on the hearth.

Jonathan followed the stare.

A big, red-bearded man stood at an entrance to the room. The man held a smoking pistol in his hand, already lowered to his side. He stared at Jonathan as if Jonathan had somehow imposed upon him.

Blinking to focus, Jonathan searched the cold face, but saw nothing there—no sympathy, no compassion. The bearded man had shot Silman as simply as he would shoot a dog.

"I told you to go home," he rumbled.

Struggling to speak, feeling faint with the first tendrils of deep, deep pain, Jonathan gasped, "Why did you..."

Casting a last look at Charon, the man turned and walked away. He ascended the stairway before turning back, stoically standing on the edge of darkness and light.

"Kid," he growled, "your father didn't want money from Silman. That was a lie. But your father *did* work for Silman... long enough to learn the details that would help Israel. But after he found out where the gold had come from, he wanted out. Only Silman wouldn't let him out." Emotion, for the first time, surfaced in the man's face. "Your father was a friend of mine, Jonathan. He helped me out, and I owed him. He loved his country, believed Israel belonged on their land, and Silman had no right to take it from them. He was...He believed in your God.

"I wish I had taken your dad's path. I couldn't save him, but I could save you. I know saving one child isn't enough to redeem me for everything I've done. I'm done fighting. It's time to see what I can make of my life. May God have mercy on me."

Jonathan was losing focus.

"Your father was a good man, kid, a lot better than me. And he knew he was gonna die." He paused. "Your dad loved you more than anything on this earth, kid. More than the job. More than the money. More than his own life. And he made me promise I'd protect you, cause he knew I could." He shook his head. "I did my best. I hid you from Charon. Hid you from Silman. From MI6. From the CIA. Hid you from everybody but my man in the FBI. But then you came back into this and I had to get into it again, myself. And, kid, I'm getting tired of saving your life every time I turn around." He motioned to the door. "Go home, Jonathan."

Grimacing in pain, Jonathan shook his head.

"I *am* home."

A moment passed; the red-bearded man frowned. "It might be over, anyway," he said. "It's about time." Then, unexpectedly, he smiled. He turned as the front doors were kicked in.

Was gone.

Logan led the way with Webster beside him and then Jonathan pitched forward.

Only at the last did he hear Logan cursing and shouting directions and then he glimpsed Logan lashing out to smash Silman flat to the floor as darkness descended from the highest place of his will to overcome everything else.

THE SCAM

An ambulance was prepared to take Jonathan to a hospital in Loughton, which held the closest trauma unit. Two members of CI-3 were in the van.

Logan leaned over Jonathan, who'd regained a measure of consciousness with the adrenaline administered by medical technicians. Logan smiled as he placed a hand on his shoulder.

"You did good, kid."

Jonathan's licked dry lips. "The guy...with the beard."

"He's gone."

"He shot Silman."

"I know," Logan nodded. "Silman told us the guy was his bodyguard." Logan paused, shaking his head. "He said that the bodyguard and Charon were trying to kill him. He says you saved his life. Says you're a hero."

Jonathan winced.

"I know," said Logan. "Look, forget it. They're going to take you to a hospital and I'm sending some CI-3 guys to protect you. Just get some rest."

Jonathan closed his eyes to sleep. In seconds they'd loaded him into the ambulance and it was streaming down the drive toward the distant highway.

With a frown Logan went back into the estate and saw Webster and Johnson arguing with over forty MI6 agents who had descended from nowhere to angrily argue jurisdictions and "defense of the realm" aspects of the situation.

Implacable, Johnson was holding his ground, staring instead of nodding, giving no agreement. Webster was frowning, appearing more than a little primed for action.

Riebling and the CI-3 team stood against surrounding walls, weapons at port arms. Already, they'd prevented MI6 agents from using their radios. But the situation was getting complicated fast and Logan somehow sensed how it was going to end.

Smoking a cigar, Silman sat in a chair beside the fireplace. Though wounded, he was maintaining remarkable control, as if to demonstrate he was above pedestrian, human limitations.

Logan made a line past Webster and took one second to callously kick Charon's dead body in the head before slapping the cigar from Silman's hand and lifting him from his chair. With a curse Logan slammed him against the stone wall at the hearth.

Silman was struggling frantically.

"You're *finished!*" Logan grated.

Others leaped on Logan's back but he wasn't pulling away. He leaned closer: "It doesn't matter if you escape this or not! You're *finished! Do you understand me!*"

"Logan!" Webster was shouting. "Let him go! Let him go! This is a volatile situation!"

Enraged, Logan leaned even closer. "I know who you are and I know what you've done! And know *this*; whatever life you've had until now is the *best* you'll ever know! Because the rest of it's going to be spent under a *microscope!*"

Logan let go and Silman fell to the floor, clutching his throat. He glared at Logan like he would kill him, but Logan knew he wouldn't. There would be too many complications— enough complications to stress a half-century of secrets and sin. He pointed a finger at the little man. "From this day, you belong to *me!*

Fear was in Silman's eyes.

Logan turned away.

The ensuing argument between intelligence agencies heated until Logan finally lost it and pulled his gun to slam an MI6 agent over a desk under arrest and Webster countered the reaction of CIA and MI6 with his own gun and a violent shoving match erupted between Johnson and *another* MI6 agent that quickly disintegrated into a hand-to-hand fight that Johnson was winning righteously until Chapel, the CIA man, burst through the front doors with the American Ambassador to England and a representative of the Prime Minister and a formidable swarming battalion of London police.

Logan spun as they entered, seeing the face of a true American diplomat and knowing then and there that it was over. He knew that Silman would walk away from all of this simply because, in the guilty souls of either government, he had committed no crime greater than the crimes that joined them. He saw it at the same time he saw Blackfoot lying dead in flames and Woodard, his face red in blood, eyes wide to see what he had so greatly feared to see.

Logan shook his head as he gazed grimly over the chaos and accusations and slowly lowered his gun, knowing that nothing...*nothing* could go beyond this.

Beyond this, he knew, there was no place to go.

Epilogue

I t was buried.

The past, the present, and justice were delivered to the ground as surely as the dead, but Logan made it a personal mission to visit the graves, to stand over each, and leave something in respect. To tell them that their deaths had not been for nothing because that would have been the greatest injustice of all.

He had done it with reverence, with sadness, and with meaning. But it didn't do any good, in the end. Because, in the end, there had been no justice. Not for anyone. And there never would be. There was only the dead and the secrets buried with them.

Now, months later, Logan stared out the window of his new office at Quantico, where he'd been reassigned as an instructor, listening to the phone as it rang and rang and rang. He had been expecting the call, wondering if it would ever come, hoping it wouldn't. Because he knew that it would finish whatever small hopes remained.

Ringing.

Slowly, he answered.

"This is Logan."

There was a pause.

"It's Webster," was the curt reply.

Logan suppressed a grunt.

"I'll meet you on the range in an hour."

THE SCAM

Beneath a somber, storm-clouded sky Logan lit a cigarette as he watched Webster's black LTD stop in the parking lot. The Assistant Director of the Federal Bureau of Investigations exited to walk slowly down the shooting range.

Calm but also somehow reluctant to approach, Webster slowed even more the final steps, pausing before Logan's stoic gaze. He seemed pale, as if the strain of whatever war he had waged in the higher levels of government had exacted a severe toll. But, though he had been surely defeated, he still bore his imperial aspect of command, something no one could take from him.

"It's going to be buried," Webster said without preamble. "I just wanted to tell you man to man."

Without humor, Logan laughed. "I figured that much." He inhaled, releasing the smoke slowly. "What's about BCCI?"

"There'll be fines levied against the Saudi who owned it," Webster responded wearily. "He pleaded guilty to foreign ownership of an American bank. But the fine is only three hundred million, nothing he will miss. And a few people will probably go down to indictments, but we can't prove they knew what was going on, so they won't do time. And the economy has returned to normal—as normal as it ever gets, anyway." He shrugged. "They've got good spin control. And the reporters will just follow the herd. They always do."

With unmasked contempt, Logan scanned the horizon. "What about Silman?"

"He'll be indicted...for something."

"For something?" Logan didn't attempt to hide either his smile or his sarcasm. "What about Blackfoot? What about Woodard? Or Hooper? Who'll be indicted for them?"

Webster sighed. "Justice says they can't prove Silman ordered the hits. They say any prosecution would be without evidence of conspiracy to commit." He took another breath, as if in physical pain. "According to their final report, Charon was a rogue MI6 operative bent on extortion and revenge. They're saying Charon was as much a threat to Silman as anyone else. And with Silman's bodyguard vanishing, the argument can stand under cross." He paused. "At least, as long as they pick the right judge. Which they will."

"All of it was a setup," said Logan. "Silman always sacrifices his own to get clear."

Webster shook his head. "Only Jonathan knows why Frazier did what he did, and if he hasn't told you, he's not going to tell anyone. If it was a plan, it was a foolproof plan."

"It was a setup."

"I know."

"So we're not going to do anything to Silman?" Logan seemed depressed. "Silman is going to walk away with everything he's got? Just walk into the sunset free and clear?"

"He'll have to pay restitution for the crimes he's willing to admit," Webster answered. "But, yeah, in the end he's going to walk. He might even go into Witness Protection again. Justice says he's agreed to testify against...whoever."

"What about Israel?" Logan couldn't believe that they'd been pressured to let it go.

Webster shrugged, shook his head. "I don't know. They might try for him one day. But it'll be a while. They're under a lot of pressure from the president to let sleeping dogs lie." He grimaced. "Money buys a lot of favors."

Logan laughed out loud. He turned to stare over winter's descending sun and he wanted to say something, but nothing seemed sufficient. He shook his head.

Webster added, "I guess it was destined to end this way, Logan. Silman just knew too much. Too many people. Too many secrets." He paused. "Just...too many secrets."

"And who did these secrets serve? Who did these so-called secrets serve, Richard? The American people? The Nazis? A bunch of rich dynasties? The intelligence community? All of 'em?" Logan stretched out his arms. *"None of 'em?"*

Head bowed, Webster finally looked up. "I don't know, Logan. It's too big. It was always too big—too big, too old, too dirty. There's no justice to it. There never will be."

They stood in silence.

"I guess the only person who found justice was Jonathan," Webster added with a frown. "But we didn't give it to him. Nobody gave it to him. He outplayed all of them and won it for himself. By cutting out Charon's heart, in the end."

Logan genuinely smiled, then laughed out loud as he flicked the cigarette out over the shooting range. He didn't look up as he walked past Webster, still smiling.

"Good for Jonathan."

Jonathan turned away from the grave. He'd been here once before, long ago. He'd come to pay his respects to his mother and father. It helped a bit to think that he'd see them someday in heaven, but it wasn't enough.

His father had died trying to protect him. That was love.

Touching the gravestone lightly one last time, he turned away. Daniela was waiting by the car.

It was a good time to make up for the sins of the past.

London fog hung in a heavy white shroud over darkened trees as they returned home.

Before the fire, Daniela laughed as he kissed her. Her face was warm, happy, and content—no trace of the bitter and angry woman of just a few months before. Her wound had healed and her body was once again strong.

Flames crackled in the fireplace, light and comforting in the opulent and newly furnished den of Falken Manor. And Jonathan knew—knew in his soul—that he was home. And he would never be leaving again. Not for the FBI, or Silman, or anything else. And with General Ariel Ben Canaan's blessing, Daniela was with him.

"I told you I'd never leave you," Jonathan said, and she laughed freely and beautifully.

She had changed so much during the past months that he could barely remember how she had been. No longer a soldier, she had grown softer, gentler, even more beautiful, and talked daily of having children again. When she smiled, she could lift his heart. Her eyes held magic for him, soft and true.

Her anger was gone. Charon was gone. They could forget him and move on.

Jonathan found himself gazing pensively at the chess-board before the fire.

Daniela's eyes narrowed, mock serious.

"What are you thinking, my love?"

A moment passed, and then Jonathan shook his head. "Nothing, really...It was right; I'd do it again. All of it...But I was just wondering...if we really won."

She smiled, "You don't know?"

He shook his head, stared.

"I'm...not sure."

Daniela reached up; her fingers tightened in his hair and she gently pulled his face closer, close enough to kiss. Her eyes laughed, so alive, so bright, so...

"We won our *freedom*," she said, and placed a hand over her heart, then his chest. "In *here*..."

Jonathan saw the joy in her smile, her eyes. He thought about that night...it seemed so long ago...when he had fought

Matsumo for the sash. The lesson that night had been that some battles were won through mercy. Jonathan fought in anger, but God had still seen fit to give him this time, this love. "A time to love, and a time to hate; a time of war, and a time of peace...A time to kill, and a time to heal..."

Jonathan knew it in her smile, her eyes.

He smiled.

"Yes..."

About the Author

A veteran novelist and best-selling author, James Byron Huggins' life story reads more like fiction than fact. His career as a writer began normally enough. He received a bachelor's degree in journalism and English from Troy State University, and then worked as a reporter for the *Hartselle Enquirer* in Hartselle, Alabama. Huggins won seven awards while with the newspaper before leaving journalism in 1985.

With a desire to help persecuted Christians in eastern Europe, Huggins moved to Texas to work in conjunction with members of the Christian underground in that region. From the Texas base, Huggins helped set up a system used to smuggle information in and out of Iron Curtain countries.

In 1987, Huggins was finally able to leave the United States to offer hands-on assistance in Romania. As a jack-of-all-trades, Huggins photographed a secret police installation, took photos of people active in the Christian underground, and also continued his work as an orchestrator of smuggling routes. Huggins was instrumental in smuggling out film and documentation that showed the plight of Christians in Romania. He even found time to create a code that allowed communication with the United States. As in Texas, Huggins' life had few creature comforts. To survive, he often remained hidden in the woods or in secure basements for days at a time.

After his time in Romania, Huggins returned to the United States and took up journalism once more. He again worked for a small newspaper and won several awards as a reporter. Later on, he worked at a nonprofit Christian magazine before becoming a patrolman with the Huntsville Police Department in Huntsville, Alabama. After distinguished service as a decorated field officer, Huggins left the force to pursue writing novels.

His first three novels—*A Wolf Story, The Reckoning,* and *Leviathan*—achieved best-seller status in the Christian marketplace. From there, Huggins broke into mainstream science fiction with *Cain* and *Hunter.* Huggins then released *Rora,* a historical novel depicting the harrowing life of a European martyr. *Nightbringer,* his first book with Whitaker House, is currently being made into a movie.

Huggins currently lives in Kentucky. *The Scam* is his eighth novel.

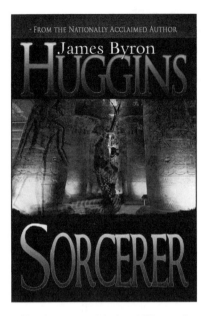

Sorcerer

the next novel by
James Byron Huggins

ISBN: 0-88368-818-2
Trade • 400 pages

Ex-detective Michael Thorn has retired from the police force, and is eager to lead a normal life for once. His days of fighting to protect the innocent are over. But his "retirement" isn't going to be the long-deserved rest he expected. His new home in rural New England has many strange stories surrounding it. But those are all just rumors...right?

Then he discovers the skeleton in the basement and realizes the rumors are true. But when the skeleton mysteriously disappears, Thorn is faced with an ancient mystery—one that leads to an even more ancient foe: the same sorcerer who fought Moses!

Now, to protect his family, Thorn must figure out how a sorcerer from ancient Egypt ended up in America and how to defeat him before he regains his full power and wreaks havoc on the world. Thorn has help from a wise professor, a devout priest, and a sect of warriors sworn to protect the church. But will they be enough?

In the end, Thorn will face even larger questions—of good and evil, and of God and the devil.

WHITAKER
HOUSE
www.whitakerhouse.com

from the prologue of
Sorcerer,
the next novel by James Byron Huggins

B *ury him alive!"*

"While we still have the chance!" another cried.

Three men with shotguns raced forward to level trembling barrels into the dark mouth of the cave. A pale host of others frantically slammed stones into crude mortar that yet another man was heaving in shovelfuls to wall up the entrance of the skull-like cavern.

The night was close and cold in the darkest hour before dawn, and some glanced nervously at the enshrouding fog, as if expecting to behold more than mist.

"Forget the mist!" the oldest man shouted. "He'll recover quick enough, and we won't get another chance!"

A young man raised his face. "What about the Logan family!"

"*Dead*, boy! Like the rest of the town! *Now*—quickly!—wall this abomination up before it kills the rest of us as well! If the thing awakes, I don't know if these rifles will stop it again!"

The boy spun to the stones, slamming them atop each shovelful of cement. Now there were two men hurling the mortar, and the wall was climbing quickly.

They stopped as a low, guttural growl issued from the bowels of the darkness—a threatening tremor inhabited by clear and cold intent. A moment, then a voice began whispering in a soft, hissing maliciousness in a language the boy had never heard.

"*Be silent in the name of Christ!*" the old man shouted.

He raised his shotgun to his shoulder and fired both barrels directly into the mouth of the cave and the others followed, six shotguns expending twelve rounds into the face of something they could not see. As the last man finished firing, the first to fire had reloaded with the conditioned reflexes of men who hunted to survive, as was the way of any man inhabiting the small frontier village.

And then—no command, no words—they were firing again. As they finished the second volley, the others had again reloaded, smoking shell casings rocketing from the chambers of the heavy-barreled weapons.

Volley after volley continued for a smoke-blasted minute, round after round after round fired point-blank into the cavern. And somewhere in the thunderous explosions of light the boy looked up to see something in the near distance—something chained to a wall.

There were flashes of silver at his manacled wrists as he—as *it*—raised and crossed forearms before its face.

It was dressed in a long scarlet robe that might have once been imperial but was now dirty and bloodied and ragged from the long battle of the past week where it had killed and destroyed so many. Those who had not been killed in the terror wished that they had been so they would not have to live with the memory.

The rising wall of heavy stones was so high now that they had only to lay the last layer of granite, and it would be sealed. The ones not still firing took suicidal risks to avoid the narrow angles of volleys, placing stone after stone solidly in place, and then it was almost done.

But the grandfather of the group took one last second to steady his aim before the final stone was set. He laid the twin barrels into the narrow aperture. His voice was enraged.

"*Beast!* This is your grave!"

The twin concussion of his final rounds was followed by, "Quickly! The last stone!"

With the words, the two men lifted the massive stone and shoved it atop cement at the crest of the cave. Another second, and they had piled shovelfuls of yet more cement atop it to completely seal the cave from light and even air, and then they stood, staring in shock at the hastily built prison.

The old man lowered his smoking shotgun, breathing heavily. His face was ghastly white and he seemed perilously exhausted.

Sorcerer

His shoulders sagged as he slowly turned, staring steadily upon the men who gazed back upon him with the respect one would give an Old Testament prophet. Then the old man turned further and gazed over the settling mist toward a small New England village.

It was a warm crimson dawn, and there should have been merchants and others strolling along the boarded walkways. There should have been children running toward the one-room schoolhouse, milkmen drawing wagons along the rows of houses, and farmers moving over hills and fields.

Yes, there should have been. But there were not. The town was as dead as a grave. And foggy, ghostly specters seemed to hover along the once busy streets like disembodied souls not yet departed from this temporal plain.

The boy quietly walked up to wait beside the old man, who stood on the edge of the hill that held the cave and whatever dark force it now contained. The boy's voice trembled.

"How many are dead?"

For a long moment, the old man didn't reply. Then, hoarsely: "Most of them, boy...All of them."

The boy's widened eyes strayed back to the cave. "Do you think the cave can hold it?"

"I don't know," the old man replied grimly. "It has escaped prisons built of stronger stuff." He shook his head. "By the odds, it should have killed us. And if I had not finally discerned who he—what *it* truly was—aye, we would be dead."

The young man looked back. "Why did it kill us? What was its reason?"

With a frown the old man shook his head once more. "It does not need a reason. It is its own reason—a cruel creature bent on mindless annihilation."

By reflex, or the remaining vestiges of terror, the old man reloaded the heavy 10-gauge shotgun, and lowered it in a single hand. He took a slow, somber step down the hill toward what was now a ghost town.

"Come, boy...We have dead to bury."

Nightbringer
a novel by
James Byron Huggins

An ancient evil has darkened the halls of Saint Gregory's Abbey
in the Italian Alps. The once-peaceful monastery becomes a murderous battleground as the monks and a group of visiting tourists
find themselves locked in a hopeless battle with an unstoppable
force. Cut off from the outside world by a sinister snowstorm, the
group of defenders must fight for their survival and for their very
souls. But from among the defenders arises an ageless holy warrior who alone has the skill and power to stem the bloody tide of
evil. In the epic battle that will decide the fate of all involved, the
warrior must not only struggle against a familiar foe of mythic
might, but also rediscover the faith and love that have carried him
through a thousand battles.

ISBN: 0-88368-876-X • Hardcover • 304 pages

www.whitakerhouse.com